REFORMING HELL

REFORMING HELL

MARILYN "MATTIE" BRAHEN

WILDSIDE PRESS

REFORMING HELL

Published in 2009 by Wildside Press.
www.wildsidepress.com

ACKNOWLEDGEMENTS

I would like to thank my friends and family who have been so supportive and understanding as I worked on this novel, especially my husband, Darrell Schweitzer, whose loyalty, love, and editorial feedback are treasured, and my mentor, Ray Bradbury, whose encouragement has *always* kept me going whenever the going got tough. Ray, you also hold an extra-special place in my heart.

I would be remiss to not thank my publisher, John Betancourt of Wildside Press, for his support and friendship over the years.

And lastly, I thank my readers who started this journey with my first novel, *Claiming Her,* and will continue and complete its tale here with *Reforming Hell.*

Marilyn "Mattie" Brahen
October, 2008

"People must believe what they can,
and those who believe more must not be hard
upon those who believe less. I doubt if you would have
believed it all yourself if you hadn't seen some of it."

— from *The Princess and the Goblin*,
by George MacDonald, 1872

"When any religion tries to enforce its superiority with
violence, it has lost the battle."

— Marilyn "Mattie" Brahen
August 30, 2007

1

Stories in the Garden

I'm looking back from the present. For those of you who never met me, my mortal name is Leigh Ann Elfman. My eternal name is Leianna, given to me 35,000 years ago when I was born to the angels Eve and Michael, their only child.

It's 2008. Sometimes you have to look back from the present to figure out where to continue telling the story. I left you guys, left off at the very beginning of 1972, and the world was so much easier to take then, when we didn't have wackos blatantly masquerading as pious vigilantes or a flim-flam president. I know there were other sleazy presidents in the past. But our current brazen bozo in the Big House is beyond sane belief.

Back then, we didn't have religious bigots telling us their beliefs were more important than democratic freedoms. We didn't have extremists who kill over cartoons, films or books, unable to handle justified criticism of their distinctly unspiritual behavior.

It's 2008. I'm 60 years old, my auburn hair is streaked through with silver, my face, I'm told, is still youthful despite a few new pounds filling out my chin and cheeks, and my brown eyes are still my best feature, even with a few lines at their corners. So much has happened in 36 years. Eve, as my mortal mother, Miriam Elfman, is 80 years old, and according to my spirit master, Quatama, also known as the Buddha, this is Eve's last mortal lifetime. She's out-lived the rebalancing of humanity's DNA, after the damage caused by the first Fall from Grace, when she and her brother Adam were trapped on Earth and interbred with mortals. That mixed angelic and human genes, but the damage has now been reversed. A subtle evolution will begin taking place; mankind will become a new, improved species.

Bear with me here. I know humanity still seems to be off its rocker. The last eight years I've been cynical, badly heartbroken, and angry. I get to *do* something about my anger. I'm the Queen of Hell now. I get to judge those who *really* sin in the eyes of the Cre-ator. This doesn't always match the perpetrator's religious belief. God doesn't particularly care what religion you are. Many souls who rise to the heavens are extremely perturbed by this at first. Then they realize that nobody's listening to their complaint. Judg-ment really hinges on ethics and spirituality, not on what religion we follow.

I'm having one of those days when I can barely make it through without my muscles aching, just getting through the day job and cleaning up the dinner dishes. I tumble into bed, fall asleep, and wing it up to the eighth physical astral plane. This is one of the high heavens I've got access to, something you might not think I'd have, since I'm the Queen of Hell. But God asked me to take that position, to relieve Lucifer of his duties.

Few mortals even know about that change in management Down Below, or all the other changes there, that I get to do the judging. Actually I'm waiting for some really large rats, human ones, to come my way. You don't just lie your way into world chaos, destroying other lives impertinently, and not expect to be called to judgment. On the other hand, Heaven doesn't approve of fanatical religious leaders killing in the name of God. None of these people are going to Heaven. They're heading for a total isolation cell for a thousand years or so to teach them the value of a human life.

I did freak out insanely in the beginning, when judging the 9-11 bombers, and initially stooped like the Furies to their violent level. But then I calmed down, put them back together, and it's been isolation cells ever since for each of those misguided fools. And, believe me, isolation hurts a lot more than physical punishment. YOU try being denied all sensation, stuck in total blackness, with nothing for reference, nothing visible, audible, sensory or structural, just hanging in a void for *even two days*. Oh, yeah, you *can* hear yourself scream.

Hell is tidier and much more logically run these days. We even have social workers and behavioral therapists on our staff.

And then there's my second job: President of the High Council of Heaven. I actually asked to be relived of that duty in 2003. They let me go for two years, and then told me I had to preside again.

I don't like it. All these well-meaning people come up to Heaven to complain and half the time they want me to do what those zealous Muslims insisted Denmark should do: pass legal judgment based on one specific religion. I've had to educate both crowds of astrally-projected Muslims and throngs of out-of-body Christians and Jews, especially the orthodox believers, explaining that in Heaven we don't bend rules to suit mortal religious beliefs. The Hindus, Buddhists and pagans have less trouble understanding that Heaven has no secular restrictions. Or perks!

Like the group that recently came, including that nauseous woman who kissed her son and sent him off to blow himself up, along with other children. They demanded that the suicide bombers be returned to the heavens and that the 70 virgins attend them. I dearly wanted to tell them that the 70 virgins married nice, peaceful boys whose mothers brought them up right. But I didn't. I only told them that their sons had committed murder and were not expected in Heaven anytime soon.

They didn't like that answer. They started clamoring and crying out to M—, but M—, though he sits on the High Council along with me, cannot change Heaven's rules to fit human delusions. He told them, what many of their eminent scholars had told them: that they were interpreting Islam wrong. When they heatedly accused him of being an impostor, he took it stoically, his eyes sad. Later on, they realized their error and sent apologies to him, which he accepted. I told him — to cheer him — that if Jesus appeared on Earth today, some people would probably demand to see his driver's license.

So now I wing my way upward to the eighth plane and rather than stop at my home there, I go straight to the Garden, heading to my favorite part, where the fragrant flower beds extend seemingly for miles. I especially love the hyacinth's sweet aroma. When I arrive, J.C., Quatama and M— are already waiting for me.

They want to talk to me. I knew J.C. 35,000 years ago, before I ever incarnated on Earth. His name was Yeshua then. He and Quatama were both my spirit masters, when I first lived as Leianna in Eliom.

You're probably more familiar with Eliom as *Eden* and with Quatama as *Gautama Buddha*. I still think of and spell his name as Quatama. He's reached Nirvana and is one with everything, and knows me beyond my own current knowledge of myself. He allows whatever will help the world reach its own Nirvana.

M— is, of course, the prophet of Islam. I know that Muslims aren't supposed to "portray" him, but I'm not a Muslim, and this isn't a portrayal . . . I'm telling a true story. But out of respect to him and his followers, I am only using his initial in place of his name.

M— was the previous Keeper of the Earth before me. Before him it was J.C. and before that it was Quatama. The Keeper, in theory, watches over the world and leaves some legacy to the Earth and its people, a legacy which helps to keep both the Earth and mankind balanced. I haven't chosen my legacy yet.

In 1971, when Quatama first told me that I was the current Keeper, I asked him who the previous Keeper had been, who had symbolically handed me that baton. But M— felt I wasn't quite ready to learn his identity. I knew nothing about Islam.

Since then I've learned that the name M—, in Arabic, means "one who is praised," an honorable name, but he isn't just any M—, he's *The M—*. I also had no idea that, for a very long time, two of my dear astral friends, Ali and his wife Fatima, were M—'s son-in-law and his daughter. At first I was upset when I found all of this out. I was in no way going to kow-tow to anyone's religious superstar. But Ali and 'Tima calmed me down and helped both M— and me to compromise and trust each other. They are a blessing in my eternal life.

Yeshua, called Jesus by most of today's modern world, lets me affectionately call him *J.C.* I never call him Jesus. During his one earthly lifetime — his name in Hebrew was Yeshua — I had both the honor and sorrow of being his mother. Today our roles are slightly reversed. He calls me Little Sister, and I still call him Yeshua.

When M— came forward and identified himself *after* September 11, 2001, I had my hackles up, my back against the wall, with radar on full alert.

I needed to let him know that I was not subordinate to him, that I owed him nothing that I didn't wish to give out of my heart's true desire, when he came around and told me that he had been the previous Keeper.

M— couldn't understand why Allah would now give that responsibility to a divorced Jewish-American woman from Northeast Philadelphia. He complained to Quatama that if I hadn't the simple courage to face my own destiny, it didn't seem likely I'd ever leave any legacy to the world as great as Islam. The only reason, he said, that he accepted my becoming the Keeper was because Allah willed it.

When M— added in a gravelly tone, "I will have to strive to understand how such a thing could be," that ruffled my spiritual wings. I very calmly looked up at him and said, "Well, we're apparently going to find that out now, aren't we?" He understood exactly what I meant, because when you are in spirit, your feelings are heightened by your words, and he very quietly replied, "You are being an irritating woman."

"No, I'm not," I told him. "I think you're uncomfortable with my *being* a woman."

For years, we verbally sparred back and forth, neither of us gaining or conceding an inch. I read about one-third of the Koran and found contradictions in it: compassion and cruelty, spiritual tolerance and religious prejudice. Other books of religion also contradict themselves, while insisting they're the last word from God. God's absolute word? Many religious passages are not about what God has to say to humans, but what *humans say to God,* asking God to sanction their behavior unconditionally, and then insisting that God does so. Who could prove this except by faith? If the "sanctioned" behavior is harmful to us, shall we blame God for it or say our prayer went unanswered? If the "sanctioned" behavior harmed others, are we denying our own responsibility for our violence, and blaspheming when we call it God's will? Humans fight for human reasons. Humans wrote these religious works. Perhaps some passages were inspired by God, but I can't consider them absolute.

Years ago, I decided never to join any mortal religion, including Judaism, but I still study spiritual texts, believe in God, and have my own philosophy. I call it *Universophy*, which is *not* a religion. The world doesn't need any more religions. It needs bridges to connect these beliefs in peace.

In 2006, M— and I had a breakthrough. We simultaneously realized hostility was useless. He accepted my individuality and I accepted his, and we learned to deal with our differences honorably, even affectionately. Never angrily. We realized if his legacy was to survive, he would have to sincerely help me with mine.

The hyacinths are staggered with rows of geraniums, tulips and borders of ageratum. A mild spring permeates the Garden today. M— waits for me, holding a large clay pot, thick with pinkish orange blooms, which he offers me. Quatama and Yeshua materialize behind him. M— explains: "For your house on the eighth plane. I know you like begonias. They are from my garden."

M— lives on the eighth physical astral plane with his wife Aishah. When he was alive, she was his third wife. Fatima has told me that her father had nine wives then. She didn't expect me to find this extraordinary, as I myself have more than one astral husband now and our astral group marriage also includes Sharlan, the only other sister-wife in it.

As far as I know, Aishah is M—'s only wife now. When we were introduced, she was polite but taciturn with me, serving us coffee in M—'s vast garden, standing off to one side while her husband talked with me. I asked him if she wanted to join us, and he said no, she had no reason to. Yet I knew that she could hear our conversation, standing near us at the edge of the patio, by the back door of their spacious, single-story home, as if awaiting her husband's further instructions.

But the woman he was instructing was me, in the history of Islam, beginning with his meeting with my eternal uncle, the angel Gabriel. My uncle Gabriel verbally dictated the Koran to M—, who wrote it down and brought it to his people.

During those lessons, the pot of coffee stayed ever full, fragrant and warm, even though we poured generous cups. A plate of sweet pastries filled with pistachio nuts also sat on a plate nearby, but these did not replenish themselves, to my chagrin, because they tasted divine. When the plate lay bare, I sighed, and then Aishah appeared, a fresh plate in her hand. She laid it down, took away the empty one and smiled briefly at me. And M— murmured, "My wife appreciates your compliment to her baking skill."

Today I accept M—'s gift, the pot of the sturdy begonias, taking it in my own hands. "Thank you. They're beautiful."

A white, wrought-iron table and four chairs appear beside us. I place the begonias, as a centerpiece, upon it and sit down. Yeshua and Quatama also seat themselves, and M— sits directly across from me. He clasps his hands and speaks: "The time has come for me to choose whether to guide my people toward change and its acceptance or to stand behind those who reject it, who insist rigidly upon the old values and the immutability of the law.

"The problem, of course, is that sharia is applicable only on Earth and only for Muslims. Allah is most tolerant and generous toward all good-hearted humans in the afterlife." He glances at Quatama, who smiles but says nothing. "The Seraphim tell me that my choice will be influenced by you, Leianna, by decisions you have made before and those you will make in the near future, and that these decisions will decide what your legacy will be. And so, I cannot make my own choice until I understand yours.

"I need you to begin instructing *me* in the story of *your* current life, mortal and astral: what you do, who you love, your challenges, dreams and hopes. And I need to understand the purpose of this Alliance, which Allah has asked you to create between Heaven and Hell. Who benefits from it? I have no knowledge of Hell. The pious never lived and ruled there until now . . . until you."

"Where do you want me to start?" I ask him. "What happened yesterday creates today and influences tomorrow. To answer you fully, I'd have to backtrack into the past."

M— considers. "I now know the truth of Lucifer's fall, and how Gabriel's brother, Michael, was your angelic father, and that Eve was Michael's wife and your mother, when you lived among the angelfolk in Eliom, before your incarnations on Earth.

"I know that Adam, your other uncle, was Eve's brother and not her spouse, and how Adam and Eve trespassed on Earth and were trapped there. And how the obedient angelfolk willingly joined the endless cycles of incarnations on Earth to rebalance the damaged genetic code altered by the hybrid offspring of Eve and Adam.

"I also understand now how Lucifer's rebellion over this caused him, his family and his followers to be flung into Hell, and how you and your betrothed — Lucifer's son, Bael — were separated for 35,000 years.

"Quatama also explained why Heaven allowed your reunion with Bael in 1971, that they wanted you to form this Alliance between his father's dark realm and Heaven's glorious light.

"What I haven't learned is the aftermath, what led up to Lucifer's release from Hell, and what circumstances allowed you to take his place. Is there really a reform movement in Hell, and can any of it be taken seriously? Can you succeed in this at all, and how could it possibly benefit our world?

"You must also enlighten me as to your plans for your mortal life, since you are Earth's current Keeper, regarding the legacy you propose to give to the Earth as its Keeper."

Sudden silence. Both Quatama and Yeshua still sit quietly, although Quatama has a mirthful look on his face. As if to say, *and you thought I put you through your paces before!*

Finally, I respond to M—'s daunting questionnaire. "You're asking for a lot. Trying to tell it only from my personal viewpoint won't let me express what other people, whose lives intertwined with mine, also experienced. May I tell it through their eyes as well, as they told me, but in their individual voices, as a storyteller would? I'll try to be as detailed as I can."

M— smiles at me thoughtfully. "Then pretend you are Scheherazade. Tell me the stories as she would. When all of the tales are told, perhaps we will greet our future with greater compassion and clearer understanding. *Inshallah.*"

"God willing," I agree.

M— and I are to meet each night, here in the Garden. There I will spin each tale and weave each into a tapestry that will hopefully reveal a better fate for all of humanity and the good, green Earth we share.

May the ending bring healing to all that dwell upon it.

2

What Went Before

January, 1977. Leigh Ann would always look back on that year as a major crossroad in her astral life, while her mortal life continued on its mundane way. She was twenty-nine-years-old, and her son Daniel, six. Her sister, Ginnie, was twenty-four, and their brother Rick (no longer called Fred by anyone, family or friend . . . he had achieved that goal) was nineteen. Their mother, Miriam Elfman, was forty-nine, and their father, Bill Elfman, was fifty-four. Their cat, Lucy Angelina, was about halfway through her sixth (human) year, although in cat years, she was older than Leigh Ann and probably much wiser. Her fur was black, as was her nose, and her eyes were a deep emerald. She was pampered by the family, put on the highest of feline pedestals, having in 1971 alerted the family to a smoldering fire in the basement before it could ignite the heater and blow up the house and endanger them.

They all still lived on Glenview Street in Northeast Philadelphia. Rick had just graduated from Northeast High School and was working part-time in Bill Elfman's plumbing and heating business, while taking college courses in computer programming. Ginnie had received her nursing degree and was employed at Hahnemann Hospital, working a 4:00 P.M. to midnight shift. Leigh Ann had a new job, working for an accounting firm as a secretary. Daniel, bright but boisterous, was enrolled in the Paley Day Care Center, where he also attended kindergarten. Paley also had an arrangement with the nearby elementary school, Farrell, and Daniel would start first grade there in September.

This is how the year began in the everyday waking world of Leigh Ann Elfman, she and her family living their mortal lives, heading to where the future led them.

But after midnight, as her physical body slept, Leigh Ann continued her eternal existence as Leianna. She was torn by her love for two unique men, both immortal: her original betrothed, Bael, and her spirit guide, Terence Dearborn.

Bael had fallen with his father, Lucifer, into Hell and had become his second-in-command. Leianna's plea, to be allowed to go with Bael, had been denied by their Creator. Instead, she incarnated on Earth along with other angelfolk compliant to their Creator's Will, rebalancing mankind's damaged DNA.

Leianna's eternal mother, Eve, and Eve's brother, Adam,

had disrupted that genetic blueprint. They disobeyed the Creator and visited Earth in the early days of Cro-Magnon man, despite being told that the Creator's new planet was forbidden to the angels.

The angels had been granted a distant glimpse of that young planet and, safely enclosed in celestial winds, were carried into space, well above the blue and green world, far enough away from its instability. The winds then returned them to Eliom, their own dimension with its village, its beautiful Garden, its prairie, woods and glistening shore. But Eve and Adam, believing they could quickly travel to and view the planet's surface and swiftly return to the winds, alighted on Earth and underwent a strange metamorphosis. Their angelic clothes disintegrated, and their bodies changed cellularly from immortal to mortal flesh. They became hybrids, half-angelic, half-human, and were trapped on Earth until mortal death released them.

Captured by Cro-Magnon hunters, Eve became its leader's second wife, and, as the clan grew, Adam formed his own clan. They bore and sired children with their mates. Those offspring, including Eve's twins, Cahn and Ahbel, raised by Adam when she died in her last childbirth, introduced angelic DNA into Earth's mortals, changing their genetic future.

After her mortal death, Eve returned to Eliom, to her angelic husband, Michael, and their daughter, Leianna. But the war in Heaven soon separated them all again.

Bael vowed to return from Hell to find Leianna and claim her as his wife. In 1971 they were reunited, unaware that Heaven had planned this as an alliance between Heaven and Hell, to end their opposition and work to heal humanity's faults.

Hell would be reformed. Or so Leianna was told by her spirit master, Quatama. Five years had passed since Bael, his older brother Ashtoreth, Leianna, and Terence Dearborn, a dead British composer, who also loved Leigh Ann, had first agreed to act as ambassadors. But Hell's rulers had steadily refused to accept the Alliance and Heaven's goals.

This formidable challenge seemed more likely to fail than achieve the smallest measure of success. Lucifer had demanded that his first-born, Ashtoreth, and his second-born, Bael, come to their senses. He blamed Leianna's eternal parents for his disgrace: Michael, for not siding with him in his rebellion, and Eve for submitting to God after Lucifer had risked everything to save her and the other Eliomese from the Creator's manipulative and unrelenting control.

For five years now, Lucifer had ridiculed his sons' fatuous claim that they were Hell's ambassadors to Heaven. He tried to persuade them to abandon Leianna. When they refused, Lucifer suggested corrupting her to bring about her own fall from grace. She could be with them in Hell for all eternity. They refused that suggestion as well. Lucifer raged, while his youngest son, Azmodeus, sneered at his brothers. He disliked Leianna and her influence on them as intensely as Lucifer did. Their mother, Affaeteres, said nothing, for Hell had long ago crushed her, and she rarely gave advice.

Bael and Ashtoreth backed off. An uneasy truce developed in that fifth year between Lucifer and his eldest sons. They went about their duties and refrained from mentioning Leianna. Lucifer never questioned their absence on certain nights from Hell, while knowing full well that they were with her on the upper planes, and that Heaven had permitted his eldest sons to enter its gate, to tempt Lucifer with the Alliance, and with the false promise of his own redemption and return from exile.

A sly and crafty lure, one he would never snap at.

And so Bael and Ashtoreth reported their father's denial to Leianna, who felt their task might well be hopeless, and to Quatama, who quietly smiled at them and asked that they be patient with Lucifer.

And Terence Dearborn paid scant attention to the whole Alliance business, believing it would either succeed or fail, while *his* business was to help Leigh Ann's earthly existence have value and purpose. There were many ways to contribute to one's world in a given lifetime. Leianna had helped him to recover his lost musical compositions after his death. Together, they had attended the debut of his symphony, sonata and nocturne at the Philadelphia Academy of Music in January, 1972. Terence, of course, had been *incognito,* invisible to both the performers and rest of the audience, but his final legacy had been salvaged and preserved for posterity.

Leigh Ann had musical talent; he was helping her master the guitar, and she enjoyed creating songs. Perhaps she could aid her world through music? He loved her with an intensity he'd never felt for any other woman. He knew she also loved him. But she felt an equal but different love for Bael. Terence had stepped back from that, allowing Bael to win her. Terence had agreed to a platonic relationship with Leianna, for anything more would cloud his judgment as her spirit guide. Her happiness came first. Bael brought her happiness. Terence would never deny her that.

This was the tangled web of love, hope and the desire to move onward, of anger, hate and the refusal to change, that marked the beginning of 1977. But Leigh Ann Elfman's mortal life, and her immortal life as Leianna, was about to change forever.

3

Surprising Lucifer

Lucifer first heard the distorted version of Eve and Adam's expulsion from the Garden of Eliom, a dimensional world parallel to Earth but not *on* that planet, and his role in it as the serpent that corrupted Eve, almost 30,000 years before this night. This story of Earth's first man and woman, of the snake tempting the woman to eat from the Tree of Knowledge of Good and Evil, and the woman beguiling her husband to taste the forbidden fruit, both intrigued and infuriated Lucifer.

The tree, its fruit and the snake were pure fantasy, merely symbols masking the ultimate truth.

But mortals repeated the tale through the ages as their hearth fires cast shadow and light on the walls of their caves and huts. They added the tale of Cain and Abel, also distorted, for the twins had not been Eve's first-born, and certainly not Adam's get. Adam had raised them after Eve's mortal death, causing the confusion over their parentage. Cwuh had sired them on her.

Lucifer had long ago ceased to be mystified by humanity's need for its religious symbols, although it still amazed him when they took their symbols at face value, as *gospel.*

Lucifer's rebellion, neither cold-blooded, nor furtive, had been passionate and honest. He sneered at the hidden sexuality in the image of the snake tempting Eve. He and Eve had been dear friends. He had never seduced her or cuckolded her husband Michael, once loved like a brother. Lucifer, before he fell from Heaven, had been faithful to his wife, Affaeteres.

Five thousand years after conquering the astral wilderness of Hell and building his kingdom, Lucifer heard the first mortal chants of the Garden, naming him the serpent within it. The reptile was maligned on Earth, despite having no greater or lesser need to survive than any of Earth's other creatures. Lucifer decreed that all snakes in his kingdom were to be treated with respect, for there were snakes and other animals in Hell. Hell had evolved like any other world in the Creator's universe. Snakes were native to Hell, Earth and Heaven.

But he would not abide any artistic depiction of the limbless creature in his kingdom and banned the snake's image and his association with it.

Hell's artists grumbled over Lucifer's proclamation, but none dared defy it. His throne room where he now sat, awaiting his eldest sons whom he had summoned, held many fantastic images but contrary to the paintings of many mortal artists, nothing serpentine. He had decorated it with images and symbols of his fall from his lost homeland, Eliom.

The right arm of his marble throne, as it faced the vast hall from the smooth, black granite dais, flowed into an eagle at rest, its eyes glaring and its beak opened threateningly, as if daring any to disturb it. The left arm segued into a crouching wolf, ears flattened and teeth snarling. The tall back of the throne held, on Lucifer's right, the standing profile of a proud, bull oxen, its tail at the end, its bovine head toward the center, turning to gaze coldly at those who stood before the dais. To its left, padding toward the oxen as if the beasts might meet in the middle, a powerful lion also turned its head to face those Lucifer surveyed from his throne, both the willing and the unwilling, its countenance harsh.

The throne sculptures represented the four Seraphim who disgraced Lucifer during Eve's trial and after it in Eliom, a reminder of his vow to one day face them again and win their atonement.

Lucifer savored the grandeur about him. Six, thick, marble, gold-veined pillars, three on each side of the central reception floor, rose up to support left and right balconies. A palace guard stood before each pillar, dressed in the manner of Roman soldiers in the reign of Tiberius, Lucifer's elite. Six more guards stood rigidly at attention: two before the elaborately carved, gold and jewel-encrusted, central throne room doors, two unseen from the throne at smaller entrances under the balconies, and two more stationed at private doors that led to and from the dais.

Below the balconies were the galleries, open areas with shadowed recesses, once lit by lamps filled with sweet oil, now replaced with softly glowing electrical light fixtures jutting from the wide, wooden, balcony support beams. Displayed upon the gallery walls, extraordinary paintings, ten feet in height and width, portrayed the long ago expulsion of Lucifer and those he championed from Eliom, their struggle to survive in Hell, and their triumphant conquest and taming of its wilderness.

Lucifer leaned forward on his throne, fingering the hard sculpted fur of the stone wolf impatiently. He stood up and strode abruptly down the three wide steps, descending the dais, and briskly over to the first painting adorning the left-hand wall. In it, rebel angels captured by the winged Seraphim were lifted into the roiling cloud above the village green in Eliom, where Lucifer had earlier argued heatedly against the incarnation of the angelfolk on

Earth. The complaisant angelfolk were shown in a wide circle around the green, separated from the disobedient angels by an energy field. Only one of the obedient dared to breech it: Leianna. The artist had lovingly painted the lethal sparks that flew about her, igniting her hair, robe and body as she blindly strove to break through its barrier. She had not reached Bael. The electrical charge threw her violently back; she'd been nursed back to health by her family and her spirit master, Quatama.

"Father."

Lucifer didn't turn. "You know, Bael, it's a wonder that electricity didn't maim her for life despite the healing ability of the angelfolk. If she had been hideously disfigured, would you still love her? I mean immortally, regardless of how prettily any mortal life might paint her."

Bael remained silent.

Lucifer slowly pivoted, facing him. "And where is your elder brother?"

Bael regarded him somberly, almost rudely, to Lucifer's thinking. He was dressed, as usual, all in black, in a long-sleeved turtleneck sweater, jeans and boots, matching his ebony hair and eyes, in contrast to his ruddy golden complexion.

"Well?"

"To answer your first question, I would still love Leianna. It might lessen my pleasure a bit when we made love."

"So this love, after all these centuries, is more than just a need for closure, to finish an interrupted passion and let it run its course? Do you intend to marry her?"

"I believe the betrothal has stood the test of time."

Lucifer nodded. "And where is Ashtoreth? I sent for him also."

"Ashtoreth is not in Hell tonight." Lucifer waited, and Bael obliged him. "He is on the upper planes, consulting with Quatama."

"The great Gautama Buddha, championing Leianna, your brother and you in this fairy tale quest. You would think that the current behavior of humankind would prove my point and end this reformation folly."

"The Alliance may — possibly — improve mankind's behavior." Bael spoke haltingly, as if trying to convince himself as well as Lucifer.

Lucifer raised an eyebrow, incredulous. "Bael, I don't believe souls damned to Hell will ever be redeemable, not even with one-third of Earth's humanity being incarnated angelfolk and the rest carrying some measure of angelic DNA, thanks to the Creator's great rebreeding experiment, going on now for what . . . nearly 35 millennia?"

"Nearly that. And most mortals know little to nothing about the angelic incarnations. But I bring other news Quatama conveyed to us. The old ones, the elders who left Eliom on the eve of Leianna's immortal birth, are due to return to our sector of the universe at the start of the 21st Century. He believes they will influence the goals of the Alliance."

His son's eyes met his deliberately then broke contact, but Lucifer continued to gape at him, as if Bael had delivered a blow, stunning him. He forced himself to swallow, to draw air into his lungs, then found his voice: "You've trumped me! Do you know who was among those elders trusting our Creator to send them light-years away to help with some newly sentient species on some unknown planet? Do you know who was taken from me and from your mother with no knowledge as to where they'd gone or when they might return? You were barely a year old, but I later told you of it. But I demanded to all who were told, that they never again mention my loss. Perhaps you've forgotten in the passage of centuries exactly who we lost."

"Your parents and Mother's parents. Your father Othorath. Your mother Ise. My paternal grandparents. And my mother's mother, Venea. And her father Mercurius. My maternal grandparents. And Leianna's paternal grandparents, Zoras and Heira. And you only became bitter, questioning the Creator's ability to safeguard them, after we were exiled into Hell."

Lucifer nodded. "And when they do return, what will they find? Eliom changed, its people scattered, their own kin lost to them in Hell!"

"Father, they willingly took on the task set for them by the Creator."

"And I didn't." Lucifer paced, agitated. "My and Affaeteres's parents will find us banned from Eliom — or whatever damned name it goes by now, their son disgraced and their daughter destroyed by this dark realm." *And by me*, he thought, *and for love of me.* "And what will you and your brother Ashtoreth, who are permitted where I may not trespass, tell them?"

"Heaven has placed rules and restrictions on Ashtoreth and me, Father."

"Dammit, answer my question!"

"I . . . I would ask that they be permitted to visit you," Bael said, his voice raising, "if you would explore a potential alliance, a long-awaited chance to heal the ostracism we've suffered, no longer rebels, but leaders negotiating for our realm's future!"

"Ah! But could *I* visit Heaven?"

Bael hesitated, staring at him. "Possibly. In time."

Lucifer sucked in air and expelled it, teeth gritted, lips twisting. "So you dangle a carrot before me, thinking me some old goat you can lead forward to your own ends!"

"Father," Bael murmured, but Lucifer could feel the anger smoldering behind Bael's quiet reproof, its sparks ready to erupt into bitter flames.

They had fought before. Bael never shied from speaking out; he would never play the role of sycophant to anyone. But a sudden, overwhelming need, to see a burden, too long carried, possibly lightened, prompted Lucifer's next words, not the stubbornness of his second-in-command. He took the carrot but would somehow control the direction of this Alliance business. "Tell Quatama that he and Leianna may visit my realm and, at my insistence, dine with me and my family. I will guarantee them safe passage."

Now Bael gaped.

Lucifer shot him a mocking glance. "I would question Quatama *myself* about our elders' return. That is why *and only why* you've won this small victory. And I make no promises beyond it."

"When, then?"

"On the next Sabbath." Lucifer turned from him, walking to the private door to the right of the dais, his voice loud in the high-vaulted room. "One A.M., Saturday, as time is measured in your lady's mortal world. Thus I even accommodate her." His guard opened the door as he approached. "To meet my adversary on the Sabbath suits my humor."

He went to his chambers, leaving Bael to carry the news to Heaven that the goat had snapped at the bait.

4

A Dinner Party in Hell

Bael had warned Leianna: "Don't ever come down to Hell without me!"

As it turned out, she had never set foot on the lower planes comprising his kingdom, despite being tempted to seek him out and explore the Netherworld. Despite her protests, Quatama had tweaked her soul's aura with some power that blocked her ability to even venture near the darker planes. Only tonight had he lifted that psychic block.

Now as a guest of Lucifer, she and Quatama were in Hell. Even so, Leianna still hadn't even left the royal palace.

She leaned over the low stone balustrade that circled one-third of its highest tier. Bael had led her outside onto this balcony. Above and directly behind them, a round, lighted dome crowned the northwest corner. It cast shadow and light onto the yellow, white, beige and brown flagstone floor that they stood upon. Leianna welcomed the dome's soft illumination; it chased away the murk of the Netherworld night.

Bael waved his hand toward the cityscape far below them: the buildings, shops, parks, and thoroughfares of the capital city of Tandour in Domain. "Here in Domain, our royal principality in Hell, and in the four other countries sharing this first level of Hell, the noble classes of Hell rule and play."

"And their servants?" Her tone challenged him. The panorama below stretched past the city limits to open country with the lights of smaller cottages, roads, a large, round stadium, and further on, darkened fields and a distant mountain, barely discernible against the black velvet sky.

"There are other classes besides servants," he answered with a half-smile. "We have industry, arts and sciences in this first level. Its citizens live here willingly. You could liken them to the freeborn citizens of ancient Rome. They, too, had emperors, some mad, some sane, but none like Lucifer, ruler of our Netherworld."

"You don't rule?"

He stared at her, as if deciphering the intent of her question, then returned his gaze to the panorama beyond the palace. "My brothers and I are royal princes, and we each share both responsibilities and power. Our word is considered law in most instances."

"Except for what?"

Now his stare became probing.

"Why do you stare at me like that?"

"I'm trying to guess your reasons for asking these questions."

"Why don't you just ask me?"

His smile widened, flashing even teeth. He looked good, dressed all in black: pants, boots, long-sleeved shirt and wide cummerbund. Looking like some dashing pirate, his thick black hair framed his face, resting temptingly on his neck. He had removed the elegant black dinner jacket he wore, casually handing the jewel-encrusted garment to a hall guard before guiding Leianna out into the warm night and the tower balcony to show her Tandour. "Perhaps I enjoy your mysterious womanly ways."

"I want no mysteries between us."

"No secrets?"

"This is no game, Bael. I need to know what goes on around here, and how I'll fit in." Despite distant starlight in the night sky, Hell was a world endlessly gray and dark, not even a moon to cast silver light upon this dimension, never a sun to rise into its sky and shed rays of golden warmth. But Lucifer had tamed Hell and used its resources, and today, electric lights chased away its darkness.

Hell had a day, too, Bael told her, but its sky shone a dull, thick silver-gray, as if an encroaching storm was forever approaching. And Bael had joked there was sulfur with its repellent stench, just as the legends said, but only in the lower circles of Hell. No brimstone assaulted her nose here. "I wonder if I could ever fit in here."

"You'd be a royal princess." He paused. "I hear both fear and determination in your words. You'll be an unusual addition to my family, but you mustn't fear them."

She turned away from the balustrade and from Bael. "Not even Lucifer?"

"Especially not him."

"Why? Does he secretly admire me and want us to marry?"

He hesitated until Leianna turned back to him, glancing sharply up at him, and then he reached over and ran his fingers through her hair, lifting and separating one auburn strand. He stroked it between his fingers. "See how the light catches your hair, giving it a golden sheen. Fire and ice, and one does not douse or melt the other." He lowered his hand. "No, Lucifer doesn't want you back in my life. He's never forgiven you for siding with the Creator. He's hoping that you'll screw up, that the millennia we've been apart have changed us."

She pursed her lips, troubled. "I think that they have. Don't you?"

"Yes, intensely so. But it seems some things *don't* change."

"My Lord," the guard holding Bael's dinner jacket interrupted them. "Your father requests that you and the Lady Leianna join him and the other dinner guests. They are about to sit down." The man nodded to another guard, who walked briskly off, having delivered his message. Both were dressed in a perfect imitation of a Praetorian guard of old Rome. Perhaps there was some significance to Bael's remark about Roman citizens, some parallel history. The guard now held out the jacket like a butler, helping Bael into it, then stood once again at attention at his post within the archway.

Leianna noticed that he held a spear, and a short sword was sheathed in a scabbard hung on a belt around his waist, but she saw no guns. Considering that Bael had said that sulfur and phosphorus were plentiful, she wondered if the guards were ever really called upon to protect their masters, or if the spear and sword were merely ornamental.

Bael held out his hand. "Come. Duty calls, Leianna."

She grasped his hand and walked beside him through the cavernous hall that connected the tower with lower palace floors. The silken folds of her lilac gown brushed the stone corridor, its petticoat undergarment rustling softly. Soft sconces positioned along their way lent a golden cast to the gown's delicate, white lace collar. The collar draped its scoop-necked bodice and covered her upper arms demurely. They moved downward to the ballroom and banquet room.

"So tell me why?" Bael said.

"Why what?"

"Why were you questioning my status here, my power? Why do you ask about servants?"

They turned a corner and now various aromas filled the air, both of baking and of roasting, rich and beckoning. Leianna wondered what they could possibly eat in Hell; it smelled inviting and she hoped the aromas genuinely matched the food to be served. "First, I want to make sure that you can protect me here. Secondly, I want to know if your servants are condemned souls, forced to serve you as slaves."

He slowed his pace, squeezing her hand. "I can protect you if I am beside you, my love. That is why I forbid you to come here without me, or to go wandering off without me or my having designated a trustworthy guard for you. I have already made it very clear to my people, as did Ashtoreth, that if any who owe allegiance to Hell should in any way harm you, be it done in Hell, on the astral planes or on Earth, they will be punished beyond severity. Aside from that, trust in the protection that Quatama, the Seraphim and the Creator have given you."

"And the servants?"

"They are all willing and loyal, whether they are condemned to Hell because of Earthly misdeeds or they have chosen to descend to our realm of their own volition."

"In mortal slave cultures, a job in the house of the master was a cushy job."

"And so it is here, but if a soul is not being punished for a serious sin, he or she is treated decently." Down at the end of the corridor large double doors opened for them. Inside, four male waiters stood stiffly in dark suits near the long dinner table set with linen, china plates, silver cutlery and crystal goblets. In the eight chairs ranged about the table, six people sat, waiting for them.

Leianna saw Quatama nod to the two empty seats to his left. Ashtoreth, his golden hair neatly brushed and wearing a Roman toga, his favorite mode of dress here, sat at Quatama's right side. Across from Ashtoreth, sat a woman Leianna hadn't seen for 35,000 years: Affaeteres, Lucifer's wife, mother of his sons. She had some minor facial lines, the only hint of those years having passed, her long blonde hair coiffed in an intricate upsweep. To her right and across from Quatama sat Lucifer himself, his own hair as thick, golden and wavy as Ash's, for Lucifer's first son resembled him strongly, although Ash's sea green eyes matched his mother's. He had not inherited Lucifer's piercing, blue eyes.

Leianna was also seeing Lucifer for the first time since he fell from grace. To Lucifer's right sat a beautiful slender woman with blonde hair a shade or two lighter than Affaeteres's and a face that could easily have been her daughter's. Leianna took her seat next to Quatama and across from this girl. With typical candor, she told her, "We've never met, I believe. My name is Leianna. Are you a family member whom I'm unaware of?"

The girl appeared confused and turned to the young, fair-haired man who sat to her right and directly across from Bael as he sat down next to Leianna. The girl asked her companion, "May I answer?"

The young man, who seemed familiar to Leianna, said, "Of course, you may, Regan. And tell Leianna who I am as well."

"Good evening. I am Regan, a concubine from the harem of Lord Azmodeus and honored to sit here at this table with him and to serve him and his family." She spoke demurely and lowered her eyes after speaking.

Leianna sat quietly for a moment and then gazed at Azmodeus,

Bael and Ashtoreth's younger brother. "I didn't recognize you, Az, until you spoke. I remembered the fourteen-year-old I once knew. You've obviously become a man, but your speech patterns haven't changed." She didn't mention the Halloween over five years ago when he had disguised himself as an obnoxious, sarcastic teenager in the mortal world and harassed her as she, as Leigh Ann Elfman, and her sister Ginnie were taking Daniel out trick-or-treating. She also hid her surprise when Regan asked his *permission* to respond to her and then described herself as his *concubine*. Now she nodded to the timid girl and said: "Good evening to you, too, Regan." The girl raised her eyes briefly to meet her own and gave an almost imperceptible nod back. "You look so like Affaeteres that I thought, at first, over the long years since we've seen one another, that she might have had a daughter."

Affaeteres spoke for the first time. "My son simply wishes to insult me by parading about a woman whose beauty is similar to that which I once possessed."

Leianna simply stared at the woman who had once been like a second mother to her. "Mother Aff? You're still just as beautiful."

"Are you blind, Leianna? I have shriveled in this realm, my skin dry, my hair dull, my nose pinched. My youngest son has to remind me of this, even on this day when I am to reunite with you, Bael's beloved, who was to be my daughter through marriage, whom I loved and nurtured when you were little and your true mother, Eve, was trapped on Earth. Azmodeus, why did you bring your trollop to this monumental dinner?"

Regan's cheeks burned crimson; she appeared torn between appealing to Azmodeus for direction, who sat there motionless, and fleeing the room. A thick, coagulating silence engulfed them. Leianna felt Quatama's hand briefly touch her arm. She looked at Affaeteres. "Mother Aff, perhaps you feel that way inside. Bael told me of how Hell has tested and tried you. But although I don't know Regan at all, I feel that she is not deliberately trying to mock you by resembling you. She has no control over that at all, and your accusation may have deeply hurt her. Az is not using Regan as a mirror to remind you of your flaws. You *are not flawed,* your beauty is your own, and any who resemble you only compliment you." Leianna sat waiting to see how Affaeteres would react, glancing anxiously at the troubled woman.

Affaeteres stared back, her eyes suddenly wet with tears. She stood up stiffly. "My dear, soon-to-be adopted daughter through marriage, it took your visit to Hell to open the thickly scabbed wound that Hell has inflicted upon me." She pulled back her chair and began walking away from the banquet table. "It still pains me, and now it bleeds again."

Leianna also stood up. "Please don't leave, Mother Aff. I need you here!"

The older woman hesitated, turning back.

"Please! Don't leave me. Not alone here," she said, sincerely uncomfortable confronting Lucifer without Affaeteres beside him. The fact that Mother Aff seemed to have succumbed to a sort of madness made Leianna all the more determined to want some justice in this sad dimension for those being manipulated within it. "Please, Mother Aff! I was only trying to help."

Lucifer twisted in his chair, confronting his wife. "Sit down, Affaeteres! And apologize to your youngest and his damned trollop."

Leianna sucked her breath in and expelled it angrily. "Father Lucifer!" Her tone plainly rebuked his insult to Regan. During the war in Heaven, Leianna had expressed herself just as plainly to him.

He apparently still felt no qualms in responding back to her just as blatantly, leaning toward her with a confidential air. "Azmodeus has many concubines. This one is nothing more than an ornament that Az has chosen to wear on his arm. And he did deliberately choose her because she resembles his mother and he knows that irritates Aff. He also probably means to impress you, Leianna, with the example of Regan's extreme subservience. Or maybe depress you with it. If I recall from that long ago time, during Eliom's short-lived war, you were anything but subservient to Bael's needs until you knew you were about to lose him.

"You and Quatama must forgive us our little entertainments. It gets so boring here in Hell and when we have extraordinary guests, we like to test them in little ways that give us a rise. Please pay these little squabbles no attention, Quatama. We are glad that you've accepted our invitation to dine and discuss, shall we say, a new tomorrow?"

As he spoke, Affaeteres had reseated herself. She held up her crystal goblet and struck it delicately with a silver spoon, creating a dulcet ring. "I wish to say something: I have returned." The dinner guests waited patiently. "I apologize to you, Regan, as Leianna has requested of me. You are most welcome at my table." She gestured with her hand to the four standing waiters. "Dinner may be served."

One of the waiters snapped his fingers and new waiters came into the room, carrying various trays of food and beverages, wheeling carts also laden with food. Leianna watched curiously as the other three original waiters surveyed the food, and sliced then lifted morsels of each dish with their own cutlery into their own mouths. When all met with their satisfaction, they gestured for the new waiters to begin serving each offering, first to Lucifer and then to his guests and family.

A thick soup ladled into large bowls held what appeared to be succulent chunks of chicken within the broth and chopped vegetables. Salad plates were heaped with green feathery leaves, orange pepper slices, ordinary cucumbers and tomatoes and pale slices of mushroom. Small clear canisters of salad dressing were placed beside each plate, a thick purple sauce within. Leianna pointed to it. "What is it?"

A waiter answered. "A plum vinaigrette, my lady."

She nodded. All but two of the waiters had thin black hair combed slickly down and back onto their necks; all wore dark suits with white shirts and were thin. The head waiter and one of the tasters were bald, and now all but the headwaiter withdrew a few paces from the table. The headwaiter placed a jeweled centerpiece on the table before Lucifer and also stepped back.

Lucifer reached over and pressed one of its ruby jewels. It lit up like a lamp, its rays scintillating and spreading out, around and beyond the table.

Leianna became startled, scraping her chair backwards, but Bael stayed her with his hand. "A protective aura," he explained, "safeguarding us. A custom long established."

"You need protection during dinnertime?!"

Lucifer answered wryly. "We have upon occasion suffered disruptions and distractions." He spooned his soup and swallowed his first mouthful.

Water in crystal decanters had already been placed on the table. Azmodeus said, "Regan." It was not a request. She rose and poured each crystal goblet full, attending to her own last and then took her seat again.

Lucifer said: "Once the force field is set, we engage a trusted servant to serve the remaining meal. This is for your protection as well. Many here suffer no sympathy or love for those who help cast us into Hell."

Regan settled her gaze upon her place setting, her soup and salad, but lifted no fork or spoon to eat them with.

She intrigued Leianna, seeming not to belong in Hell, much less subservient to its youngest prince noted for his lewdness. Leianna would pursue this later, not now. Tonight she would broach the possibility of an Alliance between Heaven and Hell.

She glanced across at Lucifer. He had finished his soup and was chomping his salad with the heartiness of a man for whom food was an art, who cherished every nuance of texture and flavor. He swallowed and said, "Eat! Eat, please! The food's been tested. It's safe."

Startled at the thought that the taster earlier hadn't only been approving the taste of their dinner items, she tried the soup, mildly seasoned, its vegetables crisp. The others did likewise, even Regan, as if Leianna were a bell, leading the rest of them.

They ate silently, slightly strained in their quiet courtesy, body language veiled.

The first course ended. Regan stood up and cleared the salad and soup dishes away. Slender and small, her shortness was the one trait completely opposite to the regal height of Affaeteres. Regan moved between two serving stations and the table, carrying heated plates filled with roasted beef and potatoes and vegetables smothered in a rich wine sauce, serving one to each diner, her own last. She then accepted from the head waiter three large baskets of soft, fragrant rolls and butter, placed them on the table, front, middle and end.

"And now," Lucifer said, "please take your time and savor our chef's culinary delights. We can reacquaint ourselves in a friendly manner while we appreciate his skills. But first, some wine!" He snapped his fingers and a rich, red Burgundy appeared in decanters on either side of the banquet table, as well as wine glasses for everyone. "It wouldn't be Hell," Lucifer joked, "without a little magic. Actually this is my own private stock, its vintage quite ancient, and its taste exquisite." He snapped his fingers again. Regan stood up and served the wine, then reseated herself.

Lucifer raised his glass. "A toast then. To a new dialogue between Heaven and Hell and to the renewed courtship of my son Bael and the beautiful Leianna!"

Bael and Leianna drank along with the others, nodding to them. Quatama pointed his emptied glass at their host. "A true dialogue will bring many benefits. Heaven wishes to reform Hell. The time for its use purely as a punishment plane, for mortals consigned by their actions or trapped into it or resigned to it by false belief, is soon to end, along with the condemnation which you, Lucifer, and your followers, who rule it, have suffered."

Lucifer swallowed his mouthful of wine-drenched beef. "By whose decision?"

"Our Creator's," said Quatama.

Lucifer poured himself more wine and sipped it thoughtfully. "We have done quite well on our own over the centuries, punishing sinners." He smiled wistfully. "Sometimes we also reward them if it suits our purposes. Does Heaven propose to forgive them all, even those most evil, lifting them sentimentally into higher planes? And do I get to ride along . . . back home?"

Quatama helped himself to more wine, drank it sparingly and set the glass down. "Heaven is aware that some of those whom you call sinners are not capable of entering Heaven, due to their soul's current negativity. But we have long known that no one is eternally damned, no more than any being can be eternally blessed. One can only *be* and in the process of *being*, learn about oneself and in learning, advance spiritually into a better self, and eventually into an unselfish state that brings accord with all things in the universe. All entities undergo this growth process. Even those who dwell in Hell, including yourself, have an eternal right to it."

"And so?" Lucifer speared a chunk of beef, waving it. "How do you propose to educate the damned in exercising this right?"

"By rehabilitating them."

Azmodeus laughed aloud, leaning out over the table, looking down it to Quatama. "And just how do you expect to do that? Prayer sessions? Send a troupe of Catholics down to sprinkle them with holy water? Have a tribe of Jews tear up bits of bread for them to throw into the lava rivers of Hell, to burn up their sins?"

Leianna leaned toward him. "The proper ritual is to throw the bread into a real river during the High Holidays to carry any troubles and wrong-doings we committed out to sea and away."

Az smirked. "Like you know everything, right. Well, we had our share of trouble and sinning down here. But, Quatama, what will your method of rehabilitation be? Hair shirts? Praying to God on their knees morning, noon and night, which it's hard to tell the difference between, here in Hell? Or perhaps leeches to bleed their sins away? Just how do you intend to reform the lost sinners of Hell?"

Quatama had pushed away all of the beef on his plate and was enjoying the potato, mixed with his salad greens. "We intend to use psychology."

Lucifer nearly choked, coughing loudly, and then calmed himself. "Psychology?! Are you serious?!"

Quatama nodded. "And meditation. And perhaps some psychiatry thrown in. We will also determine if the earthly life traits were due to chemical imbalances in the brain and body."

"Whoa," Lucifer said. "I think we've got West Side Story here, complete with the equally useless social worker, shrink and job counselor. What's that line?" He sang out: "We're no good, we're no good, we're no good, we're no good. The whole lot of us is no damn good!"

And Azmodeus said: "And don't forget our own Romeo and Juliet." He turned to Regan. "I forget the names of the couple in the Bernstein movie, not that the guy could dance as well as the Puerto Ricans."

Bael drained his wine. "Tony and Cleopatra. And I also have my right-hand man."

He flicked his glass at Ashtoreth, who put in, "But we're not going to fight you."

"Oh, man," said Azmodeus, "no battle in the barrio?"

"No," Ash told him, "this is about positive change, regardless of whether you think it's possible."

Az took Regan's hand in his. "They want me to grow. Where shall I grow, my dear?"

She didn't answer, but Leianna did: "Don't be rude!" Her tone rang out sharply, regally, visibly startling Azmodeus. He let go of his concubine's hand, saying nothing. Leianna felt certain that no other woman had ever shut his mouth in centuries.

Quatama said with a touch of ironic humor, "Behavioral therapy is also an effective tool."

They could feel Az's anger at being the butt of the joke. He now responded, his voice low, his words measured, laced with a subdued fury. "I'd forgotten how difficult it was for you to deal with conflicts, Leianna. Everything had to be proper and perfect. You should fear this Alliance you propose, but I fear that you do not know what fear is. We of Hell do. Tell her, Father, her and Quatama, what horrendous challenges waited for you and our people when you were first thrown down into Golgotha! I was spared from them, having beforehand been torn from my family and flung through the winds of the canyon into a mortal woman's womb, to be born as a mortal on the Earth. But when my mortal body died, I found my way back to my father and my family in the hellish world our Creator had banished them to. And they told me of horrors which I'm sure would have cost you your mind, Leianna. You ought to know a good deal more about our world before you so blithely invade it! Tell her, Father, tell her and Quatama of your arrival in a world you eventually came to rule."

Leianna had listened quietly and now addressed Lucifer. "Yes, I would like to know that."

Lucifer broke a bit of roll to sop up the remains of the wine sauce on his plate, chewing slowly. Leianna slowly finished her own meal, surprised at how delicious everything had tasted, certain that the meat was an illusion, but not an evil, deliberate one. On the higher planes, a roast turkey dinner was created using a form of psychic tofu for any animal flesh. "It will help me to understand what you and your people underwent."

Lucifer poured more wine for himself, sitting back. "Regan," he commanded, "clear the table and serve dessert."

The petite blonde complied. For the first time, Leianna noticed that she was dressed in the Eliomese style, a snug white gown that hugged her soft curves and resembled Affaeteres's. Regan removed the used dishes and glasses, waited until the head waiters tasted the thick berry pie and chocolate mousse, and then served them to the dinner guests. The coffee and tea were also tasted, and steaming pots were placed onto the table for them to choose and help themselves.

"Very good, Regan," Lucifer told her. "You may sit down and join us again." His tone held a softened edge of weariness. He looked at Leianna. "The last you saw of me, my family and followers, we were being lifted into the roiling cloud of blinding light. Now you ask me what befell us afterwards. Didn't Bael speak to you of this?"

"Only that you were blinded and buffeted about within that cloud, and that he fell unconscious until he arrived in a land that seemed devoid of light, except for the fiery glow of volcanoes and phosphorus pools." She glanced at Bael. "He told me that hours later a dim, misty dawn broke, and that a dark grey sky rose over the world you were exiled into."

Lucifer remembered, grimacing. "Exiled, yes! Our arrival point resembled a moonscape except that in the distance a volcano soon steamed rivers of lava flowing down its slopes, its smoke and ash obscuring the sky."

Ashtoreth spoke up. "We were all afraid, especially the women, who began to wail and beseech my father to ask the Creator's forgiveness. But it was too late for that. None of us knew this would happen."

Affaeteres stood up. "I didn't wail." She sat down.

"No, you didn't, Mother," Ash said. "You were very afraid, but you acted bravely."

"Yes, I did. When this world was at its worst, I could stomach it better." She looked at Lucifer. "Well, my dear, tell Leianna and Quatama the tale of how we survived Hell."

5

Into the Abyss

In the utter darkness — (Lucifer recalled the terror of their arrival in Hell) — he heard screams, wails and calls by his followers to their friends and family and to him. Lucifer once again took command. He called back to them, his voice booming above their fearful babble. "Everyone be quiet! Everyone! This is Lucifer!"

He had chosen his people well. Their cries died down to silence. "I am going to call out the names of my leaders one by one, who must answer me and then call out the names of their own charges, who must answer them and alert us to their presence. And once we have done that, I will call for my family. In this way we will know if we have all arrived here intact, that none of us are missing."

He started with Dagon, the only spirit master who had rebelled with Lucifer.

His eldest subcommander answered him, his voice hoarse as the gravel beneath their feet. "I am here!" Dagon called out the names of those under his command, who called out their presence in the darkness.

Lucifer then called out the names of Moloch, Adrammelech, Chemosh, of Behemoth, Mammon and Belial, of Thamuz, Phoenixious and Cimeries. All responded as did the folk under their guidance. Adrammelech complained of the suffering of his seven year old son Marech, and his mother, Maura, Adrammelech's wife, called out shakily: "He will not speak sense to us! The child utters nonsense words, and shivers, as do I in this black void."

Lucifer spoke soothingly to her. "We will find light, and we will ease your son's shock, Maura. For now, let me continue to identify us all. I call for Naamah. Answer me, lady, if you be here."

"I am here," came her voice, faintly, from what seemed like a distance from him. "Those who are under me, I will call out your names for your acknowledgment. Answer me swiftly!"

Her charges did so quickly, trusting Lucifer's only woman subcommander and voicing no complaint.

Lucifer continued: "Lothan, I know that you, your wife, Tia, and daughter, Sharlan, must be here." They all three raggedly voiced their presences to him. "Now call out to those angelfolk who serve under your command."

Lothan's strong, deep voice rang out: "Answer me, my folk, as I call your names." His charges did, all accounted for.

Lastly, Lucifer called out, "Nergal! I call you last. Are you and Shadella and your group of angelfolk safely accounted for?" Silence greeted his question. "Nergal? Nergal! Shadella was with child. Are you both here?"

A loud masculine wail shattered through the blackness. "Damn our Creator, who has stolen Shadella's unborn child from her very womb! We are here, but our child is not! Shadella's womb is flat, as if it had never blossomed with my seed! Daughter or son, I know not, but know that I have been robbed and my wife's heart torn into pieces of pain." A woman's incoherent wail matched his cry.

"Nergal!" Lucifer shouted above their outcry. "Nergal! My heart grieves for your and Shadella's cruel loss. But you must calm her and yourself. You are also indebted to the folk you took as your charges. They will be like your children now, until you and Shadella can again conceive. Put aside your grief until there is time for it. Call out to your people!"

"My people?" Nergal's voice sounded drained of emotion. "Very well. Until there is time for grief." He called his charges. They answered not only with their names, but with murmurs that consoled him and Shadella.

Lucifer nodded to himself, invisible in the blackness. "Lastly, I call to my own. Affaeteres?"

"I am here, Lucifer, but I cannot see where you stand."

"No one can see. Ashtoreth?"

"I am here, Father. And Mother is beside me. We arrived here together. I was holding her. Protecting her."

"And your brother? Bael?"

No answer.

"Bael?!" Lucifer waited, wondering if his second son had been taken from him, just as Azmodeus, his youngest, had been. "Answer me, if you are here!"

A second more of silence, then a soft mutter. "Bael is present, but his heart is lost."

Lucifer looked up, mid-memory, glancing at Leianna, who asked, "If there was a volcano in the distance, wouldn't its lava flow create some light?"

"It didn't freshly erupt until perhaps an hour or two later. Time was difficult to judge. And then we had a better sense of place and space."

Bael added: "There *are* stars in the Netherworld, a cold, faint light, but no moon. We later found that the volcano, one of many which originally dotted the landscape, had erupted earlier and the ash in the Netherworld sky obliterated the weak starlight."

His father spooned up a bit of mousse, savoring the taste, then said, "Why don't you tell of the rest of that first night and morning in Hell? After all, you were the star of the show! Despite your distraught state of mind, you acquitted yourself honorably. It was the catalyst that caused me to name you my second-in-command and heir."

"Immortals need no heirs, Father."

"I am less sure of that now than when I bestowed the honor on you. However, you still carry the title. And I again request that you continue the story for Quatama and Leianna. I weary of telling it."

Bael sighed, wondering about his father's real motive, and reluctantly continued the tale of their arrival in Hell.

He felt as if the blackness entombed him, that his father and the others spoke to him from an immeasurable and unreachable distance. He knew that a part of his very soul, his Leianna, had been taken from him, and if a foreseeable future awaited him, she would never share it. Before Lucifer's fall, during the events leading to it, the elven matriarch Chamira had warned Leianna and Bael: do not allow yourselves to be separated. But perhaps Chamira knew that their best efforts to safeguard their love, to not be torn apart, would fail. Perhaps that was why she had Elijah, the young spirit master, speak of a prophecy to Bael, Leianna and Ashtoreth.

If the prophecy was valid, countless eons would pass before he and Leianna could reunite. Until then, she was lost to him.

He had forced himself to answer Lucifer. He didn't want to be here in this astral wilderness, he didn't want to face this horrid exile. He wanted to die, as those earthly mortals did, and forget he ever existed.

And then he heard the screaming, a woman's high-pitched wail, sounding somewhat familiar. Her voice gave proof to some unseen horror afflicting her.

He heard a man call: "Sharlan?! Where are you, daughter?" Bael knew it was Lothan's daughter whose cries pierced in the black void. Another woman cried out, "Lothan! Our daughter! Help our daughter!" He heard the sound of Tia's hysterical weeping, fearful and not knowing what danger their daughter faced.

"Something has hold of me, Father! Something with scales, standing upright! And claws! They cut me! Oh, Creator!" Sharlan screamed again.

Bael moved towards her, trying to gauge her voice, calling, "Try to get away, Sharlan! Try to find the rest of us. Curse this darkness!"

He brushed against another body. "Who is it?"

"Ashtoreth. Mother is beside me."

Their mother spoke in a resigned whisper. "If only we had light. Dear Creator, do not abandon us completely!"

Peals of thunder louder than any they had ever experienced drowned out all other sounds. And then they knew it was not thunder, but the rim of a mountain top, perhaps as distant as a valley's length from them, bursting outward and upward with fire, smoke and what seemed a river of burning water, the color of bright flames, sweeping out in wide swathes and thick rivulets down the mountainside.

Its heated glow produced a faint visibility, and they saw what creature attempted to drag Sharlan off. It was small, reaching only to her shoulder, and reptilian, a sort of upright lizard, its tail snapping back and forth, the thin lids of its eyes shutting and opening rhythmically, turning towards Bael, as it pulled the struggling girl along.

The fallen angels clustered near one another in a loose circle, but at its perimeter, Bael saw other lizard creatures. They huddled and watched the progress of their bolder member's attempt to capture the screaming Sharlan.

Lothan, his daughter's distress now visible, grabbed the creature furiously. He attempted to pull it off. But its thick claws were embedded in Sharlan's arm, tearing her flesh. "Stop it, Father!" she shrieked. "It's tearing me apart!!" But Lothan didn't seem to understand, Sharlan's arm hidden from him, between her and the creature. And now one of the other creatures moved stealthily towards another of the women angels.

Bael rushed forward, facing Lothan. "Stop pulling the creature. Its claws have a hold of her arm."

Bael raised both of his hands and dug his fingers deeply into each of the creature's eyes. It howled, a furious honking sound, and released its short but powerful forearm's grip on Sharlan, its small paws sweeping up to its ruined sight and then blindly outward to attack Bael with its claws springing out again. He clenched his teeth against the pain it caused to his own arms and withdrew his fingers from the reptile's eyes, now pounding its face between its nostrils until he heard a crack. The creature stilled, sinking down to the rock-strewn ground, twitching.

He felt Sharlan touch his back. She wept, her long, black hair tangled and disheveled. "Thank you! Oh, sweet friend, thank you!" She touched the wound on her injured arm carefully. "I will need healing." She looked at Bael's own arms, lacerated in ugly, parallel rips. "So will you, again," she said, reminding him of his earlier injuries, before the Seraphim exiled them from Eliom, when he tried to reach Leianna and met an invisible barrier that burned him.

Other shouts echoed from the rim of the clustered circle of angelfolk. The men had found large stones and were aiming them with deadly intent at the lizard creatures, targeting their eyes, skulls and necks. One, nearly upon a woman it had chosen as a victim, went down, yellow fluid spraying from its torn neck. The other creatures retreated now, running off shrieking into the murk until they disappeared from view.

Tia's hand hovered over Sharlan's wounds; Affaeteres and Ashtoreth attended Bael's injured arms. They sent their healing energy over Bael and Sharlan. The torn skin stopped its blue flow of lost skane, the angelic equivalent of mortal blood, and drew together, the wounds closing, the scars fading to faint pink marks.

Lucifer joined them, his expression grim. "What *is* this place? What were those things?"

Affaeteres said, "Whatever they are, they are part of our world now." She glanced at the fiery mountain. "A dangerous world. We must guard against them."

Bael touched each of his arms gingerly. "I am glad now to know that Leianna was not sent to this world. But my heart is still sick with worry. Did she survive breaching that fiery barrier, trying to reach *me*, just as I first tried to reach her before the Seraphim lifted us up and flung us into exile here?"

Lucifer answered him bitterly. "I wouldn't worry about your precious betrothed. Our Creator, I'm sure, has plans for her. She was deliberately separated from you. Worry more about yourself and our people here!"

"He did!" Sharlan defended him fervently, standing beside him, as tall as he was. "He saved me from that beast!"

Affaeteres folded her arms. "He rescued you, yes. But the fire mountain saved us all, lifting the darkness, exposing our attackers."

Sharlan added: "It did, after you called out to our Creator for help. Perhaps you were heard, however distant we are from Eliom, our homes and the Garden."

Affaeteres shrugged. A tall woman herself, taller than Lucifer, she looked at him coldly. "What shall we do now, husband?"

He gazed about at the other angelfolk waiting for his response. "The only thing we can do. Explore this world. The Creator was very explicit: we were to be taken to a place where we would be granted free will, even the free will to disobey, a right we were denied in Eliom. Free will implies choice; choice implies things to choose from, decisions to make, here in this harsh world. But it is not a place to die in! We must learn to live in it, with its challenges, punishments and rewards. Oh, yes, our adventure is upon us!" He paused, studying the fire mountain. "I think those fluid streams are on fire, made of molten rock from the mountain and a danger to us below. We must seek higher ground away from it and hope this darkness is merely night in this wilderness."

The way still was difficult, but they noticed a lower *cahn* or hill, leading upward and followed it away from the *vulcahnoh*, the name they gave to the fire mountain.

In their language, Eliomese, *vul* meant "fire," although they had never tamed it nor had a use for fire in their lost home world. In Eliom, they only ate the fruits, nuts, vegetables and grains of their fields and orchards, and they heated their cooking and baking alcoves and warmed their residences with their own radiant energy. And as winters passed mildly in Eliom, they built no fireplaces nor knew of such things. The word *vul* — fire or flame — was reserved for the rare display of lightning and the even rarer lightning strike igniting a bush or tree. Never in all the angelfolk's experience had a dwelling or person been struck, and so they considered the sky's *vul* a display that only the Creator understood.

The word *cahn* meant "hill" and the word *oh* meant "great size." And so they dubbed the fire mountain *vulcahnoh*, the fire hill of great size, and feared it, knowing the blessings of Eliom were denied them in this hard world.

Unlike the Seraphim, they had no wings, but while in Eliom, they had the special gift of lifting, a discipline of levitation and traveling through meditative thought, off the ground a ways and flying low on air currents to their destination. They quickly found this ability stripped from them in this world.

The most extraordinary trait of the angelfolk — thought transference, an intense concentration that allowed instant travel from one place to another — was only used during spiritual learning and ceremonies conducted by the Seraphim. Adam and his sister Eve had misused it when they thought-transferred to Earth for a forbidden glimpse of Earth's surface and were stranded on that planet.

No one would dare to thought-transfer in this horrid wilderness. Creator knew where it would land them. And so they had yet to test if that talent still remained.

It seemed that the only safe gifts of Eliom left to them were their healing powers . . . their radiant energy . . . and their minds and bodies. They trudged wearily up the smaller *cahn*. Both men and women gathered whatever sharp stones could be culled from the rubble beneath their feet, for crude weapons, should the lizard creatures return.

When they reached the hill top, they gazed back across the valley below to the *vulcahnoh* and what appeared to be a dim mountain range beyond it. The *vulcahnoh* still spewed forth its streams of fire water, its crown a molten, bubbling mass against the dark sky.

They then turned their gazes in the opposite direction, but their eyes were unable to see beyond the murk.

Lucifer called the women to the center of a circle and set the men around them. "We cannot see the way ahead. I hope that I am not merely optimistic when I suggest that we have arrived in the dark night of this world and that there will be a day and it will bring more light. This hill offers some protection, but we must be prepared to fight if those creatures or others attack us. Yet perhaps we will be lucky in a luckless land."

"What luck?" Nergal said, his bulk imposingly visible now. "Is our Creator so harsh, simply because we would not incarnate and save the inferior mortals of Earth from what Eve and Adam wrought, to heave us into a land with no sustenance, no shelter or safety, and no means to find such?"

Dagon, now their only spirit master, came slowly toward them, a thin bald shadow in the half-light. "Our Creator will not let us waste away in this barren place. It would neither satisfy nor amuse the One to see our punishment as short-lived as the mortals we disdained."

"Perhaps it would," Lucifer said. "It would lend irony to the price for our disobedience. But I also cannot believe the Creator would set us upon such a path. That would invalidate the promise made to us. The Creator must keep that promise, providing us with the means to continue and face our lives with conflicts and choices involving free will. Perhaps our Maker has no inclination to ease us on our way. If so, so be it. We will do whatever is needed to survive. For now, let us rest. I wish to perform an experiment."

Lucifer bent down and began to select large rocks from those strewn on the ground. He piled them carefully, one supporting the other until they rose a few feet upward. He then knelt and held out his hands to the stones.

Dagon and Lothan, realizing his intention, lent their own radiant energy to the rock pile. Sharlan came over, reaching out her own hands, but Lucifer waved her away, saying, "Wait until we discern the nature of these stones." She backed away.

A slight burning smell tinged the air, and the brown rocks under Lucifer and Lothan's hands began to glow a dull purple. But under Dagon's hands, the uppermost stone changed rapidly from grey to dark red and suddenly burst into flame. Dagon scuttled back, but not before the hem of his robe caught a spark and flames licked its edges. Dagon knelt quickly, suppressing his radiant energy, and pounded the burning cloth with his hands, turning the fabric over and smothering it out.

Some of the remaining rocks also ignited in a shower of leaping flames, the less volatile stones now heating more, turning from purple to bright, glowing lavender. They lent light in a circle a good many yards around the folk.

Lucifer studied the different stones and picked up another cold, grey stone from the ground. "This is our fire starter," he said, pleased. "We must pile the darker stones first, then add the lighter ones in alternate layers, carefully heating the fire starters in the pile to burn and heat the darker rocks."

Lothan held out his own hands, his radiant energy contained now, to the glowing rocks for warmth. "There is a chill in this place that our robes bring little comfort from."

"Then let us gather these stones as new tools and show our people how to safely build these little fire hills, these *vulcahnahs*, for warmth and for light, and perhaps to assist in food preparation, once we find sustenance."

Sharlan held out her own hands beside her father's. "That will be good," she said, glancing worriedly both at Lucifer and Bael. "The folk have never gone without food and drink. Can we angels survive without nourishment or will we die like the mortals of Earth?"

Bael put his arm around her shoulder, hugging her loosely. "We will find water and edible plant life. The Creator did not fling us into a totally lifeless world. We have simply begun this challenge in a less hospitable part." He hid his own uncertainty from her.

Sharlan leaned against him, allowing the comfort of his embrace for one moment more. "Thank you for your words of hope." She broke away gently. "Many of the folk are weary, cold and afraid. With these *vulcahnahs*, perhaps we can rest for awhile. Their fires may even drive the lizard creatures away."

Bael nodded, beginning to comb the ground for more of the precious rocks, and he and Sharlan spent the bulk of the night teaching their people how to use their first weapons against the cold, the darkness and the monsters hiding within it.

Bael broke off from his tale, helping himself to more wine. "The *vulcahnahs* did bring hope to the exiled angelfolk that first dark night in Hell."

Leianna touched his hand, her fingers entwining with his. "It almost sounds as if you're still saying volcano."

"The last syllable is *ah*, which means small, tiny or perhaps even miniature in Eliomese. *Vulcahnah:* tiny fire hill. *Vulcahnoh:* great fire hill. There are degrees of meaning in Eliomese, just as there are in other languages, depending on context. *Ohah* means normal size, average, medium."

Leianna shook her head. "I'm afraid I don't remember my Eliomese."

He squeezed her hand. "It may come back to you eventually. For now, it doesn't matter. For now, I will say that the exiled folk wandered on and found that the terrain rose steadily upward into an immense circular plateau with another steadily rising set of hills leading to a vast mountain range at its center. That second rise led to a new, vast circular plateau with an extensive range of connecting mountains at its center that led upward to another seemingly endless circular plateau. These vast plateaus have centered mountain ranges rising ever upward, totaling seven in all, which took us over a millennium to explore and civilize. They are known in lore as the Seven Circles of Hell. Domain, of which Tandour, as you now know, is the capitol, is the ruling country of the Netherworld and is part of the first level of Hell."

"We don't call them circles," Ashtoreth said, speaking softly, almost to himself, "although Dante found that description worked for him, and many mortals have decided that his description, which has nine circles and sinks downward into pits instead of rising upward, is the only one."

"And that Lucifer," Lucifer said, "stands in a frozen lake in the ninth circle, ruling Hell from there, while he lunches on traitors."

"I think you're interpreting Dante's *Inferno* a bit loosely, Father."

Leianna shook her head. "I've never read Dante; perhaps I should."

Lucifer shrugged expansively, his expression comical and dismissive.

"From your description, Bael, it sounds like six of those circles each sit atop another like the rings of a tree, except three-dimensionally, each ring developing a new center hub or base upon which to build the next ring of land. And the bottom or seventh circle serves as the foundation for all the upper circles. Or maybe a tree isn't such a good example. It sort of also sounds like a world shaped like a Chinese pagoda with seven stories from bottom to top."

"We call them levels," Bael corrected her. "The first level of Hell, the fifth level of Hell, etc. We don't call them circles, rings or stories." He rubbed his chin, amazed that she had pictured his world as well as she did. "But your description hits somewhat close to the mark. A better way to envision Hell is to imagine each level as a vast, round terrace rising to a new and slightly less vast terrace and that leads to another until you reach this first level, and, yes, the seventh level is the foundation of Hell."

"Just how vast are these circles — I mean, levels?"

"The first level, which is topmost and the smallest, contains five principalities or countries. There is a lake between three of them, called *Lei Lello* or Star Lake, for it reflects the only natural light in Hell. Bordering it is Keth, Allonia and Domain. The edge of Gollame marks the eastern border of the first level, neighbored by Keth and Allonia, and Absaliom borders the western border of the first level and Domain is its inland neighbor."

"I must admit that your description of the levels as "terraces" sounded incongruously pretty."

Bael snorted, sipped his wine and stared at the half-full glass. "Most of it is not, I assure you."

"I'm sure it's not. Tell me more of these seven levels. I'm assuming that some of the levels are livable, as this first one seems to be, but that others, as you imply, aren't pleasant."

Bael gave her a slightly condescending grin and raised his brows. "Very well, I'll attempt a quick nutshell description for now. Below this level is the second. The expansive waters of Lei Lello, through connecting rivers, flow downward to it, so intensely from Keth and Domain, that they create the second level's Great Lakes. We were so amazed when we discovered truly fertile land and sources of water from the third level up, that we named these lakes reverently: Lake Hope, Endurance Lake, Hidden Lake, and Lake Blessing. The second level also holds forests, farms and livestock ranches that now feed Hell.

"The lakes are bordered by a mountain range that climbs downward and covers nearly a quarter of the third level. We call that territory the Cahnohiom, the Great Hill Land, and Hell mines precious metals and jewels from it. The mountains are flanked on one side by Ajan Helvert or the Dark Green Wood and on the other side by Ajan Morvert or the Gray Green Wood. On the far side is a territory called *Talith* which means wonder in Eliomese. We named it after discovering it held a wealth of wild but edible vegetation and fruit, growing with barely any daylight, hence, our wonder.

"Below that, on the fourth level you'd be quite uncomfortable. The horrific aspects of Hell begin here: the dwellings of the damned, the demons and Hellspawn creatures; Sin City, where demons and fallen mortals who are serving us are permitted to entertain themselves; and our military barracks and prisons for souls incarcerated behind sturdy, psychic bars.

"After that it steadily gets worse. The fifth level is a punishment plane with burning deserts, suffocating quicksand, immense barren stretches of land with volcanoes, and vast facilities filled with torments and horrors to terrorize fallen sinners in need of intensive correction. The sixth level of Hell is where my father and our people landed when the Creator flung us here, a primordial world with more volcanoes, swamps, salt marshes and sparse vegetation that was barely edible. Had we been mortal, we would have starved in that world, but our angelic bodies allowed us to survive.

"And lastly, we descend to the final, seventh level, the foundation of Hell, a world of frozen waste with ice glaciers and steppes and tundra, and also a curiously cold, nearly endless stretch of beach that we call the Barren Sands. Surrounding the seventh level is an ocean the likes of which you have never experienced, not made of water, but of mist. When we finally explored all of Hell, those who ventured into the Sea of Mist soon became lost and were never seen again. We could hear them calling to us, but those who went in after them were also swallowed by the mist. At one point, only a century or so ago, we had an expedition venture into this sea with ropes tied around their bodies and one end of those ropes held firmly by others on the shore. We were able to bring those explorers back from the Sea of Mist this way, but they never found any of those who had previously been lost. Those who entered the mist had been horrified by it. They said it felt as if it were a plane of nonexistence, and once within it, as if they, too, didn't exist. We sometimes sent the irretrievably damned into the Sea of Mist. There's very little maintenance; it's an excellent garbage disposal for souls too evil for even Hell to bear, sucked away and never again seen on our unsacred shores."

"That's horrible, Bael!"

"This is Hell, Leianna."

"Yes, Bael, it is, but we're supposed to be working for a possible alliance, through which reforms and improvements can be made in Hell."

Across the table, Azmodeus spat out his wine in a rude spray, laughing hysterically. Red splatters dotted the white table cloth. "Excuse me?! Did you say you want to improve Hell?! For whose benefit and by *what* authority have you embarked upon your lofty enterprise? Bael! Ashtoreth! Are you planning to mutiny against dear old Dad?"

Ashtoreth's fingers tapped against the stem of his wine glass. "No, Az. We're simply here to discuss a possible reconciliation, pending Father's approval, to mutually benefit both Heaven and Hell."

"What could we possibly offer Heaven?"

Leianna cut in. "The redemption of lost souls."

Az studied her incredulously, no longer a recalcitrant, lanky boy dogging her and Bael's footsteps to surreptitiously watch their love-making and failing in his quest. He had grown tall, although Ashtoreth was taller and Bael even more so, but Az was as trim and firmly muscled. A man now, handsome with his waves of blond hair, his green eyes, he could play the young Apollo. But his comeliness was marred by his sneers and scowls, the emblems of his perpetually adversarial nature. He leaned toward her now, elbow on the table, hand cupping his chin. "Why? Does Heaven lack its quota lately?

She looked to Quatama, taken aback. He pushed away his untouched dessert, cupping his hands on the table. "Leianna speaks too soon. But you could offer forgiveness."

Lucifer sat up straighter, his anger plain. "Forgiveness?! What sin has Heaven committed that demands our absolution? Does Heaven even consider itself partially to blame for the events leading up to the exile of my people, after crushing my peaceful rebellion!"

Quatama turned to the right, facing Lucifer while he answered him, a gesture of respect, and held up his hands palms outward. "We would ask you and your folk to forgive us for abandoning you for so long, for not healing the rift between us sooner, and for being closed to compromise."

Lucifer leaned slowly back in his chair. "What changed your mind? And let me ask a second question: what does Heaven want of me *after* I forgive you, yours, and our Creator? Do you propose to serve in Hell now and usurp me, making those improvements Leianna so innocently wants?"

"Not to usurp you, but to restore you. We hope to rehabilitate the souls of Hell, as Leianna said."

Lucifer smirked, clearly befuddled by Quatama's proposal. "And will she wear a name tag as she works: 'Welcome to Hell! My name is Leianna. I'm your social worker?'"

Leianna ignored his joke. "Father Lucifer, don't you want to return to Heaven?"

Lucifer gaped at her, then pushed back his chair and rose. "This initial meeting of the dubious alliance committee is concluded by my say so. I'll think upon your offer and perhaps lay down some terms and conditions for Heaven, if I seriously consider it. After all, this is my world now, built by my people and our toil, with no thanks to Heaven, and I would protect it from Heaven's frivolous dichotomy. Heaven may know the difference between right and wrong, between good and evil, but Hell enforces it!

"You will both be escorted safely by Bael and Ashtoreth beyond the borders of Hell. Good night." He held up his hands. The force field around the table flared briefly for a moment, then disappeared.

As he walked away, Leianna spoke: "I would like to stay awhile to visit with Mother Aff . . . Affaeteres."

"As you wish," Lucifer said over his shoulder. "I'm sure it would do her some good." He left the dining room.

Affaeteres was staring at her, both her resignation and emotional hunger plainly showing. "That would please me very much."

6

Sharlan

Ashtoreth elected to escort Quatama back to the upper planes, while Bael and Leianna followed Affaeteres to her private chambers in the palace.

In the halls connecting the royal residences, a statuesque, dark-eyed woman came toward them. Her light green, Grecian-style gown accentuated her voluptuous figure and her rich, raven hair swept over her shoulders and down her back. She stopped abruptly; her gaze flickered first to Bael and then to Leianna. Her full lips opened in surprise, her expression almost frightened, puzzling Leianna, who posed no threat to her.

Bael and Affaeteres also paused, Bael's hand on Leianna's arm also halting her stride. He swept a hand toward the unknown beauty. "Leianna, Sharlan. Sharlan, Leianna."

Leianna barely recognized her as the pleasant but shy girl she had know in Eliom, 35,000 years ago. They had never been close, not as close as Leianna and Chloe, now incarnated as Leigh Ann's sister, Ginnie, had been. But Leianna and Sharlan had shared a simple friendship in the tight-knit community of angelfolk before the rift in the heavens tore them all apart, exiling the rebels and sending swells of the obedient to be reborn on Earth, heeding their Creator's command to heal humanity's genetic imbalance.

Sharlan attempted a smile. "Leianna. I had heard Bael found you. Has he brought you to Hell now?"

"I'm just visiting." Her answer sounded flippant, despite its truth. But Sharlan's question unnerved her. Would she have to live in Hell if the Alliance succeeded? Could she adjust to and survive in its environment emotionally? The fact that Bael lived in Hell had always been a charged and unsettled issue, since she had never even been allowed down here until tonight.

And Sharlan was now exquisite. Leianna suddenly felt inadequate, short and bumpkinish. Why hadn't she paid more attention to her astral appearance and choice of gown? She must look like a purple turnip left out overnight in a frost in her purple and lace gown. She recovered her voice — they were all staring at her — and forced a note of warmth into it. "Bael told us during dinner of the terrible ordeal you underwent when you first arrived in Hell."

"The saurian creature? Yes, Bael rescued me, a terrible ordeal for him as well. Afterwards, he worried over whether the beast's death at his hands broke the Creator's command never to injure any angel or animal."

"I would say death is a fatal injury, yes." She adjusted her lace collar uneasily. "But the creature would have done the same to you."

Sharlan shook her head. "You don't understand. We were no longer under the Creator's jurisdiction. But Bael had never killed anything before. None of us had, until we were forced to survive here in Hell. He was terribly upset. He felt tainted, as if he would never be clean again. I had to convince him otherwise, and we eventually put the experience behind us." She smiled a bit too fondly at Bael, then turned her gaze back to Leianna, who had to crane her neck to return her gaze. "Bael, of course, told me of your reunion seven years ago, and I was happy for both of you. I hope things will work out for you."

Leianna noticed that Bael was altogether too silent, even if his nature was naturally taciturn. "Yes, well, I'm glad you survived the ordeal. The Fall from Grace happened so long ago, sometimes it feels as if I'm remembering someone else's story, not my own and Bael's. It's good seeing you again," she added, although she wasn't sure she totally meant it.

A look of amusement crossed Sharlan's face, and she gave Bael another quick glance. "Likewise. If you'll excuse me now, I'm sure Affaeteres is looking forward to your company." Sharlan nodded to Bael's mother and then to Leianna and Bael, saying, "Good night," and continuing past them.

Affaeteres said, "My chambers are just around that corner up ahead."

Leianna and Bael followed her, Bael leaning down to murmur in her ear: "As one can in the upper planes, those in Hell can often read thoughts in someone's mind, if they're loud enough."

"Was I that obvious?" she asked.

"Yes," he answered her bluntly. They entered Affaeteres's sitting room.

Affaeteres gestured to a loveseat beside a low table with tea set upon it. They sat down as she made herself comfortable in a stuffed velvet armchair. "There is so much to catch up on, children." She looked at Leianna. "And by the way, darling, Sharlan is Bael's head concubine and has been for thousands of years. His father, I'm sure, was planning on telling you this at dinner, but you and Quatama changed the subject and spoiled his anticipated fun."

This time Leianna didn't find her voice; this revelation rendered her temporarily speechless. She glared at Bael instead.

Affaeteres continued. "Bael's relationship with Sharlan is only one small part of what you will have to deal with. But really, son, you should have told Leianna seven years ago."

Leianna had parked herself on one-half of the loveseat, but now she moved deliberately closer to her far end, away from Bael. "What she said," she agreed angrily. "You should have told me seven years ago."

Bael remained as still as stone. "Leianna." His voice held a warning note.

"*Yes*, Bael?" She waited, clamping her fury, wanting to scream at him.

"We'll discuss this later." He glanced at Affaeteres, then lowered his gaze. "I wasn't expecting Mother to spill the beans."

"Well, she's spilled them and they stink! For Mother Aff's sake, I won't kill you right now."

"I'm immortal."

"I'll find a way!"

All three sat silently for a good two minutes, then Affaeteres spoke. "I had to tell her, Bael. If you delayed any longer, it would seriously jeopardize your and Ashtoreth's hope for this alliance with Heaven. And your relationship with Leianna would not survive further deception. I'm sure once you explain to her about Sharlan, she'll understand."

"I *will*?!" Leianna couldn't help herself. "What's to understand? He cheated on me!"

"No, he didn't, dear. Actually, technically, he's cheating on Sharlan with you."

"He's married?! Are you married to Sharlan?"

"No," he said, "and I'm not cheating on Sharlan or you. I have a relationship with both of you. I just haven't worked out your sudden reemergence in my life."

"Sudden?! It's been seven years!"

"They went very quickly. Look! Do you want me to explain or not?"

At least they were facing each other on the loveseat, Bael's eyes connecting firmly with hers, rather than his standing, towering over her. At five feet two inches, it mattered very much to her right now that they weren't standing, that she wasn't staring up at him, all six feet four inches of him. How often had his tall, muscular frame made her feel protected; how often had he delighted in her smallness, calling her his little one. Now she simply felt small, small as a trinket to be used at his whim. But she'd let him explain. Paybacks could come later. "Go ahead. Tell me why I should understand."

"All right." He stood up, pacing a few steps.

"And don't stand up!"

Bael stared at her, and a look that was halfway between mirth and sadness crossed his face. He sat down, facing her again. "Please forgive me. I never meant to hurt you. Having you back in my life was a treasure, one I wasn't sure would last if this alliance project failed."

"Bael, we were reunited."

"Shh! Let me explain please." He took her hands in his, holding them lightly, and she allowed this, keeping silent.

"When we were first cast into Hell," Bael began, "it was a vast wilderness and untamed. These lizard creatures were later found to have some intelligence and a rude language of grunting, hissing and honking sounds. After we destroyed a large number of them, they took to leaving piles of tribute to us, first the rocks they saw us gather as fuel and weapons, and, later, food: strange, multicham-bered berries on thorny bramble branches, a sponge-like fruit that yielded sweet water when cut, and, to our dismay, dead lizards and snakes and crustaceans of an unknown species. They began to follow us as we traveled on, and when we caught them sneaking about our shelter, they lay down, seemingly fearful, exposing their scaleless bellies to us. We knew enough of animal behavior to recog-nize their submission to us.

"After a long while, they conquered their fear, but not their awe and curiosity. They made constant noises, attempting to communi-cate with the folk, and Nergal began studying their sounds, sorting them out. They took to his interest intensely. He soon discerned the rudiments of their language and began teaching them a rudimen-tary version of our own tongue. Over time, he succeeded.

"We learned the name they gave themselves, the *Guggithim*.But among ourselves, we simply called them the *saurs*, which meant lizard in our own language. Over the millennium, they evolved, adopted our language and now are part of Hell's population."

"They don't sound very safe to have around," Leianna ven-tured.

Bael laughed softly. "You know how it's said that books should not be judged by their covers? The *saurs*, it turned out, were not attacking us. They were trying to pull Sharlan over to meet their tribe. They hadn't realized their claws were cutting her. My counter-attack, killing that *saur*, confused and terrified them. When we continued to kill them when they came too closely, they finally made their signs of submission, to communicate their inten-tions and to stop our violence."

Leianna pulled her hands from his. "This is all very fascinating, but doesn't help me to understand about you and Sharlan."

"It will," he said. "The *saurs* traveled with us and pointed out the real dangers in Hell. Their territory encompassed the sixth and fifth levels of Hell; they had never been above them before. On the sixth, there were vast swamps with large reptiles resembling your crocodiles, except that their tales were stumped and their bites poisonous. And there were wildcats as large and treacherous as your extinct saber-toothed tigers, and other mammals and reptiles that posed a threat, as well as a rather oversized bird that resembled a griffin that seemed to enjoy aerially attacking the angelfolk. To guard and protect our womenfolk from these dangers, and others that developed over the centuries, the folk created a harem structure."

"New dangers?" Leianna asked.

"The same dangers that drove men on Earth to create harems to sequester their women. The danger of a male not authorized to be with a woman."

"Bael, harems enslave women."

"Not necessarily. They were created to protect the females of the household."

"So your harem has nothing to do with, umm, you know what." She glanced at Affaeteres, who had listened to this whole exchange placidly, until now. She said, "Sex, Leianna. The harems may have been initially for protection here, but now they are mostly about pleasure and property, with women chosen for the harems by Hell's upper classes. And, yes, some women, like Sharlan, are in them simply to keep unwanted attentions by unwanted men at bay. These females are fairly free to come and go as they please, as long as they do not favor any male other than their appointed masters. Even today, especially in Hell, there is an advantage to having a societal *hands-off* sign, even if you have to give up your freedom for it."

Leianna shook her head at this concept. "Are all the women in Hell in harems?"

"Of course not," said Affaeteres. "Only those still desirable. I, for example, will never be in one. It's a matter of status."

Leianna, confused, protested. "You're still beautiful."

"Yes, but there is another reason, besides no longer being attractive, to refuse harem protection. I long ago ceased to let Lucifer or any other male apprise me of my worth or decide my actions for me. I suggest you never allow Bael or Ashtoreth to judge your own values for you, not unless you agree with and support those values."

Bael, chagrined, added: "You are also the wife of Hell's emperor, although he considers his name as sufficient as a title, and you are the mother of his sons, Hell's royal princes. You are protected beyond any harem structure."

Leianna leaned toward her. "Are you queen?"

"I, too, eschew titles. I am known as the Lady Affaeteres, and none would harm me for other reasons. I have powers of my own, although Bael and his brothers and Lucifer consider them negligible."

"I'm sure they're not," Leianna said. And to Bael, "Get back to Sharlan."

He sighed. "We were alone in an unknown world. I was grieving for you and needed the comfort of friendship. She was grieving for Eliom and her own loss. We became close. When the harems were set up — initially for protection and called *leiths*, which translates as "enclosures," not as "harems" — Sharlan would not enter any man's *leith* but mine, not even her father's. Her parents permitted this. I think they hoped that time would dull your memory and that Sharlan would take your place as my betrothed and eventually as my wife. But Lothan made it very clear that no other woman must exceed Sharlan's authority in my *leith*, in my household. This was long before we even heard of the word "harem" or connected it with pleasure. Sex only occurred if both parties were willing. The women of my *leith* were not "owned" by me. They were rather my charges under my protection and guidance as we conquered Hell."

Leianna nodded, not really convinced or comfortable with his explanation. "So what happened, in those days, if your charge fell in love — with someone other than you — and wanted to marry and leave your harem."

Affaeteres interrupted. "A woman could do so, but she and her husband had to choose a new *leith* for her to live in or return her to the original *leith*."

"So they really were just a form of protective housing for women?"

"Yes, for at least a millennia or two. Not that there wasn't sex then. There was always sex. But marriage was the prevalent form of ownership rights, even if wives were sequestered elsewhere for safety's sake. The men's quarters could be arranged for privacy, a wife temporarily sharing her husband's sleeping cot."

"It doesn't sound like a very loving system, Mother Aff."

"There was no time for love, Leianna. We were busy taming Hell."

"For two thousand years?"

"For three thousand. That was when we reached the third level of Hell and discovered its fertile land and the forests of Ajan Helvert and Ajan Morvert. They provided us with wood and other supplies, and we slowly returned to a system of private dwellings. In the later centuries, the *leiths* slowly became what mortals call harems."

"That still doesn't rectify Bael's long liaison with Sharlan, Mother Aff."

Bael began to speak, but his mother shushed him again. "Some of the women left the harems then. Others stayed by choice. And sometimes, the choice was due to love."

"But if Bael loved Sharlan, after all those years, why didn't he marry her?" She turned abruptly to Bael. "And she can't be the only women in your harem today . . . your mother called her your *head* concubine . . . that means there are others."

He sat rigidly, eyes locked with hers. "Yes, there are others. Being a concubine of one of Hell's princes does convey status."

"Your mother suggested her status was due to *not* being a concubine."

Bael glanced at his mother. "Mother is being sarcastic. Being a wife still conveys a higher status than being a concubine."

"Uh, huh." Leianna nodded. "And none can be higher than Sharlan in your household." Affaeteres let out a small titter of laughter, covering her mouth to subdue it. Leianna ignored it. "So is that why you haven't asked me to marry you?" Affaeteres was having a hard time holding in her laughter, her cheeks puffing with breath. "Mother Aff, what do you find so funny about this? Even if he does marry me, do you think I'll put up with his harem?"

Affaeteres opened her mouth, letting out breath and laughter, grinning wildly. "Will you even let him have his harem if he *doesn't* marry you, Leianna? You won't disappoint me, will you? You *know* there's something wrong with men having harems beyond the *leith's* initial purpose, now long gone. You *know* this is not Heaven's way!"

"Not unless they let us women have harems of gorgeous men, all built like stallions and standing at attention for our every need!"

Now Affaeteres did burst out laughing. "Now *that* will end the harem system, if we women demand equal sexual power."

"And when we're done with them, we'll make them clean the house!" Leianna herself couldn't resist laughing. Bael sat woodenly, waiting for his mother's and Leianna's tittering to subside, then said: "It is very hard to dissolve a system that has been in place for so long, ladies."

Affaeteres looked at Leianna. Leianna looked at Bael. "Watch me. Just watch me."

Bael shook his head. "You cannot do it, Leianna."

"Where is your harem, Bael?"

Affaeteres tapped her hand. "It's on this floor. Go to your right as you exit my chambers. Go two, full, corridor-lengths past two intersections. At the third intersection, turn right and continue down that corridor, past Bael's apartments on the left, to its end. You'll see large brass doors guarded by two house wardens. Tell them Affaeteres bids them give you entrance to Lord Baelzebub's harem to see the Lady Sharlan. And please, do have a nice talk with her and Bael's other concubines." She rose from her chair. "I will see you at another time, I hope. I have missed you, my dear, and worried after you."

"I'm sorry, Mother Aff." Leianna also stood.

Bael got up reluctantly, asking her, "You're not seriously going to confront them, are you?"

Leianna ignored him, reaching out and clasping Affaeteres's own pro-offered hand. "We didn't even have any tea or get a chance to talk with you about other things."

Affaeteres squeezed her hand. "We spoke on what we had to."

"Mother Aff, I will try to get down here again soon, to see you and spend more time. But, in the meantime, is there anything I can do for you? Try to do for you?"

Affaeteres patted her hand, then let go. "Get me out of Hell." She said it quietly, unemotionally. "That will be sufficient, and if Lucifer can't follow, that's his fault. Now, go! Go!" She ushered them briskly out of her quarters, which Leianna saw were unguarded. Perhaps servants with protective powers lurked unseen.

Affaeteres smiled broadly at Leianna, a twinkle in her eye as she shut the door, saying: "Now don't let me down. Have fun in the harem, Leianna!"

7

Leianna Raises Hell

Bael kept protesting as they turned right, the brass doors and the harem's wardens guarding them visible at the end of the passage. "You don't have to do this, Leigh Ann. I can arrange a meeting between you and Sharlan later, privately. This will only upset the other women!"

"*Your* other women!" She stole a quick glance to her left as they passed the elaborate double doors to his private apartments, perhaps also guarded by the harem wardens, well within their sight, standing their vigil up ahead. The doors to Bael's quarters were adorned with inlaid ivory sculptures in bas relief; she had no time to study their subject matter as she continued on. There would be time enough to explore his chambers after she straightened out the neighbors.

The guards looked confused as they watched her and Bael approach. Both men were dressed in the same pseudo-Roman style worn by the guards on the balcony. The one on her right, seeming older than the other, turned his broad face to Bael. "My Lord?"

Leianna walked over to him. "I see Rome hasn't fallen here yet," she quipped.

She felt Bael's hand on her shoulder. "Leigh Ann." He kept his voice low.

She didn't turn around. "Why do you keep addressing me by my mortal name?"

"To remind you that you *are* mortal and should not be flippantly interfering in Hell as if you owned the place."

This only brought her hackles up. She said to the older guard, "The Lady Affaeteres bids you give me entrance to this harem. I am to see the Lady Sharlan."

The warden glanced worriedly from her to Bael. She continued: "I am not one of his concubines, by the way."

The man visibly blanched. "Oh, no, my lady! I would never think that!"

Bael edged to her right, facing her at any angle. "He *knows* who you are, Leianna," he said, voice thick with exaggerated patience and male exasperation.

The younger guard, dark-eyed and dark-haired, cracked a minuscule smile. The older guard appealed again to Bael. "My Lord?"

Bael flung his right hand outward, waving at the doors. "Let her in then. Maybe she'll want to stay!"

Leianna laughed, her laugh not amused but incredulous. "In your dreams."

"No, my dear," Bael countered, "yours. After all, you are astrally projected."

The guards were beginning to enjoy her and Bael's verbal sparring a bit too much. Leianna could feel Bael's increasing ire, as if it were his honor on the line and not hers. Well, his male pride would just have to heal. "Open the doors, please," she told the wardens.

They turned to obey her, but before they could touch the brass handles on either side, both doors swung slowly inward, creaking loudly. Leianna couldn't see who labored to open the heavy doors wide enough to comfortably permit her and Bael's entrance. She suspected the concubines themselves from the slow pace, but Sharlan herself stood a few yards back from the doorway, tall and proud in a diaphanous, nearly see-through white negligee and golden-heeled sandals.

The doors continued to protest audibly before their movement finally ceased. Leianna stared, perturbed, at Sharlan, then at the confused wardens, who obviously couldn't decide who was trumping whom and who wouldn't dare bet on a favorite.

Leianna drew herself up as regally as her petite frame allowed, hands on her hips, and eyed both guards. "You really have to oil those hinges, guys." So saying, she lowered her hands from her hips, her fists still curled into balls, and strode into the harem foyer, past Sharlan without looking at her, and into what appeared to be a large, main room with couches and chairs on both the lower floor and two raised floor levels, each three steps up on either side. The levels were circular and decorated in red and gold. "My goodness," Leianna said as she reached the room's center and turned around to face Sharlan and Bael, the wardens, and a set of two women each on either side of the partially opened brass doors. "Look at this. You've built the main room to resemble the three lowest levels of Hell."

Sharlan approached her, her gait relaxed, and stopped halfway. "I see Bael gave you a geography lesson at dinner." She turned to the guards." You really don't have to protect us. Those hinges screech so loudly that an intruder might as well carry a loudspeaker and announce his intentions."

The younger guard knelt on one knee. "My pardon, my lady, my Lord. We will report it immediately to the head palace custodian as soon as we are off duty."

Bael walked to a point between Leianna and Sharlan. "Sharlan, you know they cannot leave their posts until their replacements arrive. And I do not believe those doors creaked before tonight." He eyed Leianna. "At least, I have not heard such."

Leianna waved her hand nonchalantly. "He hasn't been around here lately, you know. He's been commuting these last seven years . . . to Earth and to Heaven." She glanced at the other women, the four near the doors and eight more lounging in various other areas of the room, besides Sharlan, all in attractive and revealing lingerie. "Well, I must thank you all for dressing up for my visit to your harem."

"Lord *Baelzebub's* harem," a short, blonde girl, much thinner than Leianna, in a conspicuous, genie-type costume, drawled. "And we ain't dressed for *you!*"

"Well, that's what I came to talk to you about, actually. You don't have to lower yourselves in this manner. No woman should be subjugated by a man. Not even in Hell and certainly not by my betrothed. I'm going to make him free you, and then you can go off and live your lives fully. There's going to be changes in Hell, and this is the *first*." She swiveled toward Bael, watching his reaction.

He pointed to the wardens. "Leave and close the doors." They quickly complied, the hinges protesting. "And get those damned things oiled!"

"Yes, my Lord," they each said and pulled the doors harder until both closed with a resounding clang. "Now," Bael said. He covered the distance between him and Leianna. She backed up an inch or two. "Who do you think you are, telling them what to do?"

"Your future *wife!*"

He sighed theatrically and turned in a half circle, grinning to his concubines. "I'm surprised that she still wants to marry me, now that she's met you, my lovelies." And to her, "Leianna, things cannot be changed overnight."

"This can."

The skinny blonde inched closer. "Tell her to leave, Lord. We love you and won't speak back to you."

A tall, fiery redhead, her hair styled much like Sharlan's, in a black, silky nightgown, folded her arms defiantly. "Yes, Lord. We take your demands. We do not make them on you."

Leianna addressed them quizzically. "Don't you understand? He doesn't *love* you. Not really. If you dared to be yourselves, outside of your sexual subordination, to challenge him for your rights, would he still find you lovely?"

"Leianna," he said. She could almost see his muscles tensing.

"Well, would you?"

The little blonde came right up to her. "We don't wanta challenge him. We wanta please him. He fucks real good! I bet you just lay there like a wet piece of spaghetti." She giggled. "Bet your tits are flabby and floppy!"

Leianna, mouth opened in dumbfounded amazement, just stared at her. Another blonde, this one with ringlets and a girl-next-door smile, sauntered over, her baby-doll nightie of silk and lace showing her long legs and pert curves. "Yes, we love serving Lord Baelzebub. He's a stallion. Freedom is overrated when you have a stud that good."

"So," Leianna said, her tone measured, "he never leaves you lonely and you're planning a large family to perpetuate your love."

The baby-doll blonde's innocent smile twisted into a snarl so nasty, Leianna almost felt it as a physical slap. "The great Leianna!" The girl's voice now held a razor-sharp sneer. "The woman whose memory haunted him. So considerate, so kind and loving was she! But now she's a haughty little bitch who reminds the women who comforted him that they can't *conceive!*"

"Yeh, that's right," the skinny blonde put in. "Maybe you're barren, too, all shriveled up inside your *cunt!*"

"*Enough!*" Surprisingly, the reprimand did not come from Bael, but from Sharlan, her voice firm and resonant.

The tall redhead moved toward her. "But, Sharlan, you, out of all of us, should hate her."

"Yeh, the tiny blonde muttered, "after what he did to your . . ." She stopped herself, mid-sentence.

Bael pinned her with his gaze. "*What* did I do, Sally Louise?"

She was obviously frightened. Leianna wondered what additional beans the girl had almost spilled. The little mealy-mouth struggled to apologize now. "You know me, Lord. Sally the sassy!" She laughed weakly, shooting a glance at Leianna. "None of her business, I suppose."

Sharlan came over and, laying her hand on Sally Louise's nearly flat chest, shoved her back brusquely, away from Leianna. "It *is* her business. It's none of *yours* to tell it, something you heard second-hand, for I never shared my true memories with the likes of you. Now go. Return to your room and stay there until you are summoned." When the girl hesitated, lifting her blue eyes timidly to Bael in appeal, Sharlan reiterated in a tone of absolute command. "*Go!*" The girl fled up and out the three levels and through a hallway leading beyond the harem's common room.

Sharlan came closer to Leianna and spoke in a much softer

voice, as if shielding her words. "Please restrain yourself, Leianna. Let the others alone for now. There'll be time enough for change after you and I have talked."

Leianna opened her mouth, a question forming, then shut it, complying.

Sharlan asked Bael, "May I meet with Leianna alone?"

Bael shook his head. "She is in Hell, and while I may trust you, I do not trust others. She is under my protection until I bring her home."

Sharlan nodded. "Will you come back to my quarters?" she asked Leianna, who also nodded. She followed the tall woman, Bael trailing behind her, up the two levels, past them into the hallway, then down it into an open entrance only blocked with strings of colorful beads.

The beads made a clicking noise as they pushed through them into another small but lavish sitting room. Beyond it, Leianna could see two exits, one toward the right that led to a short, shaded hall, and another on the left leading directly to a dining room and, behind that, what seemed to be a small kitchen. Sharlan ushered them into the dining room, sweeping her hand at the highly polished cherry wood table and chairs, the latter cushioned with upholstery embroidered with red roses. "Please be seated while I make some refreshments. Do you take tea, coffee or cocoa, Leianna?"

Leianna sat on one of the beautiful chairs, very much admiring Sharlan's taste, despite her disgruntlement. "Coffee, please."

Sharlan did not ask Bael. She went into the kitchen, and returned carrying a black tray with white china with more roses adorning them upon it, and set filled cups on saucers before all three of them. Bael's and Sharlan's held a fragrant tea.

Sharlan took a sip and set down her cup. "You may ask your questions now, Leianna. I'll do my best to answer them."

Leianna sighed and lifted her cup to her lips. The coffee was rich, expertly brewed. She wondered if Sharlan had been expecting them, not just listening behind the brass doors and sending someone to prepare refreshments in anticipation. "I don't know where to start. Is it true that every woman in this harem is barren?"

"Yes, all are now. At one point, I was not."

"You had a child? With Bael?" She tried to keep the disapproval out of her voice and failed.

Sharlan opened her mouth to speak, but Bael spoke first. "I do not wish this to be discussed right now, Sharlan." He seemed extremely uncomfortable with the subject matter.

She hesitated, then murmured. "It will have to be told, sooner or later. You'd do well to get it out into the open between the three of us now and spend the later days trying to heal the damage. What you mother said was true. You shouldn't have waited this long. But I will let you make this decision."

He didn't respond.

"Sharlan, how do you know what Affaeteres said?" Leianna asked.

Sharlan stared at her. "Bael's mother has recently discussed this with us."

"Oh. I thought you had somehow listened in on my and Bael's meeting earlier tonight with his mother."

Her rival's quizzical look remained. "We can sometimes read thoughts and expressions accurately, but long distance eavesdropping? No."

Leianna wasn't convinced. "And you seemed to foresee my visit to you tonight. This coffee is brewed."

"I *anticipated* your visit and Affaeteres's determination to reveal the truth to you."

"She wants me to end the harem system."

"Yes."

"And apparently there's some truth still yet to be bared."

Sharlan nodded. "Borne, Leianna; it will have to be borne, if Bael will forgive me for I mean no pun. But it is a burden we bear. And it will affect the way you see Bael. That is why he fears it so much, your knowledge of it."

Leianna watched Bael lift just his eyes, wide with alarm, to Sharlan, who shook her head, as if to comfort him.

Leianna sighed. "Why should he fear me knowing that you two had a child? I'm divorced with an eight-year-old son named Daniel on Earth. If we weren't together — Bael and I — when you bore his child, why should I hold this against the two of you?" She sat up straighter, not quite looking at either of them. "So. Am I going to meet this child or is that to remain a mystery, too?"

Sharlan said nothing. Leianna waited, puzzled again. Finally Bael spoke. "You can't meet him."

"Why not?"

"He's dead."

Now the silence thickened. She could feel the pain radiating from Sharlan and Bael, the heartbreak, and something else. A silent scream hung in the air.

Leianna felt heartsick at the thought of losing a child. Her empathy came out in a low, nearly nonverbal moan. "Ohh . . ." She wanted to hug them both, to tell them that she understood why they had been reluctant to tell her all of this.

Then Bael spoke again, his voice lower than normal, nearly a whisper. "I killed him."

At first, Leianna thought she hadn't heard right. Then she knew she had, and there was no going back, she would have to hear the whole story and live with it, hate it, reconcile it, heal it.

Because she still loved him. "Tell me," she said to him. "I'll find a way to forgive you and save you from your own pain and suffering. But tell me."

8

Bael Confesses

"This has tormented me. Telling you of my role in the death of Sharlan's son, my own as well, is painful. I fear your hatred, Leianna, even if Sharlan herself has been an angel — never failing in her forgiveness, in her understanding, long before I deserved it. But even if *you* forgive me, as Sharlan has, it ultimately doesn't matter.

"I feel the shame, even now, feel that there was no excuse, and that neither those who are in Heaven nor those of spiritual enlightenment on Earth would think me worthy of forgiveness, because I can't forgive myself. If you can't forgive yourself, no one else will think you worthy of forgiveness.

"And so all I can ask is that you and others may find it possible to understand what I did. There was a reason, if not an excuse. But it's hard to confess. To you, Leianna. Knowing I will never be fully cleansed of this sin, and you may not wish to have its taint associated with you."

"Bael . . ." Leianna reached out her hand toward him, but stopped short of touching him, as if his words rang all too true. "Just tell me."

Sharlan sat solemnly, eyes downcast, staring at her tea cup.

Bael rose slowly, leaving his chair, pacing. "I'm trying to. There's so much to it, but it must be told. All stories must be told, even those too horrifying. We want to hide from them, from the picture they paint of our folly and our fear. And our pride . . . terrible pride!

"Before I begin, know that there was absolution from Sharlan for me, and it humbled me before her. And before I end the tale, know that if you find a single drop of forgiveness for me, Leianna, that I will savor it as a blessing from Heaven.

"Sharlan, this tale will not be short or easily told. If you believe at any time that we need our refreshments replenished, please do so quietly. And I pray that your own heart will not be newly burdened by my retelling this to Leianna."

Sharlan said, "It has to be told. Tell it. Tell it from *your* heart."

He nodded and began. "We found out, after our forced arrival in Hell, that none of the fallen angelfolk could procreate. We wondered if this was why Nergal's wife, Shadella, arrived with her womb emptied of the infant she had nearly carried to full term before our exile.

"Shadella was devastated, frantic with wondering what had become of her child. Nergal soothed her by promising that she would bear another someday, but he confided to my father that an infant would probably not survive in that dark, astral wilderness. We had no idea where we were or what we would find. Food was nearly nonexistent. We found sparse vegetation and little water on the sixth, fifth and fourth levels of Hell. Yet, strangely, we found we could survive on little or no food and drink . . . but not thrive. Our energy waned, our tempers flared, but we trudged on.

"It was only when we reached the third level that we found the Taleth plains, *taleth* meaning "wonder," and discovered their miles of edible, wild vegetables and fruit, all growing lushly in hardly any light. For the first time in nearly 400 years, years three times longer in the astral realms than in the mortal worlds, we felt real hope. And when we found the third level's two great forests and its mountains, its hills, and more fertile land in valleys with streams and rivers of fresh water, we nearly fell down in prayer, praising the Creator's leniency, thinking we had gained absolution, that we had been forgiven.

"Even Lucifer couldn't stop some of the lost angels from kneeling down, words of thanks upon their lips. He simply asked them to let him know when they received an answer back. He reminded them that their own determination in the face of centuries of suffering had led them to the Plains of Taleth, not the Creator. That their free will had simply, finally, reaped a reward instead of hardship. That they were still in the *Heliom*, the dark land of their exile.

"Lucifer soon took to saying we were in *Hel*, in the *darkness*, for only starlight and a darkly grey daylight reached this place, never sunlight.

"But our spirits lifted, knowing we had reached a part of Hell much closer in habitat to our lost home in Eliom. We wondered what other creatures, beyond those the *saurs* had shown us, might exist in the great forests or in the mountains. We found a great variety of bird and beast. They kept their distance from us at first, and we from them, for we couldn't yet know if the beasts in Hell were as peaceable as those in Eliom.

"The *saurs* were afraid of the forests, never having seen the third level. They sniffed at the tall tree trunks and backed away as if scenting a predator. And then the air filled with ululations. What seemed to be very small children came swinging down on ropes on the tree branches, or just as quickly climbed up into the sheltering foliage, using chiseled-out hand and foot holds in the tree trunks.

"We later discovered that they were fully grown, adult natives of the third level. They seemed to especially admire our women and took to following them, clasping their hands and stroking them, especially their hair. They fearlessly studied both us and the *saurs*, who seemed to fear them, avoiding them wherever possible.

"We called these woods people the Ajanese in our language. It took another century before we learned one another's languages fully. They liked ours more than their own and adopted its fuller spectrum of words into their own.

"Although the Ajanese could procreate, they weren't an especially fertile people. The tallest among them was about half my size, an inch or so over three feet, their children about half that. Their females had very small breasts, nearly as flat as a man's, even those nursing infants, and hips so slender, they resembled undeveloped girls. I never saw a pregnant Ajanese woman. Perhaps they had a taboo about that.

"Perhaps the sight of fully developed Eliomese women intrigued them. They constantly offered our women gifts: nuts and berries and fruits of the forest, and vegetables from the Plains of Taleth, and surprisingly, beautifully carved objects, some utilitarian, such as bowls and spoons, and others decorative, intricate pieces of art depicting animals and trees on jewelry and hair ornaments.

"Over time, they showed us where to gather nourishment, and they eventually led us to the mountains, hills and valleys on the other side of the third level, the Cahniohiom."

Leianna interrupted him. "What does that mean? When Quatama told me of my eternal mother Eve's mortal sons, Cahn and Ahbel, he told me that *cahn* meant strength, but you earlier told me that this word meant 'hill' and the Eliomese '*oh*' meant 'of great size.'"

Bael sat down and sipped his tea. "The word has a double meaning: strong, tall, of high rank and power, as well as a land that rises. A hill. *Cahniohiom* basically means 'mountain land.' In its ranges, we met stouter relatives of the Ajanese, whom we named Cahnese or hill people. But in time we found that these mountain folk preferred their own language and their own name, both for themselves — the Teleperi — and for their forest cousins — the Talaperi or forest folk. *Tele* meant 'stone,' appropriately, as the Teleperi worked the gifts of their mountains loose. These first aboriginal miners of Hell worked flint, copper, tin, silver and precious stones into tools and ornaments, which they traded with the Talaperi for food and animal skins. They also fished in the mountain lakes for sustenance and shared their catch with the forest folk.

"Through these natives, we learned Hell's version of the Earthly practice of hunting and fishing, of killing beasts, of taking their flesh for food, and their fur, hides and skins for warmth and garments, and even their bones and certain organs as tools. Accepting this practice was gradual among the Eliomese, many of the fallen angelfolk speaking out adamantly against it, but in private, so as not to upset the native folk with what might be construed as a curious or harsh criticism of their customs.

"The Talaperi and Teleperi had another unpleasant need. They could not simply meditate negative energy away from their bodies, as we angelfolk could, purifying our bodies by thought alone. The natives expelled their bodily waste physically, and they buried it in secluded areas chosen for that need."

"They had bowel movements? In Hell?" Leianna found this ludicrously humorous, and wondered what all this had to do with Bael's confession, but didn't challenge him on that yet.

"Yes, Leianna, something that you would have been just as amazed and shocked by, had you been exiled with us. They also marked partial boundaries within their territories which we clearly weren't permitted to cross, these waste burial areas among them. We respected these boundaries, when the forest and stone folk indicated them, without at first understanding their purpose. We were slow in understanding this extraordinary difference between them and the angelfolk.

"To this day, the fallen angelfolk are still free of such need, but many inhabitants of Hell are not. The civilized sections of Hell have sanitary systems in place, a great improvement. No one wants to live in a cesspool. But I digress, perhaps avoiding the painful point, but this does lead to it."

"It's all fascinating," Leianna agreed, "but it doesn't seem to have anything to do with you and Sharlan."

"It will." He watched as Sharlan silently brought out a teapot and freshened his and her tea cup and returned again with a tray holding a smaller coffee pot, sugar bowl and creamer. She placed it beside Leianna, who helped herself before Sharlan could pour for her. Sharlan smiled her thanks, sitting down again, sipping her tea.

Bael continued. "In contrast to the nearly endless suffering we experienced on the sixth, fifth and fourth levels, we became enamored of the peace and seeming plenty found on the third level of Hell. Content, we sought to settle there, and were unwilling to continue journeying up another rise to the next level far above us. We had no guarantee that it would offer any improvements. We were bone-tired and needed rest as a people.

"And so we built a small village on the Plains of Taleth near Ajan Helvert and sought to restore some normalcy to our lives in exile. And I, lonely and no longer believing I would ever see you again, Leianna, I began to truly court Sharlan, no longer seeing us as only friends. I knew she loved me, although she had never admitted it to my face.

"Our system of *leiths*, of protecting our women and the older children originally exiled with us, was firmly in place, but on the third level, we loosened their restrictions. One male, instead of three, guarded each *leith*. The prominent families still maintained each *leith*, but if a woman desired to leave it completely and live in her husband's or parents' home, we felt we were on safe enough ground to do so. Many did. The remaining *leiths* became a social center for our women. Even those who had left them visited those who hadn't, attending to their duties in feminine camaraderie.

"My *leith* still held five women and one older boy. It was built of stones and wood and hardened resin, connected to a smaller cottage, which held my sleeping alcove and a larger, common room for meals and the few leisure pursuits we finally had some time for. Sharlan was still among the five, treated by the others as my favorite with feminine good humor." He stopped speaking, staring at Sharlan across the table, breathing heavily. "I cannot tell this! I simply cannot tell this. Leianna will hate me! *You* may hate me anew."

Sharlan shook her head. "We won't hate you. You must go on, or it won't be told at all. I cannot tell it. It has to be from *your* point of view if you want absolution."

"Excuse me, children, and my intrusion . . ."

All three looked to the doorway where Quatama stood smiling apologetically, holding up three, small, multi-colored hoops, his brown monk's robe drab against their vibrant hues. Leianna immediately recognized them as V-Re-E devices, allowing the wearer to experience the virtual reenactment of his or her own or another person's memories as if they were reliving it. She had worn similar hoops on her head when reliving the events leading up to and at the original Falls from Grace, both Eve's and her brother Adam's, and consequently, Lucifer's, although those hoops were each a single color.

Quatama approached them. "I know that the memory can alter events retold long after they happened, and that Bael wants you, Leianna, to know precisely what occurred between him and Sharlan. And so, I have brought V-Re-E hoops, three copies of the actual events, keyed to Bael's point of view, as Sharlan suggested. Once you place them on your heads, you will all relive it." He handed each of them a hoop.

Bael felt the shiny pliable circumference of the hoop. "Reliving it. I don't know . . ."

Quatama gently interrupted him. "It is important that all three of you review this painful memory together. To ease your grief, I will tell you that the child will one day live again."

Bael's eyes widened with surprise; Sharlan put her hand upon her heart, her quickened breath audible.

Leianna, also comforted by Quatama's prediction, but not surprised that reincarnation might occur in a dimension other than Earth's, said: "I know that you and the Seraphim tracked the angel-folk who incarnated on Earth, but how could you track the fallen angels in Hell? They never prepared themselves for tracking. They never allowed you to capture their images on the tracking stones."

"No, they did not," Quatama agreed, "but the Seraphim, through our Creator, prepared them for tracking as they were lifted into the roiling cloud above Eliom on the day of their expulsion."

Bael sat forward. "That blinding light before I blacked out!"

Quatama nodded. "For want of a fuller explanation, your souls were being photographed and tagged. Our Creator and the Seraphim knew everything that occurred from the moment your father and his followers arrived here."

"And since?"

Quatama paused, then confirmed: "And since."

"Big Brother is among us."

"More so your benevolent parent, but we are not here to debate your Creator's responsibility to you or lack of it, but rather your responsibility towards each other, then and now. Are you ready? When the program is finished, the hoops will deactivate, and your consciousness will return to normal. Or," he added with a hint of mirth, "as normal as the three of you could ever be."

Leianna was shocked. "Quatama!"

"Ah, Leianna. I am allowed my tiny moment of humor."

"The subject hardly lends itself to humor, master."

"Perhaps not the subject. I have noticed, however, that people worry far too much over things that time will heal. Please place the hoops onto your heads and lower your hands. Sharlan and Bael, it will feel like falling into a dream . . . ah, you are already there. Leianna, what are you waiting for?"

"Courage."

Quatama said softly: "It was not as terrible as Bael remembers it to be, only sad and tragic."

Leianna raised the hoop above her head. "Please let him not be to blame," she murmured. She lowered it, immersing herself in Bael's memories.

Such a simple act, taking Sharlan's hand. For centuries, it had been a friendly gesture, but now it sparked a sensual longing, a fire smoldering and building up to a blaze. For months now, they had explored one another in the dark of night, tasting each other, joining as one. Their pleasure was her first ever, and for him, an awakening which broke the centuries of emotional repression following his loss of Leianna.

Her parents, Lothan and Tia, had at first expected Bael to declare Sharlan his betrothed, as he had done with Leianna, before the rebellion in Eliom had separated them.

But Bael refused betrothal, pointing out that the laws of Eliom did not apply in the Heliom, the dark land of their exile. Even if, technically, his betrothal to Leianna had been broken by the Fall, he still loved her, despite also loving Sharlan. He preferred no ceremony be performed between Sharlan and himself. They had declared to each other in private. Sharlan backed him on this, assuring her parents that Bael and she considered their vows binding.

Tia and Lothan relented, but insisted on hosting a celebration, calling the couple wedded, despite Bael and Sharlan calling themselves mated and, each other, *mate*.

He made one firm concession to her parents: that he would never desert their daughter, so long as she wished to stay with him. And he declared this aloud to her and to Tia and Lothan before their family and friends within the community of fallen angels, along with some saurs and Talaperi who had snuck curiously into the festivities.

That night, he and Sharlan returned to his dwelling. The four other women and boy-child of his leith bid them goodnight. Sharlan accompanied Bael to his sleeping alcove, as she had for awhile now. She removed her robe and began to climb beneath the covers on their cot.

Bael stopped her, heating a fire stone in a dish with energy from his hands, its glow shedding soft light and amber shadows about the room. "Let me look at you. You're so beautiful."

Her long, black hair covered her shapely back. Her tallness, her full breasts with their dark nipples and her long, strong legs projected a regal sensuality. Her dark eyes blinked at him, the nostrils of her graceful nose flared slightly, and her full lips pursed as she watched him watching her. A blush spread over her cheeks and chin and other areas. "I often wonder if you are comparing me to Leianna when you stare at me naked."

"There is no comparison. You are tall and dark. Leianna was small and fair."

"No similarities at all?"

"Why do you ask, Sharlan?" When she shrugged, he relented. "Yes, you have some things in common with my lost betrothed. You both have bright, beautiful eyes, although Leianna's are brown and yours are black. You both have small, rounded noses. And while your lips are slightly larger, you and Leianna, if my memory serves me well, have smiles that are nearly identical." He began to disrobe, loosening his belt. "Do you feel better now, knowing that I find you just as beautiful?"

"Yes. And now may I cover myself? This night holds a chill."

"Go ahead. I'm right behind you." He followed her into bed and cradled her against him, caressing the plumb underside of her breast. He leaned toward her and met her mouth with his own, pressing her stomach and thighs against his, his hand gliding between her legs to gauge her readiness, his penis erect and seeking her.

Sharlan was moist and able to receive him, an eager lover since his gentle deflowering of her. He entered her slowly, savoring it, knowing it pleased her as well, then rhythmically increased his thrusts, feeling her reaction beneath him, within her, as she met him and matched his motion. Her legs hugged his back, giving him full entrance, and as they reached climax, nearly together, his lips crushed hers in dual unity.

As he leaned sated, against her and within her, his penis surrounded by her flesh and his own secretion, she squirmed happily under him, pressing him against her. His semen within her seemed to add a final level of excitement to her pleasure.

He lay against Sharlan, suddenly remembering that Leianna also luxuriated, so she told him, in the warmth and wetness of the feel of him, both his penis and its offering, as they lingered inside of her. And the memory, centuries old, hurt him.

She who would have been his wife, lost to him forever! Never to bear his sons and daughters. Never to bear his love again.

Sharlan shifted gently under his weight, until his head rested beside her own, and hugged him. "What are you thinking about?"

He hesitated. "Nothing."

"You were thinking about Leianna. I could sense it."

Bael shifted to look at her. "Only about how you were similar to her . . . in the way you express your devotion."

Sharlan smiled languorously and gently pushed against him. He unlocked their bodies, but maneuvered himself into cradling her once more.

Sharlan snuggled back against his arm. "Then we will be sisters, Leianna and I, should we ever meet again." She gazed at Bael, holding his own gaze. "I want to promise you something."

"What?"

"If you are ever reunited with Leianna, and you wish me to release you from your vows to me, I will. And I will not hold it against Leianna, should she reclaim you. I will accept the love you've given me until such time, and let it comfort me."

Bael smiled wistfully at her. "Silly Sharlan. I've promised you and your parents that I will always take care of you."

"Yes," she agreed, "But you still love her. And you may find each other again." She sighed, not happily.

Bael thought awhile before replying, then finally said: "I can't deny any of that. I will always want to find Leianna someday. I will always regret that we never married or raised a family. It surely would have been, if my father hadn't rebelled, if the Creator and Seraphim hadn't cast us from Eliom and into darkness."

She was silent for so long, he thought she had fallen asleep. But then she spoke, softly, almost timidly. "Perhaps we may have a child, Bael."

He chuckled softly. "Oh, Sharlan, you know we cannot; no angelfolk have conceived since we were flung here. Even those few youngsters who were exiled here with their parents do not seem to grow up at the pace they would have in Eliom."

"Mmn. Perhaps we will grow old here eventually, even if we do not die. We have no Well of Being here to keep us in the prime of our maturity."

"No," he said, "we don't have the renewing vapors of the Well, yet still we don't age like mortals. Perhaps the Creator has been lenient there, but not lenient enough to grant us offspring."

She snuggled closer. "We can hope."

A deeply-buried anger reacted to her hope, bringing to the surface the plain fact that he wanted no children by any woman but Leianna, that she alone was his fulfillment, and that Sharlan, despite her love for him, was his comfort but not his completion.

The shallowness of that truth made him turn away from her in silent shame. "Do not hope," he told her. "It is not meant to be."

She lifted herself up, leaning over him, appearing unconcerned. "How can you know what is to be? You're not the Creator! I just hope, if you ever do find Leianna, that you and I will have had enough happiness and gained enough wisdom as a couple to weather the storm of change that it will surely bring."

Bael finally turned back to her, stroking her angular cheek. "If I ever could find Leianna, the three of us would have to sit down and talk and work out a fair and honorable solution. Now go to sleep. It's late."

Sharlan sighed, and he drew her to him, until she slept and his own eyes became heavy, and he nodded off.

The angels of the Heliom had settled enough of the Plains of Taleth to begin cultivating its fruits and vegetables, the fallen folk now tending their own dark version of the Garden of Eliom.

Bael went out every grey day with the others to work upon the dark soil and tend the native plants which they now harvested for themselves, the saurs, and for trade with the forest and mountain natives. A comfortable community developed and now thrived.

His brother Ashtoreth now worked beside him, aerating the soil and digging up the weeds, no longer given equal care as they were in Eliom. These weeds didn't coexist peacefully around the vegetables, fruit and flowers. They choked and overran the other plants. Ash uprooted and held a large red weed, with sharp barbs tipping its leaves, by its base. It grew prolifically. He threw it into a pile of other weeds to be dried out and used for tinder. "How goes it with you and Sharlan? It's been three years since your declared mating? You seem happy enough together."

"We are." Seemingly unbidden, Bael could sense the image of Leianna arise not only in his mind, but in Ashtoreth's. He ignored it and forced an image of Sharlan over it. "She keeps going on about wanting a child."

"All things are possible now," Ash said. "This is a place where a child could be birthed and raised."

"I do not want a child," Bael said shortly. "The sky here is either grey or black and never bright with the rays of a sun. We are eternal and need no offspring, if those dangerous beasts of this world will leave us be. But we are not indestructible, as was shown us in such harrowing detail, when some of our people suffered deaths on the lower Heliom levels."

Ash grimaced, remembering other lizards of the swamps of the sixth level, three to five times larger than the gentle saurs, which tore five of their people to shreds and pulp, before the folk learned to ring their camp with heated fire stones and keep them hot and glowing. For whatever reason, the monsters avoided all heat, and as they hunted only at night and stayed within their natural territories, the angelfolk — and the smaller, intelligent saurs — rejoiced when they finally climbed to the fifth level and found only deserts, barren lands, volcanoes and scare vegetation and little water, but no giant, vicious saurs. There, however, quicksand traps claimed the lives of two angels in a scouting party, and the people quickly learned to make ropes from the fibers of stringy desert plants and to carry supplies of sturdy branches from the stunted trees of that level, both for testing the terrain and for protection, if needed.

On the fourth level up, the land was nearly as bleak, but not as inhospitable, and its wildlife resembled more of those peaceable animals in Eliom, except that they were not always peaceable. The folk suffered injuries there, but none that couldn't be healed, and continued their long trek to the third level to find a land, in comparison to the lower levels, of plenty. A land that allowed for their long-awaited rest and relief, they diligently sculpted it into their home, with few still wanting to explore the last two levels, towering in the far distant skies above them.

Most could contentedly stay a few more centuries here before curiosity and wanderlust might breed an urge to explore farther, Bael thought. To Ashtoreth, he added: "At least, we have suffered no deaths here."

"No." Ash moved on to another patch of weeds and began prodding their roots loose. "I wonder what became of their life essence, those who died, if they truly are no more."

"Before the Fall, Eve and Quatama's wife said that the dead on Earth are reborn as new babes — just as the angelfolk who agreed to heal the genetic imbalance would be, when sent to Earth. Reincarnation, she called it." He paused in his own work. "I cannot remember her name," he said, chagrined.

Ash searched his memory. "Mirisham was her name, I believe. And Leianna is either on Earth now, as a mortal, oblivious to her angelic roots and us, or back in Eliom, between incarnations."

Bael stopped working, slumping, leaning one hand against the cool soil. "I miss her even now."

Ashtoreth stared at him sadly. "She will not be forgotten. But perhaps it would do you good, be it possible someday, to have a child with Sharlan. To see the present as it is, and not dwell on what it can't bring you, no matter how much your heart grieves for it, Bael."

"I do not wish it," Bael reiterated, and then they heard the horn of Cimeries, signaling the end of the day's labors, that night was coming on, that their homes and hearths and respite from their work beckoned them.

9

Sharlan's Child

Sharlan lit the candles in the common room of their cottage, two on the shelves near the only window, night coming through it, and three on the long tables. She quietly threw the lit taper into the hearth's small blaze of burning wood and tinder and banked the fire carefully, before removing the vegetable pie from the small oven they had built into it.

Bael rose from his chair at the table, shuttering the window. Sharlan wrapped her hands in strips of old cloth and carefully lifted the pie in its hot stone dish, bringing it over to him as he sat down again. He looked at her, noticing that her figure seemed more curvaceous than usual, and smirked. Had she been eating too much? Still, the slight excess wasn't unattractive. "Do you want me to help?"

"No, stay, Bael. I'll only be a minute more." She returned to the hearth and lifted the kettle from its hook, taking it to the table. She filled their cups, the aromatic tea leaves bobbing to the top and swirling within them to flavor the boiled water. Fruit in a bowl and a half-loaf of bread baked earlier also graced the table as Sharlan again hung the kettle in the hearth and then sat down to Bael's right on one end. No places were set for the other five members of their leith.

"Where are the others?" he asked.

"They're out visiting other family and friends. They'll eat there."

"Why?" he asked again, curiosity and a twinge of alarm in his voice.

"Because I have something of importance to tell you and wish to do so without others about." She smiled. "Although, eventually, everyone should know. Only the women of our leith know of it so far. It should have great meaning for our people here." When he remained silent, she continued, nearly breathless with excitement. "I am with child, Bael. We are going to have a baby!" When he continued to sit there, staring at her, his mouth agape, she reached over and touched his lower arm. "Aren't you happy? Oh, please, be happy!"

Scraping his chair back abruptly, he came to her and wrapped his arms about her, bending over, his cheek against the crown of her hair. "Oh, Sharlan . . ."

But his brief, fleeting thought was of Leianna, how she would not mother his first-born, and how this — more than anything — proved that his beloved from Eliom would never return to him.

He reseated himself, taking Sharlan's hand in his own. "Yes. I am happy for both of us. If this is true, it will be a blessing for our people."

"It *is* true," she said eagerly, then blushed. "I am sure that Eve, when she returned to Eliom after being trapped on Earth, didn't tell you and the men how mortal women differed in the signs of pregnancy, but we women learned of it from her. In Eliom, as on Earth, the belly swells and feels queasy upon awakening in the morning. But we never bled in Eliom, once every month when *not* pregnant, as women do on Earth when they come of age. On Earth, when a woman's monthly bleeding time stops, it means that a baby is growing within her womb."

He frowned. "I had no knowledge of this. Are you bleeding? Do you need healing?"

"No, no! What happened in Heliom, upon our reaching this third level, is that our women suddenly developed these monthly cycles, just like Earthly women, although only for a day or two with little flow, barely spotting. Not all the men were told. We were thankful that Eve told us of her womanly trials on Earth, of these 'moon cycles,' as they call them, and of birthing children there, for we now believe our own bodies have changed to resemble those of Earthly women. We don't know why, but it means that birth may not be as easy or as beautiful as it would be in Eliom."

She remained silent, contemplating it for a minute, before brightening again. "But that was how I knew I was with child. These 'monthly blues' stopped for me, the signal on Earth that a woman is becoming a mother," she said, adding shyly, "Our women have named these cycles the 'monthly blues,' being that our skane traceries flow blue within our bodies instead of the red flow of mortal bodies. But all this talk of bleeding is hardly helpful to our appetites, and I am eating for two now!" She rose to cut up and serve the hot pie, piling a healthy portion onto each of their plates.

Bael scooped up a spoonful and tasted it. "Very good," he said slowly. "Sit and eat. So when will this baby come, and when shall we tell the others?"

She reached for some grapes in the fruit bowl. "I thought we should tell your parents and mine first, and then announce this new miracle at month's end, at the Council meeting."

"So be it, then." He drank a bit of his tea, then turned to her uncertainly. "You are absolutely sure of this?"

She wore a satisfied smile, the very picture of certainty. "I am completely sure. And if our new female nature follows the same pattern as Earthly women, you will be a father in about nine months. Eve said that sometimes the babes come earlier, but that was not good, for they could die or be born too weak. So pray that I and your son or daughter stay healthy and have a healthy birth."

"Who will I pray to?" he asked, ignoring the tears wetting his face.

Her fingers softly wiped his cheek. "Don't be afraid. And pray to our Creator. We are still not the makers of our miracles, only of our continued endurance."

"I'll try," he promised her.

That night he often hid his tears from her, and made no mention of the silent farewell that his heart was sending out to Leianna. But in the morning, he felt like a man again, and his eyes stayed dry and clear.

As in Eliom, not so in Hell.

Lucifer had created this rebuff to the laws of the Creator in Eliom, but even in Hell, some laws became necessary to protect the folk from division or danger, and so Lucifer created the Heliomese Council. Similar to the Eliomese High Council, his subcommanders from the Fall comprised its senior members, who now in turn chose junior members from their small populace based on willingness to study, debate, enact and preserve the new laws of Hell. Lucifer, of course, presided as Head Councilor and Commander of Heliom, and no one contested his leadership.

And although Bael had often wondered if his father had erred in rebelling against the Creator's will in Eliom, he also couldn't accept his or his loved ones incarnating endlessly on Earth, all to repair the mortal genes flawed by Adam's and Eve's inbreeding with humans. It jarred him to think that their so-called Creator couldn't correct this defect omnisciently without disrupting the lives of the angelfolk for centuries. Even if Bael had refused his father's rebellion and sided with Leianna and her father and Quatama, she still would be taken from him, and him from her, for one long Earthly life at a time. Who knew what such long absences would do to their love? Perhaps estrange them just as irrevocably as they now were, being flung dimensions away from each other.

It was best to accept his new life fully, to let his past go and settle down now with Sharlan beside him.

Originally his father and their people had no time to convene a law council twice weekly, as was the practice in Eliom on the first two afternoons of each week, to discuss the law and its nuances, to hear arguments and debates, and to settle disputes. Lucifer's word acted as final say, and none contested that. Nor was there time for gatherings of a spiritual bent at the week's end, and little capacity in the fallen angels for belief in any caring power beyond their own bravery and will. Lucifer never banned prayer, but neither encouraged it. As far as Council meetings, he determined that once-a-month gatherings would suffice in overseeing their community, its conduct and concerns.

At these meetings, anyone could attend and observe and, following the Council's agenda, non-council Heliomese could participate, ask questions, give comments or bring news for the Council.

Bael remembered when the fallen angels first began to mark their days in Hell, approximately one year after their exile and arrival there. The folk stripped the bark from a pliable swamp tree on the sixth level, dried it and carefully peeled its layers to make a writing surface. Another plant yielded a reddish-black sap that could be watered and then heated to form a fast ink. Sharpened sticks provided a hard tool to write with, as no opportunity arose on that level for gathering hairs for a proper brush. The scarce animals remained unmolested, except when they attacked the folk, but even then, in those early days, any need to kill a living thing was a new and hated task. The idea of using their carcasses for anything practical, was anathematic and taboo.

The thin, irregularly-shaped pieces of bark marked with the yearly days, weeks, and months were light enough to carry, rolled together into tight scrolls, and carried by the Heliomese, as they now unanimously called themselves, while journeying through the levels of Hell.

Their relative ease now, settled on the Plains of Taleth, allowed a more leisurely social structure. They numbered their weeks by seven days, their months by four weeks each, their year by thirteen months, and found that this count matched the seasons in Hell accurately.

The thirteenth month, with its dry, chill air, ended the harsh snow, ice and rain of Kholluth, the wintry twelfth month, and was called Mizzuh, meaning the completion time, a proper and successful ending to a task or cycle. Celebrations were held, for Mizzuh heralded the coming of the Heliomese Spring, a time when the land replenished itself before the new growth budded, and planting could begin on the land the Heliomese now cultivated.

It was now 497 H.U. — Hell Ukavamasil or Hell Year, the 497th recorded year since their exile, on the seventh day of the third week of Mizzuh. Bael sat with Sharlan and his mother Affaeteres in the circular back row benches of the Council Hall, a large, round building of wood, thatch and hardened mud erected nearly four years before.

Phoenixious, still looking extraordinarily young with his pale hair and slender frame, finished speaking, giving his tally of the remaining harvest stores from the past year. The centuries in Hell seemed not to mar his ever-eager, poetic nature. Yet the youngest senior council member proved to have a sharp eye for figures and an aptitude for managing both crop supplies and the barter trade with the Talaperi and Teleperi. The Heliomese rejoiced to hear of the surplus their hard labor had created. Their Mizzuh celebrations in the coming week would be filled with plenty and much to be thankful for.

Lucifer acknowledged Phoenixious's contribution and report with his own thanks, both to the boy and their people. He glanced toward the back rows at Bael, who had twice refused to become a junior council member, and then at Ashtoreth, his eldest, who sat to Lucifer's far right within the council members' inner circle.

Bael glanced at Ashtoreth, who raised his eyebrows and offered a wry smile. The brothers knew Lucifer's disgruntlement with Bael's refusal. But Bael had no interest in Heliomese law and government; life in Hell had always felt like an endless waiting for release from itself, for a pardon and forgiveness that might return him to his lost, real world. When that never came, life in Hell reverted to simple survival and acceptance of what small pleasures it might allow him.

Sharlan might have altered his outlook, improving those pleasures considerably, but not until her surprise announcement had he felt any demand to plan responsibly for their future.

And now his father was saying: "We now welcome our people to participate in this Council Forum, to bring any news to it that they deem important, to question anything you feel must be discussed. Speak up, my friends, and share with us what you will."

There was a murmur from the folk crowding the public back rows, and a thin, brown-haired woman stood up. Bael recognized Maura, the wife of Adrammelech.

"I have asked my husband to discuss this with his other council members, but have heard nothing from you today concerning the Ajanese men, or Talaperi as they prefer to be called, harassing our women. They follow us all about, obviously enamored by our beauty, their own women are so small and thin and plain and rarely seen. While I appreciate this compliment, it worries me. What are their true reasons for all of their attention?" She sat down, waiting for their response.

Lucifer eyed Adrammelech who stood, signaling that he would answer her. "My wife's concern — and I apologize to her as I meant to tell her of this — is unnecessary. Both Nergal and Dagon, who have mastered the Talaperi tongue, have questioned the chieftain of the little wood folk as to this behavior. Quite simply, Maura, we are told they are protective towards our women. It is their way of saying, should you be endangered, they will come to your aid, that while you are out and around, they are aware of you and your needs."

Maura stood again abruptly. "Husband, how can such small people protect us?!"

Her spouse looked aggrieved. "I don't know, wife. Perhaps they have talents we are unaware of. I simply point out that you and your gentle sisters are not in danger from them." He sat down.

Maura looked about her and did the same. "Thank you."

Lucifer looked out over the gathering. "Is there anyone else with something to contribute?"

A man stood to Bael's left. "Will there be a distribution of some of the harvest and bartered surplus to our households?"

"Yes, Jediah, there will be, on the eve of the Mizzuh celebration, one week from today. We will measure an extra share of fruits and grains to each home. The vegetables are being used for barter in the new year with the forest and mountain folk, in exchange for wood, flint, coal and a supply of fish."

The man nodded and reseated himself. Lucifer looked expectantly over the crowd, and Bael slowly rose to his full height, offered his hand to Sharlan and bade her stand as well. She wore a long cloak against the remaining cold over her winter robe and held it closed. The two braziers with burning coal on either side of the council hall did not warm it sufficiently. Affaeteres stared at both of them curiously and drew her own cloak more snugly about herself.

Lucifer nodded at them. "My son, Bael, and his mate, Sharlan, apparently have some concern to share with us. I'm pleased to see you taking an interest in our affairs, Bael. And you, Sharlan."

Bael noted Sharlan's father, Lothan, among the council members. He glanced at her and Bael quizzically.

Noting Ashtoreth's own questioning gaze, Bael put his arm around Sharlan, drawing her close. Sharlan's mother wasn't present. "We would like Tia to be present before we speak. Will someone please fetch her?"

There was movement behind them, and a woman's voice said,

"I'll get her."

Sharlan whispered to him, "That was Shadella, Nergal's wife. Our news may bring her hope."

Sharlan's parents lived close enough to the Council Hall. Tia soon appeared, making her way to Bael and Sharlan as Shadella reseated herself. Tia sat next to Affaeteres, asking, "What are these two up to?"

The murmur in the Council Hall suggested many others also wondered. Affaeteres said, "I don't know. Perhaps Bael will be good enough to clear up this mystery. What is so important that Tia must be hauled here?"

Bael smiled softly at her confusion. His mother, despite their better life here, seemed weary of late. He noticed, in another section of the public seating, all of the women from his leith waiting patiently, their faces revealing nothing, although they alone knew Bael and Sharlan's surprise.

Bael turned to his father, but spread his arms to include the entire gathering. "Sharlan and I have something of great significance to share with you all. She tells me we have conceived, and that she will bear a child. If this blessing goes forward unchallenged by fate, ours will be the first child born among the Heliomese!"

Stunned silence greeted his remark, as if the entire gathering took a deep breath and were holding it.

Then Lucifer stepped out of the Council's circle, walking slowly towards Bael and Sharlan as, at the same time, Affaeteres and Tia stood up, reaching out to Sharlan, and Shadella scurried from her seat, racing up to Sharlan, grasping her by the arm.

Shadella's eyes implored her, glazed with fear, as she cried out: "You mustn't! You mustn't. The Creator will take the child! It will vanish as my baby did."

Bael gently removed her hand from Sharlan's arm. "No, no. No, Shadella. That was long ago. This will be different."

Shadella wept soundlessly now, and Sharlan held the smaller, dark-haired woman, soothing her. "Ssh, ssh! Perhaps we have regained our child-bearing strength here. We women already know our bodies are changing here. Perhaps your long-held sorrow will one day be forgotten, perhaps there'll be another chance for you and Nergal to conceive."

Lucifer, Lothan and Nergal now stood near, and Nergal slowly led his wife back to her seat, comforting her.

Tia and Affaeteres, both as tall as Sharlan, confronted her, Tia cupping her daughter's face in her hands and asking, "Are you sure?" Affaeteres echoed her. "Yes, are you?!"

Sharlan nodded silently and shrugged off her winter cloak, smoothing her hands down over and under her swollen stomach.

Affaeteres asked, "How many months?"

"At least five now, Mother Affaeteres."

"You must not exert yourself. You must rest and nurture the unborn child."

The four other women from Bael's leith now rushed over to them: hearty, blond Cilah; petite Carin with her curly, light brown hair; pale, black-tressed Battah; and dusky Rhiah with her ebony mane, all speaking at once.

"We've been taking good care of her!"

"We couldn't say anything until they did."

"Sharlan's been hiding it until we were certain."

"We'll make sure she's all right!"

Lothan continued to stand there, his mouth agape, looking from Tia to Sharlan, a smile slowly forming and widening his lips.

Lucifer had made his way back to the Council circle. He now clapped loudly for attention. The women surrounding Sharlan quieted, looking toward him.

Lucifer said: "It appears that my second-born has made a contribution to our people, one which I was not expecting."

'He didn't do it alone!" Battah shouted, causing laughter to ring out in the Council Hall.

Lucifer held his hands up again for quiet. The expressions on the faces of the folk filled with wonder and uncertainty, Bael noted, Lucifer's included, as his father addressed him and Sharlan. "Your news, Bael, indeed brings us joy. Your mother has told me of the bodily changes many of our women, especially our younger ones, have experienced here, so similar to what we were told that mortal women on Earth experience. It is possible that giving birth will follow that pattern and be difficult."

Sharlan moved slightly toward him. "If it is, I will find the courage to face it for the sake of our child. For the sake of the Heliomese, and with hope that others among our women will be blessed with quickening as well."

Lucifer nodded. "Brave words, Sharlan. We, your people, will watch over you in your unique condition, and indeed hope that all will go well. But keep in mind that our home is now Hell, no matter how improved our lot may be here, and that the Creator did not send us here to be blessed."

Bael saw Sharlan visibly withdraw from Lucifer's warning, backing up again, as if away from an omen of evil. "Father," he said loudly, "I know how much you disdain any faith that our punisher may relent, but I might remind you that our crime was one of omission, in what we would not do, and not in anything we actually did. Oh, yes, our rebellion in the village green as the other angels were being prepared did create a physical dispute and chaos until the Seraphim appeared, but again, our motives were honest, and our actions not evil. Yes, we disobeyed the Creator, and were sent here. But is it not possible that our punishment is ended, that we have been forgiven, as shown by the relief and good fortune we have found on the Plains of Taleth?

"And is it not possible that Sharlan's pregnancy is another proof of our Creator's return to leniency, a special gift to her by virtue of her never having lost her own faith? For this I know; she hasn't. Not in the darkest of days. What do you say to that? Is there not the slightest cause for celebration here nor reason to hope again?" He drew Sharlan to him, embracing her gently.

Lucifer appeared befuddled, not speaking for a long stretch, and neither did anyone else. The hall remained silent. Finally, beginning in a low voice, he said, "I hope . . . yes, I hope what you say is true. This third level of Hell does seem like a reprieve, after our former torturous assent, with its fertile lands, peace and plenty. But I see no proof of forgiveness, regardless of how little there was to forgive, if anything, for in my mind, we were wronged by the Creator, treated harshly and unfairly!"

An audible gasp and murmurs again ran through the assembled folk, but Lucifer raised his hand. *"This has not changed.* It was not forgiveness we lacked, it was fair justice. My son . . . Bael . . . and Sharlan . . . recall two things during the events before our exile: that the Creator only promised us freedom to determine our own paths here, and the Creator said that I, Lucifer, as leader of the angelic rebels, would have to judge humans worthy of heaven before I, myself, could return to it, to our lost Eliom. I assume that means my followers also remain here until that judgment. We were offered nothing else, no other *blessings."*

Bael interrupted. "And yet they have come . . . blessings."

His father nodded briefly. "Perhaps we create our own; perhaps they are a happy coincidence. But I would caution you — caution everyone — to be wary of blindly trusting what seems wonderful and fortunate. Keep a constant vigil to make sure it continues. And," he looked firmly at Bael and Sharlan, "keep a small space in your hearts for the unexpected, for disappointment. We have settled on the Plains of Taleth for just over one hundred years now. Why is it only now that our women change so and one of them conceives? And will others conceive? We will have to wait and see. For now, I call this council meeting to a close."

He walked briskly over to Bael and clasped his shoulder, then abruptly hugged Sharlan and released her. "Dear girl, if you bear a healthy child, I will be the proudest grandfather. And all of our people will rejoice."

Sharlan impetuously hugged him back. "Oh, Father Lucifer, have just a little faith, and I know it will be rewarded. I feel the child within. I tell you it will be healthy!"

Tia moved protectively next to her. "Do not make ill omens, Lucifer. Our grandchild will be the gift Bael predicts."

Lothan added, "It cannot harm us to have hope," as Tia and Affaeteres swept Sharlan along, with her cheering leith-mates, to receive the well wishes of the others in the Council Hall. Lothan followed them.

Bael, attempting to join them, was stopped by his father's quick hand. Lucifer held him fast, his eyes searching Bael's, troubled, saying: "Now that Sharlan is out of hearing range, I tell you: expect *treachery!*"

"Father!"

"If none comes, you can rebuke me harshly, and I will allow it. But we, the fallen, refused to help the Creator's precious mortal children. Why now would we be allowed to bear our own here? I tell you, our punishment may yet continue, Bael. Guide Sharlan to nurture hope but not to trust it blindly. Guard her against the cruelest of disappointments. Shadella knew that grief."

"This is *not* the *same*, Father."

"I hope so. You see, I *do* hope."

Lucifer's words curdled within Bael's chest, constricting him with anger and depression. "Just once, Father," he hissed, "just once, do not be a leader bent on controlling everything and everyone! Leave us to our own determination, to that freedom which we have so painfully won. And let us decide things for ourselves!"

Bael turned on his heel and strode furiously away from him, joining the others. He felt no temptation to look back at Lucifer. He could imagine the effect his criticism had and the angry, impervious expression his father wore.

In the black night of Hell, even unclouded starlight only gave off faint illumination. Hell had no moons, as Earth and Eliom did. The fire stones, which the fallen angelfolk had carried with them from the fifth and sixth levels, could be heated by the angelfolk's radiant energy and cooled endlessly to be used again and again. They often sat in earthen pottery bowls to be heated as night lights.

Bael awoke to the strong glow of the fire stone on the table between his and Sharlan's cots, her swollen stomach making the sharing of his cot far too cramped in the last month of pregnancy. He saw that she sat on the side of her cot now, her hand hovering over their firestone, increasing its light. He asked, "Are you all right, Sharlan?"

She shook her head, her hand withdrawing from the stone to clutch at her belly beneath her robe. "I feel pain, cramping."

"I thought we had three weeks yet before our child's arrival."

"We should, but something seems to be wrong. Awaken our other women and tell them the birth may be early. We must go to the House of Healing. They must attend me and awaken the healers if I have need of restoratives, salves and teas, and their own healing energies through this trial, if it chooses to begin tonight."

"Can you walk?" He picked up the lamp bowl, its outer coolness shielding him from the fire stone within.

"For now. Let's get down the ladder stairs to the common room and wake them in the leith. Go now! I will follow carefully." She pulled on her winter boots, for it was only the first week of Pahluh and the month's brisk winds often chilled them, especially in the night.

Bael belted his robe, donned his boots and descended the stairs, putting the lamp bowl onto the table and rapping loudly on the inner door to their leith. Murmured voices sounded behind it, and the door opened up a crack.

Rhiah peered out, her ebony hair mussed from sleeping, then noted Bael, and then Sharlan moving painfully toward them. "Sharlan! Is the labor beginning?"

Sharlan nodded. "Something does not feel right, Rhiah. I want to go to the House of Healing tonight! Rouse the others."

Rhiah nodded quickly back and returned inside the darkened leith. A tiny glow began and built in a fire stone lamp as she added her energy to it, its light swelling to brighten the dark room. "Up, ladies! Get up! You, too, Mak! Sharlan may be in labor, and we must all attend her in the healing hut. If this be a false alarm, we can return here to sleep later. But up now, up!"

A flurry of activity answered her call, as Carin, Cilah and Battah, and Battah's lanky son, Mak, still a youth appearing no more than fourteen years, rose from their cots, tightened their robes, donned boots and cloaks and converged in the common room, surrounding Sharlan and wrapping her in her own winter cloak against the cold outside. They led her and Bael out the door, Mak and Battah leading the way holding two bowls of lit fire stones for illumination as they walked in the dark to the House of Healing.

The hundred-plus years in Taleth, as they named their village, had seen innovations, but none so helpful as the House of Healing. The Heliomese occasionally suffered injuries and minor sickness, and the little native folk had taught them the art of the healing plants. There were few instances where an angel became seriously ill or hurt; they still had strong bodily systems and recovered quickly. But maintaining a healing hut where both nurturing could take place and restoratives could be kept and applied was approved by all.

Bael supported Sharlan on one side, Cilah on the other. Other Heliomese emerged from their huts along the way, and some ran to the House of Healing to alert its three healers, chosen to oversee it, to make ready to help Sharlan.

When they reached the house, word had spread and a large crowd gathered around it. As Bael and Cilah helped Sharlan inside, Tia and Lothan, standing anxiously near the entrance, greeted them. Lothan stroked his daughter's hair. "Shadella came and told us. She's on her way to rouse Lucifer and Affaeteres now."

Sharlan smiled feebly, then abruptly hunched over.

Bael grasped her tightly. "Pain?"

"Yes!"

Dagon, the primary healer of the Heliomese, and their acknowledged priest, gestured for Bael to bring Sharlan from the vestibule, through the large inner treatment room, past it to the two sick rooms, and into the one on their left. Both rooms held a small fireplace for warmth and heating remedies, a softly cushioned bed cot, two stools and a small table with a fire stone lamp upon it. Logs and coals burned in the fireplace of this sick room and in the larger fireplace in the outer treatment room. Bael had noticed that the sick room on the right was dark and not in use. Now he bluntly asked Dagon, "Will you be delivering our babe?"

Dagon, running a hand over his bald head, just as bluntly answered, "I am frankly not at all knowledgeable concerning mortal childbirth. If we were in Eliom, this would be so much easier, safer as well. Naamah and Tilley, our female healers, have advised me that this will be best overseen by them and the other women, that it is done that way on Earth. They believe that an instinct will be aroused, and that instinct will guide them through this. Come, Sharlan, lie on the cot and let the fire warm you." She did, and he covered her with a soft fur, a gift from the Ajanese. "Ah, here come

Naamah and Tilley, who will attend you with your leith-mates as you've requested."

As he spoke, Rhiah and Cilah entered the room, followed by Battah and Carin. Mak poked his head in briefly, but Battah pushed him out, saying, "Stay with your father outside. I saw him in the crowd. This is no place for a boy."

Sharlan reached out weakly for Naamah's hand. The only woman council member and one of Lucifer's subcommanders during and after their exile, her luxurious black hair and sea-green eyes projected a feminine allure that complimented her strong-minded nature and drive for survival. She refused any concept of failure. Everything had its place and use, and problems were viewed as challenges to be thought out and learned from. She tightly clasped her fingers around Sharlan's hand and shut her eyes in concentration.

"Ah," said Dagon, "Naamah is sending her healing!" He nodded at her and at Tilley, who struck a startling contrast to Naamah with her soft, straight, blond hair and sky-blue eyes, her short, thin frame and unimposing persona. "I will remain in the main room if any of you need my advice or assistance." So saying, he left the room, drawing closed the curtain in its open doorway, affording Sharlan and her attendants some privacy.

Tilley moved to Sharlan and ran her hand over her pregnant girth. Sharlan arched her back as another contraction coursed through her, then quieted as Tilley began to send healing into her belly, to the babe, to relax them both. She turned to Lothan and Bael. "I believe that fathers and husbands should leave the room, so that we can examine Sharlan more thoroughly. You can stay in the treatment room, where it's warm as well, but from this point on, we women will assist your daughter and wife." When both men hesitated, she added: "We will call you if Sharlan needs you. Or after the baby is born."

Bael noted a sigh, barely audible, of relief escape from Lothan. He kissed his wife Tia's cheek and then Sharlan's, and exited. Bael moved to Sharlan's side, bending over the cot, lightly kissing her lips. He noted how dry they were, how pale she looked. "Do not be afraid. Remember your faith!"

"I love you," she said simply and shut her eyes.

He was only silent for a heartbeat. "*I* love *you!*" It surprised him to realize that he meant it. She had achieved his heart, had healed it, and now she would bear his child.

Sharlan opened her eyes and offered a frail but pleased smile.

In his mind, he prayed incoherently that she be protected, that this all might go well, as he smiled tiredly back at her. Turning, he left her to the care of the women, pulling the heavy curtain well-closed behind him.

Only later did he consider that Tilley had called Sharlan his wife and he, her husband, when all of Taleth knew they were not formally wed, only mated. Only later did he wonder if that contributed to his turmoil, that his prayer had been so foully rejected or perhaps not heard at all, because he *had not* broken all ties with his past. Or perhaps because he finally believed that Lucifer had been right.

He remembered his bravado at the council meeting, but if Sharlan's moans and occasionally much louder outcries, increasing as the night wore on, was what childbirth on Earth was like, he pitied both his mate and those mortal women. At one point, he had tried to gain entrance to the room again, thinking his close presence would comfort her, but Cilah, as tall and as strong as he was, had rudely shoved him back out, emerging briefly with him.

She said, "You mustn't come in. The baby has moved further down the birth canal. Thankfully, Eve told us of these things when she returned to Eliom. But you must wait outside until the birthing is finished!"

He nodded dumbly, and she went back into the room. Feeling numb, he sat before the large hearth, stoking the logs and coals, glancing at Dagon who also sat, eyes shut, leaning back in a chair, asleep, mouth slightly opened. Mak and his father Tihbal sat on the floor in another corner of the room, also dozing.

Most of the other Heliomese had been sent home by Dagon with an assurance that he would send word to the people when the birth occurred. Bael found it strange, that only a few of the folk had trailed Sharlan and him here, and that even Lothan had returned home to await Tia's news, when the baby arrived. And Bael's father, mother and brother had not come to the healing hut. Shadella had told them; in fact, she was in the room with Sharlan and the others now, determined to be there, needed or not, fiercely protective of Sharlan.

A cry rang out from Sharlan and he jumped; it angered him, feeling useless. Soothing voices came from the room, mingling with Sharlan's murmured whimpers and then silence.

Dagon woke briefly. "Shouldn't be long now," he mumbled and went back to sleep in his chair.

Tihbal looked at Dagon, at Bael. Mak still slept against him, as he quietly told Bael: "We men must be patient. It takes awhile, but it will be worth it."

Bael offered him a wry, crooked attempt at a smile. "I hope you are right." He shut his own eyes, trying to sleep a bit, for Sharlan had quieted. Perhaps they had given her more healing energy, letting her rest awhile.

A gust of wind came through the vestibule, waking him again. Lucifer entered the healing hut, followed by Affaeteres and Ashtoreth, drawing the door closed behind him. Through it, Bael saw that the grey dawn had arrived.

Lucifer strode straight up to him. "Has she?"

Bael shook his head. "Not yet, it seems. They haven't called me in."

His mother bent down and squeezed his hand. "I'll go in and see how she's doing," said Affaeteres. She straightened up, stroked her younger son's shoulder, and headed for the birthing room, lifting the side of the curtain quietly as she slipped by it.

Bael, Lucifer and Ashtoreth watched the curtain fall back in place. Only murmuring broke the silence beyond in the birthing room.

Lucifer's own voice, low, nearly a whisper, broke their own silence. "Something is wrong."

Bael briefly shook his head, his own fears wearying him more than the long night's vigil. "We do not know of these things. It may only be a delay."

Ashtoreth said nothing, his expression taut, as if the miracle they all awaited was tainted, an approaching disaster, and not a blessing. His mouth creased downward, a frozen frown.

The murmurs of the women now changed to a babble, increasing in volume, filled with alarming wails, and Sharlan's voice carried over it, building to a shriek. "No! You cannot. It lives. You CANNOT!"

Bael stormed past his father and brother, flinging aside the curtain, invading the room. The women, startled, turned tear-stained, anxious faces toward him.

Sharlan lay on the cot, looking pale and worn. In her arms, she clutched a small bundle wrapped in a small blanket, only the top of its head visible, her own naked body covered by the Talaperi's fur blanket, its lower half stained with the blue of her skane.

He stared at her for a moment, then asked, breathing heavily and feeling inane, "Are you bleeding?" His eyes kept drifting to the quiet bundle she clutched tightly against her chest.

She lifted her eyes to his, her own tears flowing from them, unchecked. "It's stopped. The bleeding has stopped." She lowered her blanket to expose her breasts and drew the bundled baby to them, its face down. She uncovered it as its mouth sought her nipple, and it began to drink its mother's milk, sucking strongly.

As Sharlan drew down its tiny blanket, pulling it off, the baby's smooth back, arms and hands revealed, Bael stared at its small buttocks and the stumps below it where the thighs and legs should have been and were not. Bael felt rooted to where he stood, as if he had lost all power in his own legs, as if he, and not the babe, were deformed.

He asked, inanely again, "Is it boy or girl?"

Sharlan only looked at him, seeming hesitant to answer him.

He heard the curtain being pulled back behind him. Sharlan quickly covered the legless baby up with its blanket and then again with her own, shielding its deformity from view.

Lucifer walked past him to the cot. "So. The child's been born."

Sharlan clutched at it protectively.

"Is it boy or girl?"

Bael watched as Ashtoreth slowly entered the room and edged between him and their father. Ash's face took in the swaddled child held fast against Sharlan's breast; still he said nothing.

The child chose at that moment to turn its face from its mother's nipple, showing itself in profile, its black hair matted softly against its small head, its tiny nose and mouth perfect, but sunken skin covered the sockets where its eyes should have been.

Bael very slowly reached for both blankets around the child, grasping them, and even more slowly, pulling them down. Affaeteres, standing beside Tia on the other side of Sharlan's cot, slapped her hand down onto Bael's, stopping him. Bael drew his gaze sharply to his mother's determined face.

But Sharlan pushed both of their hands weakly away with her own. "This is my child, born to sorrow, and I will protect him."

Bael said nothing, but Lucifer said, "A boy then. And blind."

Affaeteres asked, "Will you let it live then?"

Lucifer glanced at his wife. "It will be burdened by its lack of sight, but as Sharlan said, if protected, the child will have a life of sorts."

Bael lightly touched Lucifer's arm. "Father . . ."

Lucifer raised a quizzical eyebrow. "There is nothing more to say. I was right! The Creator brings no blessings to us in Hell. Be thankful this is not worse and hope that no other Heliomese women bear children, for I fear they would bear even more monstrous infants than your sightless son!"

As if Lucifer's words had wounded the baby, it began to wail and squirm, its small stumps waiving in odd susurrations under the thin blankets. Lucifer stared at it; Bael saw understanding dawn on his father's face.

Bael leaned over Sharlan, his hand gently cradling and caressing her face. He gazed at her, and then at his mother and Tia, and said simply, "You cannot hide it."

Sharlan drew the covers off her son again. "I will not have him destroyed! His life is not ours to end!"

Lucifer touched the child's flailing stumps. "Worse!"

He looked at them all, all of the women clustered around Sharlan and her son, save for Naamah and Lilley, who stood to the side near the small hearth, its banked blaze incongruously cheerful against their despair. "Naamah. What do *you* advise?"

Naamah lowered her head, her dark hair falling about her face, half hiding it, a gesture unlike her. She softly replied, "I have advised Sharlan to let us destroy it. Blind, without legs, it will be a burden. It may be angelic by birth, but we have proven in Hell that even angels can die. But Sharlan will not agree with me, and Affaeteres and Tia are protective of *her* and also won't allow me to put the creature out of its misery."

Affaeteres said in a voice thick with disapproval. "It is *not* a *creature!* It is our grandson, and I do not know how long it will live if we nurture it." She locked eyes with Lucifer. "But if there is a curse, we must do our best to counter it, love the child, for as long as he survives, help him to survive!"

"Aff . . . the child is severely deformed. . . ."

"My child will *not* be put to death!" Sharlan interrupted. "Bael, do not let them hurt Nikki!"

"Nikki?"

Lilley squeezed Bael's arm. "Sharlan named the child."

"Nikki?" Bael repeated and looked at Sharlan. "You named it Nikki?" In Eliomese, *nikki* meant *courage.*

Sharlan nodded. "He will need it, will he not?"

Bael shook his head in wonder. To name the child was to recognize it as a divine spark of the Creator, to accept its existence in eternity. But their Creator had cast them out, abandoned them. Bael turned to Lilley, the other master healer. "And what do you say? What do you advise?"

Lilley, too, lowered her head, but then abruptly lifted it, her blue eyes hard. "I say let the mother decide. It is the mother's right."

"And its father's?" Bael asked.

Her stubborn expression never wavered. "The father must accept the mother's decision. It may be his right to disagree, but never to decide. That is a woman's choice."

Lucifer cut in. "So be it, then! Tragedy has befallen us. Yet a new mother cannot bear the thought of losing her child, even a misshapen, blind one, and has named him for courage. So be it. But in this world, there will be no Naming Day! Why could our Creator want to be presented with a child maimed as an ongoing punishment, to settle my score? What Creator would do such a thing?!"

Bael gathered the child in both hands and lifted its sightless, legless body upward, saying, "We have no Well of Being to hold my son over, and he will never stand nor see, but I hold him up and declare his name to be Nikki to whatever power will hear me and declare that I, too, deny this curse and claim my poor son and will protect him!"

He lowered the babe, who had remained strangely docile throughout this declaration, to Sharlan, who cradled Nikki gently.

She smiled her relief at Bael and kissed the baby. "No one will hurt you, little soul. No one will harm you, my son."

10

Nikki

On the third day of Nikki's birth, Sharlan recovered enough to return home, walking silently through the pathways of Taleth, supported by Battah and Cilah. Bael flanked them, holding his son.

They arrived at their leith and cottage as the sun set. Caren and Rhiah greeted them, the supper laid out on the table. Mak sat stiffly, looking anxious, in the middle of the long bench facing the door as they entered. He seemed not to know what to do with his hands, resting them on the table top, then jerking them below it, out of sight. He stared at Bael and Nikki, almost, it seemed, without realizing it.

Bael addressed Mak quietly. "It's not his hands that are missing, Mak."

The boy colored. "I know. I didn't mean . . ."

"I know you meant no harm, that you're simply nervous. But Nikki is not a pariah to be shunned; his needs are the same as any other infant's right now. It is when he grows that he will face challenges. But right now, his needs are simple: to be fed, cleaned, nurtured and protected."

Mak nodded. "At least he isn't like the native folk."

"What do you mean?" Bael carefully lowered Nikki into the cradle he had built for him, soft cloth lining it.

Mak wrinkled his nose. "Their terrible body function. They cannot meditate their waste away as we can. But you can even help Nikki to purify himself, using our radiant energy, until he grows up and can learn to do it by himself."

"Well, yes," Bael agreed. "From what we can tell, Nikki is one of us. Sharlan already rebalanced the baby's aura when it," Bael grinned, "overloaded."

Mak nodded, glancing at Battah. "My mother had to teach me, when I was old enough to understand."

Cilah led Sharlan to one of the two carved chairs at each end of the long table. Bael took the other end chair near the cradle, while Cilah and Battah each flanked Mak on the far bench. Caren and Rhiah sat opposite them on the other bench.

The meal consisted of bowls of thick vegetable soup and flat bread baked with crushed berries. A pitcher of water sat on the table, their cups already poured.

They all bent their heads to the food, spooning and swallowing the hot broth and chewing the cooked carrots, celery, potatoes and beans, as well as the sweetened bread, not speaking. Even the infant remained silent.

Finally Sharlan put down her spoon, looking with uncertainty at her leith-mates and then at Bael. "Nikki lives," she said. "My child lives. And he is more frightened than you, living in darkness, not knowing what he is, only knowing comfort and companionship through our touch and our voices. I pray that someday he may speak, and we can answer back through our own words, and Nikki will know he is not alone." Then she lowered her eyes and said nothing more.

Bael glanced uneasily at the cradle. "He sleeps."

Sharlan nodded, drinking a sip or two of water. They continued their meal silently, nothing more heard than a sigh or two escaping worried lips.

And then the outer door to the cottage slowly pushed open, and yet no greeting sounded and, at first, no one appeared in the small opening gap.

Bael started up to close it, thinking an errant wind had blown the door open, when a small, curly-haired head peered around it. The Talaperi man lifted his gaze uncertainly to Bael, surveyed the others, and then stared directly and sadly, Bael thought, toward Sharlan.

Sharlan spoke as the small native walked a step in, clothed in soft cured skins and strapped sandals. The Talaperi and Teleperi weren't shy, but they preferred contact in their own villages or in the Council Hall for barter-trade, and rarely entered the Heliomese cottages and huts. "Why did you journey here, little friend? Please come inside."

He moved a foot further in, still watching her, then spoke in Heliomese, his tongue forming the non-native words with care. "We wish to help. Your sorrow. The newly-born in sorrow. We will help you do the hard. Take away the sorrow." He now spoke his own language more rapidly, his face turned back to the door. *"Cheecha asima palatagh dundee."*

A Talaperi woman entered timidly, no taller than the man, both the size of children no older than eight, Bael thought. What shocked him was the miniscule baby the native woman carried, held fast against her tunic. The baby wore no clothes as the woman held him out to Sharlan, as if for her inspection.

Bael felt anger sweep through him, gazing at the Talaperi infant, fully limbed and sighted. It squirmed in his small mother's arms, looking about.

Sharlan nodded, her face as troubled as Bael himself felt, at the small mother and her tiny babe. "Yes," Sharlan told her, "he's pretty." The woman kept holding the baby out to Sharlan.

Bael approached them. "I think she wants you to hold her baby."

Sharlan glanced at him, then held out her hands for it.

The Talaperi mother seemed anxious, turning to the man, saying, *"Pahl ah!"* The man spoke sharply back at her. *"Pahl tuh!"* She gave him a look of anger and then one of despair and placed the tiny infant into Sharlan's hands.

Sharlan, obviously confused, cradled the child, saying. "You have a beautiful son." She then held him carefully out to his mother, to return him to her.

The woman shook her head and began walking stiffly to the door, but Bael was swifter, blocking the doorway, stopping her. "What is this all about?" he demanded.

The Talaperi man held out his hands, as if to ward off Bael's fury. "We give you good child, small but whole. The other ... cannot stand ... cannot see." The little man's face took on an ominous cast. "Cannot survive. Bad." He struggled again with their language. "Must ... must treat kind. Give to me. I will do what is kind."

Bael shook his head. "We are already treating Nikki with kindness. We know that he's legless and blind. We will take care of him. You don't have to do that for us. And we cannot take your baby."

Battah stood up. "This is a misunderstanding, little folk. We are well. Go home."

The Talaperi man folded his arms. "Not well. Child sick. Not good. Do what is right. Talaperi give you new child, good child. Pain will be less. Mother's pain will be less."

Sharlan looked at Bael, confused. "They seem to want to give me their own infant, so that I won't feel so badly about Nikki's ... deformities." She fixed her gaze on the Talaperi mother. "But I can't take your son." She stood up to bring the babe back to its mother and saw the little man heading for Nikki, reaching into his cradle and picking him up with surprising ease. Sharlan rushed toward him. "No! Put him down!"

Cilah, closer, jumped up from the bench and forcibly took Nikki from the Talaperi.

The small man wore an expression of total amazement. "We try to help! Give me sick child. You cannot do it. Too hurtful. We will do it. Pain will ease. Child suffer only little, not all its life. Do what is right."

Bael took Nikki from Cilah, cradling his whimpering son protectively. "You keep saying that. We *are* doing what is right!"

The Talaperi man shook his head vehemently and glanced at his woman, standing hesitantly before the door, Bael no longer blocking her, Sharlan still trying to give her back her baby.

Bael asked him, "What are your names?"

The question threw the little folk off, but the man answered. "I am Pent, my mate, Salik, our son, Turic. You perhaps name him different name."

"I will do no such thing. You and Salik will take your son back, Pent. I don't understand why you wish to exchange children. We would never allow you to raise Nikki, burdened as our baby is. We can treat him just as kindly as you."

Sharlan held Turic out to Salik, urging her, "Please. He belongs with you. Not with me."

Salik looked to her mate. Pent, disgruntled, pleaded with Bael. "You will bring trouble and ruin doing this! It is not a right thing! The vine will dry; the berries will sour."

Bael spoke briskly to Salik. "Take your son Turic back!"

Again, Salik looked to Pent, who nodded, once, curtly. She held out her hands to Sharlan, who placed Turic into them. Bael then handed Nikki to Sharlan, walked to the cottage door and opened it wide, frowning at the Talaperi couple and their infant son. "I am sorry for the misunderstanding, truly I am. But you also must understand that our decision will stand. Go home, Pent. Salik, take your son Turic home to your village. Now."

The Talaperis slowly exited the cottage, Pent again gazing ominously up at Bael, repeating, "Trouble and ruin," as he left. Bael shut the door firmly behind him. He said, walking up to Nikki and Sharlan, and briefly stroking his son's cheek, "You were born in the month of Pahluh, when the cold winds buffet Taleth and sway the tree tops. And blow strange offers to our door. But you are safe, little son." And to Sharlan, "Perhaps there was more substance to Maura's complaint last Mizzuh than we thought. The Talaperi have no shyness when it comes to pushing their ways and customs on us."

Nikki began to cry, and Sharlan sat back down at the table, opening her robe demurely to feed him unobtrusively. The others also took their places again and began to eat, Bael seating himself last. "We must watch out for well-meaning Talaperi," he warned.

Sharlan shook her head. "It was a misunderstanding. Did you see the relief on Salik's face? She did not want to lose her son either. Whatever Pent's reason or belief that caused him to suggest such an exchange, he knows now that he was wrong."

Bael studied her face, still etched with worry over their son, over the foolishness they had just endured, and he wished he could soothe her. But he knew the road ahead was best walked stoically. "I have no idea how they thought they could care for Nikki better than we can," he muttered and returned to his soup.

"I'm afraid it's not very hot now," Rhiah commented, sipping the broth.

Bael stirred his bowl. "No matter. It tastes fine. Let's finish it before it does turn cold."

They did so in silence again, but the quiet now soothed them, as if the night and rest would bring them peace and renew perhaps a glimmer of hope in their hearts.

The rainy month of Parrauh came and went, but these were not the cold, icy rains of Kolluh. Warm, drenching showers replenished both the cultivated fields and the woodlands.

The Teleperi, the slightly-larger, mountain-dwelling cousins to the forest folk, traded freshly caught fish to the Talaperi and the Heliomese in exchange for foodstuffs and another curious trade item: the angelfolk's ability to create the vulmakoth or fire stones. The Teleperi praised their radiant energy and often asked them to use it to heat stones to stoke the forges where they worked the metals they mined in Cahniohiom. The heat energy transferred to the vulmakoth lasted five times longer than any coals or wood alone and the stones could be reused.

They lived in small villages close to the mountain lakes. Their cousins lived in Ajan Helvert — the dark green wood that bordered the left side of their vast mountain ranges — and in Ajan Morvert — the grey green wood to the right of those mountains. The Taleth plains stretched across the opposite ends of those woods. And in the center of all, the land rose again to the next higher level of Hell. But the Heliomese were weary of climbing onward and saw no reason to push higher. For at least five more centuries, they would have no knowledge of that second level of Hell with its vaster lake system and rich lands, or knowledge of the topmost level above it with its great central lake, Lei Lello, and the surrounding lands that would one day become powerful principalities of Hell.

The village of Taleth sat close to Ajan Helvert. The angelfolk and the saurs, both preferring the plains, still traveled freely on the third level and were accepted by its natives. But the saurs who had followed the angelfolk this far onward were few, theirs a small community, and they had developed no real bond with the third level natives, allied only with the Heliomese, their protectors and mentors.

The third level held one other, stranger trait, which the angel-folk were unaware of until they traveled upward and onward and reached the second and first levels of Hell. The first, top level, with its large territories and central lake, was dimensionally a continent long and wide. The second level, below it, held its own vast tracts of forest and fertile lands, as well as a great system of four lakes fed through Lei Lello above it. These lakes, in turn, fed downward to the lakes of the Cahniohiom, the home of the Teleperi on the third level.

Logically and physically, the third level territories, its mountain land, its parallel forests and its Plains of Taleth could not have been near enough for daily travel between each territory by a simplistic society. And yet the distance was minimal: by foot, approximately a day in each direction between plain and mountain through either of the forests.

The angelfolk assumed the two upper levels were simply small rises, top and final plateaus, although mist surrounded each rise, obscuring each plateau until they eventually reached it.

It was not until they finally reached the final two, that they knew some magic or trick of nature existed on the third level, for its territory could not be that compact and still hold and encompass the higher continents of the second and first levels, not without overlapping the third and covering and crushing it completely.

The angelfolk later discovered, as they developed scientific understanding and knowledge, that the last three levels of Hell were spatially distorted dimensions — and while it took them five hundred years to travel upward from the sixth to the third level, it would only take them 100 years to travel the final two rises to the top. And when they did reach the first level of Hell, they would spend the bulk of their eternal lives there, building the five great lands of Hell around Lei Lello — Star Lake — which sat in its center. They would then extend their empire downward again, controlling all the levels of Hell, from Domain, its capital principality on that first top level.

But for now, they only knew their home village on the Plains of Taleth and their contentment in settling on the third level, a comfortable land with all of its territories easily traveled by foot within a day or two.

The angelfolk often ventured into the nearby forest knolls and small meadows of Ajan Helvert for outings in the milder times, its peacefulness soothing and reminiscent of old Eliom in the heavens.

And so, two months later in Kallaiuh, the month of "beauty time," Bael and Sharlan and Cilah took Nikki for an afternoon in the forest near a running brook that Sharlan found relaxing and cool. They carried a blanket and a basket of food and drink to share. Nikki rode in a cloth pouch that Bael had constructed. It wrapped securely around and in front of Bael's shoulders and waist, and Nikki was held fast inside of it.

Bael still cradled Nikki with his arms, for both he and Sharlan believed that their touch communicated their love and more to their son, that it challenged his blindness.

"Can you see me, little one of mine?" he asked his son. "In your infant mind, can you picture my hands holding you?"

They had reached the brook and its grassy banks.

Cilah bent down and spread the blanket in a spot relatively level, her blonde curls falling against her face, momentarily hiding it. She straightened up to her full height, lifting her arms overhead, stretching her muscles. "The ground is fairly smooth, the grass new and soft. A lovely spot to rest and eat."

Sharlan placed the basket onto the blanket, taking out the cups and the two tightly knotted skins, a large one filled with a sweet wine, fermented from the white grapes the Heliomese grew, and the other, smaller one, a less potent juice made from a native fruit called *pala*, which tasted like a spongy apple but had a dark blue outer skin against its pale lavender inner fruit, its juice easily squeezed.

Next came the fresh bread that Rhiah had baked for them early in the morning, a special loaf, not flat, but thick and soft within, speckled with walnuts and raspberries and another local fruit they had hitherto been unfamiliar with, a single chamber berry, red and as deliciously edible as the blueberry they all missed, for Hell seemed to have replaced that tasty Eliomese fruit and its bush with a red version.

Lastly, she brought out the small block of white cheese, for the Teleperi had tamed the mountain goats and milked them and turned that into cream and butter and cheese, which they traded with their woodland cousins and the Heliomese.

Sharlan sat down, beckoning to Bael to give her Nikki, baring one breast to feed their baby, kissing his small forehead as Bael placed him into her hands. Nikki gurgled and cooed at the feel of his mother's lips, reaching up to grasp her hair, pulling on a long dark strand. Sharlan gently extricated her hair and lowered Nikki comfortably against her breast. His tiny hand now sought that, touching her nipple, and his mouth followed, suckling contentedly. Sharlan shut her eyes, equally content. "You two eat now," she told Bael and Cilah. "I'll wait until Nikki's done nursing, then one of you can hold him while I eat."

Bael watched her as he ate, her eyes still shut, her head nodding. He lightly touched her cheek.

She slowly opened her eyes to study him. "Yes?"

"You were falling asleep."

"It's the warmth of the day. And the rhythm of Nikki's suckling."

"I thought you had had a bit of that wine before we left."

"No," she laughed. "But I would like some when I'm done with Nikki."

Cilah picked up the wine skin, made from the bladder of a deer and bartered from the Talaperi, and untwisted the stopper. She poured all three of them a cup. "I think if anyone deserves some sweet relaxation, it's you, Sharlan."

"Thank you. And after I eat and, yes, drink a bit of that wine, although not too much when I'm nursing, what I really would like is to take a stroll just a little ways down the bank with Bael. Not too far and not too long. Just to have a little time to ourselves out in these beautiful woods on this tranquil day."

"And you would like me to watch Nikki for you," Cilah concluded, downing her cup of wine and pouring herself another. "Well, considering how relaxed *he* is after his feeding, that shouldn't be hard. I'll just lie down beside him and watch him nap."

Bael cut a slice of cheese with the small knife, another Talaperi good. He placed the cheese on a hunk of bread and chewed them with gusto, stroking Nikki's stumps. The baby broke away from his feeding to turn his head in the direction of this father's touch, smacked his tiny lips, and then resumed his own meal. "Even if you fell asleep," Bael told Cilah, "it's not as if Nikki could go anywhere."

And Sharlan added, "At least not go far. He has begun to try to crawl, but it's more of a dragging motion, pulling himself across a rug."

Bael raised a brow at this. "Then we must encourage it. It will also help him develop strong arms. Perhaps one day we will find a way to help him adapt, to become more mobile."

"Yes." Cilah nodded. "He's already responding to our voices, turning to us when he hears us, as accurately as a sighted child would. Nikki may surprise us after all." She reached over the blanket, tickling Nikki's soft chin, but he had fallen asleep at Sharlan's breast, sated in the afternoon warmth. "Here, give him to me, and eat and drink, Sharlan, and then take your romantic walk with Bael in the woods. But don't be too long, in case your son wakes and protests your absence." She took Nikki in her arms, rocking him a few strokes, and then gently laid him down on the soft blanket. He squirmed a minute then fell back to sleep, his small chest rising and falling.

Sharlan ate some fruited bread and cut a large slice of cheese, washing them down first with the cup of wine Cilah had poured her before, then with a fresh cup of *pala* juice. "I don't think Nikki will wake too soon," she told Cilah, "if his pattern these last three months stays the same. He usually sleeps rather heavily after feeding." She got up, smoothing her lightweight robe down, and Bael followed suit. "We won't be away long. And thank you, Cilah. I need this tranquility."

Bael drew his arm around her and pulled her close. "And we promise to behave."

Cilah made a face and began to put away the remainder of their meal and implements, back into the basket. "Ah, but you don't say how, which leaves you a wide assortment of various types of behavior."

Sharlan laughed and dragged Bael away. "Come on, before Cilah asks us for a list. We won't be long."

Cilah lay down next to Nikki, her one hand resting lightly atop his stomach, her head against her other lower arm, pillowing it. "Don't get lost," she murmured.

They had gone about a hundred yards along the river bank, hand-in-hand, enjoying the peaceful privacy, the first time they had both been away from Nikki since his birth. But Cilah was strong and still near enough to call if needed. In fact, the outing had been Cilah's and the other leith-mates' idea, something to put fresh color into Sharlan's wan cheeks, a touch of fresh air and freedom from worry over Nikki.

The woods ran closer to the bank here, the brook narrower, easily waded across. He squeezed Sharlan's hand. "Do you want to go across?" he asked, gesturing at the cluster of trees on the other side. "The thick trunks of the trees will shelter us from any other folk in the woods."

"What do you think you're going to do? Or did you write a list?"

"Just enjoy my beautiful woman's sensuality. For a few minutes without our son."

"Well, I would like to wash my feet in the cool water, tired as they are from the brisk walk from Taleth to Ajan Helvert." Sharlan removed her sandals.

Bael followed her example and they stepped into the cold water. It streamed over their feet as they carefully crossed the brook and climbed up the small bank. He put his sandals back on, then held her steady while she followed suit. "Come on, now. I think I see a small glade between those trees on our right." He led her there, a nearly circular set of trees surrounding a secluded center of lush, tall grass. Bael sat down and pulled Sharlan toward him. She didn't protest, letting him guide her to the ground.

She leaned over his hips and legs. He put one arm around her neck and the other around her waist and leaned back toward her, holding her, kissing her. Sharlan sighed deeply and relaxed, letting him cradle her head and shoulders.

He loosened her robe, exposing one plump breast, lowering his mouth towards it, but her hand pushed him gently away.

"Why?" he asked, and then, "Why not?"

"Nikki's milk is inside of it."

"And he cannot share it with me?"

Sharlan shivered at the thought, her desire evident, but said, "It will not be clean if the baby requires feeding again. I know he would not normally drink again so soon but . . ."

Bael put his finger across her lips, hushing her. "There is a brook, lady of my heart. We can wet my robe and wash your precious nipple clean. Only let me now drink a bit of the nectar you feed our son." He lifted his finger and brought his lips against hers. She melted into the kiss and made no further protest as his mouth traveled down to her swollen breast, covered the nipple and suckled it, drawing the warm milk into his mouth, and then swallowing it.

After a minute he released it and, still cradling her, laid her down on the bed of grass, lifting her robe and his own, and then her hips rose to meet his eager erection. Her body felt warm and welcoming around his penis and he rocked her within, knowing his pleasure matched her own from the grasping of her hands on his back and the sighs and gasps she uttered.

They climaxed together and lay sated for a while, then got up tiredly but happily and walked back to the brook.

There, Bael stood guard while Sharlan washed herself, shook off the excess water and put her robe back on. And then Bael did the same, while his mate admired the view.

He laughed as they put on their sandals and headed back to Cilah and Nikki. "Now *that* was long overdue, my lady, for both of us!"

Sharlan answered softly, "I'm glad you enjoyed it, my husband."

Now Bael was silent, fumbling for her hand, clasping it. "I am like your husband, aren't I? Even though we haven't pledged that formally."

Sharlan gave no reply, only squeezed his hand as they approached the picnic blanket and Cilah and Nikki, both asleep in the lengthening afternoon.

Suddenly Sharlan stopped, staring at Cilah and the baby, Nikki wrapped in a small blanket, his head and body covered up.

Bael paused beside Sharlan. "I don't recall your bringing that blanket for the baby."

"I didn't!"

"Perhaps Cilah?"

"I don't know. I don't think so."

They walked quickly over to their friend and shook her awake as Sharlan uncovered the baby and cried out in a strangled voice, "Oh, no!"

The Talaperi infant Turic gazed up at them.

Cilah, awake now, stared in horror at the tiny boy. "How?! I would have heard!"

Sharlan shook her head. "No. You weren't expecting such a thing. The forest folk are very nimble and move silently." She grasped Bael's arm. "We must go immediately to their village and get Nikki back!"

Bael nodded morosely. "Pack up, Cilah, and go quickly back to Taleth and bring help. We must stop this foolishness for once and for all. Get my father and some of the other Council members and tell them to meet us in the Talaperi's village. Sharlan and I will go there now to bring Turic back to Pent and his wife Salik. And Creator help them if they have harmed Nikki in any way with their foolishness!"

Cilah stuck their remaining food and drink in the basket as Sharlan picked up the Talaperi child, wrapping him in his blanket. The child made no protest, his eyes large, their pupils rounded. Cilah folded their picnic blanket, flung it over her arm, the basket in her other hand, and started off. "I'll be as fast as I can. Go now! The Talaperi live half an afternoon's brisk walk from here. They cannot have gone very far."

Sharlan glanced at Bael. "Perhaps we can catch up with them before they get to their home. Nikki is not as light as Turic. He would weigh them down, make them slower!"

"Possibly. Cilah," he called to her, "we will head for Talaperi village even if we find Nikki and his abductors first. The angelfolk must never let this happen again! Creator bring our son back to us," he added softly, wondering at his last vestige of hope in a power that still cared and could help them.

He started briskly in a northeasterly direction with Sharlan holding Turic lightly in her arms.

Cilah turned southeast and began hurrying back to Taleth.

Bael's anger gnawed at him. "I want to slay Pent like the forest creatures his people slay for food!"

"Do not say such a thing, Bael. Please!"

"Why not? We are no longer subject to the laws of Eliom. We have been given free will to choose as we will. We chose to love our child born legless and sightless, and the Talaperi chose to believe they could force this replacement on us. And now it is our choice to react as we wish to such effrontery!"

"I know we must confront the Talaperi," Sharlan said, struggling to keep pace with him through the forest. "But they *think* they've given us a *better* baby. Yet I cannot comprehend why they want to take care of Nikki in our stead. Do they think that they have some special method of protecting a deformed baby? That will care for Nikki better than we can?"

Bael stopped so abruptly, she had to turn back, her expression asking why he had halted. He gazed tensely at her. "Pent kept describing Nikki as a burden, as bad luck. He kept saying he would do the right thing with Nikki. We assumed that meant to care for him and protect him."

Sharlan asked, confused, "And what else would he mean?"

Bael hesitated before answering, breathing heavily at the realization. "He may mean to kill Nikki!"

"No!" Sharlan shook her head vigorously, gazing at Turic, so quiet, whimperless. "Why does this child make no sound? Have they fed it something to subdue it? And they would not kill Nikki. They would not harm him or blame him for being born as he was!"

Bael said slowly, "I can only hope I am wrong. We hardly ever see their children until they're nearly grown, and those we do see are all whole and healthy. But the more quickly we move, the quicker we'll stop them, whatever they intend, and get Nikki back."

They increased their pace, hurrying to the village of the forest folk, and finally reached its outer boundary as the grey daylight began fading from the sky.

Bael and Sharlan had not caught up with Turic's parents as they entered the outskirts of the Talaperi village. Pent and Salik had eluded them, must have reached the village first, but the other villagers also seemed to expect Bael, Sharlan and Turic, lining up or milling about in groups in the large clearing where their ground huts formed a circle against the trees, and others watched from higher up, leaning out of their tree huts, watching them, Bael thought, with an air of caution, and if his instinct proved true, an almost palpable touch of disdain. Why? Because he and Sharlan chose to raise Nikki? Was there ever such a choice?

Torches affixed to sturdy poles and burning at safe distances from anything flammable dispelled the deepening shadows of early evening. Sharlan held up the Talaperi infant, shouting in a loud and ragged voice: "Where is Salik?! I have brought her child back to her, and I want my own baby in return! Where is he?! Where is my son, Nikki?!"

The native folk only stared at her.

Sharlan held the baby higher, flinging her arms over her head and behind it. "I will dash this child to the ground if you do not answer me!"

A babble of voices arose in alarm, but none answered in her own language or moved toward Sharlan, and she flung her arms forward, Turic clutched tightly in her hands, as if she *would* heedlessly throw him. But she didn't, halting her arm swing in front of her, Turic still held out like an offering.

And now the Talaperi infant wailed, frightened out of his stupor, and Sharlan's gambit worked, for in the second before she had halted her swing, its intended threat caused a high-pitched scream from within the natives clustering before them, and a woman pushed fiercely out of the crowd and stood exposed a few yards from Sharlan, halting as Sharlan lowered her arms and cradled the infant.

The woman held out her own arms for Turic, but Sharlan shook her head. "You cannot have him, Salik, until you bring Nikki to me. You will bring him now. You will bring my son to me!" Grief and anger heated her words, but Salik slowly lowered her hands.

Bael realized she did not understand, did not speak Eliomese. And neither he nor Sharlan spoke the native tongue. "Who is here who can translate for us?!"

He watched the crowd.

An elder stepped from the crowd and strode up to him.

"Do you speak the angelfolk's tongue?"

The man nodded, his posture stiff, his head thrown back to gaze directly up at Bael. "I am Seerbith, brother to Khallah, the head clansman among us. You may keep Salik's son only if you do it no harm. Turic is a healthy child."

Bael heard Sharlan's sharp intake of breath as she said, "I never meant to do this child real harm. I only meant to shock Salik into appearing. We do not wish to keep him. We wish our own son back. Where is he?"

The clan elder stared up at her for a minute and then returned his attention toward Bael, addressing him. "Your *toawlag* is not here. It,"

"What is a *toawlag?*" Bael interrupted angrily.

Seerbith wore a passive patient expression. "It is failed birth, where evil warps that which should have been child. Its mother must ask Great Spirit to forgive her for failing, and that which is unwhole must be destroyed. It is given back to the Spirit in our highest place, left for the Spirit to take back to the Place of All Beginnings and Endings. Thus is the evil taken from the clan, cleansing us of its curse."

Bael only remained silent for a moment, horrified that they might be too late, before snarling at Seerbith, "Where is my *son?!*"

"Gone." The small elder waved a hand at Turic. "We are not given replacements. Our people face what must be faced. But we try to soothe your pain, make you accept what you want to deny. Your wife birthed a *toawlag.* It was not child. It is bad spirits, evil spirits; they destroyed your son before he could be born. We only now destroy the *toawlag.* Now go home and know we have done good for your wife. She has whole, well baby. Small, but good." He turned briefly to Salik, who stood waiting, uncertainly, grieving for her own loss by her posture and dull expression. Seerbith told her, "Go."

She raised red, swollen eyes to Turic and then to Sharlan, looking equally dismayed. Salik turned, walking woodenly away.

Sharlan began walking after her. "Salik, wait!" She caught up with her, sprinting ahead and in front of her and placed Turic firmly in his real mother's hands. Salik protested feebly, then hugged her infant to herself, turning back to look at Seerbith.

Sharlan strode over to him. "Where are Pent and my son?"

"Gone."

"Gone." Sharlan shook her head. "Where is your brother, Khallah, your head clansman? We will talk with him!"

"He is gone as well."

Bael cut brusquely in. "*Where* have they gone?!"

"To the high place," Seerbith answered just as brusquely. "You cannot go. Secret. Sacred place."

Bael very quietly said, "They have gone there to kill the *toawlag.* Am I right?"

"Not kill. It will be left for the Great Spirit. Great Spirit will take its . . . energy . . . back. You do not wish Turic? You and your wife can make new child, maybe healthy, maybe whole." He nodded to Salik, who breathed a heavy sigh and, clutching her son to her, edged into the crowd and was gone from their sight. "You understand now? It will bring blessings to do the right thing. No bad luck. Great Spirit must be obeyed; the people do the right thing."

"Where?" Bael repeated, all too quietly, feeling the vicious anger swelling slowly up inside him. "Where are Pent, and Khallah and my son Nikki?"

Seerbith shook his head. "Sacred place. You cannot go." He smiled as if Bael surely would see reason. "Go home to Taleth. Rest. We do what we must do."

Bael himself was amazed at how fast his hand thrust itself towards Seerbith's throat and closed tightly about it, as if his mind hadn't been aware of his actions. He lifted the small man off the grass.

Seerbith struggled, his own thin hands covering Bael's long-fingered hold, his own fingers trying to dislodge Bael's as they squeezed away his breath as Bael chanted: "Where is Nikki? Where is Nikki? Where *is Nikki?!*"

And now the other Talaperi swarmed around him, trying to pull Bael's arm down, to lower Seerbith, but Bael held on, applying more pressure to the elder's neck until the Talaperi blurted out: "Cahniohiom!"

Bael dropped the elder unceremoniously onto his back on the ground and, before Seerbith could scurry away, pressed his sandaled foot hard on Seerbith's chest, pinning him there. "Where!?"

"It is sacred!" Seerbith protested. "The Great Spirit . . ."

"I will destroy your Great Spirit. You will worship *me! Tell* me!" He pressed his foot hard enough to crack at least a few of the small native's ribs and heard a satisfying crunch.

Seerbith screamed in pain, but Bael calmly told him, "The next push will kill you, will crush your heart, as you and your people would like to kill my son. Where is he, Seerbith? Where did Pent and Khallah take him?!"

Panting, the elder raised his hand. "To the Teleperi village in Cahniohiom, and to the Great Peak above it."

Bael nodded. He knew this place. He had once gone on a trading expedition to the mountain folk. But none of the Heliomese had ever climbed the Great Peak, the tallest mountain beyond the lakes and the village, rising up into the clouds and merging with the ascent to the next, the second level. The Heliomese had respected the fact that the Teleperi held it to be a sacred place, had avoided even going near it, asking no questions so as not to break their taboo. They had no clue as to what the wood and mountain folk did at the Great Peak; they did not pry.

Now Bael knew at least one of its functions and was doubly horrified. It would take him at least a day's time to reach his son, who might not survive whatever Pent and Khallah did to him, in whatever way they made the "Great Spirit" take Nikki's energy. That was his first horror.

His second was that these small natives felt they could impose their beliefs and superstitions onto the Heliomese without discussion or permission. And because of what they had done, there was no recourse except one. The Heliomese would have to impose a law system onto all other beings in Hell and rule and control them.

Bael lifted his foot from Seerbith's chest as other Talaperi men attempted to restrain him and Sharlan. He flung them from him fiercely; his anger mounting again and lending him extraordinary strength.

He walked to Sharlan, and the other Talaperi holding her let go, backing away. Bael swept his gaze over all of them, a commanding gaze mixed with a madman's ire. They shrunk from it, knowing now that their actions had brought a response none of them had ever expected, that would bring irreversible change to their lives forever.

All this his eyes threatened and they knew he would keep his threat.

He pointed to Sharlan. "This, as you know, is my wife. I am going to Cahniohiom to seek my son, and Sharlan will stay here, awaiting my kinsmen who are on their way here. You will treat her with respect, for you have no choice. You have meddled in our lives, and now we will meddle in yours. You have no separate authority. The angelfolk are your authority, their laws are your laws, and your Great Spirit must bow before us, for we are your chieftains, above any of your headsmen, and will command your lives from this day forward." He placed his hands on Sharlan's shoulders. "Tell my father where I've gone. Tell others to follow me, if only to witness what I find and subdue Pent and Khallah."

"I want to go with you!"

"No. Stay here."

"Please?"

"They will not harm you, and someone must be here to explain when our people arrive here."

"They will not harm me," she agreed, and her face took on a fiery expression of unrestrained fury. "But you must hurry." And now Bael saw the tears she blinked back. "Get our son back. Get Nikki."

He squeezed her shoulders. "If I can. If I'm in time!"

Sharlan collapsed against him, her face hidden against his shoulder. He held her for a second more, then gently pushed away. She straightened up, standing stiffly, determinedly. "Go! Do what you must. I'll wait here for you."

"With luck," he said, "I'll reach the Great Peak by dawn, and if all goes well, I'll return here by late afternoon or early evening. Tell my father what I've told these Talaperi, that we will rule them — and control them — from this day on."

She nodded. "Hurry, Bael. Go now. Creator keep our poor son safe until you find him."

He saw the tears resurface in her eyes and wiped them gently, giving her a soft kiss. Then turning to the remaining Talaperi, including Seerbith who lay nearby while his kinsmen put a poultice on his chest, binding it, Bael said, "I will return by tomorrow before the grey day of Hell turns to its black night. You will give my lady shelter until I return and any other of my people that arrive here. Until today, my people have shown yours respect. You have repaid us poorly and must work to earn our respect again. Will you heed me?"

One of the men attending Seerbith stood up and spoke rapidly in a contrite tone to the others. There was a quick response, and he turned to Bael. "We will heed you."

Salik emerged from the crowd and approached Sharlan. Turic was not with her. She called over to the man, and he translated: "She wishes you to spend the night in her hut. Her mate will not be there tonight. She will serve you with humility."

Sharlan nodded to Salik, who carefully responded in Eliomese: "Is . . . good. Forgive . . . hurt."

"Yes," Sharlan said, "I will." And to Bael, "Go now. I'll be all right."

Bael nodded, looked over the Talaperi again and in the fiercest voice he could muster said, "I will return!"

And walked toward the crowd, which parted immediately at his approach, and they let him pass swiftly into the forest of Ajan Helvert.

Bael had been traveling steadily north through the woods, aware that night would soon darken the forest and very little good starlight would do him, blocked by the tree tops. Then he heard the snapped twig, the rustle of leaves under feet other than his own. He was being followed; perhaps the other Heliomese had caught up with him. He turned slowly, his eyes searching the paths between the trees and saw the saur huffing toward him.

It was slightly taller than the others, a male saur, the top of its scaly head crested and level with Bael's chest. It approached Bael, carrying something lumpy in a small sack that jutted out on one side sharply. "Angelmale," it called in a hissing but not ominous tone, "I am Lishtov, was going into *ajan* to gather food, saw your small one taken, knew you would pursue. Your people kind to my saurs. Ajanese not. Afraid Ajanese eat saurs; they eat others. Now they take your little hurt one and you pursue. Lishtov say you go far to find your baby. Hell night will come. Lishtov run back to saur den and get fire stone and holder and come back, but you do not see me. I follow you and your lady to the Ajanese village, hide watching you find where baby, then follow. Lishtov help you."

The reptilian native took a breath recovering from both its journey and lengthy explanation. The saurs had learned to use the fire stones, asking the angelfolk to heat them with radiant energy or warming their dens the old fashioned way, striking the stones until they sparked and caught fire to feed the tinder.

Bael regarded the saur curiously. "Having something to light my way as I travel will be a blessing, and I thank you. But you do not have to travel with me. I still have a long way, and I must move as quickly as I can. You can return to Taleth, and I will find a way to reward you most gratefully for this. And I do not think the Talaperi intend to eat saurs. They've never bothered your people."

"No, but we no friends. Do not trust. Now they steal your baby, say they take it to die, no? Yes." A look of anxiety crept into Lishtov's eyes. "Maybe eat? They eat rabbits, birds, others in forest. Maybe saurs. Maybe angels next."

Despite his own anxiety, Bael smiled. "No. Let me see what you've brought." He pulled six fire stones out of Lishtov's sack and a rectangular stone holder made of pottery. It had six recessed areas for holding each fire stone in place. "This is perfect, Lishtov. You have my gratitude. But I still don't understand why you wish to accompany me to Cahniohiom and the Great Peak."

The saur folded his slender arms stubbornly. "Must be witness!"

"Witness?"

"For my people, my saurs, witness wrong thing, help angelmale accuse Ajanese!"

"Ah, you're representing your folk."

Lishtov nodded quickly.

"Very well, but you'll have to keep up travelwise. Whatever time we've lost will be well made up by these fire stones. Let me get them started. Night is nearly here." The forest sank into gloom, dark greys and blacks obscuring its landscape as Bael held his hands over the stones, using his radiant energy to heat each one, until they glowed brightly and shed an arch of light before the holder, enough to navigate. Bael held the tray out by its handles, and they moved on. "You know that you have nothing to fear from the Ajanese or the Cahnese now," he said. "Those allied with us are now under our protection."

Lishtov nodded again in reply, and they continued their northern journey to the Great Peak.

Traveling in a straight line through Ajan Helvert, the eastern forest of the third level, would bring them to the mountainous lake region of Cahniohiom. The Teleperi lived in an extended village that circled both the eastern and western banks of the most eastward of the three great lakes, whose source actually flowed downward from the second level of Hell. But the mountains rose upward so high, the clouds obscured any path to its final plateau and that next level. The Talaperi and Teleperi called those uppermost heights the world of the Great Spirit, a world they considered both sacred and forbidden to them.

The first lake flowed lazily northward, and then met a land bridge between it and the second or middle lake. The second lake meandered westward, thinning eventually out and meeting another bridge of land between it and the third lake, a rounder, more placid body of water on the westward side. These uneven oblongs of land occupied the lakes' inner banks. The Teleperi village, occupying the first land bridge, was only reachable two ways, once Bael and Lishtov emerged from Ajan Helvert in the grey dawn.

Walking a bit longer through the open plains that led to the mountains and lakes, they came to the mouth, the source of the first lake, on its eastern banks. The Teleperi called it Pahka Dahm or Mother Lake, because its water flowed from the sacred places far above. With their forest cousins, they had fashioned small, floatable dugouts from the trunks of trees, sturdy enough to hold up to six of the small folk, and capable of supporting at least two to three angels. Small wharves with the log boats tethered to pilings were maintained by Teleperi to let travelers row across Pahka Dahm from its eastern to its western bank. Otherwise, they would have to journey along the entire eastern border of the lake, then across the northern boundary of Pahka Dahm, and then backtrack along Pahka Dahm's western banks to the Teleperi village and the mountains that rose above it.

Lishtov froze when he saw the small boats and the expanse of Pahka Dahm. "No cross water," he hissed.

"We have to cross water. We cannot waste time walking around the entire lake." Bael pointed to the other side to a part of the mountain that seemed to jut out in a great slab or shelf far above the Teleperi village below it. Above the shelf, the mountain rose in a triangular peak, and beyond that continued to climb towards the second level. "That is the Great Peak, where they have taken my son, and we must use these boats to get there quickly."

Three Teleperi men had emerged from the wooden huts beside the closest wharf and were moving toward Bael and Lishtov. Lishtov looked fearfully at the lake. Bael realized no saur had ever taken a dugout, at least he had never seen a saur do so. The few times they had come to the Teleperi village, Bael thought, they must have walked the entire circumference of the first lake. He told Lishtov again, "You don't have to come with me, Lishtov. You've witnessed Nikki's abduction. That's enough."

Lishtov shook his scaly head. "No! Witness all." He looked up at Bael. "I am leader of my saurs. Will go on lake! Will do it. Run to child. To save child!"

Bael studied him, saw his sincerity, his determination. "Together, then."

The three Teleperi had reached them and were speaking in their own tongue excitedly. Their conversation stilled. One wiry little man with a mass of tangled black hair approached Bael. "Go home," he said in Eliomese.

"No. We need passage across your lake," Bael told him.

"Go home," the man repeated. "Come back different day. Today sacred!"

"Yes, I know why today is sacred," Bael slowly told him, "and you will give me a dugout to go across the lake and find my son!"

One of the other Teleperi, an older man with graying hair and a whiskery chin, struggled to explain in Bael's tongue. "No . . . no good. Let . . . go!"

Bael patiently said, "We will take a boat ourselves." He and Lishtov started toward the nearest wharf, but the Teleperis ran ahead, turning to face them, waving their hands, blocking the entrance. The one with the black hair told Bael: "You want go to Great Peak? Walk around Pahka Dahm! And for good luck, walk all around three lakes, around Tahla Dahm and Pahla Dahm, too, the sister and the daughter lakes." The sneer of disdain in the little man's voice and face was unmistakable. He considered Bael a fool for not disposing of Nikki, for having no rite and no god for disposing of monsters. "Walk far, walk far so that you do not stop the Great Spirit from taking your *toawlag*, you who do not understand!" And the small man brought out a sharp dagger he'd concealed in a pouch beneath his tunic.

Bael put his hand in front of Lishtov, palm down, fingers spread, to indicate it was not the saur's battle, that Lishtov should back away. The saur immediately complied.

Four more Teleperi men emerged from the huts, all brandishing daggers, joining the others, circling Bael, herding Lishtov back beside him as they surrounded both angel and saur.

Bael held out his hands to show that he was weaponless. The angelfolk still had little concept of violence, and neither the Teleperi nor Talaperi had ever threatened them until now. "You have no right to take my child or to judge his right to live! You cannot force your beliefs on the angelfolk!"

The dark-haired man pointed his dagger first at Bael and then at Lishtov. "You come here, our land, our way. No *toawlag*. No disobey Great Spirit. No bring evil to us! Go now, or we cut you!"

The threat spoken, Bael decided to bluff them. "We will leave if you put away your weapons."

The dark-haired one hesitated then nodded to the others. Bael saw that the daggers had been concealed in sheaths hung on belts under their tunics. The Teleperi withdrew from Bael and Lishtov, waiting for them to leave. Bael spoke softly to Lishtov. "Pretend we are leaving. Once we are free of them, you will return to Taleth and find my people and bring help. Tell them the Teleperi are threatening us, and we must bring weapons to subdue them. But I do not wish you harmed. I will return alone to sneak past them and take a boat."

The little saur nodded as they began walking away from the wharves, watching the silent mountain folk, who watched their departure with equal silence. Bael and Lishtov finally passed beyond their sight, nearly at the northern entrance of Ajan Helvert, and Bael leaned down, putting his hand on Lishtov's shoulder, locking eyes with the saur. "Go now swiftly! Bring my people, prepared to fight the Teleperi!"

Lishtov nodded again, but his eyes bore his worry. "You should not go alone, angelmale."

"My name is Bael."

"Bael. Do not go alone."

"I have to. My son's life is at risk. You go now. I'll be careful." He straightened up.

The saur stared at him, then headed back to the forest. Bael turned to return to the lake, wondering if his size would be any advantage if he needed to outrun the Teleperi. They would see him approach again if he made straight for the wharves. Perhaps if he approached from the west slightly, they would not be looking in that direction, and he could possibly slide down the bank, if it held walkable paths that also hid him until he could steal a log boat.

"Bael!"

He turned back again and saw at least three dozen angelfolk approaching him with Lishtov happily accompanying them. But, Bael thought, did they bring anything that might be used as a weapon? As they came closer, he saw that they had: knives that were used for pruning and cooking and eating, gardening tools such as digging stakes, spades, and hoes, as well as daggers traded by the native folk and used, until now, for domestic and artistic needs.

His father led the rescue party, and behind Lucifer, Bael spotted Lothan, Nergal, Behemoth, Thamuz and Cimeries.

"Father," Bael called. "The mountain folk also have daggers and have refused to return Nikki to us. They believe he will bring evil luck and that he must die. They took him to the Great Peak. I must get there quickly before they harm him."

Lucifer nodded, reaching and walking beside Bael back to the wharves. "It may be too late. But I know we must try. We had to fight some of the Talaperi in Ajan Helvert. They succumbed to us shortly after two of their people died. Their bravado quickly fled. And this rebellion by the mountain folk must also be controlled."

"No," Bael said. "It must be utterly crushed, and then *they* must be controlled and threatened with violence as they have threatened us, if they dare to disobey us!"

He knew Lucifer heard the fury in his voice and was sure his father knew his intent.

Lucifer's next words proved him right. "You are suggesting that we rule them, force them to obey the laws of our Council?"

"Yes."

"A rather large and distasteful task."

"No, Father, an easy one, provided you threaten any disobedience with swift punishment and, if necessary, destruction."

"You're suggesting we kill those who further refuse our law?!"

Bael paused before answering then said, "Only if they attack us in their dissent. The Ajanese and Cahnese — the Talaperi and Teleperi — have no qualms about killing other living things. I fear we angelfolk shall very shortly also find we must accept this remedy, no matter how distasteful, if the native folk will not respect our boundaries and choices.

"As we approach the wharves, I need you and the other men to cover Lishtov and me when we take one of their log boats. Lishtov has asked to go with me to represent his people and be a witness to whatever they have done with Nikki. I first refused him, for the mountain folk would have cut us both, had we tried to defy them. I don't want him harmed, not after he aided me and proved his loyalty to us. But if you create a diversion, engage the Teleperi in conflict, we can steal one of their dugouts and start swiftly across the lake."

Lishtov had caught up with him and Lucifer, walking beside Bael, listening to his plan. Bael continued, repeating, "You must utterly crush them, Father, and gain full control of these wharves, docks and boats. Prevent them from following us over to the western bank. Then some of your men must stand guard on these wharves, but some of you must take other boats across to subdue the Teleperi village on the western side of *Pakha Dahm*. I must reach Nikki, no matter what I find. Pent and Khallah of the Talaperi have taken him to the Great Peak for some ceremony concerning *toawlags* — deformed infants — and possibly some Teleperi headsman is also taking part in this horror. Possibly two of our men could subdue whoever we find at the Great Peak, but time is not my friend and I must hurry. There are the wharves, Father. Alert your men."

Lucifer halted his rescuers and spoke with them in quiet tones while Bael and Lishtov waited a few yards away. The Teleperi had emerged again from their wooden huts. Bael noted with satisfaction the alarm on their faces upon seeing the Heliomese.

Lucifer came back to Bael. "We will go down first and engage them while you slip by us and take your boat. Cross the lake swiftly. As soon as we teach these mountain folk some manners, we will follow and meet you on the western bank, or follow you up the mountain, if you're already heading for the Great Peak."

"Be careful, Father." The Teleperi had unsheathed their daggers and stood rigidly along the wharf, blocking the nearest dock and its log boats. "They will not listen to reason."

Lucifer smiled. "We do not intend to use reason."

"Use war then."

Lucifer smirked. "I did not lose the heavens to be subservient to native upstarts in Hell."

He waved the other men over to him, and they moved into position past Bael and Lishtov, their faces determined, their posture stiff, holding what once were tools for growth, as if they had always brandished them for violence.

Bael watched the dark-haired, belligerent Teleperi man running blindly toward Nergal, dagger pointed futilely toward the huge man's stomach. Nergal's hoe, its metal lip forged by a smith using ores bartered from the Teleperi, split the small man's head.

That morning, the blue blood of the angelfolk flowed, but the red blood of the mountain and forest folk surpassed it in terms of who spilt whose blood.

Bael and Lishtov snuck quickly around the wharf and made for another dock. They took a log boat, putting its paddles to hard use, reaching the western bank of Pahka Dahm, a short while later. As they climbed up the bank, having guided the log boat in a good distance from the western village, away from its own wharves, they looked back over the lake. Five more log boats were sailing towards them, making for the sloping bank where Bael had steered his boat and secured it in undergrowth on a thin strip of beach. He hoped those who followed were his own people and not the Teleperi, as he and Lishtov headed up the mountain paths to the Great Peak.

"Here," Lishtov said as they trudged up the steep trail to the overhang above them. He still carried his pack with the cooled fire stones and pottery holder, but now he pulled two sharp knives from the sack, giving Bael the longer one. "We can fight! Not be defenseless!"

"Where did you get these?"

"Lucifer, he gives them to me for us."

"My father came prepared."

"Got from Talaperi," Lishtov said, adding, "Not give. Took."

"Spoils of war."

"What is war?"

"Fights between groups of folk, sometimes to get something you want, sometimes to stop others behaving in unacceptable ways. Angels fought each other briefly in the heavens hundreds of years ago."

"Where is heavens?"

"Far from here. We lost everything. Our homes. Our land. Those we loved who fought on the other side."

"You lose war?"

"Some think we did. We didn't get what we wanted in the heavens. We got it here, but it's little consolation."

Lishtov remained silent for a bit, as if digesting Bael's words. Finally, he asked, "You leave heavens and come here to Hell instead to get what you want, to find your way?"

Bael shook his head, looking up the path. The mountain shelf and the Great Peak loomed closer, and he wondered how best to approach it. "Finding your way means living life the way you decide is best and not letting another tell you how to do so. My father disagreed with our Creator, the Power that controls the heavens and beyond. It's a very long story, but we lost and the Creator exiled us to Hell, but promised us free will here, that right to live life as we choose to."

"When you have war, you have to kill other angels?"

Now Bael hesitated, remembering the almost innocent hand-to-hand fighting between the angels. The Seraphim had quickly put an end to it, using their strange powers. And then the Creator had arrived and challenged Lucifer and found Lucifer's response lacking, banishing him and his family and all of his followers, lifting them from the very ground they stood on, up into the fiery light in the sky, stripping them of their consciousness and any memory of how they had traveled to Hell. They knew they had lost the war when they awoke in the dark night of Hell.

"So you kill other angels," Lishtov concluded from Bael's silence. "A sad thing."

"No, no," Bael corrected him. "We never killed our own. We were extremely long-lived. We rarely knew death, until two of our people went to another world called Earth."

"Good. Good that angel not kill angel."

He nodded. "We learned that angels can die here in Hell, but only if harmed by others. Angels were going to Earth, too, when we were exiled, but they were the angels who obeyed the Creator. They were transformed, reborn for a new life on Earth. And when those mortal lives are done, they, too, die, but return to Eliom, the heavens, restored to their angelic selves again."

"You loved girl who go to Earth."

Bael stared at him. "How did you know that?"

"Your lady, Sharlan, she told me. That your heart is sad for long time. I understand. Saur can die, too, lose other saur."

Again, Bael stared at him. "Did you lose a loved one, Lishtov, a lady saur?"

Now Lishtov spoke so softly, Bael couldn't understand.

"I didn't hear you. You don't have to tell me, if you find it too hurtful."

"Yes, still hurts. I speak louder, the hurtful thing. I no lose mate. We lose child. Saur baby."

Bael, very quietly, said, "That's why you're so upset about Nikki."

"Lishtov have saur son, but it born badly, too. It die. So I worry for Nikki, watch him, and that is why I see Pent take him and leave Ajanese baby in blanket. And run back to get fire stones. Lishtov know you follow Pent, and woods get dark. But you gone when I get back, so I go to Ajanese village, but get scared and hide when you hurt little man. Then you leave, and I follow and find you."

"Thank you," Bael said.

Lishtov nodded, a bond formed between them.

"Look." Bael thrust his chin toward a bend in the road. "The mountain shelf below the Great Peak is just beyond that turn. We'll move slowly as we come around it. If Pent and Khallah are there, we should subdue them, but not kill them if Nikki isn't there. If neither they nor the baby are there, we'll have to try to reach the Great Peak, even though that climb is sharply angled and precarious."

Lishtov asked, "If they *and* Nikki there?"

"Then, from what I've seen of their behavior, we must attack and disarm them quickly, for they may have weapons. Kill them if necessary."

They moved quietly toward the bend, Lishtov nosing around the rock wall paralleling the ledge and then inching back to Bael, whispering, "Pent, Khallah, sitting on ledge near edge. Nikki not there!"

Bael peered around. The two Talaperis sat quietly before the edge, facing it. Bael whispered back, "Extend your knife. Move silently but quickly! Whatever they do, get your weapon into a fatal position. I need to threaten them to find out what they've done with Nikki." He silently hoped his son was not lying crushed on the rocks below the ledge.

Bael crouched low, and Lishtov bent into a sprinting posture. They rushed to the Talaperis and nearly reached them before Pent and Khallah half-turned, startled, alarm in their eyes. Then Khallah, closer to Lishtov, scowled at him, exposing his own dagger in his left hand as he leaped to his feet, facing the saur.

But he hadn't counted on the normally meek saur's anger. Lishtov extended his sharp claws on his free left hand, his knife clasped in his right, and dug those claws into Khallah's right shoulder, the knife deflecting Khallah's dagger as Khallah thrust it underhanded toward Lishtov's round belly.

It was a lucky move on Lishtov's part. His knife not only parried Khallah's dagger away, momentum drove Lishtov's knife into Khallah's left wrist, slicing through muscle, tendon and vein. The dagger fell from Khallah's hand as blood sprayed from his wrist.

Lishtov's claws had raked Khallah's right arm. Khallah frantically squeezed his left wrist with his right hand, ignoring Lishtov who shouted, "Where is baby?!"

Both saur and Talaperi looked toward Bael and Pent, Khallah obviously seeking aid from Pent, Lishtov ready to aid Bael if needed.

But Bael needed no help. His left hand held Pent by his slender neck. In Bael's right hand, his knife was poised to slice Pent's throat. Bael's long arms held Pent far enough away that the small man's flailing arms and kicking legs could do him no harm. Bael had also stabbed Pent's palm, disarming him and throwing Pent's dagger a distance away.

Bael also held the struggling man just at the lip of the ledge. If Pent tried to pull Bael's fingers off with his good hand, he might lose his balance and fall, and if he used his injured hand, the slickness of his own blood might make Bael lose his grip and Pent would plummet to the rocks below. Pent's feet dangled and danced, trying to touch the rock ledge.

Khallah, seeing no help would come from Pent, fell to his knees, weakened by blood loss. He reached out toward Pent and Bael. "No good. Great Spirit already take your *toawlag*. But you kill. Bring more bad luck on us all. Cannot disobey Great Spirit."

Bael gave him a quick glance. "The bad luck will be on your people forever more." He shook Pent and pushed the knife tip against the small man's neck artery. "Where is my son?!"

Pent stared at him, dazed, then stared upward toward the Great Peak. His voice came out warbled.

Bael pulled Pent slightly forward, barely away from the edge, letting go of Pent's throat in one swift motion and grasping the Talaperi's thick red hair in his hand. Bael wrenched Pent's head to the side, the knife still at his neck, shouting, *"Where?!"*

"On Great Peak," Pent gasped. "We not kill him. Left to die."

"My son is up there?!"

"Yes! Let go! Let me go."

Bael stood silent as death and murmured, "Salik will miss you." He swept his knife across Pent's throat, the Talaperi's blood spurting out, his scream quickly cut off. Pent's body slumped as he lost consciousness. Bael pushed him off the lip of the shelf, flinging him from it to the rocks below.

Khallah also lay dead at Lishtov's feet. The saur looked anxiously about. "Where is baby?"

Bael pointed to the dangerous climb above, its least steep passage to the right of the ledge. They walked over to it, staring upward.

"You are too big. Let Lishtov try. I am smaller."

"Together," Bael said grimly, and started up the steep climb with shallow purchases and small, unstable overhangs that pocketed the way. "Nikki is in one of those, I think."

Lishtov followed. "Please let me go first! I can see if ground not weak."

Bael sighed and moved slightly to the side to let Lishtov pass him.

They continued upward slowly, carefully, the path becoming steepest right before the crown of Great Peak.

"Nikki!" Bael called. The faintest whimper carried back to him, but he couldn't tell if it was his son or an errant wind moaning.

Lishtov pointed a few feet above them. "There!" There is Nikki!" Ground too bad here. You wait. I get Nikki."

"No," Bael said. "I'll go!"

"You *WAIT!*" Lishtov's tone was not a request. "You stay!" The saur gingerly moved higher, as loose pebbles and rocks scattered down toward Bael.

Bael thought he heard the saur emit a soft cry. "What is it, Lishtov?" He started following the saur. His foot slipped on gravel and he came down hard, sliding three or four yards before halting his near fall to the ledge and possibly over it.

Above him, Lishtov said, "I have baby! Will go down slowly to you. You go down, too. *Very* slowly. Me and you."

Bael complied, his heart beating fast as more rocks fell away beneath his feet and other stones rained on him from above where Lishtov, carrying Nikki, labored to also descend the crumbling mountain's face. An uncontrolled fall could fling them over the cliff. "Be careful," he called, not knowing if the saur heard him as he wormed his way downward. Finally his feet touched the path leading to the ledge. He stood, looking up, and saw Lishtov. He held Nikki tightly in his left arm, the baby's head lolling, and Bael felt a deep ache within.

Lishtov reached the last few feet of the descent, straightening his squat body. With a sorrowing look, he cradled Nikki in his thin but wiry arms and brought the dying baby to Bael.

Bael held his naked son. Nikki's small chest shuddered up and down, his blood leaked blue from his small ears and nose, his skin frosted grey and chilled to the touch. He whimpered faintly, with an ominous gurgling noise as if he were drowning internally.

Bael handed Nikki to Lishtov. "Hold him one more moment." Lishtov took the baby while Bael removed his robe and with his knife cut a large brown swath off from its bottom. He put the shortened robe back on and lay the swath on a patch of grass. He took Nikki back and placed him on the cloth, wrapping it around him, attempting to warm him. "Oh, Creator!" The baby began coughing up the blue blood, the *skane* of the angelfolk, some of it clotted. "Oh, my innocent child. Why has this been done to you?! All of this." And to Lishtov, "I'm going to try to heal him."

He placed his hand on Nikki's cold body and called forth his own radiant energy, feeling his hands tingling, vibrating with his gift of heat and healing, willing it into his son.

Nikki lay still under his touch as Bael's hands moved over his infant body, his leg stumps, his chest, his little arms and finally his head with his blind, flesh-covered eyes. His soft black hair and scalp beneath it were nearly frozen to Bael's touch, his radiant energy not warming them.

Suddenly Nikki let out a shattering cry and vomited curdled globs of skane blood, his small body heaving and shaking.

Bael leaned over him, pulling the robe fragment more securely around him. "No, no, no!" he moaned. "Live, Nikki. LIVE!"

But the baby's cries became piercing, his small arms flailing, tiny hands fisted.

Lishtov grasped Bael's shoulder. "In great pain. Nikki dying! In great pain."

"No! I can heal him!"

But the bleeding worsened, staining the brown cloth a viscous blue.

Bael sat wearily on the ground, clasping the crying baby to his chest, rocking him. "Hush, Nikki! Hush! We'll get you back to Taleth. Take you to the healers. They'll know what to do, know what I do not!"

Nikki's tortured screams still pierced the air.

"Bael . . . your son will never survive the journey home."

Bael turned to see his father and Lothan standing near him on the ledge.

Lothan crouched down. "Bael, Nikki is afflicted with the pain of dying. If your healing made it worse, hastened him toward death because it is the only healing *left to him*, even our combined energies won't save him."

"We must *try*, Father Lothan!"

Lothan glanced upward to Lucifer.

Bael saw none of the other angelfolk. Perhaps they waited a distance down the mountain path, out of respect and sorrow. "Father, we must try!"

Lucifer nodded and Bael laid the suffering baby on the grass, as Lothan and Lucifer and he all placed hands on Nikki's shaking body. Their hands heated, glowed, but when the combined glow faded, Nikki's loud shrieks still punctured the quiet mountainside.

Lucifer said, "He's dying, son. Your only choice is to let him suffer until his natural end or to help him by ending it now. To end his suffering for him!"

Bael glared at him.

"Your choice." Lucifer held out his own knife, still tinged with red from the recent battles.

Bael's ears rang with Nikki's terrified wails. He picked up his son, cradling him in his left arm, and with his right hand, brought the torn cloth from his robe up to the baby's face. He stuffed small ends of the cloth into Nikki's nose and mouth until his breathing was cut off, then hugged his son tightly in his arms, holding the rest of the cloth over the baby's head with his left hand, holding his tiny hands fast in his embrace, clasped within his right hand, murmuring, "We love you, Nikki! We love you, Nikki! We are so sorry!"

Nikki's muffled squalling quickly became weaker, his small chest stopped its frantic heaving and stilled completely. Bael relaxed his hold, Nikki limp and lifeless in his arms. His small soul had fled to wherever souls fly to in Hell.

He felt a soft touch on his shoulder, looking up, seeing Lishtov's grieving reptilian face, his yellow eyes wet with tears that moistened his snout.

He hadn't known that saurs could cry.

"Come," Lishtov said. "We carry Nikki home, have him on sacred fire, its smoke and flame send soul to sky, chant farewell."

Bael merely gazed at him.

"You want I carry Nikki?" Lishtov whispered.

Bael nodded woodenly and lifted his dead son into Lishtov's care. And then he saw his father and Lothan on either side of him, grasping his arms.

"Come on, son, stand up," Lucifer murmured. "It's a long walk back home, and your heart can do some healing along the way."

They helped him up and led him down the mountain paths to the western harbor of the Teleperis and their log boats. The native folk had been subdued in ways that would never again allow them to question Lucifer's sovereignty in Hell.

But Bael only noticed his surroundings and those around him in a misted way, as if a fog covered all, his mind dulled and his heart hidden within it.

He had come to save his poor son, had failed and, in the end, was forced to end his Nikki's life.

They returned to the Talaperi village by early dawn. In the central clearing, a large wooden bier had been raised about six feet off the ground and, on its bed of tightly piled branches and tinder, five Talaperi men lay dead. Around the bier stood both Talaperis and Heliomese, including Ashtoreth and Sharlan. When they saw Lucifer, Lothan and Bael approach with the other rescuers, they ran to them, eager hope in Sharlan's eyes until she saw Bael had arrived empty-handed, his robe torn and his own eyes haunted.

Her faint hope crumbled when she saw Lishtov hand him the stain-covered bundle. Bael carried it to her, unwrapping Nikki's blanket and exposing his still face.

Bael had washed away all trace of blood on Nikki as they sailed back over the lake, rinsing out the makeshift blanket as well, letting it dry on the return journey. But the stain remained, discoloring the cloth a deep purple, and Bael knew that Sharlan knew. She reached out, touching Nikki's face, her eyes only briefly questioning Bael's. No hope. No miracle. He gently shook his head, and she slumped against him.

He held both her and Nikki, saying nothing. But she asked, "Did he suffer?" Her voice so soft, it might have caressed. Instead, her question tore at him.

"Yes," he told her. "Nikki was in great pain. Our attempts to heal him failed. You know what happens when the body cannot be healed, when its life is being drained by whatever cursed it to fail, when our healings fail. It heals in the only way it can, by hastening death and ending life."

"And that is what happened to Nikki? How he died?"

Bael shook his head. "Not completely. Our fathers and I tried again to heal the baby, although they advised me against it. It did make it worse. But Nikki didn't die quickly. Sharlan, he was in greater pain." Tears flooded his eyes, and his voice choked and wavered. "He was vomiting his life out, his body dying inside, his screams assaulting my heart. My father handed me his knife, handed me the choice of letting our baby suffer or ending his misery. But I could not spill his blood myself!" He felt her fingers digging into his flesh as she clung to him, listening, grieving. "I smothered him with this cloth I had cut from my robe to warm him in. He was so cold, Sharlan. The exposure, the bitter mountain winds, destroyed him, before we could reach him — Lishtov and I. Lishtov brought him down to me from his dying place, a small ledge set in the top of a mountain in Cahniohiom called the Great Peak. There are a number of recessed niches there. Lishtov saw tiny skeletons in two. The mountain and forest folk leave deformed or seriously ill infants there to die, believing them to be bad luck for their clans."

Sharlan grasped the baby from Bael, crushing it against her breast. He felt her tears soaking his neck, his shoulder. He tightened his embrace, as she murmured, "But why Nikki? He was *our* baby, not *theirs!*"

Bael had no answer, not now, but he had a solution. "They will never again interfere with our lives. Now they know what their folly cost them."

Sharlan nodded, cradling her dead son as Bael released her. She looked beautiful and heroic, despite her sorrow. "Our baby!" She looked to the funeral bier. "They're going to burn the fallen Talaperi warriors. Their death rite. Salik wanted to know if Pent . . ."

"I killed him," Bael said curtly, watching her eyes squeeze shut, as if to shut out the news of more death. "At least Salik still has a son. And Lishtov killed Khallah, who was trying to kill Lishtov. And no, I do not want our son's body cremated with those of his abductor's people."

Lishtov, who had been standing quietly nearby, came over. "Poor Sharlan lady! Take Nikki home. Send him to sky world there. Angelfolk and saurs will gather to chant his farewell."

Sharlan drew her son's body closer. Bael saw her emotional pain and reached out his hand to caress her face. But she turned gently away from him. "Leave me my pain. I have a right to it and need it to heal."

"As do I," he said, not hiding fresh tears.

"Both of us," she said, nodding as Ashtoreth finally stood before them, having found his voice.

"I have killed now," Ash said, "and I have seen death and now know it is the worst goodbye any living creature must face. My heart has grieved for you both since the birth of your child and grieves as bitterly at his death. Let us go home, my brother and sister-mate, and I will help you say that goodbye."

Their father came up behind them with Lothan. Lucifer clasped Ashtoreth's shoulder, father and eldest son, their golden hair bringing brightness to the dull morning light. "We have the village secured with our people," Lucifer said. "The Talaperi now know of the death of Pent and Khallah and their mountain cousins. We will leave them to their death rites and carry Nikki and our own dead home to Taleth to arrange our own rites."

To Bael's questioning look, he gruffly added, "We lost two angels to fatal blows. One was Thamuz, the other was a younger angel named Caleb, one of Naamah's cousins. We must never forget that immortality has no guarantee in Hell."

"But where does the soul go, our Divine Spark, which we were always told is indestructible?" Bael asked.

Lucifer cast him a weary glance as they all walked on through the forest, returning to Taleth. "You believe our Creator's promises, son."

Sharlan, walking silently beside her mate, holding their dead child, suddenly spoke. "I will hold our Creator to this promise. If Nikki's spark of life is indestructible, I will see him alive again, whether I bear him in my womb again or another woman bears him. And I will see him whole and happy and blessed with a life his world values and respects!"

For the rest of the way, her tears spoke of the emptied places in her heart.

Leianna felt the hoop being removed from her head. Bael's and Sharlan's had already been removed, and he sat near her, holding her, as she cried silently, just as Leianna had seen her crying through Bael's eyes at the end of the virtual reenactment of Nikki's life and death.

She walked around the table, hugging both Sharlan and Bael. "Oh, Sharlan. Oh, Bael. I am so sorry!" She didn't know what else to say. If anything happened to her own mortal son Daniel, she would be devastated. She could empathize with their loss of Nikki, despite its occurring thousands of years ago. The curse of cognizant immortality . . .

"Quatama," she said to their spirit master, who stood quietly at the end of the table, holding the three virtual reenactment hoops, "That was intense. Bael, I understand you did what you did to end the baby's suffering. I don't hate you for it. How could I? It was a tragedy."

Bael sat straighter in his chair. "I had a thought, all throughout that tragedy, that I shared years later with Sharlan, although it was hurtful to her."

"Whatever it was, it was only a thought," Leianna told him, seating herself again next to Sharlan. "Your actions spoke louder."

Bael shot Sharlan a glance.

She nodded back to him.

"We want you to know what it was, for Sharlan has always loved me in the shadow of my love for you. I told her that I feared through the debacle of Nikki's short life and death, that it was brought on by my thwarting my true destiny. That I was meant to remain by your side during the Fall from Grace, to follow our Creator's demands and wait for your return to Eliom after your mortal lives on Earth.

That I was only meant to have my children through you, and that any child I fathered on another woman would be doomed and not my true heir. That Nikki was cursed from birth because you were not his mother."

Leianna stared at him and Sharlan. "That's ridiculous. We might not have had any children, I was so busy incarnating for all those centuries. Lord! I'm busy now with this last lifetime of mine, if it is my last! It might be quite a while before we have any children, still."

"Children," Quatama interposed, "it is true that Bael leaned toward his father's rebellion during the war in the heavens, but he did not intend to separate from Leianna and did not thwart his true destiny. What happened was meant to happen in the realm of closest probability. And Nikki was born deformed because there are elements in Hell that warped his development in Sharlan's womb. It was not a curse or any fault on Bael's part that doomed him. His soul would have eventually fled, even if the third level natives hadn't had their cruel beliefs about *toawlags*, a practice Lucifer wisely put an end to."

Sharlan whispered, "Then he would have died anyway. But Quatama, will I ever see him alive again, or will the Creator refuse my bold demand made as I carried Nikki home to the village of Taleth for his funeral rites?" She sighed. "Will I even recognize him, if another woman bears him?"

Quatama offered her a gentle smile. "Tonight we made excellent headway in forming an alliance between Heaven and Hell for the sake of all souls, including those on Earth." He grinned at Leianna, who nodded back tiredly. She wondered what *time* it was on Earth and if, rejoining her true or astral self with her physical body that slept blithely on in Philadelphia, she would feel rested when she woke up on Sunday morning and had to deal with the demands of laundry and her overactive son. But deal with him, she would, and much more patiently now.

Quatama continued cheerfully: "We've done so well, in fact, that I think we should plan a wedding for Bael and Leianna."

Leianna was well aware that her lower jaw had dropped an inch in surprise. She quickly clamped her lips together, then opened them to speak, having found her voice. "Uh, Quatama, you mean like, uh, while I'm still mortal?"

"Yes," her spirit master nodded. "I think that it is time."

"But he can't take out the garbage for me. His hand will go straight through it. Unless it's Halloween. This means I have to do it 364 days a year. Uh, uh! I'll wait until I have *astral* garbage! When I'm done my mortal life. I mean, can you imagine what it'd be like if

I got pregnant and our baby was invisible?" She paused. "Oh! I'm sorry, Sharlan."

"It's all right," her rival assured her.

"It's just that Quatama's shocking me. I really think we need to wait on this marriage thing, master. I can still work with Bael and Ashtoreth on this Alliance stuff while I'm single. Well, divorced on Earth, at any rate." She shook her head, befuddled and not sure where Quatama was heading with this.

Bael, wisely perhaps, had been silent during this, but now he asked Quatama, "Why *does* she have to marry me now because of our work on the Alliance? I don't see the connection. Not that I would mind it. She's been stalling me on this, using her mortal life as an excuse, her talk about the garbage being just that: garbage, an excuse. I think she still has a crush on Terence."

"Bael!" Leianna shot him a look. "Okay, Quatama, please tell us what you're up to, so I can go home to Earth and get some rest, body *and soul.*"

Quatama offered her another happy grin. "If you really don't wish to marry Bael, I suppose we can work around it. But you *are* pregnant by Bael and will have your astral first-born in the astral equivalent of nine months, which will measure about three months on Earth in your mortal body."

Now not only Leianna, but Bael and Sharlan gaped back at him, slack-jawed, Sharlan's eyes looking haunted again. But Quatama continued, turning to the dark-haired head concubine. "And Sharlan, the soul who was Nikki is now growing in Leianna's astral womb."

"Will it . . . will it . . . ?"

"It will be born whole and healthy, Sharlan. So I have been told and believe."

Leianna looked at all three of them. "Am I going to *show* on *Earth?!* And what if I start to give birth while I'm awake in my mortal body?! What if I'm at work?!"

"Calm down, Leianna," said Quatama. "We will attend to your needs. You will not look pregnant, perhaps gain a few pounds if you eat too much, but that would happen anyway. But I still think you and Bael should marry. And you mustn't worry once this child is born, for Sharlan will happily mother it while you attend to your mortal duties."

Leianna and Sharlan exchanged looks, and Leianna said, "Not in Hell."

"Leianna," Bael chided her.

Quatama laughed. "Of course, not in Hell. Sharlan will be

moving to the upper planes, once the child is born, but you will have to spend some time in Hell, Leianna, after you and Bael marry. After all, you are Heaven's ambassador, and there is a great probability that you may one day become Hell's queen."

Sharlan stood up abruptly, her expression resigned yet determined. "Leianna, you and Bael should marry. I've always known that you, one day, would. Let me to be your Maid of Honor to show both my world and yours our friendship. I will be your friend and care for the baby as if he were my own son, once he's born, wherever you wish me to."

"From what I'm told, he *is* your son."

"And yours as well. It's you who will bear him this time. And you don't have to name him Nikki, if you don't want to."

Leianna gave a shuddering sigh, feeling weary. "I don't think who bears him will matter the most to him, but rather who *loves* him. If we share this soul as *our* child, yours reborn as mine, then I, too, pledge friendship to you, Sharlan. I'm going to need all the womanly advice I can get. And I have another small problem, Bael and Quatama."

Bael asked, arms folded, "Which is?"

"I've told Terence Dearborn that I'd marry *him.*"

Bael glared at her. "What?!"

"I didn't think I could deal with Hell, Alliances and saving the world. I didn't think *we* could work everything out. And Terence is a loving, good-hearted man, filled with music and laughter and joy. I'm sorry, Bael, but I just cannot imagine being the queen of Hell!" She glanced at Quatama. "Sorry."

Sharlan came over to her, putting her arm around Leianna's shoulder, her height making the gesture rather motherly. "We're having a baby. I'll stand beside you, and together we'll find a way to work this out, Leianna. I've never met your Terence, but Bael's spoken of him and he sounds likeable."

"He is," Leianna said.

"Yeh," Bael agreed. "But can he take out the trash?"

Quatama laughed again and walked up to his mortal charge. "Why not marry both Terence and Bael?" he said.

Leianna's eyebrows raised an inch. "Is that allowed?"

"Yes, in certain cases," Quatama assured her. "In Heaven, there is no jealousy. But your first child will be Bael's."

She looked at the spirit master dubiously. "Then my first marriage will have to be to Terence . . . if he'll still have me. That way, I hope he'll feel he came in first on something."

Quatama told her: "I have already spoken to Terence about

this."

"You have? What did he say?"

"He is not overjoyed to have Bael as a brother-husband, but he said he would stand by you. And now, Leianna, it's time to take you back to Earth and take our leave of Bael and Sharlan."

Sharlan, her eyes bright with wonder and happiness, hugged Leianna. "Take good care of our baby, little sister."

"I'll do my best, big sister," she quipped, looking up at the raven-haired beauty. "I'm still in shock!"

"I know, Leianna. So am I. But we'll be all right."

She nodded. "Okay, Quatama. I'm ready."

Bael took her hand. "I'm going with you. I need to be with you tonight. Sharlan understands. You're not the only one in shock."

She gently pulled her hand away. "I'm still afraid, Bael," she admitted. "I'm sorry I sprung the news about Terence on you. Everything's just happening too quickly."

"I know. But I'm not giving up on us, just because you're hot for Terence." He held up his hands. "Maybe it's the real thing, but he's just as astral as me, not mortal, and Quatama seems to think we're both qualified. I think you need both of us. And since you're carrying our child, I'm owed some time and consideration."

Leianna sighed, exasperated with everything. "Okay, come back with me. But please don't haunt me tomorrow. I've got too many things to do."

"Deal. Sharlan, I'll see you tomorrow."

"Fine. Quatama, watch over her," Sharlan told the spirit master, and to Bael and Leianna, "I love you both."

Quatama offered Leianna his hand, which she took, and told her, "Close your eyes. We'll get back the quick way. Bael can follow us. Good night, Sharlan."

Leianna shut her eyes, hearing Sharlan's murmured response, and suddenly awoke in her room in her mortal body in Northeast Philadelphia. The clock read three A.M. She felt Bael's invisible astral form slide onto the bed beside her and hold her tightly.

I love you, he said telepathically. She drifted back to sleep in his astral arms, knowing she had not accurately expressed herself to Bael.

However, Quatama plainly knew her true feelings.

She did love Terence and had agreed to marry him, feeling a unity filled with the light and happiness of the heavens with him. Yet the other fact that confounded things was that she still also loved Bael.

How this fit in with her being the "keeper" of the world and what she could possibly do to keep it turning on a positive track, she still hadn't figured out.

She just didn't think getting astrally married — or becoming Queen of Hell could have anything to do with it.

11

Life Goes On

September, 1977.

In the morning, when Leigh Ann awoke to the bright sunlight of a beautiful Sunday, it looked strange and foreign after reliving Bael's memories in the drab dimension of Hell, which seemed to have no sun. Something lit the days there, but its sky never warmed to a shade of blue atmosphere. At best it glowed with pale silver with the occasional white cloud; beyond that, its sky showed pewter, milky or a storm-laden grey. Depressing. It probably worsened the maladies of its inhabitants. How could Quatama ever think she could live in such a realm, even temporarily, let alone become its queen?

Remembering Bael's trauma, the reenactment of Nikki's life and death, Sharlan's struggle to nurture and protect their deformed son, also depressed her. The initial shock of finding out about Bael's harem, and the other leiths in Hell, an archaic, chauvinistic system, upsetting as that was, had faded into secondary importance after reliving Nikki's life and death, and Bael's and Sharlan's valiant attempts to thwart the inevitable. And now they were told that Nikki's was now within *Leianna's* astral womb, courtesy of Bael. She was pregnant, and yet, in her mortal body, she wasn't. It didn't make any sense. And yet Quatama assured her it was true and what's more, that it would pose no problem for her!

This was not the best way to start a new day on Earth.

She put a hand on her flat belly gingerly, but it felt no different than it had yesterday. She shook her head and checked the clock. It was 11:00 A.M. Her family had let her sleep late. Ginnie wasn't there. Leigh Ann heard no sounds upstairs. Everyone was up and about except her.

She got out of bed, mentally searching to see if anyone astral was hanging around. She couldn't pick up on any unseen presences. Bael had apparently left, returning to Hell and Sharlan, and Terence might be avoiding her if he knew about her astral pregnancy.

"Hey, Mom?" Daniel peered into the bedroom. "You up yet?"

"Yes, I'm up. Someone should have gotten me up earlier."

Daniel came in, his brown hair shaggy and Beatle-styled, his brown eyes looking somehow wiser than a six-year-old's should. He had put on a pair of denim shorts, a tee shirt and socks and sneakers, something comfortable. Summer still lingered in Phila-delphia. "Grandmom said you've been looking really tired and to let you sleep."

"I'm looking tired?"

"Yeh. She said it's 'cause you work all week and schlep me back and forth to daycare."

"Well at least your daycare is affiliated with the elementary school, and *they* schlep you back and forth to first grade. By the way, did you do your homework yet?" She got out of bed and stretched, her long, cotton nightgown lifting slightly as she raised her arms overhead.

"Yes." Daniel raised his eyebrows in a mock gesture of exasper-ation. "I wrote all my vocabulary words down and did my numbers. Listen, Mom, school's just started. A kid has to have some time to play."

"Well, if you did your homework, you can go play." She started down the hallway.

He scampered ahead of her, going down the stairs. "Great. I'll call Jeff and tell him to come over.

"Play outside. Get some fresh air and sunshine while you can."

"Why? Is it going away?"

"It might rain tomorrow."

"Tomorrow I'll be at daycare and school."

Leigh Ann shook her head as they entered the kitchen, Daniel grabbing the phone.

Her mother sat at the table, drinking coffee and reading the Sunday *Inquirer*. Miriam put down the entertainment section and gestured at her grandson. "Who do you think you're calling, young man?"

"Jeffrey."

"Make sure you dial the number right."

"Grandmom! I'm almost seven. I know how to dial a phone number!"

Miriam picked up the paper again. "All right. Just don't want strange numbers showing up on my phone bill."

"Hey, Jeff! It's Danny. You want to get together, ride bikes or play ball or something? Okay, I'll meet you outside." He hung up the phone. "See you, Mom, Grandmom."

"Stay within shouting distance," Leigh Ann said.

"Aw, Mom! I'm not a baby anymore."

She just looked at him.

"Grandmom, tell her."

Miriam looked at him, then his mother. "You are a bit overprotective, Leigh Ann. Daniel, just stay on our block and be careful crossing Glenview Street if you boys decide to go back to Jeff's house."

"Will do, Grandmom." He ran down the kitchen steps leading to the side door and basement, going out the door.

Leigh Ann poured herself a cup of coffee, still warm in the pot. She added sugar and milk and sat down opposite her mother. "I was in Hell last night."

"Oh? And what did you do there?"

"Relived the birth and death of a child."

Miriam lifted her gaze from the movie page. Leigh Ann quietly told her the story. When she finished, Miriam quietly said, "And so now the soul of Nikki is within you."

"Yes, and I don't know how to deal with it. Mom, I don't even know if I believe it."

Miriam reached across the table and squeezed her hand. "You don't have to. The astral life is like living in a parallel, dreamlike dimension concurrently with your mortal life. You just have to let God guide you and attend to your duties in each world. Have you told Terence?"

Leigh Ann pulled her hand away. "No, I only found out last night, but I somehow think he knows."

"You have to discuss this with him. He's a part of it."

"But a baby, Mom! How can I nurture a baby when I'm not even there with it?"

Miriam's smile seemed to hold a tinge of sadness. "I'm sure they'll provide an astral nanny. You have a whole network of astral friends on high, Leigh Ann. I'm also certain that this isn't just a coincidence. You have to trust events to work themselves out."

"I'm sharing a baby with Sharlan, Mom, and I only met her last night. Well, except for a passing acquaintance with her 35,000 years ago in Eliom."

Miriam ignored that. "And what do you think of her now?"

Leigh Ann hesitated, then: "I like her. I'm impressed by her."

"And jealous?"

She thought about that. "At first. Not anymore. I know she sincerely loves Bael and helped him through the dark years in Hell. Maybe I should just give them this baby when it's born and relinquish my right to him. Especially in light of my love for Terence."

Miriam shook her head. "I don't think so. You don't hold anyone's love by 'right,' only by their returning your love. And this may not ultimately be about the four of you. I think it's about Lucifer and your helping him to abandon his rebellion against Eliom and the Creator."

"Where did Lucifer enter into this?"

"Bael is his second-in-command. If Bael changes, Lucifer will be involved, like it or not."

Leigh Ann smirked. "I'll *bet* he will, and I'll be looking over my shoulder." She shivered.

Miriam squeezed her hand again, then let it go. "Lucifer won't harm you." She got up. "Now I have to go grocery shopping to feed this brood of ours."

"And I have to do laundry if Daniel and I want clean clothes for this week."

"Would you do me a favor? I left a small load of sheets and pillow cases in the dryer. Would you fold them and put them into the basket on top?"

"Not a problem."

"And Leigh Ann, I have just one more question: do you still love Bael?"

She paused for half a heartbeat. "Yes."

"Then how can you give him up?"

"But how can I *share* him? That's so harem-like, and I'm not sure if *that's* right!"

"So it's impossible to love two people at once and have both love you back with no jealousy."

"Don't you think it is?"

"No. And by the way, I'm not only talking about you and Sharlan loving Bael. I'm including the possibility of Bael and Terence both sharing *you*."

"Mom, you're talking about polygamy."

"It's called polyandry when the wife has more than one husband."

"And what is it called when there are *both* extra husbands and wives? Because it looks like we might have a full house, if we get another player."

Miriam grinned at her joke. "You might invite Ashtoreth in to play. At any rate, I would call that *family*, but if you want the specific term, it'd be a group or communal marriage."

"Oh, boy. . . ."

Miriam collected her coat from the dining room closet and her handbag from where it sat on the table. She fished in it for her car keys; she had recently learned to drive. Bill had bought her a used car on their anniversary.

Leigh Ann knew her mother loved the freedom it gave her, even if she didn't drive too far outside the neighborhood yet. "Hey, Mom, where is everyone?"

"Your Dad and Fred went fishing, and Ginnie is working her Sunday shift. Thanks for folding that laundry for me."

"No problem." She headed upstairs to dress and sort her own load of clothes as her mother went out the front door.

She had just loaded Daniel's clothes into the washer and was measuring the detergent when Terence showed up. Being a ghost, there was technically nothing to see or hear, but Leigh Ann knew, within a foot or two, where he stood in the laundry room. She could see him through the detailed image of Terence in her mind, and could hear his words as clear thoughts separate from her own. And he spoke without preamble, straight to the heart of the matter: — *I want us to be married* first. —

Leigh Ann knew exactly what he wanted and why he wanted it, his need coming through as sharply as his words.

Since everyone in the family was out, she felt it safe to respond aloud. "That's fine. I don't know how these things are arranged in Heaven anyway. Or in Hell." When he didn't answer, she added: "What did Quatama say about it?"

His pique only lasted two seconds before his voice filled her mind again. — *That we can get married all together or married separately, but that I must allow you to marry your handsome devil as well as me.* —

"All together? You, me, Bael and Sharlan? Do you know about Sharlan?"

— *I knew about her before you did. But Sharlan is refusing Bael's hand in marriage, mine not being part of the equation, since we haven't met yet, me being heavenly and she still stuck in Hell. Quatama said she could leave there now, sort of being pardoned, but she wants to stick by Bael when he's home in Hell* —

"That doesn't make any sense, sticking by him, but refusing marriage. Is it because of me?"

— *Yes, but not from jealousy. She's told Bael that you're his true love and she won't usurp your rightful place as his wife. She's bloody sincere, too, acting like you're pure and saintly, while she's a fallen angel, lucky to be allowed to worship you.* —

"Worship? Are you sure you're not sensing sarcasm here?"

— *No, Leigh Ann. According to Quatama, Sharlan really does worship the ground you walk on.* —

"Why?"

— Apparently because you sacrificed yourself for God's cause all those years ago. Noble of you. —

"No, I didn't. I was forced by the Seraphim, pulled away from Bael, separated during the Fall from Grace."

— Would you have gone with him to Hell if you hadn't been? —

That stumped her. "I . . . I don't know . . . yes, I do know. I wouldn't have been able to defy the Creator's will."

— Mmn. And the Creator knew that. And so does Sharlan. —

"But no one knew what was going to befall the rebel angels. They were trying to compromise."

— Well, apparently their terms didn't convince the Creator of their sincerity. —

She opened the dryer door and took her mother's bedclothes out, folding them as she talked. "It was totally unfair. Being asked to leave our homes and loved ones for thousands of years, never even knowing if the sacrifice paid off. If the genetic code of mankind would ever be rebalanced."

— Will ever be rebalanced. The rebalancing isn't done yet. You sound as if you now believe God was unfair. —

"I do," she said softly. "Look at our world, Terence. What good has the interbreeding of angel and human done for it? For every ounce of love and kindness, you find three ounces of hate and intolerance. It's a troubled planet, and I don't know how to heal it."

— Oh, it's not so bad now. Just wait till the turn of the century when things heat up. —

"What?!"

— Oops, I wasn't supposed to tell you that! —

"Good try, Terence. Cheer me up by making me think things could be worse." She picked up the basket of folded bed wear, carrying it up the basement stairs, and met Daniel on the middle landing by the side door.

"Hey, Mom? Who were you talking to in the basement?"

"Huh? I was talking to myself, Danny. Thinking out loud."

Her son peered down into the shadows below. "No, really. I heard some guy talking to you."

Leigh Ann stared at him; he was blocking her way unintentionally. "I have to get by, Danny, and bring this upstairs for Grandmom. As far as a man's voice, you heard something from outside. I was alone."

He moved slowly to one side to let her pass. "Okay, Mom. I must have imagined it." Daniel followed her through the house as she climbed the stairs and put the basket down on her parents' bed.

He said, "I came in to ask if I could go to the roller rink to skate. Jeff's dad said he'll take us."

Leigh Ann held up a finger, gesturing, "Wait," then picked up the phone in her parents' room, dialing Jeff's house across the street. Jeff's father picked up. "Hello, Mark? This is Leigh Ann. Danny says you offered to take the boys to the Palace to roller-skate? Uh, huh. Okay, I'll give him a ten for admission and skates and a snack. No, that's okay, I can pay for him." Pause. "Well, okay, if you insist. You're very sweet. All right, I'll expect him home by six. Thank you again." She hung up. "Okay, Danny, you can go. Mark says it's his treat, but let me give you a five, just in case of emergency. My wallet's in my bedroom."

He followed her there. "There won't be any emergency, Mom. We're protected."

She stared at him, got up her courage, and asked, "Who told you that?!"

Daniel fidgeted. "Um, I saw this little old guy when I was playing in our backyard." He stared back at her.

"Did this man say what his name was?"

"Um, no; he said he knew you. I saw a bee and got worried it would sting me. And when I turned around, he was there and told me we were all protected. He was dressed funny in a brown bathrobe, and he said the bees were God's creatures." Danny grinned at her with wonder. "And then he did something weird. He held out his hand, and the bee sat on it and looked up at him. He asked if he should tell the bee to sit on my hand, but I said no, that I was still a little scared. He said that was okay, and lifted his hand and the bee flew away. And Mom, when I turned to watch the bee, the old man disappeared! Like magic. I didn't tell you 'cause you might not believe me. But he said God protected my family and me."

Leigh Ann knelt down and hugged him. "Danny, you can always tell me anything you think is important. I trust you to tell me the truth."

"'Cause you're my Mom, huh?"

"Yes!"

"So it was okay."

"Yes, it was okay." She took a familial leap. "I *do* know that man. He's an angel watching over us. But be careful telling anyone else about it. Maybe they'll believe or maybe they won't."

"Keep it secret, huh?"

"Yes. But you can always tell me when weird stuff happens."

"Okay, Mom."

"Take the five anyway. Give it back to me if you don't use it." She handed it to him, and Daniel tucked it into his pocket. "Now, go, before Mark and Jeff wonder what's keeping you."

Daniel hugged her and planted a kiss on her cheek, then headed downstairs, calling, "Love you, Mom!"

"Love you, too," she called back.

Leigh Ann switched Daniel's wash load into the dryer and turned it on low, then started filling the washer with her own clothes. She sensed Terence enter the laundry room and greeted him telepathically. — *Hi. I think we'd better not talk aloud after what happened with Danny.* —

— *He heard me, Leigh Ann! I think he's inherited your talents.* —

— *Maybe more than mine. He recently saw and spoke with Quatama in the backyard. Quatama apparently cured him of his fear of bees and the like with a demonstration to prove we were protected.* —

— *Danny saw him?!* —

— *Brown robe and all.* —

— *Hmmn.* —

— *We'll have to be careful. He's only six.* —

— *Nearly seven,* — Terence quipped. — *I wouldn't worry. He's a sensible lad. Despite having a few genes from his mortal father, he is the current incarnation of your eternal father, Michael, from your long ago days in Eliom.* —

— *Nobody must mention that he's also Michael. He's Daniel in his current lifetime and that's that.* —

She felt Terence sigh. — *You're right. It wouldn't do for him to find out that his grandmother Miriam was once Eve, his wife in Eliom.* —

— *That was centuries ago. There's a good reason why people forget their past lives. It keeps us sane and centered on the here and now.* —

— *Ah, well, that's sensible most of the time, but sometimes knowing your past can help you sort things out and put your future in perspective.* —

— *Like knowing about Bael and our past? All that's done is complicate my life, mortal and astral.* —

She suddenly felt another presence, her inner radar alert, unsure yet if it were a mortal or an astral person about to appear. But the house above remained silent, and the image of Bael congealed in her mind. "Oh, it's you," she said aloud.

— *Forgive me for eavesdropping, but I want to know if you want a divorce.* —

— *We're not married yet.* —

— *Then we could drop the whole charade and save ourselves the trouble, if you don't love me anymore. Forgive the clichés.* —

She didn't even consider that she was astrally pregnant when she replied. The mere fact that he had *offered* to end it, if she *had* stopped loving him, created a gut response in her. She never could, *ever,* imagine herself completely away from Bael. "I love you," she said, very softly under her breath, audible only to him and to Terence. It was also an answer to Terence. Then she said, telepathically, — *Terence wants to marry me first, if you don't mind.* —

12

Back in the Garden

The weather has cooled in the higher planes of Eliom, but pleasantly so, as we head into the astral Autumn of 2008. In M—'s garden, we still meet outside on his patio, Aishah still serves fragrant beverages and sweet Middle Eastern pastries, and she now sits quietly in a chair a few feet from the table where I and M— sit, also listening as I tell him my tales of how I became both Queen of Hell and the chosen President of the High Council of Eliom.

Both jobs are hard. I must judge and make decisions that impact the lost souls of Hell and the disposition of worldly conflicts. Yet in the end, both lost souls and recalcitrant mortals must enact their own atonement. Before God can forgive them, and regardless of my judgment and recommendations, they must forgive themselves with alternate acts of good will towards whomever they have wronged.

Evil only visits its victims; those it hurts eventually go on with their lives and are healed, learning and becoming stronger, whether still mortal or returned to their eternal forms. We all get chances to work things out beyond the hurt, to lead a better, balanced life. That's when the soul hears a whisper that finally promises it peace.

"So," M— says as I sip the spicy tea. "You married both Bael and Terence on the higher planes."

"Yes, but I wasn't quite ready for one of those changes," I tell him. "I was afraid of Hell, of becoming trapped there, and a little bit afraid of Bael, despite everyone in Eliom telling me he was sincere. And despite loving him myself."

M— studies me. "If you were an ordinary woman, I would say you were wise to distrust a lover from Hell, regardless of his saying he wished to reform." He strokes his beard and sighs. "But you are no ordinary woman. You are one of God's chosen. May Allah bless you and the path you travel."

I incline my head in thanks for his well wishes. "And may I honor you as well on my path," I return, adding, "as best I can."

M—'s placid expression wavers, amused. He offers me a wry grin and nods his own head, reiterating, "As best you can."

"Considering I am not a Muslim."

"Considering you are Jewish, nontraditional, with equal traces of flower child hippie and Buddhist in you. You want instant peace, love and brotherhood in a world filled with violence born of self-aggrandizing politics and religions, both fueled by greed and egotism."

I murmur, "It's a thankless job, but somebody's got to do it," and he chuckles at my slightly serious joke. "Continuing my story, Terence and I were married in Eliom on the 8th plane on October 9, 1977. I wore a white satin Regency-style gown that gathered under the bosom and hung loosely. I was technically about six weeks pregnant by astral standards. Although only two mortal weeks had passed since conceiving, the astral measure of time is, as you know, three times as long as mortal time. A mortal pregnancy lasts about nine months, but an astral pregnancy only three months, in which time moves at triple the measure. So each month felt as long as three months when I was on the astral planes, and back to normal when I was awake on Earth."

"Did Bael attend your and Terence's wedding?"

"No, but Terence did attend both my marriages to Bael. I'll explain that in a minute. And they both agreed to a communal marriage."

"And Sharlan refused to join your communal marriage?"

"At that time, she refused. She did, however, unofficially join our household at my insistence. But that's not the most intriguing part of this story."

"Tell me."

"Terence and I were deliriously happy together, and Bael left us alone to enjoy our privacy, while he planned his own wedding to me. He insisted that the ceremony be conducted in Tandour in Domain, the capital city of Hell. Although this troubled me, I left all decisions concerning that marriage between Heaven and Hell to my spirit master, Quatama, the Buddha. At least the first one," I grin, and continue. "Quatama agreed to the wedding in Hell, a royal ceremony necessary to cement the future terms of an Alliance with Lucifer, with all the pomp and frills. But he also demanded that Bael wed me beforehand in Eliom. As I was pregnant, Bael agreed, almost eagerly, and suggested we hold the second, Heliomese royal nuptials *after* our child was born."

M— cuts in: "Heaven's marriage is the valid one."

"I think the vows we make to our loved ones as a pledge before our Maker, witnessed or not, in Heaven or not, are what makes it real."

"But your Maker is not in Hell."

"But our Maker can hear us everywhere," I say. "However, at that time, I also believed the marriage in Eliom was our valid one. I simply didn't trust Hell. The idea of a ceremonial marriage there, a marriage of state allying Heaven and Hell, seemed more political than romantic. Waiting would also get my girlish figure back. So, on October 31, 1977, All Hallow's Eve, Bael and I were married in Heaven by Quatama. Immediately following the ceremony, Bael returned me to Terence, prepared to relinquish me to him for the most part until the Heliomese ceremony."

M— interrupts me. "You are aware that a marriage must be consummated for final legality?"

"According to old tradition, yes, of course. Terence picked up on that right away. We knew that Bael had chosen October 31st to placate certain political factions in Hell that opposed the Alliance. And, no doubt, others had considered that if Bael didn't consummate the upper plane marriage, it would be invalid. And so Terence insisted that Bael spend his first wedding night with us."

"Platonically?" He asks this with equal measures of quiet mirth and incredulity.

I pause before replying with another question. "Do you want the truth or a diplomatic withholding of the truth?"

He considers those options. "What two men and their wife do in private does not involve me personally. Perhaps provide a small hint to answer the legal aspects concerning this."

"All right," I agree. "Bael was no stranger to multiple partners sharing his bed, being from Hell with a wild and well-established reputation, once believing me lost to him forever. He didn't object to a loving — and legal, I may add — *ménage a trois*. And Terence acted as our witness." I add: "This was, after all, also a royal wedding."

"A rather unusual one," he points out with another wry smile. M— knows I am sincere. There is nothing tawdry about my marriages.

And I say, "A few of today's religions still allow for more than one wife. In Heaven, women have more equal rights, and relationships may ebb and flow with a freedom based on what is right for the couple and not on dusty rules and outdated customs."

"Are you speaking of me and the religion I founded?" he asks.

"I'm speaking of any religion that asks women to do what it doesn't require of men — outside of childbirth, which men just can't manage. As far as polygamy goes, I could just as easily mean the Mormon faith. As far as polyandry goes — where the woman can have more than one husband — none of the major Earthly religions allow that. Yet they're willing to ignore the high divorce rate and the economic instability for families, where both parents work to survive, and the negative impact on their children, left behind to fend for themselves with surrogate daycare."

He shakes his head. "And communal marriage would fix this?"

"Of course," I say, "but that's not what we're here to talk about. We can discuss the benefits of group marriage another time."

"Agreed. So your Eliomese marriage to Bael was valid, and he was planning the politically-motivated wedding to be held in Hell after the birth of your child. What is the intriguing tale you promised me?"

"Simply this: Lucifer met with us in early November and said he would refuse to accept an alliance with Heaven unless I met one condition."

"And that condition was?"

I sit there very quietly, remembering my shock, and the arguments that finally made me accept Lucifer's condition. "He asked that I take his place in Hell."

M—'s face reflects the same shock I felt then. "Free him of his punishment and exile? But where would he go?"

"I see you are incredulous. I was, too, and the tale gets even stranger. Where, you ask, could Lucifer go?" I pause. "One of his terms was that he be returned to Heaven in my place."

M— shifts in his chair and glances at Aishah, whose eyes question her husband, perhaps as to both my sanity and my revelation, neither of which they seem prepared to believe in. M— turns back to me. "I believe I would know if Lucifer had been restored to Heaven. I would think everyone would know of it. For only Allah could permit such a thing as Lucifer's redemption, for only Allah could forgive his transgressions."

I nod. "Allah does as Allah wills. And who is to say that we know the manner of our Creator's will and the timing or the way of it?"

He inclines his head in agreement. "And so Lucifer's terms were refused."

"No," I say. "They were met. Lucifer requested that no one know that he had been returned — quietly — to a corner of Eliom, and his wife Affaeteres with him. As far as his redemption, that is between him and God."

M— is very quiet for a minute. Finally, he says, "Forgive me. But if you took Lucifer's place, why are you here? In Heaven?"

Now it's my turn to hesitate, trying to form the best answer. I wish that Quatama were here to help explain and then I wonder if that would even help. "You do know in Hebrew that the word *satan* means judge?"

"Yes." M— nods. "The symbolic judging of mankind's sins, the very sins Lucifer cited as the reason why humans should not be permitted in Heaven."

"In Eliom," I clarify. "That was our home before the Fall from Grace. And Lucifer also argued that humans, at that time, could never be equal to the angelfolk, and therefore were undeserving of any sacrifice, even if two of the angelfolk, my mother Eve and my other uncle Adam, caused a deviation in the future DNA of humans. And even if only the angels could repair it, it was still a terrible sacrifice, the solution we were asked — some might say *forced* — to provide."

M— pauses, and then speaks hesitantly. "I, too, am a product of the angelic and human incarnational crossbreeding you speak of. So I was told by your uncle, the angel Gabriel, when he appeared to me to dictate Allah's will, but modesty prevailed. I spoke nothing of it to my followers, for I felt the great Gabriel spoke symbolically only."

I catch myself frowning and curb it. "I am glad that you think so highly of my uncle, and your modesty spoke well of you. But allow me to backtrack a bit, for we've gone off our aim."

"Ah, yes. Lucifer as judge."

"Yes, and his punishment was exile from Heaven until such time as he could finally find and judge humans to be as worthy of Heaven as the angels were. But Lucifer still condemned mankind as the lesser creatures."

"Just so, and the reason for my incredulity that you and he could, shall I say, exchange places."

"Yet we did. I became Hell's *Satana,* a feminized version of the word, because of the conditions our Creator placed upon Lucifer's exile and punishment: if a human of pure heart and soul willingly took on Lucifer's doom and did it out of love with a willingness to serve our Creator, then Lucifer could return to Heaven and repent of his folly to God. For that pure human soul — subject to and rising above all the temptations and flaws of mortality — was equal to the original angels, which Lucifer placed above mankind. This proved to Lucifer that his condemnation of humanity was unfounded."

"Yes, but you are one of those original angels, Leianna."

"I was, but I have incarnated many lifetimes as a mortal, and have been subjected to mortal cares, flaws and temptations. Therefore, I am changed, grown, evolved. I am the test subject that proves the experiment. And while I have occasionally lost my temper and crabbed, grumbled or wept over my fate during those lifetimes, I have never committed evil against humanity. I have emerged unscathed. *I am the new angel.*"

"You have never sinned?"

"Not mortally. I have also upheld the laws of Eliom — the laws of the angels taught to me in my first, eternal life — with one exception. I have eaten animal flesh, long unaware of my angelic past and the vegetarianism of the Eliomese people until Quatama restored my memory of it during this current lifetime."

M— looks at me, silently, making me squirm.

"Okay, I did kill a bug or two, but even there, I try to shoo the bug away or take it outside."

Silence.

"Well, some bugs are too horrid to put up with or move them. Yuck!"

He grins, chuckles, then studies me quizzically. "Aside from that, in all of your mortal lives, you have never killed anything?"

"No, and there are many just like me. I'm still trying to change my eating habits on Earth right now. Old habits are hard to break, but I have cut out all lamb and veal. Baby animals, you know. Totally wrong to kill them. And beef and pork aren't good for us, if you eat too much, so I'm substituting chicken and fish. But, no, I've never taken a life and never will, and I've also never taken anything that didn't belong to me, and I've never lied."

M— rubs his chin. "You must have driven people crazy," he laughs, and Aishah is also smiling again, amused.

"Well, I'm not exactly Galahad."

"Ah, the Arthurian legend's pure soul."

"Yes. But while Lucifer hadn't made peace with most of humanity, he had to acknowledge that souls like me were encased in mortal flesh and we were worthy of heaven's welcome by anybody's standards, including his. And I was willing to take his place in Hell and free him after he repented of the falsehood that mankind could not aspire to and achieve angelic ethics, for some of us could and did. And so Lucifer acknowledged me as one who had gone through the fire unburned, only filled with the light of its cleansing flames. And therefore Heaven is not forbidden to me, even if I've taken this job in Hell."

M— shuts his eyes, lost in some private thought, then opens them to ask, "But why? Why did *you* take Lucifer's place? Even if you made him rescind his condemnation of mankind, theoretically, based on these few souls like yourself, then why should you, specifically, have become his replacement? I cannot picture you as a judge in Hell. Could not our Creator find someone else to replace Lucifer, rather than you?"

I sigh. "Aside from the fact that Hell existed and had a complete social and political structure that would undergo far-reaching changes from our exchange, our Creator was trying to utilize some of the infrastructure already in place amenable to the proposed Alliance. That meant introducing those changes through Hell's crown princes Baelzebub and Ashtoreth and allying them with Heaven through my marriage to Bael, who intended to shorten his name to its original after our wedding, as a symbol of the new climate, forgive the joke, in Hell.

"However, I had another good reason to agree to rule Hell as its Queen and Satana. It was the only place where I *could* be a judge. On Earth and in Heaven, I may do what good I can manage to help my worlds, but I am not permitted to judge or interfere with anything evil, for I am one of the *lamed vov.*"

Aishah looks confused at the Hebrew term, but M— merely nods as if all this makes perfect sense now. "One of the 36 unblemished souls born on Earth, Allah's treasure through whom the world is kept balanced. They are the reason God intervenes and heals the hurts mankind inflects upon itself, so that life may go on. The 36 pure souls are a beacon to the rest of humanity and an example sent from our Creator's heart of what humanity can one day be."

M— gestures with his right hand, palm up, the gesture as gentle as his voice. "Please . . . go on with your story."

"I will," I say. "Humanity still doesn't know that on November 17, 1977, Hell underwent a complete change. I may have taken Lucifer's place, but I was merely a vessel whose contents within represented the judgments of her Creator. God was really in charge, and Hell has never been the same since this change in management."

"Tell me," M— says once more.

And I do.

13

The Reformation of Hell

Lucifer sat alone in his throne room, this grand hall where he had ruled Hell for countless centuries. He awaited Bael, Ashtoreth, Leianna and Quatama, having requested their attendance on a matter of supreme concern to that Alliance they proposed. And what *he* now proposed would put an end to it!

For the Creator would never lift his exile unless the conditions set upon him during his Fall were met.

While many might agree to rule Hell in lieu of him, none who could prove that mankind was absolved of Lucifer's judgment would willingly take his job. As Hell's ruler, he prepared to demonstrate this exercise in futility and end this charade of an Alliance once and for all.

That Bael had married Leianna in a legitimate, higher plane ceremony was irrelevant. Once the status quo returned to the Netherworld, Bael's and Ashtoreth's passports to the heavens would be revoked. All who fell with him must remain with him; so had God cursed them all. Leianna had also married her British musician, planning a polyandrous union with him and Bael. Well, Terence could comfort her, and she would soon accept Bael's loss as inevitable.

She was a feisty woman, that Leigh Ann, both as her mortal persona and her eternal self. He sympathized with Bael — and Ashtoreth's — feelings for her. His eldest son seemed only destined for friendship with the girl, not that Ash hadn't attractive women in his own harem, though smaller than Bael's and Azmodeus's.

He'd heard of Leianna's astonishment upon learning that the princes of Hell had harems. She hadn't been told of his own harem, and if he hadn't known her almost as a daughter since the days of Eliom, he would have been tempted by her himself. But deep within his memories, Leianna was forever tied to the lost days of happiness among his friends and family in the Eliom that the original angels had known. She was tied to his cherished friendship with her eternal father Michael and her eternal mother Eve, remembered as their precious daughter, and as Bael's betrothed before he and she were torn apart by the war in the heavens. Lucifer might have many faults, but he would not sully one who was pure before he was outcast nor disrespect Bael's beloved, now his wife.

And so he waited, somewhat wearily, for them to appear, and to straighten them out, so that he, the Emperor of Hell, could go back to ruling his realm his way without Heaven's well-meaning intrusion.

Before him a large swath of air shimmered and shapes within it began to congeal into four people. A few seconds later, Bael, Ash, Leianna and Quatama faced him on his throne.

A fifth figure shimmered to their left and became visible: a moderately tall man, fair of complexion with long blond hair and blue eyes. He wore a white tee-shirt with colorful lettering proclaiming **BEATLES FOREVER**, blue jeans and tan boots. "Hello," he said to Lucifer. "I'm Terence. Nice of them to wait for me!"

The others seemed surprised to see him. Lucifer stood up and walked down the steps of the dais, holding out his hand. If Terence hadn't come with the negotiating team, then he must have fixed on Leianna and traveled astrally and alone here to Domain. A courageous act; he might have taken a wrong turn, ending up in the pits, literally. "Terence Dearborn? Welcome to Hell."

Terence looked at Lucifer's hand, then up at his face. "I'm not staying all that long. I'm here to protect my investment, one dear to my heart. She won't take one more step in this realm unless I make sure she can do so safely!"

Lucifer stared at his still-extended hand and slowly withdrew it. "It wouldn't have burnt you," he quietly told Terence, then turned to the others. "I assume you are the real negotiators for this proposed Alliance, although Mr. Dearborn has good cause to worry about his new bride."

Quatama came forward, facing Lucifer. "You have called us here, but I have important tidings for you. The old ones, our elders who were sent nearly 35,000 years ago from Eliom to help in another world in the galaxy, have returned to the heavens. Your parents, as well as Affaeteres's parents, are among them. They grieve to hear of what occurred in their absence, of your rebellion and exile, and the sorrow called Hell and its long defiance of Heaven. They have sent their love and fervent wish that you will strive to heal this long-festering wound."

Staring angrily at Quatama, Lucifer felt his muscles stiffen at hearing so abruptly of his father Othorah and mother Ise, along with Aff's father Marcellus and her mother Venea, and their unexpectedly early return, for they were not expected until the dawn of the 21st century. He spat out, "What wound?"

Quatama answered patiently: "The wound they say you opened in your heart when you denied and defied our Creator."

Lucifer gaped at the unobtrusive spirit master in his brown

robe and simple sandals. "No doubt Michael's parents, Zoras and Heira, are also back then. Have they all not had time to look at the history and current state of humanity on Earth? Have they been told the truth about the price the Creator asked of the angelfolk and that my dissent was honorable and reasonable? And yet my efforts were twisted by our Creator, called selfish, and my plea for angelic independence from the follies of Eve and her brother Adam mocked. In return for my fervent honesty, my family and followers were exiled to this distant and dismal land to be *free* in!"

"All this, according to your viewpoint, is true, and the Earth, yes, still filled with violence and suffering at the hands of humans who will not evolve beyond their selfishness."

"So the great experiment that ripped Eliom apart for centuries has failed!"

"I assure you, Lucifer, the Earth and humanity would be much worse off, if the angelfolk who did incarnate on Earth and acquiesce to our Creator had followed your example instead. Our Creator's plan is simply unfinished as yet."

"No proof of that," Lucifer retorted, "and better to have an angelic realm free of the taint of human evil, thanks to Hell, and let the mortals destroy themselves on Earth in their spiritual blindness."

"I should think you would have more empathy for mortals, being that your own people can die in your realm, which you've made the repository of human evil."

"Humans are here to be judged and punished for their evil, spirit master, not coddled by angels in an attempt to correct them. As far as my people having at least the potential danger of death, it occurs very rarely, never by natural causes, only by grievous, unhealed injury. Luckily, however, mortals consigned to my rule after *their* death, as lost souls, do not die, no matter what we subject them to, another sign of the leniency of our Creator."

Quatama quietly said, "That is because our Creator has new plans for those lost souls. And for your own people, if you are open to change."

"Yes, yes," Lucifer said impatiently, "this Alliance. Social workers in Hell. Save those poor murderers, fornicators and thieves."

Ashtoreth cut it, "Not all in Hell have sinned so grievously, Father."

"Nonetheless, they believed their sins worthy of Hell, or they wouldn't be here."

Bael folded his arms. "Not true. Many murderers think their sins justified and themselves worthy of forgiveness, and still find themselves damned. They don't think they're evil. They think they're heroes, from Robespierre to Pol Pot, to name a couple from a short list that doesn't include all of Hell's long suffering egotists, convinced they've been misjudged by mankind, Heaven and Hell."

Lucifer waved his hand dismissively. "The soul knows evil, even when the conscious or subconscious mind denies the truth. Their souls make that judgment call, not their egos. We only judge their acts, not their conscious beliefs." He leaned toward Leianna. "Did you know that? All souls weigh their own scales of justice? We can't snare them unless they secretly determine, deep within the unexposed, hiding places of their hearts, that they're guilty."

Leianna offered him a crooked smile. "Do they have the ability, spiritually, to judge themselves fairly?" she asked him.

"I don't know, dear. You'll have to ask your Creator, who never stops them from condemning themselves to Hell. In fact, you'll be having many conversations with God, if you insist on this Alliance going forward. I've decided on an ironclad condition before I give my blessing."

Ashtoreth grimaced. "We already know your condition: that you be returned to Heaven."

"And you know damned well, Ashtoreth, that God will not lift the criteria which would allow that, placed on me when I fell from grace! There must be a pure soul among humanity, willing to take my place in Hell, to sacrifice his or her freedom out of sympathy for all the damned and hope for their redemption. Thus proving to me that I was wrong to rebel, that humanity is capable of peaceable and selfless love and is equal to the angels. Well, I have decided on that human sacrifice for my freedom, and if I don't get my way, there will be no Alliance. You, my sons, will also eventually be forced to return to this land of exile. My punishment is still shared by you, as was my rebellion. Our Creator will not forgive you simply because Leianna loves you. So kiss her goodbye or tell her hello."

Terence bounded in front of Leianna as if to shield her, his back to her, glaring at Lucifer. "What the hell are you talking about?"

Lucifer smiled wryly. "Simply this: Leianna must take my place in Hell as that pure soul." He glanced at her. "After all, you often said that eternal damnation is wrong, that souls must be permitted to work towards redemption. Perhaps you can work toward redeeming Hitler or his maniacs who destroyed Jews and others in the Holocaust. Perhaps Jack the Ripper will warm to your sermons. They're all waiting for you to rule them as their gentler, kinder Satan! Will you accept or will common sense prevail?"

No one spoke. He had them speechless. He chuckled. "I

thought so. You see, Leianna, I know that you are one of the *lamed vov,* and because of that, you are *forbidden* to make judgment or take action against anyone. You cannot fight evil. You cannot control evil. And you cannot become Satan and judge either of the fallen, neither angel nor human. You are only an observer, praying for good, for righteousness, in the world around you. You are only able to hold it up, intact and safe from final ruin by the hope in your heart and the strength which that lends to your will. But I will have no other successor but you! Otherwise, you will have no Alliance."

Bael said, "A stalemate. But what if we refuse and force the Alliance upon you? Turn to the people of Hell to gain their support?"

Lucifer raised an eyebrow. "Foment rebellion against me? You cannot. The choice lies not with my minions but with God. You cannot oust me. This *is* my destiny until instructed further. And so, Quatama," he turned to the spirit master, "do you speak for God, or shall we call it quits?"

Quatama ignored the question, asking another. "Would you accept Leianna if she gave up her place among the 36 pure souls and willingly took your place?"

"Now, wait!" Leianna interrupted, alarmed. "Even if it was allowed, I don't think I could judge people and punish them, no matter how deserving. I just don't think I'm built that way, Quatama."

"Hush, little one. You will not have to judge alone, and your life has prepared you, as a careful observer, to judge fairly."

"My mortal life?"

"No, Leianna, the sum total of your life as an eternal soul, including the lessons of each mortal life. Even your role this time around as a *lamed vov-nik,* balancing the world with the other 35 righteous souls or *tzaddikim,* was to prepare you to respect the act of judgment, to never treat it capriciously."

"And my work as Earth's current Keeper?"

"That is a function of the most special *lamed vov-nik.* You may recall that God told you, as an immortal babe in Eliom, that if you were ever in need of help in fulfilling your destiny, to call out to the other Keepers. The Creator meant the other *tzaddikim.* And you did reach out to one: your mother. But there is always a central soul among the *lamed vov,* which means '36,' a pivotal Keeper, in each century, who is called upon to leave a legacy to the Earth and its people, one that will help them further balance their world. Sometimes that soul is born again into a new century, because its work must be completed, if it was thwarted in the previous lifetime and loose ends left untied."

Bael interrupted abruptly. "What does all of this have to do with my father and the Alliance?"

Quatama regarded him patiently. "He or she who leaves the legacy is permitted to make judgment on their world with two conditions. The first is that they judge truthfully, no matter how difficult, painful or socially, politically or religiously unpopular that may be. And the second is that they must never force any other soul to accept their judgment. All souls may willingly accept the judgment of the chosen Keeper, or they may reject that judgment. And no one may chastise them for their acceptance or rejection of the Keeper's judgment. Not even God. For all souls must evolve freely without coercion.

"Lucifer is right, in that each soul blesses or damns itself, facing its own truth within. Our Creator has built us this way. All other assumptions are an illusion. All else that influences a soul is merely human dialogue."

"Then how," Bael asked, "can Leianna punish the damned if, in her judgment, they deserved retribution?"

"She cannot. She can only judge them to have done a wrong that requires correction, but she cannot force them to undergo correction."

Ashtoreth waved his hands upward, angry and exasperated. "Then how, in this world, can Leianna agree to my father's demand?! What is she supposed to say to the damned? 'Excuse me, but do you mind letting me punish you?'"

Quatama laughed, and even Lucifer grinned at that absurdity. He had won. He had to have won. Even if she could judge, one could not politely ask a sinner to torment his or her own self. But Quatama's mirth concerned him. Why laugh when you're about to lose the game? "I myself wonder how you can possibly answer that, Quatama."

Quatama gave Lucifer a nod. "I shall do my best." He gazed up at Ashtoreth and Bael. "Leianna may not order punishment, but both of you may do so, allowing her judgment to guide your sentencing of the miscreants and seeing that the sentence is carried out. The two restrictions do not in any way restrict Leianna from having emotions, whether positive or negative. They do not put the impetus on her to only judge kindly, nor do they stop her from expressing her horror or fury if an evil act engenders these emotions in her and others."

Quatama walked the few steps to Terence and took his hand, surprising him. Then he gently took Leianna's in his other hand, lifting both of theirs in his own. "Leianna is permitted to judge, in fact, *must* rule the lost souls of Hell, for her destiny is to lead them onto a path of enlightenment and renewal. And furthermore, her destiny is to raise the consciousness of mortals on Earth. She will give them new tools that will guide them to evolve into better human beings. She will prepare them for a spirituality that will no longer need a heaven or a hell, only their own souls evolving honestly and honorably within the dimensional universe!" He lowered his hands, still clutching Terence's and Leianna's tightly. "And, Terence, you must permit Leianna to fulfill this destiny." He released their hands.

"What? Let Leigh Ann be buried here in Hell? Never to see the sunlight again? And what of her mortal life? Her son, Daniel, who happens to be your old friend Michael reborn? Does she die and leave him motherless to fulfill this destiny?" Terence took a deep breath and looked aghast. "Oh, damn! I don't think I was supposed to say all that about Daniel and Michael. Especially not here."

Quatama smiled. "It's all right. You've done no harm."

Lucifer asked, incredulous, "Michael's incarnated?" He glanced at Leianna. "As your mortal son? And Miriam Elfman's grandson, she who was his wife Eve, when he lived in Eliom? What twisted mortal relationships."

"Not at all," Quatama assured him. "Michael wanted to be near both Eve and Leianna as they worked out their last mortal lifetimes, to help them in any way that he can. It's very proper." He turned again to Terence. "You ask if Leianna will lose her mortal life and become confined to Hell. Of course not. Leianna will continue to live in every way that she is accustomed to living, both mortally and astrally. The Creator has requested that she meet Lucifer's demand, as privately confirmed to me by the Seraphim, that she shoulder Lucifer's burden, judging the lost souls of Hell. But she must also work to bring them relief from their follies through whatever means possible. She will have Heaven's help with this, and her sojourn in Hell as its judge shall not be one of exile, but of choice, with access to Heaven, should she wish a respite from Hell."

Bael asked, "And her mortal life? If she accepts this sacrifice, you should provide some ease and comforts in her wake-a-day life, so that this double life — no, this triple life — doesn't weary her."

Leianna glanced at Bael, not looking very happy. "This isn't your normal deal with the devil, Bael. In fact, it sounds pretty perkless. But thanks for thinking of me."

Quatama stroked her hair as if comforting a cherished daughter. "Leianna, the Creator will protect you, for you are a catalyst for change within creation. And while you will live comfortably," he glanced at Bael, "there will be no special accommodations, other than the means to fulfill your destiny. If you examine the destinies of those who led great lives, such destinies are not always easily won. The journey is an important and integral part of the destination."

She asked, "And what *is* my destiny? How am I to do all you have suggested? And offer it to the people for their acceptance or rejection," she added, remembering the limitation to her legacy.

Quatama said quietly, "You will find that out when you achieve it." He pulled out a scroll from within the folds of his robe. It appeared to be papyrus. Quatama offered it to Lucifer. "The agreement you demand."

Lucifer slowly unrolled it and silently read it:

It Is Hereby Declared:

On this 17th Day of the month of November, in the year known predominantly on Earth, wherein resides all mortal souls, as 1977 A.D., but equally as valid for all other versions of this day in time in all other human calendars, and furthermore as it may be marked and noted in Heliom (Hell) and in Eliom (Heaven), it is hereby declared and universally authorized by Myself and Ourselves, individually and collectively as the Creator of the Universe, and the Universe Itself, that Lucifer Morningstar's rebellion shall be forgiven and his exile be overturned and ended if the following conditions be met:

HE SHALL RELINQUISH all rights allowing him to judge mortals or any other creatures given the breath of life by Myself and Ourselves. He shall cease to rule Hell as the judge of said mortals, acknowledging without dissent that some may be pure of heart and soul and worthy of Heaven, and he shall transfer all holdings and interests in Hell and in Earth to a representative chosen by Myself and Ourselves to manage the Estate of Hell and all related holdings and interests on Earth.

THAT REPRESENTATIVE, WITH HER FULL CONSENT, shall be the soul eternally known as Leianna, and currently on this day on Earth as Leigh Ann Elfman. She shall have no restrictions upon her acceptance, becoming My and Our Representative, for I and We trust her to fulfill the demands and commands placed upon her in this capacity, even if she should refuse them or fail.

FOR I AM ALL-KNOWING AND WE ARE ALL-SEEING, AND BY THEIR AGREEMENT AND SIGNATURES ON THIS SCROLL, both Lucifer Morningstar and Leianna, She Who Seeks The Farthest Star, shall agree to bring both change and further balance to My and Our Universe, and to further seek their destinies, according to their Creator's Dictates.

LUCIFER MORNINGSTAR

LEIANNA (SHE WHO SEEKS THE FARTHEST STAR)

He stared at the two lines below these lofty words, which neatly held his and Leianna's name below them. "It doesn't say that I am allowed to return to Eliom."

"But you are and will be. Allow me to demonstrate," Quatama said, and in an eye-blink Lucifer stood in Eliom upon the Shore of the Seraphim with the smiling spirit master beside him. "You will recall that Well?" Quatama pointed to the Well of Being, sitting on the beach, its stone circumference glinting like gold in the sunset.

Lucifer crumpled to his knees in the sand. So many ancient memories! He lifted his head to the sky, gazing out over the foam-flecked waves that led beyond the sea to the mysterious habitat of the winged Seraphim. Here on this beach he had prayed to and believed in his Creator. Here, he had defied and questioned his Creator. Here he had been silenced by the Seraphim, and here he had stirred his rebellion.

He turned away from the sea, gazing over the dunes to where the elven woods and the pristine prairie and the cultivated Garden of Eliom lay, and beyond that, the village he and Affaeteres and their sons had lived in. And beyond that, the Canyon of the Winds and its citadel where the Seraphim tracked the incarnated angels and monitored their Earthly lives. "Is it . . . ?" he faltered.

But Quatama knew what he asked, and answered, "Some of it is unchanged; some of it is changed. Even Heaven expands, Lucifer. The village of Eliom is larger, modern and a pleasant community that oversees the sacred lands of the Garden and beyond. Some of the past is always preserved."

"The Well." Lucifer pointed to it, vapors rising in long wispy lengths from its shaft. "The breath of eternal life emanates from its depths again! No longer dried up."

"I understand," said a different voice behind him, "that it sprang back to life just today." Lucifer turned to see his old nemesis, the angel Gabriel, smiling wryly at him. "Apparently the war between Heaven and Hell is about to end. Can I trust you not to kick me unexpectedly in undignified places in the future?" He referred to a long-ago altercation between them during Lucifer's rebellion.

Lucifer stood up, facing Gabriel. "We were all . . . ," he fought to describe it in a conciliatory way, "foolish, confused and afraid."

Gabriel nodded. "Yes, we were. So. Are you about to let my niece Leianna take over for you and give up a grudge held for far too long?"

"Did our Creator send you here to ask me that?"

Quatama answered: "No."

Gabriel explained. "I came here on my own to assure you that Leianna will bring healing to your people and that you should accept her as your successor."

"Do I have a choice?"

"Have you signed the scroll yet?

Lucifer held it up, still clutched in his left hand. "No. And neither has she."

Gabriel held out his hand to Lucifer. "She will. And Hell will never be the same. Not that mortals will know it for quite some time to come." He did not withdraw his hand and now locked his gaze quizzically with Lucifer's. "Will you not take the hand of your old enemy, in the hopes that I might become your friend again?"

Lucifer slowly met Gabriel's hand with his own, reluctantly. "Forgive me. I could not accept the loss of my free will, all those centuries ago. I still can't. But I can ask to be forgiven for that flaw, for I am only the man the Creator molded me to be."

Gabriel still looked hauntingly like his twin brother Michael, Lucifer's old friend and Leianna's eternal father. But Michael would not be greeting him until he completed his mortal lifetime. By the time that happened, most likely, they would all come home to Eliom, although Leianna and his sons would still have responsibilities in Hell.

Gabriel grasped Lucifer's hand. "To a new day," he said.

Lucifer finally returned Gabriel's handclasp firmly. "To a new day. An extraordinary day," he agreed, and they released their hands.

"Then I will see you again, soon," Gabriel said and slowly faded from Lucifer's view, his voice fading as well as he added, "I look forward to seeing Affaeteres again, too."

Lucifer stared at the now unoccupied space where Gabriel had been. "Doesn't anyone walk home anymore in Eliom?"

Quatama offered him a weary grin. "Are you ready to return to Domain and sign the scroll?"

Lucifer stared at him and realized, for the first time in centuries, that his own soul was bone-weary and in need of the sweetness of spiritual redemption and rest. "Let's go," he said. "You've just called my hand. After all of my experience as a card-shark, you've beaten me and won the final game."

In another blink, they stood once again in Lucifer's throne room. Bael, Ash and Terence stood near, arguing, while Leianna watched them, her arms tightly folded across her chest.

They all turned as he and Quatama reappeared, and Quatama took the scroll from Lucifer's hand. "Leianna? Would you like to sign first?"

She looked at him warily. "Are you sure there are no restrictions on me?"

"I am sure."

"Are you sure I'm supposed to do this?"

"There is no other way, Leianna, to create the Alliance. To fulfill your destiny."

"I don't know."

"And, as Lucifer correctly deduced, the only way to free Bael and Ashtoreth from the confines of Hell. If you do not, then you deny within yourself the selfless purity and the love that Lucifer requires to relinquish his condemnation of mankind."

She sighed and looked at the three young men who each loved her. She asked Terence, "What should I do?"

"Actually," Terence said, "it was Bael and Ash who don't want you in Hell. They don't trust what's going on."

"And you?"

"I? I — this is a gut feeling, Leigh Ann — I want you to follow your destiny. But I can't make up your mind. I can only tell you I'll be there for you. With you!"

She slowly smiled at him and then at Quatama. "And this is what God wants?"

"I have it on the best authority."

"Do we have a pen? she asked, raising her eyebrows at the mundane question.

Quatama quietly handed her one, a golden pen, and then the scroll. She looked at Bael and Ash.

Bael slowly extended his right hand, palm upward. "We want to read the scroll, Leianna, before your final decision."

"I haven't read it either. I'll read it with the two of you." She unrolled it as the brothers came over, reading over her shoulder.

Bael stroked her cheek. "It seems there are no restrictions on you, other than to do your best down here. Ash and I will also help and watch over you. But this is still Hell. Are you sure you still want to do this?"

"Come closer, both of you." She stood on her tiptoes and they bent down as she kissed them each on their lips. "I love you both and I know you're worried for me. But I have to do what must be done." She sat down on the first step on the dais and spread the scroll. "What name do I sign as?"

Quatama said, "Your eternal one."

Lucifer sat down next to her, holding the scroll flat for her. "Go ahead. I'll sign after you."

She *tsked*, as if disconcerted by his seemingly easy-going willingness to implement one of the most extraordinary changes in their universe. "You're going to go through with this?"

"My terms have been met," Lucifer assured her.

She slowly signed her name and even signed its translation, which the Creator had written in after it.

Lucifer signed his name in the space above hers.

Hell had changed hands.

Hell had changed its meaning, its purpose and its character, but nobody knew this yet.

Lucifer stood up, stretched, nodded at Leianna, Terence and Quatama, and then glanced at his eldest sons. "If you'll excuse me, I have to tell your mother that we're going home."

14

The Lull Before the Storm

Leianna still sat on the step of the dais. Terence had joined her. The others stood, everyone silent after Lucifer had vacated the throne room, each sorting through the impact of what had just passed.

"I don't know," Leianna finally said. "I feel as if there should be some sort of explosion. Or maybe a fanfare, angels trumpeting. Or harping or something. Anything but this . . . emptiness. As if we had simply transferred a deed to an ordinary property and not the ownership of Hell."

Quatama said, "You do not own Hell. Lucifer did not own it. He merely controlled it, shaped it, governed it, as best he could."

"Okay," Leianna agreed, "but it's so *quiet*. Shouldn't there be . . . shouldn't I feel . . . I don't know . . . something monumental? It's so quiet. As if nobody knows and nobody cares."

Quatama sat down between her and Terence. "Acts of great importance are not always accompanied by public drama or pageantry. Sometimes quietude speaks volumes and resounds throughout time without the need for amplification. Such is this moment in time."

Bael put in, "No doubt, it will have an eventual great effect on all three worlds: Heaven, Earth and Hell. Now it's quiet. The explosion will come later."

Quatama stood up, brushing down his robe. "Not necessarily for years yet to come. Decades to come possibly. The world's religions, at least the traditional ones, were created at least partially on the basis of the Fall from Grace," he explained. "Now that Heaven has forgiven Lucifer's disobedience, because he has repented, vast changes will occur in the way evil is judged. Evil's main prototype has just been taken off the religious market, so to speak, and yet its believers are still influenced by it and will continue to be. Earth will not know of the Alliance until it is told through whatever message the Creator chooses to unveil it with, and not until mortals can comfortably believe it. Heaven will know of it and participate in the redesigning of Hell. Hell will know of it as these changes affect its inhabitants. All this will take much time. It will follow the river of time until its proper destination is reached. The Alliance will not be fully acknowledged or its impact felt until then, many years from now."

Ashtoreth, still looking wary, asked, "So what do we do now?"

"As the mortal night will pass soon, I suggest that Leianna rest. In the upcoming weeks, you and Bael can acclimate her and Terence — no humor intended — to your dimensional world, to Hell's people and their governance. I suggest you initially avoid showing Leianna and Terence any aspects that might disturb them."

Leianna said, "I'd also appreciate that. I didn't like Lucifer's earlier comment about Hitler." She looked up at Bael. "He *is* here, isn't he?"

"Of course, he's here. You don't have to deal with him, if you don't want to."

"I'll have to, eventually. My judgment of souls will be very different from your father's former judgment. But I don't want to deal with him or anyone just yet. Rest sounds wonderful right now, and just in case the walls have ears, I think the new, umm, Queen of Hell, should stay here tonight. Could we sleep in your quarters, Bael? Is there room for Terence and me? I wanted to see them anyway. Curiosity."

Bael grinned widely. "My bed should accommodate three."

"Good. We should sleep well then." She looked at Terence. "Is that all right with you?"

"We're just sleeping there, right?"

"Of course, silly. Ash has his own quarters, and I am really tired. It's amazing how tired one can get in one's astral body."

Ash reached out his hand to her. She took it and let him pull her upward. "It's emotional, Leianna, the type of weariness you're speaking of." He glanced at Terence, who pulled himself up. "I'll be fine. You two go with Bael to his suites."

Leianna smiled at Quatama. "Are you staying with us?"

"No, I will return to the Heavens. Return the signed contract to the Seraphim. But you are watched over and in good hands."

"Good to know. Come on, Ter."

He took her hand. "I'm a bit tuckered out emotionally, too."

They all left the throne room, Leianna glancing warily at the murals on its walls. She winced at the one that showed her braving the electric force field, trying in vain to reach Bael in those last minutes before Lucifer's quelled rebellion separated Bael from her for thousands of centuries.

As they neared the royal apartments, Quatama gently and uncharacteristically touched her arm, stopping her, and hugged her wordlessly. Then he faded from their sight, returning to the upper planes.

Leianna pursed her lips and sighed. "Boy, people do come and go quickly on the astral planes."

Terence smirked. "Flighty."

"Not Quatama."

They walked on to the end of the corridor. Ashtoreth leaned down to kiss Leianna's cheek. "I go to the right now. My quarters are at the end of this hall, if you ever need me."

Leianna smiled at him, then glanced down the hallway to their left. It led to Bael's apartment and, at the corridor's end, his harem, where Sharlan and his other women were housed. "We'll see you in the morning, unless I travel back to my physical body spontaneously before then," she told Ashtoreth.

He nodded. "Sleep well." He turned, walking to his own residence, not looking back. But she had seen the sadness emerge in his eyes, unveiled for one moment.

"He still loves me."

Bael said, "He always has."

The same two guards flanked the doors to Bael's harem, straightening their posture as he appeared, followed by Terence and Leianna.

Bael paused before his own chambers, besides his ivory-adorned double doors, and curled his hands around two of the elaborate ivory sculptures that served as door handles, but he neither pushed nor pulled them. He removed his hands. Leianna watched each door slide back into slots in the adjoining walls, like the doors on the elevated train she rode in the mornings of her mortal life, traveling to Center City Philadelphia. "What did you do to them, to make them open?" she asked Bael.

"They're keyed to my touch. Did you notice what those sculptures were, on either side?"

"No. Your doors are covered with ivory bas relief, and your hands covered those handles too quickly. What were they?"

"Perfect female breasts, one on each side."

"Bael!"

He laughed and glanced at Terence. "I'd like your opinion on the workmanship. I modeled them after Leianna's."

"Bael!" She felt her cheeks redden.

He put his arm around her shoulder and ushered her and Terence into his quarters. The ivory-covered doors slid shut behind them. Leianna heard a soft click, probably a lock. She turned around. The backs of the doors were smooth dark wood.

The vestibule to Bael's chambers was dimly lit by flame-shaped electric lamps in wall sconces, throwing seductive shadows about. A dark velvet curtain — either black or a deep red, she couldn't tell in the gloom — covered the entry to the rest of his abode. He pulled it aside, letting them enter the huge room beyond it.

An immense bed covered with a dark satin quilt and soft, inviting, white satin pillows filled most of the far wall. An elaborate dresser of lacquered wood with an ornate matching mirror flanked the right wall. An armchair upholstered in some tapestried scene hugged the corner near the entrance curtain, and a standing lamp of sleek black metal with three, hooded, flower-shaped bulbs, perhaps roses, stood bchind the chair. Bael moved over to it, turning the central bulb on. The bed chamber brightened, and Leianna saw that the quilt and curtain were fulgin, a red so deep, it was nearly black.

To the left of the bed and at its foot were two wooden chests, each as richly sculptured as the ivory entrance doors, but embellished tastefully with gold. There was no left wall; instead, an archway led to another chamber. Through it, Leianna saw a sizeable sunken pool, also lit by low electric flames in sconces. Its tiles were as smooth and black as onyx, and the floor around it was black granite. Huge pottery urns sat at the pool's various corners, filled with something sweet-smelling, perhaps bath oils, salts or soaps. A long table, also of dark wood, held neatly folded towels. To the right of the pool, elaborate, glass French doors had been opened to the endless night of Hell. A caressing breeze blew into the room. Beyond the doors, a patio and sculptured garden paths intrigued Leianna. Then she drew in a breath, realizing she was viewing a myth she had only heard about before, a tribute Bael had long ago created in her memory. She moved to the doors. "The dark garden!"

"Yes. The Night Garden, I call it," Bael told her, "created for you, both hoping and fearing you would follow me to Hell. But if you had, I wanted it to hold its own beauty, a dark counterpart to the bright world of Eliom. The flowers within it only bloom at night."

Leianna moved past the small patio with its white, wrought-iron chairs and table and out onto the paths of flagstone and gravel. White stone benches flanked the garden's walkways at intervals, as did more pottery bowls and urns, but these were filled with flowers and leaves, thickly stemmed.

A water fountain, its pool nearly six feet from its central sculpture, bubbled and frothed in the middle of the Night Garden. Leianna gasped as the sculpture: it was of her in an Eliomese summer robe. The marble hair seemed to flow about the stone face and shoulders. The statue's expression was one of pure tranquility. "Did I really look like that?"

"No. You were twice as beautiful. But this statue captures your essence well."

She shivered, not from cold. "God, what happens to my essence, my soul, now? Will it become corrupted in this world of yours, Bael?"

"Never. I don't believe your soul could . . . turn evil."

"Jaded, then, given time? Are there things here to twist a soul?"

He shrugged. "Quatama said you are protected. I assume that means mind, body and soul."

Terence moved over to her; his arm encircled her. "I don't believe it's about what Hell might do to you. The whole point of this challenge is about what *you* will do with Hell. I have faith that your backbone will prove strong enough for anything, Leigh Ann." She hugged him tightly, pleased by his vote of confidence, as he assured her: "And, of course, I'll be with you to protect you, no matter what."

Bael folded his arms against his chest. "None will dare to harm you, Leianna."

"I hope not. Because I don't intend to be a token queen. I feel a deep responsibility to your people. To all people. That's just the way I'm built. But now I am literally responsible for the souls of Hell, and the major question is how can I help them, even those who have committed great sins?"

Bael yawned. "I don't know, but let's tackle that tomorrow. My bed beckons, and Terence can play with us if he wants. We're both your legal husbands by the authority of the higher courts." She opened her mouth to protest, but he jumped in first. "Don't tell me you're too tired. I know you'd enjoy it, and it'll relax you. If you want, you can lean back and think about your empire. . . ." He grinned.

"What empire?!" She didn't know whether to smack him or grin back.

"Heliom. The Netherworld. You are now in charge, whether anyone else currently in power knows it or likes it. Your judgment even supersedes mine and Ashtoreth's."

"Bael, I would depend —"

"Yes, but you will also be facing the shockwaves caused by this sudden and irrevocable change in Hell's politics, dealing with the reaction of our people, highborn or low, free souls or damned, and of those damned, the acquitted ones and the punished ones. You have, love, taken on a great responsibility, as you say, and it's going to cost you in your time, serenity and energy. Ash and I can help. I was the chosen heir to the throne. Even under that contract, I can legally declare myself King, if you prefer that to Emperor."

"Yes. But what does this have to do with sex?"

His look mixed weariness and desire. "You should take every opportunity to nurture yourself and those you love." His tone gently pleaded with her. "You're not going to always have privacy and peace after tonight. I want to make love before the chaos erupts, to please you, to have you please me, and Terence, too, if he wishes. After all, we were a threesome on my wedding night upside."

Terence intervened. "Haven't you noticed, Bael, that Leigh Ann's belly is rather large now?"

Bael struck a pose, left hand cradling his right elbow, right hand cupping his chin pensively. "Let's see. Leianna is pregnant with our firstborn, something I never thought I'd ever see. As I checked with Quatama when he first informed us of Leianna's delicate condition, I happen to know we conceived our son around September 25th, which would make Leianna's due date around December 25th, three months of physical time or the equivalent of nine months worth of time astrally.

"She is about five mortal weeks away from birthing our son. Times three, that is the same as 15 weeks. If she were mortally pregnant, that means she would be three months and three weeks away from birthing our child. Subtracting that from the symbolic nine months of pregnancy, that makes Leianna, right now, five months and one week pregnant."

Terence glanced at Leianna, who shrugged her shoulders. He said, "Honestly, mate, I'll take your word for that, but doesn't that make it a bit unwise to do the bouncy-bouncy with her?"

Bael laughed. "Terence, Leianna, I have talked to an astral doctor, Dr. Mateus, whom you'll be meeting shortly. Leigh Ann, he's your assigned physician. He'll be delivering our first born and, by the way, he's upper plane, not lower plane. At any rate, I asked him about sex."

Leianna glanced down at her swelling belly. "And this Dr. Mateus said?"

"Up to the sixth month, anything goes. But after that, only do it on the side or with you on top. That way we won't cause you to go into labor."

"So we're allowed."

He plucked a white moonflower from its vine and stroked her cheek with its petals. Its sultry fragrance filled her nostrils, but the spell it cast was natural, no further casting needed. She took it from Bael's hand and offered it to Terence. He breathed in its rich aroma.

He and Bael led Leianna back through the paths of the walled garden, holding hands, a swatch of stars dotting the Heliomese sky above. They passed by the patio, through the French doors, past the sumptuous pool and returned to Bael's bedroom.

It was only when Bael knelt down and kissed her clothed belly, that Leianna even noticed what clothes she wore. Being out of body was similar to dreaming; the mind focused itself on certain mental or emotional symbols and paid little attention to mundane concerns unless events forced it to look at them.

And so she noticed that she wore a sort of flowing, dark green, velvet Renaissance gown, fitted loosely over her expanding waistline, long-sleeved with a scooped neckline that accentuated her breasts. Her shoes were thin, T-strapped dancing slippers. Other than her astral wedding rings, she wore no jewelry, and her auburn hair fell loosely about her shoulders.

Bael seemed focused on her pregnant stomach, staring at it, slowly stroking it with his right hand. "Doesn't a woman whose belly is full with your seed look beautiful?" he asked Terence.

"I don't know, mate. Leigh Ann looks beautiful to me all the time."

Leianna added, "And I'm pregnant with your seed, not Terence's." But his words and his circling caress had aroused her. His left hand now gently squeezed her buttocks, kneading each as if she were dough he shaped. He kissed her stomach again and said, "Terence will have his time. You'll bless us with many children, Leianna."

Terence, standing to the right of Leianna, much closer to her face, his own slightly flushed and obviously affected by Bael's lead, bent down to kiss her. She responded eagerly, their tongues fighting one another's, their lips locked.

Now she felt Bael relinquish her derrière, lifting the skirt of the gown in his left hand, his mouth and tongue gliding up her bare leg. He didn't let go of the velvet hem; it rose with his face, alternately rubbing his cheek against her inner thighs as his mouth sought her pubic treats. She became aware then that she wore underpants, challenging his quest.

He held her skirt above her waist with both of his hands. His mouth kissed the top of her undies and his teeth grasped its elastic waistband, attempting to pull it down, but her swollen belly held it in place. Terence, meanwhile, was still kissing her mouth, while his hands provided pleasure to her still-covered breasts, then inched lower and met Bael's dark head of hair. Glancing down, giving Leianna's mouth a breather, he noticed Bael's dilemma and pulled down the other side of Leianna's panties to mid-thigh.

Leianna felt Bael, obviously grateful to his brother-husband, pull the other side of her panties down until they fell between her legs. She stepped out of them as Terence gently pulled her gown off over her head. She lifted up her arms and hands to help him, freeing the sleeves. The dress fell on the floor as Bael's mouth hungrily fixed itself to her clitoris and vagina, and Terence's tongue began circling her exposed breasts. She hadn't been wearing a bra, and his mouth was enjoying Sugar and Spice, as he'd nicknamed her left and right nipples. She groaned at the onslaught above and below by her husbands and felt herself climaxing.

Bael must have also sensed it. He stopped his vigorous suckling before she exploded and stood up, gently putting a hand on Terence's shoulder. Terence straightened up, looking dazed.

Leianna, naked except for her flimsy shoes, aching with desire for them, looked from one to the other. "It's no fair," she breathed, "you guys not taking off your clothes, too."

Bael laughed. "Go lie on the bed, Leianna."

"I'd expect one of you to pick me up and carry me there," she teased, still nearly breathless.

"Go lie on the bed," Bael said again, before Terence could react. Bael began to remove his own clothes. As usual he was dressed in black: tee shirt, jeans and boots. Terence still wore his **Beatles Forever** tee-shirt, blue jeans and tan boots, his blond hair framing his school boy complexion and sky-blue eyes, which were now seriously awash with arousal.

Leianna, almost entranced, walked slowly to the huge bed and climbed onto it. Behind her, Bael said, "Pull down the red satin cover." She did. Under it, white satin sheets matched the plump pillows. She turned back around to face them.

Terence had once again followed Bael's lead, although Leianna knew he would have gladly carried her to the bed, were they not with Bael. He and Bael had discarded their shoes and shirts and stood in their jeans, facing her as she waited, her body waited, for their ministrations.

Bael was grinning, but Terence looked impatient. Her handsome British composer started to unzip his jeans. "If I wait any longer, I'm going to go bonkers, Leigh Ann. I'm achin' for you, sweetie." He stepped out of his jeans as Bael quickly discarded his. Both wore no briefs; both were fully erect. Leianna shivered, instinctually moved her legs apart.

Bael dived onto the bed first, landing beside Leianna's right; Terence hugged her left side seconds later.

"Now, boys," she giggled, "don't fight over me," and a delicious desire to tease them further made her grasp their thick penises in each of her hands. Bael's head bent to her right breast and Terence's to her left breast.

Terence said, "You've got Spice and I've got Sugar," and they both covered her nipples with their mouths, sucking energetically.

She was going to burst, both above and below again. "I love you," she whispered huskily. "Both of you."

Terence relinquished her breast. "We both love you," he said, giving her a quick kiss, then grinning. "And now I'm going to enjoy Everything Nice!"

She blushed back and he bypassed Bael, still enjoying Leianna's right breast, and slid down to her vagina, lapping it as a man might lap a delicate wine. She had let go of him, to let him keep his promise below, but now her vagina, on fire, almost beyond her control, ached with wanting them to enter her, to become one with her, and it didn't matter whether Terence or Bael went first. "Choose," she murmured. "Complete me, one of you after the other."

They knew what she asked. She let go of Bael's hard member and waited for them to decide. She felt Terence offer her a long sliding lick of his tongue and then lift himself up. From her prone position, she saw her two husbands look at one another, a silent communication.

Bael took her right hand and placed it back on his hardened penis, then leaned back slightly, giving Terence room to mount her from above. She felt the swollen head of his penis rub against her clitoris, spurting a little, moistening her with his semen. Then he arched backwards and, keeping his weight off of her stomach, Terence slid his penis fully into her. She groaned. His chest above her rose and fell, his handsome face flushed as he moved himself slowly back and forth within her, then increased his speed until they both rocked to the right rhythm. Her hand on Bael's penis squeezed it to the same beat.

And then Terence's climaxed completely, his hot semen flooding her insides, warming her and bringing her own climax on. They clung to each other, Leianna's one arm around Terence's back, her other hand still held Bael's unrelieved erection.

Her vagina felt both deliciously happy and still hungry, both aching with pleasure received and wanting more at the same time.

She rocked a bit more against Terence and squeezed harder on Bael's love offering, knowing he was ready to accommodate her.

Terence leaned over, kissed her sensuously, gave each of her breasts a quick suckle and then withdrew himself, laying down on her left again.

Her hand now stroked Bael's back as he, too, kissed her breasts and softly said, "Sit up. I'm going to put you above me."

They switched places, Bael on his back in the middle of the vast bed, Leianna on his right. His long penis, thick and eager, stood at attention.

Bael smiled at her. "My weapon awaits your sheath, my lady. Only you can contain its power." His finger slid into her, tickling and preparing her again, until she squirmed with need.

She swung her leg over him, straddling him, about to mount him, when his hands clasped her waist and literally lifted her into the air above his pulsing penis. He lowered her onto it, slowly, slowly, until he filled her completely, their groins pressed hard together.

Leianna groaned as Bael began to buck like a rodeo stallion, his hands gripping her buttocks, holding her tightly on, as he rode her wildly. His penis grew hotter and hotter, grinding against the walls of her flesh, yet bringing no pain, only an excruciating rough ecstasy, until she felt that she could not keep up with his furiously pumping member. She sat atop him, eyes shut, feeling the speed with which his racing penis rode her vagina, her mouth open to the extreme sensation, Bael's hands still holding her derrière in compliance to his demand.

And then she felt a hand on her right breast, gently squeezing it, knowing it was Terence who caressed it. The gesture brought her shatteringly to climax; she felt her warm discharge rushing in a flood over Bael's penis as he lunged upward to meet her completion, exploding his semen into her like fireworks, to mingle with her own creamy offering.

She stayed above him, panting, watching as his own chest slowly stopped laboring, his arms untensing. His hands stroked her backside gently before sliding to his sides in happy exhaustion.

She pressed down on the wetness between them and smiled at him and then at Terence, lounging with a lopsided grin beside them. "You were hot," he said.

"I love you," she said, "and you!"

Bael also grinned, not asking her to get off of him. She was glad. She loved the afterglow, the aftermath.

He played with a strand of her hair. "It amazes me, this lack of jealousy. Even in my harem, there's some jealousy. But among guys, I would expect it to be worse."

Terence sat up. "When you truly love a woman, you allow another man to share genuine love with her, if she loves that man, too. Real love isn't restrictive, and real love is responsible. No treating each other like a piece of ass to be discarded when you're done; no placing restrictions on each other, either. Equality among the sexes is a reality in the heavens. Nobody plays the ownership game there, mate."

"Well," Bael said, "maybe not, but our lady here owns my heart, and I can deny her nothing." He patted her arm. "Come on. Let's all get bathed in my sunken pool."

She leaned down briefly, kissed him and slid off of him. They walked naked to the pool and stepped down into it, enjoying the warmth of the scented water, washing each other's backs, occasionally teasing in other spots, but really too sated to do more than clean and dry themselves.

Before all three of them snuggled back under the covers, they had folded and draped their clothes on the upholstered chair and shoved their shoes beneath it. Then Bael had turned off the flowerbulb, just letting the low lamps in the wall sconces lift the darkness, and Leianna fell asleep between her husbands.

15

Regan

People do sleep in their astral bodies, if they need it. If they are currently engaged in a mortal life, they sometimes sleep in both bodies at the same time and do not separate and go about their astral business. Or they do travel and attend to their astral lives and, if rest is needed, fall asleep in their astral surroundings. When they awake from astral sleep, they may have returned to their physical bodies and wake up physically as well — this is the greater occurrence — or they can wake up in their astral surroundings, either because rest was completed there, or something astral woke them up.

In Leianna's case, after that eventful night of November 17, 1977, something disturbing broke her astral sleep in Bael's suites, also waking her husbands.

She and Terence came awake first, Leianna saying, "I heard something." They looked at each other in the low light and then heard the moan, moderately pitched, sounding feminine, seeping through from outside.

Terence murmured, "It's coming from one of the royal quarters."

It sounded again, longer this time.

Bael propped himself on one elbow, listened, and flopped back down. "Ignore it. Someone's having sex."

"God," said Leianna. "I hope we weren't loud."

"God has nothing to do with it."

She turned to him. "That's not true. Who let us find one another after 35,000 years? Who put the soul of Nikki into my womb as our son? Who has just gotten me to take your father's place?"

"I just meant . . . God has nothing to do with our having sex."

"Don't be too sure of that. God created sex."

A jolting shriek silenced them. Shouting followed it, a woman's voice, incoherent and pleading, and then the low voice of a man, too muffled to make out the words. Then another shriek.

Bael sat up. "Damn that brother of mine!"

Leianna and Terence also sat up. Terence asked, "You mean Ash?"

"No." Bael grimaced. "Azmodeus. His harem is directly across the hall from us, although the entrance is down the side corridor. It's fairly large, and he has a penchant for mixing pleasure with pain."

Terence rose from the bed. "And keeping others awake." Leianna saw that he had instantly materialized pajamas onto himself, white with blue stripes. Now he sat on the bed's edge, putting on new slippers. "Well, let's go tell him to keep his titillation down to a low roar. Come on, Leigh Ann."

She stared at him, then at Bael.

"Well?" Terence asked. "Do you want to put up with this each time we bunk here? After all, a queen needs her beauty sleep, and torturing women as a cure for erectile dysfunction ought to be outlawed for reasons well beyond disturbing our peace! Get dressed."

Leianna retrieved her clothes and shoes, putting them on slowly. "It's quiet again." She asked Bael, "He really doesn't hurt them, does he?"

Bael merely frowned at her.

"Maybe we should confront him in the morning over break —" The woman's screams drowned out Leianna's words.

Bael jumped out of bed, strode naked to the chair and pulled on his jeans, shirt and boots. "He's doing it on purpose. He probably knows you're here. He's not usually this blatant."

"Do you think he knows what happened last night, Bae?"

"Don't know. I doubt if my father had time to tell him, and it's not Dad's style. He'd call a conference with the family and his councilors." More cries erupted, carrying through the walls, more muffled pleading. "Terence, are you actually going to confront my brother, the chief demon of debauchery, wearing long-sleeved cotton jammies and leather, open-toe slippers?"

"Too sophisticated? Hold on. I'll fix it." He looked down at his feet; the slippers turned into bunny slippers. He strode to the curtain and held it for Bael and Leianna as more voices sounded from down the hall. "Shall we?"

Leianna went into the vestibule. "Can I open the doors without you?"

Bael came over, placing his hand on the smooth wood. It slid open. "It's a protective device. Also assures my privacy. I'll have it rekeyed to respond to your touch and Terence's as well."

She nodded. "So lead us to Az."

Bael turned right down the hall, as the ivory doors slid back into place behind them, then turned left down the first intersection. About halfway down on their right, another set of elaborate doors decorated in gold and showing lascivious acts made Leianna bristle. She started to put her hands on one of the upright, golden door handles and realized they were shaped into penises. She snatched her hand back, telling Bael, "You open them."

Bael shook his head. "This isn't his harem. These are his personal quarters. His harem is at the end of this corridor on the left."

She sighed and started walking to it, as sobbing erupted from behind the left wall. Az's harem doors, of heavy brass, were flanked by two huge brass statues of masculine demons, whose phallic treasures had permanently risen to new heights, and whose brawny arms and hands held spears aloft.

Bael, behind her, said, "Wait!" but Leianna eyed the obscene door posts disdainfully and put her hand on the thankfully normal door knob.

One of the brass spears swiftly fell within an inch of her hand. She followed its shaft up to the huge hand of the brass demon, which had suddenly sprung to life. It spoke dully: "You are with Lord Baelzebub, and so I will not tear you apart without his permission. But entry to the harem of Lord Azmodeus is forbidden to you."

She backed away, gulping down her apprehension, staring at the monstrous face, not quite convinced of her power in this world, if these brass things could challenge her in it.

Terence spoke softly behind her. "Leianna, you *are* Queen. And protected." Bael said nothing, perhaps waiting for her cue.

She asked: "Do these creatures know that?" as the second brass demon clanked toward her.

Terence said, "Ask."

"Excuse me?! Umm, these two have long spears, stand about 15 feet high, and I'm just supposed to say, 'Hey, in case you didn't know, I'm the Queen of Hell now, and would it be too much trouble for you to obey me?'" She looked at their metallic faces, eye sockets filled with a murky red light. They both grinned.

From within the harem, another heartrending shriek jolted her. She glared at the brass demons furiously. "Yes, I *am* the Queen of Hell, you brass rejects from Oz," she snarled them, "and I'm not putting up with this crap in *any* of my worlds, Heaven, Earth or Hell. So move your metallic butts out of my way!"

Both creatures stared at her, grins fading. The second demon asked Bael, "Is she mad?"

Leianna put her hand on the door knob again. "Yes, I'm mad! Mad as all Hell! I'm also your ruler." She swung the huge door open as the second monster's spear thrust violently toward her — and melted in its hand. Metal burned metal; a strange, groaning whistle of pain escaped its mouth, its injured hand partially destroyed.

Terence looked warily up at it. "She is who she says she is."

And Bael told them, "As of tonight, this woman, my wife, is

your sovereign. Had your spear harmed her, I would have had you dismantled."

Leianna watched as the brass guards each went clanking down on one knee before her, bending their heads, one after the other, saying, "Majesty." She told them, "Remain there until I tell you otherwise. And lower those things between your legs to half-mast."

The two brutes looked confused, and then the other door opened from within. Azmodeus stood there, dark rage on his face. "Their brass pricks don't move, you bitch!" His own was standing at attention, his wiry body, about five feet six inches, naked and tensed. He looked at the ruined hand of one of his guards. "I don't know how you managed that." He glanced at Bael. "Did you do it? Why? At any rate, it's time for you to fuck off and mind your own business! Maybe you can borrow defective brass boy here, and let Leianna sit on him. Mellow her out."

Instead, Leianna shot him a killing look and strode past him, moving quickly into the main room, and stopped, her mouth gaping with shock.

"Hey, you bitch. Get the fuck out of here before I rip your cunny with my bare hands!"

She heard his subsequent gasp and gurgle and glanced back. Bael held Az by his neck, his feet dangling of the floor, and growled at him: *"Never speak to my wife like that again!"* He let Az go.

She turned away as Az crashed down, staring again at the victim of Az's abuse, unable to understand why Az resorted to such rape.

Azmodeus's harem followed the same circular design as Bael's. On its first level, with her hands and feet chained to four posts on either side of a small altar and her upper body spread out on its length, with her arms stretched upward and back and her legs pulled taut and open above the altar's edge, a petite, blonde woman cried wordlessly and turned her face away from Leianna's horrified expression.

She bled from her mangled breasts, from between her legs. Leianna moved closer and saw a handle sticking out of Regan's spread vaginal lips.

Leianna felt her gorge rising. "Dear God, you bastard! What have you done to her?!"

Azmodeus had picked himself off the floor, his ego undamaged, swollen and crude. "Had to cut her open, prepare her for my enormous cock. You'd —" He immediately dropped what he had planned to say as Bael came over, saying instead. "Besides, I like 'em nice and wet, and blood makes fucking fun."

Leianna turned to Bael. "I know these people, many of them,

are passed over, but I always thought that spirit bodies can't really be hurt. I mean, they're already dead!" She beseeched him and Terence, who had also approached and was staring at Regan with the look of a soldier viewing an atrocity and itching to pay its perpetrators back big time. "What I mean is, will she feel pain if I take out the knife?!"

Az sprinted up to Regan, bent down between her outstretched legs, and said, "Would you like to find out? I'll use my teeth to pull it out. That will take longer." He moved his mouth toward the handle, but Terence was faster, his hand shooting out and smashing into the right side of Az's face, knocking him to the floor.

Terence kicked Az squarely on his naked butt for good measure and smiled with cold satisfaction when the debauched princeling screamed. A small square of flesh was missing from Az's ass, the puncture bleeding bluely. The bunny head on Terence's slipper chewed slowly, then gagged and threw up.

Terence took a small, wireless phone out of his pajama pocket and held it to his ear without dialing a number. "Hold on, Leigh Ann." She had seen these before in the heavens. They amazed her, allowing instant communication between the dimensional planes with whomever you needed to speak to. Apparently, they worked in Hell. "Okay," he said to his party, "Yes. Okay. Thank you.

"That was Dr. Mateus," he told her. "I asked him how to remove the knife."

"I didn't even hear you ask the question," she told him. "What did he say to do? Can an astral person bleed to death if we remove the weapon from the punctured area?"

"Not normally. Not deceased mortals. But abruptly pulling out the knife could make her lose enough essence to become catatonic. Dr. Mateus said to slowly remove it with one hand, while sending healing energy into her wound with your other hand. Envision the energy packing the puncture."

"Umm . . ."

"You can do this, Leianna. Remember, you control this world now."

She offered him an incredulous, tiny laugh, staring at Regan and finally noticing fully that Azmodeus's other concubines were present, standing or sitting within the circular lounge levels as motionless as statues. Some looked sultry, some looked cold, some looked frightened. But she saw their eyes staring unflinchingly at her. Their eyes, the window to their souls, sided with Regan, with Leianna's saving her.

She quietly placed her left hand on Regan's stomach and her

right hand tightly around the knife handle. The girl's body tensed and started trembling visibly with fear.

Leianna spoke soothingly to her, remembering her own fear and pain during mortal childbirth. "Now, I need you to relax your body, Regan, to let me withdraw this from inside. Did you ever have a baby? Sometimes they have to cut down there, to give it room to exit the mother's body. Sometimes in natural childbirth, the vagina tears and bleeds and has to be stitched back up after birth. But we women survive all of it. I'm going to start taking this out slowly, one inch at a time, and whenever you feel pain, I want you to hold your breath until I stop the movement and the pain subsides. Then you'll rest another second or two and we'll start again."

She was improvising. These weren't contractions Regan faced, but it might help her through. Holding the handle rigidly, she called forth a white healing light, knowing it came from a source beyond herself, from the Creator and the universe, although the energy seemed to pulsate from within her diaphragm and outward through her body. Soon the shimmering light glowed around her and Regan, like a force field of revolving diamond-flecked dust.

She still felt the healing energy inside herself as well, and now she directed its flow to her left hand and fingers, resting on Regan's belly. Leianna wondered if she should have used her right hand for the healing, but she was right-handed and needed that hand's dexterity to confidently grasp the blade and control its withdrawal.

It doesn't matter, she thought to herself. *Healing is healing!* She envisioned a scintillating circle of healing light coursing from her left hand and through Regan's stomach to the puncture wound. "Okay. One inch." she drew the knife out one inch.

Regan cried out, then checked herself, taking a long breath, holding then releasing it. Leianna directed the white energy, filling the puncture, staunching the bleeding. "Next inch." And so it went, the altar high enough that Leianna didn't have to shift her position as the knife finally slid fully out.

She heard Terence say, "The bleeding stopped, Leigh Ann! Your healing staunched it. On her breasts, too." She stole a glance at the knife in her hand and dropped it in horror. It had not been a slender blade the size of the handle. The blade had been double that.

Terence came over with a basin of sparkling water and a wash cloth. "It's got healing energy in it, too. I went and got it while you were performing the operation."

She wrung the cloth out and gently cleaned Regan's wounds, already closing from her care and healing. "Undo her shackles," she commanded, and heard Bael say, "Take them off her, Az."

Leianna handed Terence the wash basin and cloth, then confronted Azmodeus. "Free her, or I'll throw you into solitary confinement."

"What?! What the hell is all this crap about your ruling Hell now? I mean, you marry my brother, screw him, and then act like you're some queen. I think you'd better talk with our old man, Leianna. With or without your higher plane tricks and my brother's help, you're still just an in-law, babe. So thanks for cleaning up my concubine. I'll even forgive you for interfering with my pleasure. But if you'll excuse me, I'm going to fuck Regan's brains out now, you got me so hot watching you play with her, *sister-in-law!*"

Terence had been slowly removing his pajama top as Az made this speech. Now Terence took the long-sleeved top and wrapped it swiftly around the waist of Azmodeus, tying its arms together in back. "There you go, mate." The rest of the shirt hung down the front, covering his nudity. "An apron's just the thing for you. Wear it while you're cleaning up your *own* act, you foul piece of crud."

"You know, *mate*," Az smirked back at him, "You're not from this world, but I can command some pretty nasty residents to make you regret setting foot in Hell." He tried to fling the shirt-made-apron from him and found it knotted fast. He turned it around, furiously trying to undo the knot, looking ridiculous, his erection wilting.

Leianna walked over to him. "Where are the keys to these shackles?"

"If you're so all powerful, break them yourself, bitch! By the way, they're keyed to my touch."

"Doors, and now shackles!" She threw Bael an angry glance. "Doesn't anybody use old-fashioned keys anymore?"

Bael smacked Az savagely on the side of his head. "Undo Regan's chains!"

"Will all of you bastards stop attacking me?! Regan's my concubine. I can do with her what I want."

Leianna corrected him. "No, you can't. And I'm not merely your sister-in-law anymore. *I am the law!* You father has relinquished Hell to me!"

"What?! She's crazy." He still struggled with the knot, which held fast. He went over to Regan and touched each chain, releasing her from the bondage. Her wrists and ankles came free of the shackles, the chains swinging down and around the posts, then quieting to a stop. Regan's arms and legs sank, dangling from the altar.

Azmodeus approached her like a petulant child. "Regan, get up and help me get this stinkin' knot out!"

Leianna saw Terence smirk, eyes narrowed, looking at his handiwork.

Regan struggled to rise, but she had lost too much blood, despite the healing. The floor was sticky with red, for only angelic blood, including blood from the fallen angels, ran blue. Azmodeus stared down at her face. "You're tired? Okay, so turn and lean over the altar and untie this. I know you're good with domestic shit. Obey me and I'll let you have the next night off."

Regan pulled herself onto her side, her hand tugging feebly at the ends of the knotted shirt. Leianna came up on her other side and pulled her away from Az, as Terence moved over to Az and swiftly untied the knot, pulling the shirt away and handing it to Leianna. Then Terence helped Regan to stand, while Leianna put the shirt onto her. Leianna buttoned it down. It covered Regan's small frame like a short night gown.

Terence picked Regan up, cradling her in his arms, as Leianna addressed Az. "We're taking Regan away from you. You don't deserve her."

"You can't remove her. She's one of the damned!"

"First off, I can do anything I damn well please. Secondly, I've never seen anyone more likely to be a case of mistaken damnation than Regan. Something's telling me she doesn't belong here."

Regan finally spoke, breathlessly but audibly. "Please. Don't take me from Lord Azmodeus. I displeased him. He has the right to punish me."

"Not that way," said Leianna. "And I somehow don't think Az's judgment of right and wrong is very accurate."

Azmodeus looked at his other concubines, watching, waiting. Leianna knew he was trying to save face, and Regan's desire to remain with him, to give him the right to abuse her, certainly seemed to justify his actions.

She would have none of that. "Why do you want to stay with him?"

Regan answered simply, "I love him."

"I'm sure there's more to it than that," Leianna told her, "but if you really do, Az will have to earn the right to that love, Regan. I have spoken. You're to be taken to the higher planes and healed. If, someday, Az earns the right to your love, we'll allow him to see you."

"Please! I don't want to go!" She struggled in Terence's arms, but Leianna nodded to him, and both he and Regan faded from sight.

Azmodeus sneered at her. "Separating lovers against their will. Some Queen of Hell."

"Why, Az, I'm only doing what my new job calls for. Punishing those who sin. Put your clothes on, kid, and return to your quarters across the hall. Alone. You're grounded for the night."

Az shot Bael a questioning look. His older brother simply said, "Obey her." Then he added, "We'll work it out."

Az slowly materialized blue jeans onto himself. "It's true, then."

Bael nodded. "Father will probably call a Council meeting in the morning to announce it."

"Well, I don't *want* to go back to Eliom with all its flighty, little, do-gooder angels."

"I don't think you're included in the deal."

Az looked startled. "And you are?"

"No. I get to stay here and help Leianna. As does Ash. Although some travel restrictions have been lifted. For Ash and me."

Azmodeus shook his head and looked about his harem at his still silent concubines. "I will be back," he told them brusquely, then briskly left the room, heading for his personal suites across the hall.

Leianna also gazed about at the concubines, about twenty other women of varying appearances. They had watched it all silently, but now a tall, willowy brunette came down to the first level and solemnly regarded Leianna. "We thank you, our Queen."

"You're welcome. Please retire to your chambers. In the future, report any abuse to me. Please."

The woman nodded, as did several others nearby. "We will."

She and the other concubines slowly turned and exited up the levels to their sleeping quarters beyond.

Bael and Leianna left Az's harem, closing the brass doors behind themselves, the two brass demonic guards watching them as they emerged. The first one asked, "What are your orders, Majesty?"

Leianna looked up at both. "Guard these women. Let no men enter unless I have authorized them to do so."

The second guard asked hesitantly, "Not even the royal princes or the Emperor Lucifer?"

"Not even them," Leianna reiterated. "And Lucifer is no longer in charge of Hell." She cupped her hands, palms up, and a glow formed inside of them. The intense light was reflected in the demon's eyes, changing the red light within them to a burning gold. The melted hand of the second demon reformed itself, becoming whole again.

It inclined its head in compliance. The first demon said, "We will obey," and they took up their positions again.

She and Bael walked back to his suites. Once inside, he kissed her, leading her back to his bed, throwing off his clothes and boots, climbing under the cover. He leaned back against a pillow, but Leianna took her time undressing, joining him. She sat up in the bed. "You didn't offer me much input or help during all of that chaos. In fact, most of the time, you stayed pretty quiet."

Bael put his hands behind his head and stretched. "I didn't have to. I let you do your new job, and you were doing it quite well on your own."

She slid down on the bed, facing him, pulling the cover snugly around her. "Was I?"

She pondered this, wondering if his confidence was really justified. The only weapon she had in this realm was her faith and the help of those who loved her. She could feel her power, but she wondered. Would it be enough?

His arm went around her. "Yes, you were. Doing very well."

"The only thing still bothering me is that Az seems to have gone unpunished in any serious way. I mean, sending him to his room doesn't fit his crime. Something more should be done, even if he is a royal prince of Hell."

"Still angry?"

"Yes!"

"I'll take care of it personally," Bael assured her. "After all, he's my brother, and I'll handle it as a family matter."

16

Council Meetings and Lucifer's Farewell

It surprised Leianna when she woke up astrally in Hell the next morning. And then she found that it was very early in the morning, approximately 4:00 A.M. The alarm clock on her dresser in her bedroom on Earth wouldn't buzz until 6:30 A.M. there. Being that time moved three times as fast astrally, she had the equivalent of seven and a half hours here before waking up physically.

Bael had awakened her, saying, "Get up, Leianna. My father is summoning us and all of Hell to the Throne Room."

"At this hour?"

"There are very few hours available where you won't be pulled back to your mortal body and the priority of your mortal life. But you have to be present to witness Lucifer's abdication of and your ascension to the throne of Hell. And all of my father's councilors must see you ascend to it and know that Lucifer has allowed your replacement of him as sovereign."

She slowly asked, "And this will make it all right with them?"

Bael remained silent for a minute, then sighed with an air of uncertainty and said, "You have to face them, Leianna. The High Council of Hell. Not all of them will be pleased with this abrupt regime change, which places a 29-year-old mortal woman of no particular distinction other than being God's chosen advocate and appointee to Hell at its helm. They found God's ways incomprehensible 35,000 years ago during the Fall. They're not really good with the Creator's mysteries and this may represent a brand new one beyond their comprehension."

She nodded. "So what do I do?"

He thought about it. "Act as if you're going to need their help, instruction and advice, because you will, and offer to reward them as soon as you find the means to."

She considered that. "In other words, let them know that I need them on my team."

"Exactly. But make them know it's *your* team, that you're the leader."

She shook her head. "No. It's *our* team, yours and mine, Bael. You're second-in-command here, your father's erstwhile heir. I'll need your clout to give myself ballast, or else this ship is going to sink."

He stared at her; she felt his approval. "Get dressed." He

pointed to her green winter gown draped on the chair. "It won't do to be late." She slipped on the gown and her shoes as he dressed himself, pulling more formal attire from his dresser drawers: black pants and suit jacket, dark blue shirt, a tie of blue and gold, black socks and shoe boots. Everything flawless and shiny as if freshly laundered and pressed.

"Why didn't you just think your dress clothes onto yourself?"

He grinned. "I could have. I could even have called a manservant to dress me. But I like having you watch me." He held out his hands, striking a pose. "How do I look, babe?"

"Like a male in great need of domesticity."

"Baby will make three." He offered her his arm. "Shall we?"

She slipped her arm around his. "Lead on to the throne room, your Majesty, and let's get this show started."

Lucifer sat stiffly, filled with misgivings, upon his throne. Above him, in the left and right balconies, his twelve subcommanders, comprising the High Council of Hell, were seating themselves and their families into their private boxes, six on each side. But this was not a normal council meeting Lucifer had abruptly called.

He could feel the alarm, the palpable tension in the throne room, as if some telepathic grapevine had informed his councilors of the extraordinary agreement he and Leianna had signed under Heaven's auspices, and of the chaotic restructuring it would force upon his people. He must explain it to them in some manner that would bridge the gap between his rule and Leianna's. He must not allow them, not even in the slightest way, to accuse him of abandoning them. Yet he knew, initially, some would.

Seeing Eliom again had shocked and blinded his judgment, its light slaking his centuries' old thirst for redemption, and so he had signed, especially knowing his eldest sons would also be overseeing Hell's reformation, and trusting them as a father must.

But he had not immediately considered his followers — those who had lived through the Fall and the creation of Hell during those long centuries, building it in all ways, physically, economically, psychologically and, yes, philosophically, for religion was really a philosophy to deal with the concepts of good and evil. His followers had no promise of release from Hell. He must address this and rectify it. His leave-taking must champion their own hope for their release from Heliom. He could not betray his people for his own betterment.

The lower floor of the wide room was packed with those officials, courtiers and palace staff he had privileged with a summons to this meeting. The press corps, for Hell now had its own news media empire, now gathered in the wide central balcony just above the heavy throne room doors, their equipment hastily set up as they waited for the scoop. They seemed as perplexed as Lucifer's councilors. Except for possibly one — Horace Pearleigh.

Horace had the curious advantage of resembling Bael so closely that they were often mistaken for each other at a short distance. But Horace's face held sharper angles, looked craggier, less pretty-boy handsome. Bael looked sensual, Horace, more intellectual. The resemblance had cemented a close friendship between them; Bael often leaked information to Horace, but the truth was that Horace was an ace newsman and could be trusted to present an accurate, nonbiased report of any event.

Bael had discussed the goal of the Alliance with Horace before. Horace's editorial on it had expressed optimism for the idea but questioned its practicality between two realms with little in common. Had Bael told him that Heaven was finally horning in on Hell, and that he, Lucifer, would be given the ultimate reward for relinquishing his rule in the land of his exile? Tomorrow's headlines would be made tonight.

On his left, the private, side door on the dais level, leading to and from the royal quarters, was opened by Lucifer's personal guards, allowing the royal family to enter. Lucifer gestured to another guard at his right, who worked some wall switches. Sections of the dais floor slid back and secondary throne chairs of simple design rose up, locking into place, on the dais, three to Lucifer's right and one to his left.

Affaeteres took the seat to his right and Azmodeus and Ashtoreth took the other right-hand chairs. Azmodeus had purple bruises on his face, the right side of his lip swollen, but there was no reason to ask him what fight he'd gotten into. His face would heal.

Bael stood before the chair to Lucifer's left, and Leianna stood to his left. Both looked regal and serene, but Lucifer could feel their apprehension. His mind raced to seek the best opening to explain what he must to his councilors and people. He watched Bael seat Leianna in his place upon the throne chair and move to stand behind her. Bael gazed at Lucifer, waiting.

Lucifer rose, facing the throng of wary Heliomese.

"My people, I have called you here to explain the unforeseen events of the last few hours and the tremendous impact it will have on Hell."

He could feel their shock, hear the buzz of whispers that arose, as he continued. "I did not believe it possible. You may not remember, but our Creator made it clear that I, as the author of the war in Heaven, could only be released from exile if a pure soul who had experienced mortality would rule Hell in my stead, willingly, out of pity for the damned. That would prove that a mortal could equal an angel in empathy and reverence to our Creator and therefore be fit for Heaven . . . and prove my own disdain for mortals wrong. Such a mortal is among us tonight, and although she was originally one of us in Eliom — an angel — she did not disobey our Creator, and she incarnated countless times as a mortal after we refused to help the mortals and were exiled from Eliom. Many of you knew her as Leianna — and still do. Leianna, will you stand, please?"

He watched her glance up at Bael. He nodded. She stood uncertainly, gazing at Lucifer and outward to the assembled Heliomese.

"Leianna is my son Baelzebub's wife, as well as the wife of Terence Dearborn, a classical composer from the upper planes from Heaven. My eldest son Ashtoreth, and my second son Baelzebub . . . who was originally named Bael in Eliom, before he was damned and briefly went into the exterminating business in Phoenicia and Babylon . . ." (he waited for the burst of laughter to fade), "have been permitted to visit the heavens — the present Eliom — long before last night, when I was briefly returned to the Shore of the Seraphim.

"Those of you who fell with me will remember what sat on that shore: the Well of Being, emitting the vapors of immortality from its shaft, where we at birth and our children after us received our Creator's blessing and instruction on our Naming Days. The vapors had ceased rising from the Well during that contention which led to that final rift between the angelfolk and our punishment.

"Tonight, when I returned to that shore, I saw that the Well had been restored, its vapors of longevity rising from the shaft again. And the sunset glowed upon the gold-flecked foam on the Seraphic Sea. I was told, if I allowed Leianna to govern Hell, to replace me as that pure soul, and if we allowed her to create an Alliance between Hell and Heaven, that I would be released from my exile and be permitted to champion your own eventual release from Heliom, should you wish it."

Chaos broke out among his listeners, and he heard Leianna say, "That's not exactly what the agreement says!"

He spoke brusquely to her, his voice lowered. "Do not dispute me. I am trying to smooth the way for you, and I do intend to champion their return to Eliom."

Leianna hissed back: "As does Heaven, Father Lucifer, but that release doesn't rest in your hands, but their own, after the Alliance begins."

Lucifer leaned closer to her, his anger rising. "Allow me the luxury of appointing myself as their champion, after 35,000 years as their leader, girl!" She stepped backward away from him, but said nothing more as Mammon's voice thundered from the left balcony.

"Why is our release *eventual* and yours imminent, Lucifer? Are you being rewarded for throwing Heliom into the lap of this woman? Are you a rat deserting his shipmates for a better shore?" He stood indignantly, his quivering bulk half-hidden by the balcony box, dressed ostentatiously in velvet and satin, his blond hair a mass of waves, his broad face florid.

In the box beyond his, Phoenixious, still seeming a slender, flaxen-haired young man, stood as well and upbraided Mammon. "How dare you speak to Lucifer as if you were his superior! He is our commander, our Emperor. He would not force any changes onto Hell without the High Council's approval unless circumstances forced his hand." Phoenixious leaned over the balcony, pointing directly at Leianna. "You, woman, explain yourself, the role you expect to play in Hell, and our Lord Lucifer's expectations in Heaven if this Alliance is to be forced upon us."

Leianna merely stared up at the youngest councilor of Hell, as others shouted recriminations of disloyalty, desertion and abandonment, and others still shouted at the accusers to let Lucifer speak, for surely he had not, at their expense, bargained for his freedom from Hell. Still more shouted that there was no freedom under the Creator's thumb, a Creator who exiled those who disobeyed Heaven's unreasonable demands. Lucifer saw Leianna's fear, the look of confusion on her face.

"I will not abandon you!" Lucifer shouted above the chaos, his voice heard. The roar about him died down to muttering and murmurs. "I am going to oversee this Alliance, but from Heaven's portals, and Leianna will be here as my representative, ruling not alone but in conjunction with my sons, who will remain as your princes and form a triumvirate."

Azmodeus quickly cut in, "I wouldn't return to Heaven if you paid me! So I still rule, Father?"

Lucifer said, under his breath, "I heard about your surgical play tonight! If you value this world as you say, listen silently and let me shape this night's meeting as it needs to be shaped."

Instead Az screamed, "I am Prince Azmodeus!" His voice carried over the once-again rising tumult. "And I will never abandon you! Hear my Father out!"

Lucifer glared at him, but Az had turned his face pointedly away. Lucifer glanced instead at Bael. He knew his second-born son was both loved and feared by the Heliomese. Leianna had little idea of the ruthlessness Bael could display; she only saw the youth she had loved as he had been in Eliom.

Bael took Lucifer's signal and strode to the front of the dais. The crowd, including the councilors in the balconies, quieted again and listened to him, knowing Bael — more formally, Lord Bael-zebub — was second-in-command and had been acknowledged heir to Lucifer's throne in the event of any leave-taking. Lucifer knew, in declaring his sons a triumvirate, that a single heir was now invalid. Let Bael fight for supremacy. Lucifer had no intention of making things too easy for Leianna. He sat back on his throne to hear what Hell's most popular prince had to say.

Having achieved silence, Bael addressed the councilors: "I call upon the High Council of Hell to understand that change is sometimes unavoidable. Tonight's events were not truly sudden. They have been building for years, ever since the Creator, communicating through the Seraphim and Heaven's spirit masters, realized that the genetic restructuring of mankind to repair the damage from interbreeding through Eve and Adam, was nearly completed. And when it is complete, further incarnation by the angelfolk now being born as Earthly mortals will be unnecessary. The incarnated angelfolk will be able to return, after mortal death, to their eternal bodies and identities and return home permanently to Eliom. And due to this, when this happens, there will be no further reason to continue to punish those who refused the incarnations, since the problem will be resolved. The Heliomese people will be permitted release from Hell, if they will follow Heaven's rules in the future."

Bael paused, running his glance around the balconies, making eye contact with each of the twelve councilors: beautiful Naamah; the slight, effeminate Chemosh; darkly handsome Lothan; black-skinned and lofty Cimeries; swarthy, wheedling Adrammelech; fat, pouting Mammon; the poetic but sensible Phoenixious; the bear-like Nergal, always reliable and reasonable; the ugly and skinny Moloch who was immovably loyal to Lucifer; the fallen spirit master Dagon, who relished the punishment of mortals; Belial, weasily and bland, except in his enjoyment of vice; and Behemoth, a corpulent tower of flesh and muscle who always believed any threat to Hell would emerge from the mysterious Sea of Mists on the seventh and lowest level of Hell. All of them returned Bael's glance, waiting anxiously, some perhaps reluctantly, for him to explain further.

"If you will follow Heaven's rules," Bael repeated. "But not all of you may wish to do that. Perhaps you wish to stay in Hell and help it build its new day, for change, I repeat, is inevitable. Heaven intends to reform Hell, and its goal is to redeem the lost souls, both highborn and low, and you and I must remain here to demand our rights and have our say in this reforming of Hell! Do you have any questions?"

Dagon stood up in the middle right balcony, stick-thin and bald, sharp-eyed and sharp with his tongue. Lucifer knew why he had chosen to oversee the punishment planes as his job, his calling; he held all mortals responsible for the angelic fall. "How can Heaven save souls that are already damned, Prince Baelzebub?"

Looking directly up at Dagon, Bael gestured to Leianna and said, "Answer him."

Leianna gulped visibly, opening her mouth, from which nothing emerged. She took a deep breath, and finally told Dagon, "They're going to reform them."

Dagon crossed his skinny arms. "How?"

"By . . . by psychological and behavioral therapy." Her voice barely carried despite the silence now in the throne room.

"And if they refuse to respond to this?"

Leianna swallowed hard. "Well, maybe they'll have to stay here until they *are* healed of their negative behavior."

Dagon nodded. "Feel free to engage my services, young lady, when their behavior becomes too hot for you to handle. I am in charge of the fifth level of Hell, the punishment planes, and there we use methods that never fail to make the damned regret their *negative behavior*. Not that regret ever gains them a reprieve." He slowly sat down, his black eyes piercing and challenging.

Nergal stood in his box, one forward of Dagon's. "Bael," he addressed him informally, "do you approve of this?"

Bael placed his arm around Leianna. "As you love your wife, Nergal, so do I, mine. But she has been asked to fulfill our Creator's new plans and take on the immensity of our people's needs, and the needs of the lost souls, damned to our world for both real and imagined sins, based on the arbitrary and often archaic dictates of mortal religions. She has been asked to rule, judge and, in her own way, be as a mother to our people, here by choice or by circumstance, and she has willingly agreed to this. Why? Not only because she loves me and wishes to change the world I live in for the better, but because, she tells me, no soul should be forever damned. She believes that each soul should, at some point in eternity, naturally progress toward understanding and resolve whatever conflict originally caused it to commit its sin.

"Do I approve of her faith, of her willingness to steer Hell at its helm? What would I gain by disapproving? The status quo? The status quo separates us from the rest of the dimensional universe. I vote for controlled change."

Nergal nodded. "Then I will stand behind you. And Lucifer, you tell us this is an agreement already executed?"

Lucifer stood up. "Yes. Leianna and I signed the agreement, which was carried back to Eliom, for housing in the Hall of Seraphic Records. My wife Affaeteres and I will be leaving tomorrow. I have created a separate document, my last legal proclamation, appointing my sons as a royal triumvirate, with Bael overseeing government affairs, Ashtoreth regulating treasury and financial matters, and Azmodeus overseeing military matters, to be tempered and advised by the wisdom of the High Council, of course, which shall remain in charge of the trusts I originally bestowed upon them."

Naamah, the only woman councilor, stood on the far right balcony. Lucifer watched Horace lean toward her from the press box. Naamah, her black hair neatly pulled into an upsweep, attired sedately in black and gold, quietly asked Lucifer: "And Leianna? What is her legal status in Hell when you leave? Is she our Empress now? Shall we bow to her and obey her every whim?"

"Leianna," said Lucifer, "will you answer Naamah? I don't truly know the answer. Only you do."

The two women looked at each other across the throne room. "Naamah, I am not your Empress," Leianna said. "I choose to be your Queen, with Bael by my side, if not as your King in fact, at least as my King in my heart. I have been told that I will take Lucifer's place. I suppose that makes me your ruler, and perhaps my ability to rule will come from my own strength and Heaven's guidance at times. Perhaps my ability to rule will at other times be based upon the assistance and good advice of the royal triumvirate and the High Council. I will depend on all of those factors, on all of you, and both Bael and Ashtoreth shall act as my personal advisors. I shall strive to be a fair queen, a queen who loves her people and seeks to heal their hurts and fulfill their goals and visions. But you ask if you must obey me? I would say only if by not obeying me you would harm yourself or another. Then you *must* obey me. In all other things, I would expect my councilors to exercise intelligence and wisdom and even offer suggestions through which I may improve my leadership."

Naamah considered her words, then said, "With Lucifer's approval, I suggest the High Council vote on these extraordinary changes, a vote of confidence, with majority deciding whether to accept Leianna's ascension as Queen of Hell, or to dispute her, with further deliberations as to what her legal status should be, regardless of her marriage to Lord Baelzebub."

Lucifer shrugged, feigning nonchalance. "Vote, then, and I will exercise my right to serve as tie breaker, should you split evenly. I have my own opinions as to Leianna's potential as your ruler, but speak your minds first now, and my appointed scribe will record the results. Horace?" He gestured to the newsman, who nodded and produced a pad and pen to write down the results, knowing a transcript of this meeting in whole would be faithfully produced and provided for the palace records. Lucifer would ask Bael to send Horace a copy. "Naamah, we will start with you."

"I vote for Leianna's acceptance. I do not believe that *she* will remain unchanged in Hell, but perhaps that will be for the better."

"Chemosh?"

"Oh, dear." He glanced at Naamah. "I vote yes. For Leianna."

"Lothan?"

"She carries Bael's child, who my daughter Sharlan tells me is also the soul of my long lost grandson Nikki, and she has also offered Sharlan the sincere promise of friendship." The murmurs about the throne room rose audibly at this. "I vote for Leianna's acceptance."

"Cimeries?"

"Yes. For Leianna."

"Adrammelech."

"Oh, well, I can't see what harm she can do. Yes."

"Mammon?"

"I am displeased by everything that has occurred tonight. The Creator is once again manipulating our lives, even in Hell. I vote no. We do not need this queen. Let her please Bael and leave the rest of us alone."

Lucifer nodded. "Phoenixious then."

"I vote . . . despite reservations . . . for Leianna."

"Nergal?"

"I will accept her as our queen, as she has described her role."

"Moloch?"

"I vote nay. No doubt she will close down Sin City Mall on the fourth level, and no one will get their proper due or have any fun. And I do not accept her in your place, my Lord Lucifer. If necessary, I will be loyal to you from afar, if you truly must leave Hell for Heaven. Work not for my release from Hell, but from my release from this woman's interference, for I dread it."

Again, Lucifer nodded, acknowledging his dissent. "Dagon then?"

"Again, my trust is the punishment planes and the retribution visited on the mortal sinners on whom I blame the destruction of Eliom as we once knew her. And yet Leianna wishes to reform Hell and heal damnation. I must vote against Leianna, a poor, misguided female, used by a Creator who would use us again as well."

Lucifer paused. Dagon's refusal would be the biggest roadblock in Leianna's path; even with the Creator's approval, there would be hell to pay. "Belial."

"She won't mess with me on the sixth level. Too primitive. But I don't wish to antagonize Lord Baelzebub, and I'm sure he will advise her and temper her judgment. And so, tentatively, also with due reservation, I vote yes. I will accept her, for no doubt, my dear, you will find that you can't change Hell overnight."

Lucifer wondered if he remembered how headstrong Leianna had been before Heaven's war. If not, Belial need only view the painting below, of Leianna literally aflame, attempting to reach Bael through an invisible electric barrier before Bael was taken from her, cast out of Heaven with Lucifer and his followers. "And finally, Behemoth. How do you vote?"

"I am both glad and saddened, Lord Lucifer, that the Creator's challenge to you, so long ago in Eliom, has been met. I control the seventh, most desolate level, of Hell, bordered by the Sea of Mists, from which no one has ever returned. There may be more danger from what lurks inside those mists than from a young woman attempting to reform a world she has little experience in. I suggest that Lord Baelzebub keep her safe and under reasonable control, that she does not damage that which she does not understand and make things worse, not better. Aside from that, I see no reason why she cannot wear a crown and attempt to mother the lost denizens of Hell. Every girl wishes to be a princess or a queen, and I don't believe the Creator's intent will always match her own. I vote for approval and hope that you have chosen the right path and will continue to champion our cause, as you say, in Heaven. Tell the Creator we have survived."

Lucifer quietly told him: "I shall." He looked toward Horace in the press box. "What is our tally?"

"Nine votes of confidence for Leianna. Three votes of no confidence. Leianna wins."

Lucifer allowed himself a silent moment of relief and offered Leianna his hand. She took it briefly, and moved to stand between him and Bael. Lucifer waved toward the center balcony. "Thank you, Horace. Leianna, allow me to introduce you to and explain a bit about your councilors, while I'm still here. Responsibility among my subcommanders here, after we conquered and structured Hell, was based on *trusts,* the appointing of my subcommanders to oversee Hell's seven levels and also the lands that make up this first level of Hell. I and my sons, and now *you* and my sons will rule all of Heliom, but our capitol is Domain, which means law giver. The other lands on this top level surrounding Lei Lello or Star Lake are governed by the following trustees:

"Gollame, which means Night Flower, is jointly governed by Naamah and Chemosh, because it is a large territory. Allonia, or Sea Home, is entrusted to Lothan. Keth, which means courage, also a large land, is entrusted to Cimeries and Adrammelech, while Absaliom, which means Forgotten Land, is entrusted to Mammon.

"Both Keth and Absaliom border Domain. You do not want to irritate their trustees.

"The levels below the first are governed as follows:

"Phoenixious is trustee to the second level, which has farms and orchards, as well as the Great Lakes, fed by Lei Lello above; they are Hope Lake, Lake Endurance, Hidden Lake and Lake Blessing. Phoenixious enjoys life there, living in a large estate bordering a forest, which appeals to his poetic nature.

"Nergal, with his wife Shadella, is entrusted with the third level and governs the Talaperi and Teleperi natives of that level. Nergal also manages the third level industries: mining in the mountains, fishing in its lakes, wood in its forests, and some crops grown on the Plains of Taleth.

"Moloch governs the fourth level. The Sin City Mall actually serves the damned living and working on that level. It also houses the dwellings of the demons and the damned, and also holds our prisons and military barracks.

"Dagon governs the fifth level of Hell, the punishment planes where we create physical, mental and practical means of retribution. It also holds factories worked by slave labor comprised of the lost souls. It also has charming natural landscapes: deserts with quicksand and rocky slopes dotted with volcanoes. Interestingly, Dagon, as my first subcommander, was given first choice of any trust he wanted. He chose the fifth level, as unappealing as it is, because he believes, as he said, that punishing mortals is the greatest calling, because they caused the war in Heaven and divided the angels.

"As Belial said, he governs the sixth level. It is indeed primitive, the empty level described to you as the one the fallen angelfolk first arrived here on, with volcanoes, salt marshes, swamps and sparse land. Belial likes his privacy and has created a large oasis with a forced water system for himself and his workers controlling this level. The saurs still live and work there, and it's also used as a punishment plane. But don't go visiting him without Bael. Belial is a man who likes his vice and you might be highly offended." He glanced at Belial. The short, skinny man offered him a wry smile, as if he approved of Lucifer's warning.

"Behemoth again controls the seventh and bottom level of Hell, a place of frozen wastes, icy glaciers, steppes, cold sands and tundra, all of which border a mysterious Sea of Mists, as if Hell were a seven-layered island sitting in the middle of this sea. It's true that no one who has ever ventured into the Sea of Mists of the seventh level has ever returned, and Behemoth is both fascinated and worried by those mists, wondering what lies within them, where they lead to, and why no one has entered that white sea and returned. Behemoth patrols its frigid beaches, concerned that something might emerge from those mists that could threaten Hell. Nonetheless, he maintains a huge, lavish residence on these empty lands, devoid of all life except for some small stinging insects near the steppes. He says he likes the silence; it quiets the cries of the damned. Of course, they can also be quiet when the seventh level is used as a punishment plane. Without protective clothing, the extreme cold eventually freezes its victims into silence.

"And so, these are your councilors, Leianna, each of them helping you to rule Hell along with my sons. And my advice to you is to proceed slowly with this Alliance. Give my people — your people — time to acclimate themselves to any changes you propose."

"A challenge, my Lord Lucifer!" Dagon had called it out.

"A challenge, Dagon?"

"For Leianna. I will accept her as queen in your stead if . . . she can make Adolf Hitler shed tears over his murder of the Jews in World War II."

Leianna reacted with distaste and horror. "Then Hitler is really here?"

Dagon wryly and loudly asked her: "Where else did you expect him to be, Leianna?"

Lucifer hoped that Leianna would respond carefully to Dagon's challenge, but doubted her ability to answer it. "He's housed in a prison cell on the sixth level when Dagon isn't putting him through various torments on the fifth level. Well? What shall we say to Dagon's challenge?"

"I . . . I don't know! Facing Hitler?!!"

An unexpected, gentle voice intervened. "She will accept."

Lucifer turned to his right to see Quatama, who had appeared suddenly on the dais.

Quatama held up three virtual reenactment hoops. "It is time for Adolf to walk part of a lifetime in his victim's shoes."

Leianna asked him. "What do those V-Re-E hoops relive?"

"Your previous life in Lódž, Poland until your death in Auschwitz."

"I have to relive it?"

"And Hitler will relive it also. It is necessary that you remember these events, using them as a catalyst to break through his denial, and you yourself have suffered emotional denial when dealing with Holocaust memories. Perhaps it will move Hitler to experience your fear, misery and terror. But you must also finally purge yourself of those hurts from your past.

"And Dagon," he addressed the fallen spirit master in the balcony, "you must come to see how Heaven begins a reformation and to possibly witness Hitler's tears."

Bael pointed. "Quatama, you have three hoops. All the same lifetime?"

"Yes. For three people to experience it simultaneously, Bael."

"One for Leianna, one for Hitler. Who is the third hoop for?"

"For you, of course. To understand what Leianna suffered through and to help her face it and resolve it."

Lucifer nodded and then turned to the assembly. "This meeting is adjourned until this challenge has been met, upon which I will reconvene and announce the results. Await my call."

The heavy steel doors slid open. Quatama, Leianna, Bael, Lucifer, and Dagon entered the nearly bare cell. Horace Pearleigh and his cameraman entered behind them.

Adolf Hitler looked up from the stool he sat on in the center of his cell, his face twisting with fear as Dagon slowly approached him. "No, please," Hitler murmured. "No more torturing, no more pain! I should not be here. I am innocent. I was trying to cleanse my country of its vermin. I am not evil! I should not be in Hell!"

Lucifer saw the look of confusion on Leianna's face, for Hitler spoke in German and yet all understood his words. "All languages are understood astrally through the universal mind which your soul can instantly access, Leianna. I'm surprised that Quatama never explained that to you."

Leianna shook her head. "I never understood German before. So I've turned on a universal translator? Will I recall this knowledge tomorrow?"

"Not in German; it's used when it's needed. Each soul hears the language it needs to hear. So, Adolf, you were just cleaning up Germany and your other conquests of its Jews and other undesirables, eh?"

Hitler studied him warily, cornered prey waiting for the pounce. Dagon asked him bluntly: "Do you regret killing all of those Jews?"

Hitler's expression smoothed itself out, looking blank and confused, and then he sneered. "Why should I regret that? Jews, homosexuals, gypsies, all vermin. How can you judge me for that? They should be in Hell! I should be in Heaven!"

Dagon told him, "You are going to sit here quietly and do as you're told."

An attendant brought extra chairs into the cell; Bael and Leianna sat in two of them. Quatama handed each of them a hoop, then stood before Hitler. "I am going to put this hoop on your head. It will allow you to experience part of another person's life as if it were your own. When this experience is over, you will awaken and can remove the hoop. Do you understand?"

Hitler nodded. "Will it torture me?"

"That is up to you." Quatama said and told Bael and Leianna, "Place your hoops on after I have put his on him."

Lucifer watched him lower the hoop onto Hitler's head, the front resting on his forehead. Bael and Leianna did the same. All three shut their eyes, already reenacting Leianna's previous lifetime.

Dagon asked, "How long will this take?"

Quatama told him, "Time is condensed on the hoop. What will seem like months to them will be only minutes for us. Nonetheless, we should also be comfortable while we wait." He waved his hand toward the chairs. They all sat except for the cameraman, recording Bael, Leianna and Adolf, ready to zoom in with a close-up of Hitler when he awoke, to see if he would cry.

Horace said, "It's a shame we can't see what they're reliving. I'd like to write about it while reporting this."

Quatama inclined his head. "Then with Leianna's approval, I will send you a video with a condensed version on it. You can describe the events as you see fit for your newspaper and hopefully Leianna's triumph over this challenge as well."

"I'd appreciate that, Quatama. From what I'm seeing, it appears that the Alliance has already begun in Hell."

17

Lódž Ghetto, Poland, *Hannah Liebmann, and Hitler's Tears*

"Work will save us." She whispered Chaim Rumkowski's maxim, as she worked the metal wheel of the sewing machine, her fingers numb. The Jews of the Litzmannstadt ghetto in Lódž, Poland looked to Rumkowski to save them through forced labor for the Nazis' war.

She couldn't believe it. The harassed ghetto chairman's lips spoke the Nazi lies. But the Jews of Lódž ghetto were not blind to those who were *not* saved.

Hannah forced herself to keep the wheel turning. The needle clicked on, stitching the pattern, brown thread running along the treadle, the huge black wheel catching and securing it into the tight seams of a Nazi uniform. As were the people of Lódž trapped by the Nazi machine. Everyone 14 years of age and older had to work, Rumkowski had declared. All others, too young or too old, he "trusted to God."

Hannah pushed the wheel with her right hand, guiding the patterned cloth along with her left. Hunger and anger weakened her. Last year in 1942, the textile mill in the Litzmannstadt ghetto had been built from salvaged and cannibalized equipment and parts in an abandoned factory. But work was not saving them. Workers out sick from hunger and exhaustion lost their daily food allocation. New shipments of Jews arrived in Lódž, as others were deported. Children were torn from their mothers; no one knew where they were taken.

At the end of May that year, truckloads of baggage arrived in the ghetto, filled with discarded clothing, bedding, and prayer shawls, as well as papers, personal items and ghetto currency. No one came forward to claim them. Women wearing sterile white uniforms and head coverings were set to the task of disinfecting anything reusable.

On September 1, 1942, German soldiers attacked a hospital, hauling its patients onto trucks for transport, as panicked relatives sought their loved ones in the hospital and were blocked in the street by the Jewish police. Small children had been thrown from the hospital windows into the trucks, both their screams and injuries ignored. Some Jews had fought and were forcibly removed. Anyone fleeing was shot.

Then, on September 4, 1942, the Nazis demanded that 24,000 of the ghetto's elderly and children up to age 10 be deported. Chaim Rumkowski had fought this. 20,000 were still demanded. "Give into my hands the victims," he had cried out in an anguished voice. "Hand them over to me . . . and a population of 100,000 Jews will be preserved!"

Hannah wondered if the whole world had gone mad or only her part of it. Work quotas, deportations, negotiations. Her head swam with hunger, fear, and despair. In December of 1942, Hannah's young sister Mina had been saved from this horror by their father paying two loaves of bread and a kilogram of sugar to a man who sent his own daughter instead, using Mina's name. Now, a year later, Mina was failing, malnourished and sickly. Only seven years old. The daily food ration had become so small, many people looked almost skeletal. The violence, selection committees and deportations continued. The rumor that the deported children had been resettled in gardened orphanages was not believed. One month ago, in November 1943, the Germans had put other ghetto Jews to work making armaments. As 1944 approached, the people were desperate, angry and praying for a miracle. Hannah leaned wearily against her sewing machine, giving in, letting tears flow.

Irene had been meeting her work quota, sewing quietly beside Hannah, when her friend slumped forward. Irene looked about them; the other women pretended not to notice. Irene quickly squeezed the girl's thin shoulder. "Hannah! You mustn't show weakness!"

"No weakness?" Hannah's amber brown eyes were luminous, wet, her pupils enlarged, darting. "They are killing us! We are not surviving!" She grabbed the fabric of the uniform she'd been sewing, the needle still depressed in the treadle, and ripped the cloth backward violently. The needle broke, the top half of it hanging jaggedly in the machine.

Hannah stood, slowly opened her hand and let the ruined sleeve fall. "We are dying," she said. "If I must die, let me do it with dignity."

Irene looked at the broken needle, the ruined uniform, at Hannah's sallow complexion, her hollow cheeks and slackened mouth. Her light brown hair fell in unkempt strands to her neck, in need of washing. Then she spoke again, her voice in the machinated hum of the drab brown factory hall, sounding faint and hoarse: "First they take our children, then our elders. This will *save* us, Rumkowski says. A sacrifice, he tells us, to save some of us. How many sacrifices more? Where do they go? And what of the sacrifices here?" She wavered, clutching the edge of the chair to steady herself. "What of Mina? And the children that were taken? Where were they really taken?!"

Irene stared, frozen. Part of her said, *Go back to your work. Ignore Hannah. She has gone mad.* But she could not move. Her mouth opened minutely, but fear closed it. *One movement in the wrong direction will destroy us!*

She heard the noisy clacking of the other machines, the creak of the steam driving the factory's power. The other women ignored them.

Irene didn't turn to see if the supervisor was watching. She grabbed Hannah's hand and pulled her harshly down, nearly knocking her back into her seat, whispering frantically. "Bend over your machine! Pretend to work! When the supervisor comes, tell her the machine broke by itself! Pretend!"

She immediately went back to her own sewing, head bent to the task. She pulled her coat more tightly around her for warmth, emotionally and physically, its stars of David proclaiming "JUDE" sewn onto both its front and back. Her eyes darted peripherally to Hannah.

The girl sat senseless beside her. Then she rose again unsteadily. "No," Hannah said. She pulled her own worn coat on tiredly, and began walking away. But her legs weakened, stumbling into a fall.

Irene bolted from her chair, running to her, barely catching her. Irene's arm held and supported her as they moved toward the exit. "I will take her home!" she shouted to the other women, but their faces were masked. Perhaps she and Hannah would be permitted to return to work tomorrow. Today was gone; it was nearly quitting time. Perhaps they would be reprimanded, nothing more.

She helped Hannah through the bitter winter weather to her family's four-room flat on Bryzinska Street.

There was no fuel for heating and cooking, and the cold, for many, was more painful than hunger. Mrs. Liebmann helped her faint daughter and Irene into the chilled apartment, listening with little emotion as Irene told of Hannah's breakdown at the factory. Devora Liebmann herself had just returned from the food distribution center and the community kitchen, using the daily half hour allotted to each family to heat weak potato soup and carry it home. The Nazis sent frozen or spoiled vegetables into the ghetto — the Jews salvaged what they could — better ruined vegetables than none at all. But too often, there were none, and the bread which the ghetto baked became its only nutrition and little of that was to be had.

Hannah and Irene sat at the small square kitchen table as Mrs. Liebmann spooned the lukewarm soup into bowls for them.

"You do not have to feed me, Mrs. Liebmann. You barely have enough. Especially with Mina. . . ."

Mrs. Liebmann's look reprimanded her. She set the small bowl down firmly in front of Irene, a single piece of potato bobbing within its broth. "Eat. It will warm you." She set a second bowl in front of Hannah. "You, too. No sneaking it into Mina."

"Mina has to survive." Hannah spoke for the first time since leaving the factory.

"Mina is asleep. And she could not keep what little food I gave her down today. You have given enough; you are skin and bones yourself."

Irene was twenty, four years older than Hannah. They had met at the textile factory in early '42, after Irene and her brother had been sent to work there, following their arrival from the provinces. Their parents were dead, victims of street violence. They had been deported into Lódž and lived two side streets down in a two-room flat. Irene's friendship with Hannah had blossomed in defiance of a callous world, in the hope that time would save them from it.

"Hannah, eat," Irene said, gesturing with her spoon.

Hannah spooned a mouthful of the broth and drank it. She broke off a small piece of potato, chewing and swallowing it. Together they ate in silence. Mrs. Liebmann gave them each a small slice of bread and a cup of tea. Hannah broke her slice in half, eating one piece; Irene ate the whole slice greedily and sipped at the cold unsweetened beverage.

"I'll bring you something special tomorrow, Mrs. Liebmann. We have a little bit of sugar."

Devora Liebmann seemed to hesitate then nodded.

Hannah put her spoon down. "Please, Mama, let me try to give Mina this bread. She may be awake now."

Her mother closed her eyes then opened them. Irene saw that her clothes had become too large for her. Mrs. Liebmann nodded once again, saying, "If she is sleeping, don't wake her."

"I won't, Mama."

Hannah and Irene made their way into the small bedroom Hannah shared with her sister. It held a bureau, a small lamp and their beds. Pictures of ballet dancers were tacked onto one wall.

Mina was awake, breathing shallowly on her small cot in the far corner. Two blankets were bundled about her. She stared silently at

Hannah and Irene.

Hannah stroked the rings of sweat-dampened brown hair on Mina's forehead. "Here. I have brought you a bit of bread."

Mina stared at the offered half-slice and shook her head. "I can't," she murmured.

"All right."

A knock sounded from beyond the room. Irene glanced at Hannah. Mina had drifted back to sleep. From the living room, they heard her mother speaking briefly to someone at the door, then silence.

Mrs. Liebmann met them in the kitchen, holding slips of paper in her hand, her face stiff and drained.

"We are being deported, Hannah. We must be at the train yard at eight o'clock tomorrow morning."

Hannah grasped Irene's arm, fixing frightened eyes upon her and her mother. "What will we do about Mina? The Germans have no record of her still being here."

"We will think of something," her mother said. "Thank God they did not come in and force us to leave now. They would have discovered Mina. It would have gone badly for us then." Her voice sank to a whisper. "Your father will be here soon. He went to the barber to see if there was any news. Any hope. Come and finish your tea, girls. And Hannah, you eat the rest of that bread. You must keep up your strength."

Another knock sounded, frantic, insistent. The three women froze. The knocking sounded again, more frenzied. Irene got up, walking tentatively toward the door. "Who is it?!"

"Irene? It is Jozef! Let me in!"

Mrs. Liebmann came up behind her, her fingers shaking, fumbling, then releasing the latch. Irene's brother, his heavy winter jacket rumpled, his hat held in his hand, entered the room. He withdrew two identification papers hidden in the hat's crown, one for each of them. The word "DEPORT" was stamped onto each. "We have no choice," he said. His hand rose to his forehead, massaging it.

"Why do you say that?!" she hissed through clenched teeth. "We can hide! We are not animals to be led away and herded off. We can hide."

"I cannot live like that."

"You can *live!*"

"Perhaps it will not be so bad where they will take us."

"The rumors. . . ."

"Children!" Mrs. Liebmann broke up their fearful confrontation. "We are also being deported! Go home and gather your belongings and bring them back here. Do not be alone tonight. Whatever tomorrow brings, we will face it with you. You have no family but us now."

Jozef stood stock-still then slowly nodded. Irene ran a nervous hand through her cropped blonde hair.

"Mama is right," Hannah said. "I will come with you and help you carry back what you can. By then, my father should return. He will know what to do."

"Then let's go," Irene said abruptly. "It will be dark soon — and colder."

She and Hannah covered their heads with heavy shawls and tightened their winter coats around themselves. Jozef donned his hat. Mrs. Liebmann furtively unlocked the door. "Be quick and be careful." She let them out, and locked up behind them.

They returned an hour later, laden with clothing, bedding, and whatever personal possessions they could stuff into two suitcases, satchels and their pockets.

Oskar Liebmann had returned, sitting grimly on the small sofa in the dim, candle-lit living room. He hadn't removed his own coat. Chaffing his hands to keep them warm, he regarded his eldest daughter and her friends.

The belongings of Jozef and Irene Poznowski were stacked in one corner of the living room. Irene removed a small tin from her pocket, giving it to Mrs. Liebmann. "Sugar."

Mr. Liebmann stood up slowly. "Come. Into the kitchen. It is warmest there."

He and Jozef and the two girls sat at the kitchen table. Mrs. Liebmann poured them each a cup of cold tea, spooned a half-teaspoon of sugar into each cup, and gave her husband a bowl of the remaining potato soup. Then she started for the bedrooms. "I must check on Mina."

"Devora, wait," her husband said. "I have news."

His wife stood patiently in the doorway.

"The Americans and British are fighting the Germans in Italy. The Russians are nearing Poland, but they will not reach us in time to save us. Chairman Rumkowski refuses to discuss what the Germans told him on December 14th. In two weeks it will be 1944. We have suffered two years of Hell, and there is no sign of an early end to the war. There are only three things left to do now. The first two are choices: to hide or to go wherever the Nazis are sending our people. If we hide and are caught, we will probably be shot. If we go, we are not sure where or to what. The third thing we must do, whether hiding from the Nazis or following their orders, is try to survive."

"But, Oskar? Mina . . ." his wife broke in. "What of Mina?"

"Mina cannot go. She must be hidden," he said with simple conviction.

"But with whom?"

"With me, Devora. I will stay and hide with the child. The underground will aid us."

Mrs. Liebmann's calm broke, tears flooding her eyes, her breath catching in her throat as she spoke. "But where?"

"I don't know yet. But I promise you I'll take care of Mina." He rose, walking to her, embracing her tightly. "I promise. We cannot admit that she is still with us in Lódž." Bowing his head, he added, "Perhaps God is punishing me for allowing another man to send his own daughter in Mina's name, taking advantage of his weakness and need."

Hannah placed a gentle hand on his back. "No, Father, you did what you must to save Mina. But let me stay with her. Mama will be lost without you."

Oskar Liebmann regarded her quietly. "A sixteen-year-old girl? Alone in this God-forsaken place? No. You go with your mother. I will stay with Mina. There is no more discussion."

He stood up and kissed his wife's forehead. She didn't argue back, moving through darkening shadows to check her youngest.

Mr. Liebmann beckoned Hannah back into her seat and took his own. He addressed her and Jozef and Irene.

"Tomorrow morning, you will all go with my wife to the train. Devora will say I did not return home the previous night, that she couldn't find me but did not want to disobey the order to appear. She will ask, Hannah, that you be allowed to remain with her, that you go to the same destination. God willing, the Germans will allow it. Irene and Jozef, you must ask the same. Whatever happens, my children, you must try to stay together and survive. Do not anger the Nazis in any way."

Hannah nodded. Irene sat, barely breathing, fearful, Jozef also silent beside her.

"There is nothing left in Lódž except sickness, cold and starvation." He clasped Hannah's hand. "But we, too, Mina and I, will try to survive. And when this hell is over, we all must try to find one another again. For now you and your mother must pack. Gather your belongings, my daughter, and find the strength to face tomorrow, whatever it brings."

Hannah rose in the early morning and dressed, layering as many clothes as she could upon herself.

Her mother, also clothed and ready, quietly told her that Oskar and Mina had fled in the night.

"Did they say where they went?" Hannah asked.

"Only that they will go to a man who heads the resistance. A friend of the barber. He said he would leave word . . . somehow . . . where he and Mina are." She moved stiffly, burdened by her own excess clothing, from her daughter's bedroom to the living room. "Come. Wake Jozef and Irene. Perhaps if we arrive early, it will be less crowded, there will be more time. We will not be separated."

Hannah entered the darkened living room and lit the candle. Irene lay curled up in her coat on the sofa, Jozef, on the faded carpet, a wool blanket wrapped around him to cushion the hardness and ward off the cold. She shook them awake gently.

They breakfasted quickly on some bread and water, gathered their baggage and left the building.

Outside, late December winds hit them, icy gusts pinching at their cheeks and choking their breath. Hannah wished she could pull her shawl more closely around her face, but her suitcase and satchel hampered her.

Other deportees also walked through the ghetto to the train, mostly adults, although a few still had children clinging to them. They neared the station and heard the barking of dogs, the German shepherds the Nazis patrolled with, flushing out those in hiding. Hannah shivered as they reached the train yard, the train waiting on the track to transport them, only God knew where.

They moved in a line toward other Nazis seated at tables, checking deportation orders. Their turn came.

Her mother spoke quietly to the soldier checking their paperwork, asking that they be allowed to remain together. The man, young with blue eyes and blonde hair, looking much like Jozef except for Jozef's brown eyes, asked to see her deportation papers, then Hannah's, Jozef's and Irene's. Their papers were returned and the soldier pointed to a freight car to his right, telling them to board it.

This cannot be right, Hannah thought. "Where are the passenger cars?" she asked the soldier.

"There was a shortage. You will stop on the way and be transferred to another train with proper seating." He stared at her in a way that bothered her, as if she was both vermin — and yet something else more shameful.

"Juden," he pointed, "get on that train car. It is not as crowded and you can get on together." When they stood uncertainly, he added brusquely, "Go now, Juden, or I will separate you." His eyes fell on Hannah again, but not on her face.

The Nazi soldiers were forbidden to sexually molest the Jewish women whom they considered unclean. But whispers, rumors came of those who disobeyed with small easily-hidden acts of persecution. Hannah felt her mother's hand, calmly but firmly, grasp her arm. "Come," Mrs. Liebmann said, leading her away. "We will go to that car."

They walked slowly to the freight car — Hannah, Mrs. Liebmann, Jozef and Irene — and joined other deportees filling up its empty space, hugging a wall.

When the train left, no space remained, the people crowded inside like livestock.

Unseen by any of the wretched mortals, the wide, white cuffs of his shirt and his green trousers often hidden by his billowing brown cloak, a popular fashion among Talaperi males, Picollus watched the Jews and their Nazi oppressors at the train station in Lódž. His companion, a saur named Mezzel, sniffed the air, flaring the reptilian nostrils of his snout as he savored the delicate terror in the air.

"Look at these Nazis," Picollus observed. "Whatever chaos, evil and hatred they can muster, they go at with little or no regret. It's hardly a wonder that Lucifer rebelled against mortals being permitted in Heaven."

He scratched his scalp through wiry red hair and rubbed his small nose. They were citizens of Hell, the Talaperi and the saur, and worked together as a survey and recovery team, noting human sins and collecting lost souls.

Mezzel enjoyed all of the pleasures of his work. But his favorite was to watch humans suffer and die. Unfortunately, after they shed their mortal cocoon, many of them were out of his sphere of influence.

The saur watched the girl move away from the Nazi officer, her mother clutching her protectively. He could read her mind and knew her name was Hannah. Her goodness was excruciating. If Mezzel could corrupt her just a bit before her death, even if it didn't cancel her ticket to Heaven, it would make her misery all the more enjoyable for him.

She was headed for death as were two of her companions. Their auras were fading, fluctuating between last bursts of strength and the paling colors of their mortal life force.

He offered a disdainful snort to the Nazi soldier who had secretly coveted the girl. "You could have separated that bedraggled beauty, questioned her papers, taken her to some backroom. Done nasty things to her. I could have reveled in her horror." The soldier continued to watch the Jews being pushed onto the train cars. "You Nazi crud think you're so damned superior. You wouldn't know a demon standing next to you if you smelled him!" Mezzel got a fix on the young Nazi's aura. He'd put in a request to be notified when this soldier died. The man was already corrupt. That would make it worse for him, and Mezzel could savor that misery, watching him in the lower levels of Hell.

For good measure, Mezzel farted and waved the malignant odor about with clawed hand. The Nazi's nose and mouth creased upward in disgust. He glared around, unable to pinpoint the offender.

"Twas my asshole," Mezzel said. He wished that the young fool could see him. Mezzel relaxed his tail, letting it droop toward the ground and ambled on stumpy legs, scales rippling, to the freight car Hannah and her companions had entered. He couldn't read the exact emanations of her aura, as unique as snowflakes in these humans. Something was protecting it.

It wouldn't stop a demon of Mezzel's caliber from trying to knock a few feathers off this would-be angel's wings.

He could taste her fear. He followed her to the corner where she and her mother huddled together with the other girl and young man, belongings piled between them in the cold and cramped space. He levitated himself to a comfortable position above her, eyes bulging, snout quivering, seeking out the smallest crack in her aura.

The girl was weary, body and soul, but it jolted Mezzel to suddenly feel her consciousness open up and sense evil, the recognition of *his* presence in the freight car. Although she shook the thought from her mind, he found her perception most odd.

"What have we here?" Picollus's voice said, as he materialized to Mezzel's left.

"A quarry worth tracking," Mezzel said and telepathically conveyed the girl's earlier insight to him.

"Yes, she has the gift," Picollus agreed, "but it's undeveloped. Are you going to try to soil her?"

"Of course. It's good this one will die young. If she lived a full life, the mortal world would most likely do my job for me."

Picollus stared at the girl. "There's something unique about this one. Her aura protected. And her goodness goes beyond mortal pretensions."

"So I've noticed."

"You may fail. But if you don't, she may be a prize you could offer to one of Hell's Princes."

Mezzel's eyes lit up. "An excellent idea, Picollus! I could even get a promotion."

"Happy to encourage you," Picollus answered laconically, his gaze still fixed upon the girl. "But if you succeed, I've a feeling there will be Hell to pay."

Mezzel laughed. "If it's going to cause that much trouble, I promise you I'll do my damnedest."

The freight car doors slammed shut, plunging those within it into shifting shade and darkness. A sudden lurch, a shrill blasting of the whistle, the grinding of heavy wheels on the track, and the train moved out.

Mrs. Liebmann sat uncomfortably on their baggage; stacked against the slatted freight car wall, it formed a makeshift seat. Irene and Hannah flanked her, leaning their backs against the wall for support. Jozef stood in front of Hannah's mother, his feet spread, legs balancing the jostling movement. His position was not only protective of Mrs. Liebmann in the crush of deportees around them; he had given his space against the wall next to Irene to an old man whose frail legs had failed him and now sat slumped against the wooden wall.

Other people, too, had taken what refuge they could from the clattering movement of the train, sitting on suitcases and satchels or on the cold hard floor.

The train picked up speed, and it raced from the city, through open fields, past farmland and through ravines bordered with woodland trees. Hannah and the others saw none of this. A small group standing beside a small square opening cut into the slats of the car on their left, apparently a vent, reported what they saw to the rest of the passengers.

"How far is it to Auschwitz?" Jozef asked another man standing near him.

Hannah looked up at them sharply. They had not yet spoken of the destination marked on their deportation papers.

"Not far," the man answered. "An hour. Two."

Four hours later, the fetid smell of packed bodies, tired and ill, permeated the air. Hannah slumped, leaning her head against the baggage. Irene sat, back rigid, face pale with exhaustion, hardened with anger. They had still not arrived.

"They are doing this deliberately," Irene muttered. "Auschwitz is not this far. Everyone is saying this."

There had been a number of stops and delays, followed by more travel, the reason for the halts unknown.

A middle-aged man stood near the vent opening. He held a glass container, a bottle perhaps, for passengers with urgent bladders. The bottle was passed to the needy and returned to him for emptying out the window vent.

Two more hours passed.

The train slowed down. It stopped and remained on the tracks.

"I think we have arrived," the watchers reported. An apprehensive collective hum rose immediately. Hannah felt a tightening in her stomach.

"Remember," her mother said, "we must try to stay together."

Voices were heard outside.

The freight car doors slid open, bright afternoon sunlight blinding Hannah and the others after hours spent in darkness.

A square-faced soldier with expressionless eyes stood in the brightness. "Out!" he shouted in German-accented Polish. "Out and form two lines! Women and female children in one line. Men and male children in another line."

The deportees blinked at him, weariness, worry and hope in their own faces.

"Out! Come on! We haven't got all day. Two lines. Men and male children. Women and female children. You will be inspected for medical soundness. The doctor is waiting."

They exited the cars stiffly, muscles sore, eyes adjusting to the daylight. Jozef helped Mrs. Liebmann to stand and spoke rapidly to Irene. "I will try to contact you, wherever they put me. For now, it is best I comply and join the men."

For the first time, tears filled Irene's eyes. She and Jozef embraced. "Yes," she said fiercely. "We will survive this somehow!"

"God be willing."

"God be willing." She squeezed his hand hard.

Irene hugged Jozef one last time then she, Hannah and Mrs. Liebmann joined the line of female passengers. Hannah strained to see where the women's line led to. Ahead of her, elderly women, middle-aged and younger women waited; few were mothers with children.

In the distance a man in uniform sat at a table. He seemed to wave his hand as he inspected the women. His hand flicked left. It flicked right. The women moved left. Or right.

"That doctor," Hannah murmured to her mother, "he is separating the women into two groups."

"Perhaps those who have small children, and those who don't?" Mrs. Liebmann asked. "I cannot tell from here."

Irene, the tallest of the three, stood on tiptoe, attempting to see for herself. "It is impossible to see from here. There are too many people." She looked toward the clustered line of men, further to their right. "I cannot see Jozef either." Her voice dropped, hardly audible. "Dear God, I hope we find each other again."

Hannah could only gaze at her friend, sorrow in her eyes. But Mrs. Liebmann placed a nurturing arm around Irene's shoulders. "Have faith," she said.

Jozef clutched his cap tightly in his hands as he stood before the camp doctor. He had answered the questions politely. He knew that cooperation was a means to survival. The doctor had examined him and declared him fit for work.

Now he would live to seek out Irene and Hannah, for they were both young and he had heard that the Nazis used the Jews for slave labor. He prayed for Devorah Liebmann; perhaps their conquerors would also find her useful despite her age. She appeared to be a strong woman.

To live. To outlive this time, God willing. And to find one another again and return to peace. He waited for the Nazi medical officer to finish writing his paperwork. Then they would send him to the work barracks and he would try to send a message to Irene. Nervously, he began to stuff his cap into the left-hand pocket of his coat, then realized he had placed his small book with the writings of Spinoza in that pocket. He withdrew his hand, holding the cap.

The medical officer had glanced up from his papers, gazing at Jozef, at his coat pocket. He spoke rapidly in German to a soldier beside him. The soldier moved swiftly over to Jozef and confiscated the book, handing it to the doctor who studied it, then glanced up, his eyes bland, his face angular and rigid.

"You are a Communist?" the doctor asked in clipped Polish.

"No, no . . . that is Spinoza. It is philosophy."

"Communist philosophy?"

"No, rationalist philosophy."

"This Spinoza? He is a Jew?"

"Yes, Herr Docktor."

"Mmnn. We will take this book . . . to study."

"You may take the book, Herr Docktor. Of course. But, please, there is nothing offensive in Spinoza's writings. He could not be a Communist. He lived in the 17th Century. A Dutchman."

"Ah." The doctor nodded at Jozef, and a small smile creased his lips. "A Dutch Jew. Thank you for informing me. You may go to the group on the left over there." Jozef nodded back, his hands still wringing the cap, his posture one of wary relief as he walked where the doctor had indicated.

A backward glance: he saw the doctor throw the book into a trash can. A forward glance: the group he was to join consisted of the old and the sickly, and those too young to be worked in the labor camp.

He recognized the man he had given his place to on the train. He sat on the hard ground surrounded by the others, and as Jozef came closer, he recognized the thin wail the old man was chanting.

It was the Shema.

The Hebrew prayer before death.

Jozef thought of escape, of finding some means to survive. But a deep exhaustion washed over him. He was not a fighter. He had never been a fighter.

Jozef looked at the people being led like cattle.

He looked at the Nazi soldiers guarding their prisoners, guns at the ready.

He stood beside the wizened man, reached down with his hand, and the old man, not breaking a note in his prayer, his head twisting slightly to gaze up at Jozef, reached up his own hand to clasp Jozef's. Jozef could sense death, beckoning quietly, waiting for him.

"Forgive me, Irene," he whispered.

He began to recite the Shema, his voice mingling with his elderly comrade's, whom he helped as the unwanted men and boys were marched off, herded by the Nazis.

There was a horrid burning smell in the air, and a thin coating of what seemed dust covered the ground and grass all around them.

The line moved slowly, Hannah, Irene, and Mrs. Liebmann inching forward, until there were only a dozen or so women ahead of them. They could see the long table and the doctor who sat behind it, his assistants flanking him.

The doctor was a thin, angularly faced man. Upon occasion he glanced up and his eyes scanned the waiting prisoners yet to be examined. His features were severe, long thin nose, small cold eyes, a tight mouth. His uniform appeared different from those of the other Nazi officers and soldiers, but she could not place it yet, still too far away to see it clearly. He held something long and thin in his hand, and used it to point to the left or right, to two separate lines from the one she stood within. Women, their children, moved in the direction he pointed.

Finally, only three women and a child stood ahead of her, her mother, and Irene. The first woman, a tall, strong redhead, held a little girl in her arms and approached the doctor. The doctor stood up from his seat and stretched his back, arms on his hips. Now Hannah recognized the clothes he wore, a riding habit, from photographs she had seen in magazines and from the cinema. The stick in his hand was a thin rounded strip of wood.

The doctor reseated himself and beckoned the woman and child forward. He seemed to be instructing her to send the child to the left-hand line, and for her to join the line on the right. The woman clutched the child closely to her chest; it seemed too frail to walk. She argued with the doctor. His voice rose loudly, clearly. "Damn it, woman! Do you want to die? Give the child over to one of the prisoners in the line on the left, and go to the right!!"

As he glared at her, the woman broke the oppressive silence. "Where my child goes, I go!"

The doctor studied her, his expression cold. "Fine. Both of you. To the left."

The woman carried her daughter to the left-hand line, where prisoners either very old or very young were. Had that doctor said those prisoners were to die? Hannah's skin prickled with more than the cold.

One of the women, in front of Hannah, balled her hand into a fist. She raised the fist to her mouth, gnawing on her knuckle. Hannah wondered at the smallness of that fist, until the woman turned, casting frightened eyes at Hannah. She wasn't a woman, not yet, but a tall girl, probably no more than eleven or twelve years old. Then the girl turned back, to watch intensely as her companion, an older woman, approached the doctor and was sent to the right with a flick of the little riding stick. The doctor beckoned the girl over, examined her paperwork, her. The stick pointed to the right. She joined that line to be furtively embraced by the older woman.

"Her mother," Devorah Liebmann whispered to Hannah, as they waited, next to be called before the camp doctor.

"I'll go first," Irene said, and walked forward to stand before the doctor. After a few minutes, he pointed to the right. Irene took her place among that group of prisoners.

Next Hannah approached the doctor, and was sent to the right. She breathed a sigh of relief; she did not wanted to believe the rumors circulating in Łódž about the camps, rumors that swore they were also extermination camps. Slave labor was easier to believe.

She watched her mother approach the doctor, and in short order, his small stick pointed. Left.

"No!" Hannah could not stop herself. "No! Mamma!"

She ran over to the doctor, still seated behind his wooden table, ignoring her outburst. A strong hand grasped her arm painfully.

The Nazi soldier spoke brusquely. "Come! Back where you were!"

She ignored the soldier, fighting his tightening grasp, straining to stay at the table and implore the doctor. "Please! Please let my mother come with me! I heard you tell the woman ahead of us, that woman with the child, that the left-hand group meant death. Please, please! Let my mother come with me?!"

The doctor looked at her, his face reflective. "Is that what you heard me tell the woman? But I did not say that."

"But you did!" Fear clutched at Hannah's throat, but she had to save her mother.

"No, no," the doctor answered in a soothing voice. "I sent that woman and her child to the left, to preserve them." He smiled at her. "It is the right-hand side that is fraught with danger. Now, let us play a small game." He motioned to the Nazi officer. "Bring back the mother on the left and, yes, that is your friend on the right?"

Hannah said nothing, as Mrs. Liebmann and Irene were both brought before the doctor again.

"Now," the doctor explained, "your daughter wants to be with you. She seems to know which way is death and which way is life. She listens too closely to conversations that she has no business hearing. So I will tell you all, so there is no misunderstanding." He paused, glancing with a small smile to the other Nazis. They smirked back at him. "Those in the group to your left are those we use to work the camps. Even the children, for they will grow strong and give us many years of labor. Those to your right, we have no use for. They are communists, insurgents, enemies of Germany, who will be treated accordingly. They may look innocent to you, but they are criminals who threaten the glory of the fatherland."

The doctor pursed his thin lips and held the equally thin stick in both of his hands, exerting pressure and bending it slightly. "Now, you three may think you know each other, but we know you better. You may be innocent of any crime, or you may be our enemy. You must trust in our judgment. We know you so well, we will give you a choice, and we know how you will decide when given it. So, you three must choose. The mother must go one way, the daughter and . . . friend? . . . must go the other. Choose."

He leaned back in his chair and waited for their reply, knowing they would not dare tax his patience.

Hannah and her mother looked at one another, each drinking in the other's face. "Mother . . ."

Devora Liebmann's expression grew firm, as Hannah had seen it many times before when she meant her children to know she brooked no disobedience from them. "You will go to the left, Hannah, you and Irene. I will go to the right. You will remember me at Yom Kippur, if we do not meet again, lighting the Yarzeit candle for me." Hannah opened her mouth to protest, but her mother covered it gently with upraised fingers. "You will not disobey me, my daughter." She turned to the Nazi doctor. "I will go to the right, if you will spare my daughter and her friend."

The doctor nodded genteelly. "As we knew you would decide." He pointed his stick at Mrs. Liebmann and then pointed to the right. She grasped Hannah and hugged her fiercely, then let go and walked to the cluster of prisoners on the right, squeezing Irene's shoulder as she passed by.

"You, both of you," the doctor said, "to the left before I change my mind." He smiled at them beneficently. His little stick pointed the way.

Hannah and Irene moved uncertainly off to join that crowd of women and children waiting in the cold.

Hannah felt the tears coursing down her cheeks, but she dare not turn her head and seek out her mother's face. Her mother had given her life and must be obeyed.

Picollus had jumped down from the freight car, as relieved as its human occupants, so suffocating and putrid had the human-crammed transport been. He could have left the car, astral being that he was, materializing through the roof to ride out the journey atop the train. But Mezzel had insisted that Picollus stay close and observe the girl called Hannah and her companions. She had suffered as nobly and had been just as thankful when the journey ended.

He and Mezzel followed the Liebmanns and the Poznowskis through the separation of Joseph from the women, through the condemnation of Jozef for a philosophy book in his coat pocket, through the cruel trick played upon Hannah, Irene and Mrs. Liebmann by the infamous Dr. Mengele, whose evil was already being charted in Hell. Picollus had been relieved that he had no part in that, although Mezzel was smiling as he watched Hannah and Irene go toward the line leading to the gas chambers, and Devorah Liebmann, to the labor line, thinking she had courageously saved her eldest daughter and Irene from death. Something about the girl, Hannah, still bothered Picollus intensely. She seemed to trigger an elusive memory, a memory of something long ago, some ancient tale, but somehow pertinent to the present. The memory tugged at the corners of his mind, but would not reveal itself fully.

When Mezzel wanted to follow Jozef to the death chambers, Picollus voted him down. They would stay with the girl, Hannah.

"There is something about her," Picollus said, and candidly: "I am glad I have not caused her death."

Mezzel sniffed, thinking that the Talaperi was not at all a credit to Hell, being prone, amazingly, to sympathy toward these mortals.

The women were marched to the outskirts of the camp. The ground and air were cold and often gritty with the thick taste of dust. Hannah pointed to a smokestack attached to the building they headed toward, black clouds escaping from it.

Irene nodded. "That's what is filling the air. It's ash. What are they burning?"

Hannah began crying.

"Maybe . . . maybe the doctor was lying. Your mother is not an insurgent, no communist. Why would they kill a poor woman? The doctor was lying!"

"I . . . I hope so."

"You will see her again. You will see. The rumors are false. They were meant to scare us. That's all."

Hannah shook her head, but said nothing.

They had reached the flat-roofed, single-storied building. Inside, they were taken to a room where other women, possibly inmates of the camp, took up scissors and cut off the hair of the prisoners, close to the scalp, jaggedly, nearly balding them. Then in another room, they were instructed to remove their clothing, and leave them with their belongings.

"But why?" Hannah asked one woman attendant, frightened but trying not to show it. The other women prisoners listened, waiting for the attendant's answer.

The attendant, a rough woman with a boxy build and dark apprehensive eyes, sized her prisoner up. "You have to be disinfected," she said. "For lice." When Hannah remained still, she continued. "You will be disinfected in the showers. Then you will come back here to get your clothing and belongings."

Hannah studied the woman's face. The attendant turned away, ordering them in a monotone: "All of you. Disrobe. There are other groups waiting to be disinfected. Hurry up."

Hannah removed the layered outfits she had put on that very morning, and stood in her bra and panties. Irene, beside her, did likewise.

"Everything off!" The matron said. "You are all women, no reason for shyness!"

Hannah glanced at Irene, who slowly undid her bra, revealing thin, almost adolescent breasts, and removed her underpants. Hannah, strengthened by Irene's nod, but nonetheless embarrassed, removed her bra and panties. Her breasts felt heavy, the nipples erect in the cold, unheated building. Her skin prickled with goose bumps from the chill.

They and the other women prisoners, shivering and mortified to see male Nazi guards watching them, were then herded through a doorway into a large drab room.

Within it, showerheads and their connecting plumbing hung down from the building's ceiling. There seemed many showerheads, to accommodate the many women who now crowded the room. The building seemed to have no other function than that of disinfecting and washing down the prisoners.

Irene reached out and put her arms protectively around Hannah, drawing her close for bodily warmth.

The door to the room closed with a great deal of noise.

"They are locking it," Irene whispered.

Hannah clung to her, terrified. "We are going to die," she whispered back, against the cacophony of the other women weeping, crying out in fear.

"As God wills," Irene murmured and clasped her friend more tightly.

Picollus and Mezzel had followed Hannah and Irene into the small room where the women's hair was shorn. But when the woman began disrobing, Picollus made Mezzel and himself leave, Mezzel grumbling as they waited outside. But following the shivering naked women to the gas chamber was unavoidable, and Mezzel perked up considerably, making note of the varied female figures before him.

"Shut up," Picollus ordered him, shocking the reptilian demon. "These women are going to their death, the girl among them. Look at their auras!"

Mezzel looked, shrugged. "What of it?"

"There is something about that young girl. It is driving me half out of my Hellish mind. I need to know what it is that is so unique about her. Something important!"

Mezzel smirked, not an easy thing to do with a snout, a measure of his disgust with Picollus's preoccupied passion for this unknown Jewess. "Perhaps she was your long-lost love in one of her past lives," he sneered, "one you had forgotten with all the other pleasures to be had in Hell to block her from your Hellish mind."

Picollus stared at him, finally remembering the ancient tale that had eluded him, of Lord Baelzebub and the girl he had loved before the Fall. "No, this cannot be," he muttered.

"Twas a joke, my stupid friend," Mezzel replied, obviously not gaining any pleasure with Picollus making such a mystery of one mortal girl.

"It cannot be Leianna." Picollus paid no attention to Mezzel and his ranting, keeping pace with Hannah, staring at her. "Can it?"

The women were now moving into the gas chamber, and Picollus and Mezzel, unseen and unheard by any of them and immune to the coming onslaught of chemical death, entered it behind Hannah and Irene.

"Don't know what in Hell you're mumbling about," Mezzel told him. "But I'm not complaining. This will be a feast of terror, watching this bevy of women succumb to, what is that gas? Oh, yes, Zyklon B! I hear it's quick."

"Shut up!" Picollus screamed at him. He stared at Hannah, who clung to Irene, who hugged her tightly, sheltering her. Knowing, yes, knowing, for Picollus could read her thoughts, that there was no shelter at all, only a final gesture of love and friendship.

Irene began to recite the Shema.

Hannah listened to Irene, tried to murmur the Shema, but some long-lost memory, perhaps a fantasy, filled her mind. It comforted her, seeing the boy with the dark, sleek hair and black, piercing eyes, who smiled at her, coming toward her, love creasing his lips, his lithe, young body clothed in the short tunic that revealed his smooth, tawny, muscled skin. He was coming for her, for he loved her, and she, him, and her place was with him. He would take her away from all this, this horror, take her home, and soothe her, and make her forget all of the pain, remembering only the happiness of their love. He reached out for her, and she started willingly toward his arms. . . .

The hissing above them broke her reverie. It did not sound like water. Hannah waited, waited for a shower of wetness to descend from above, but no water came from the showerheads. Something else was filling the air, some kind of gas, and Hannah couldn't breathe.

Irene grasped her still, as they slid toward the floor, hearing screams and cries all about them. But Hannah did not scream or cry. She felt the breath, the life, leave her body, but she felt no shame, only fear and regret.

Fear to be dying. Regret for the mysterious youth, of the black hair and eyes, who was fading, fading in the distance, his right arm still outstretched, fading away, leaving her, she whom he had promised to . . .

"Bael!" Her voice tore outward from her diaphragm with a last effort, expunging all that remained of her breathable air. *"You said you would find me!"*

And then there was no more breath. Her brain exploded with the suffocation, and her consciousness fled into a black void.

Hannah Liebmann and Irene Poznowski.

Died December 17, 1943.

Hannah opened her eyes and gazed about her. She was lying on a bed in what seemed to be an infirmary.

It felt as if she had been asleep for a very long time, and experienced many dreams, a nightmare among them. Or perhaps it had not been a nightmare, perhaps the horror had been real, except the terrible gas that had escaped in the showers had been a horrible mistake, stopped before lethal damage had occurred. She turned her head to the right to the occupant in that hospital bed. Irene. Asleep, breathing normally. Had the camp attendants rushed all the women and children in the huge showering facility to the camp infirmary? Had they had enough time? This infirmary did not seem large enough to house the large number of victims.

She began to lift herself up, to sit up, to look for a nurse. There wasn't one in sight. She looked at the patient on her left, surprised yet not surprised to see the young girl who had been so sickly that her mother had carried her and refused to leave her. The child was awake, and her eyes had lost the dark circles of illness. She smiled at Hannah, but said nothing. Hannah leaned forward to look at the other patients. In the next bed over, the little girl's mother slept peacefully.

"Do you know where we are?" Hannah asked the child.

The girl nodded her head. "In Heaven. God saved us."

Leianna came awake as the hoop was lifted from her head, and immediately reached out to clasp Bael's hand.

His hoop had been removed first, his expression as he met her gaze showed his pain and regret. "I'm sorry, Leianna. I'm so sorry," he whispered.

"It's okay. We're together now," she whispered back. She didn't tell him to release the pressure of his hand squeezing hers. She never wanted to be separated from him ever again. Still overwhelmed by the horrible memories she had relived, she turned to Quatama, who held the reenactment hoops, including the third one which Adolf Hitler had worn, also experiencing everything as she and Bael had. "Thank you for ending that horror with the knowledge that Heaven rescued us!"

Quatama nodded. "Heaven will always rescue good souls."

"But not all of those memories were mine," she added.

"No," Quatama agreed. "You needed to see the others, to know that Bael still sought you, and you, him. And Picollus and Mezzel were instrumental in helping Bael and Ashtoreth find you after that lifetime, as was a young German soldier by the name of Wilheim Kroeger, but that is a tale for another time. Right now we must see the results from our experiment with Adolf here."

They all turned to look at Hitler, who was leaning over, slumped on his stool, visibly shaking and sobbing. Dagon moved closer to the man. "Adolf!"

Hitler looked up at him, his face wet and red. More tears cascaded down his cheeks.

"Are you crying over the Holocaust?" Dagon, surprise on his skeletal face, asked him.

"Yes! YES!"

"Over the Jews whom you killed?"

"YES! *I am crying because of the damn Jews!*" Hitler lowered his head and continued weeping.

"Well," Dagon said. "I never would have thought to see it." He turned to Leianna. "You have won the challenge. I will accept you inasmuch as you respect the High Council in your dealings as Baelzebub's wife, and, yes, his queen. Good luck." Dagon held out his hand.

Leianna stared at it, very gracefully took it in a gesture of truce, and released it. "Thank you."

Dagon nodded and slowly left Hitler's cell, calling to the guard. "When they are finished in here, let them out and secure Mr. Hitler's quarters."

Bael stood up, pulling Leianna up as well, embracing her tightly. He glanced at Horace. "Did you get all of that on tape?"

Horace looked at his cameraman, who nodded back. "Yes."

"Go now then. I need to be alone with my wife. But thanks."

Horace grinned. "You're welcome, boss." And to Quatama, "Let me know when I can have that transcript of Leianna's lifetime for condensing with my story."

"I shall," the spirit master said, watching the newsmen leave.

Finally, only he, Lucifer, Bael and Leianna remained with Hitler in his cell. Quatama gently stroked Leianna's hair. "Leianna, child? I believe you have a question to ask Adolf?"

Leianna sighed, nearly a shudder. She turned to Hitler, who still sat in misery, an occasional tear or two dripping down his cheek. "Adolf, could you please tell me why you were crying?"

Hitler turned haunted eyes to her. "Because I am the Führer! And God abandoned *me* after all I have done for *Him*! After all I have done for Germany and the Aryan people. No! For the purity of the world!" He stood up so suddenly, nearly knocking into her, Leianna jumped back, as he paced around his cell wildly, arms flailing about. "God is so unfair that He saved that vermin, those Jews, after death, and sent me, who loved Him and wanted to cleanse the world of what infected it, to *Hell*! Oh, no! Something is very wrong, that God should allow me, Adolf Hitler, the greatest leader ever known on Earth, to rot in Hell, and save lesser beings like Jews and gypsies and unnatural homosexuals. People who defile the proud Aryan race! Something is wrong. I should not be here!" He stopped, standing very still, gazing down at her. "At least, God has sent you to Hell now, Jewess. They will put you in this cell and free me. God will release me from Hell. You are not saved. Not anymore!"

"Adolf," she began, but didn't know how to tell him that she was not damned, how to explain any of this. But she knew the man was crazy, and that she had won the challenge with Dagon by accident, not because her life had made Hitler regret anything, but because he was crying for himself, tears of self-pity. He believed that God had punished him without fair cause, and that the mass murders he and the Nazi hierarchy had orchestrated — in his mind — were not only justified, but deserving of praise and reward. "I think you're going to need a lot more therapy before you can ever leave Hell," she told him. *"Maybe a couple of centuries worth."*

Hitler sat down again on his stool, shoulders slumped again, face hanging down. "My God, my God, why have You abandoned me? And raised up Jews in my place?!"

Leianna turned to Quatama, Bael and Lucifer. "Please can we go? Before I get sick."

Quatama gestured to the door of the cell. They all exited and heard the guards clanking the door closed, its locks sliding back into place.

But before they left the corridor outside Hitler's cell, Leianna said: "I didn't win the challenge, Quatama. Hitler wasn't crying from regret, but only out of extreme selfishness."

Bael cut in sharply, "Leianna, babe, he was crying. That was the only criteria for the challenge. Don't argue when things go your way."

Lucifer added: "Actually, he *was* crying over the Holocaust, even if it wasn't out of sympathy for the Jews. You've won, Leianna. No one said Hitler had to say he was sorry."

"Are you two for *real*? You really believe that I won this challenge? Quatama, what do you think?"

The spirit master regarded her quietly, and said: "Adolf Hitler was truly crying because he regretted the Holocaust and its genocide, because he felt himself wronged by God, his actions neither understood nor appreciated. But such is the way of spiritual illness and such is the challenge that you must *still* accept, Leianna, for the challenge is not over. Heaven loves you and will always welcome you. But you are the Queen of Hell. The Alliance is *your* challenge, as God requested it and you accepted it. And so, are you ready to go back to Domain and announce your first triumph?"

Leianna took a deep, steadying breath and let it out, welcoming Bael's arms as he once again held her close. "I guess so. And then I want to get some real rest, preferably with a warm cover I can snuggle into for an hour or two more. Because it looks like I've got my work cut out for me." She remembered how the Reich had forced the concentration camp inmates to listen to the music of Wagner, a known anti-Semite. She turned back to the prison guard, staring at the sullen Hitler through the bars. "Please make sure that Mr. Hitler has Jewish Klezmer and swing music from the late 1930s and early 1940s piped into his cell at least four hours a day. And make sure you include Glenn Miller, Artie Shaw, Benny Goodman, and, oh, yes, Cab Calloway and Fats Waller."

Adolf stood up abruptly, his mouth rigid, his eyes so shocked they practically bulged. He sprung to the bars, grasping them, his nose sticking through them. "I will not have the filthy music of American Jews and niggers forced on me!"

Leianna felt her own hackles rise, like a cat whose back is

arching at a challenge. "You will not only learn to listen to it, I'm going to make you *dance* to it." She looked at the guard. "Starting tomorrow."

The guard looked at Lucifer, who grinned and inclined his head toward Leianna. *"She's* in charge now."

18

Leianna as Satana, George and Gracie,
and Mephistophele's Pink Slip.

At 5:00 A.M., November 18, 1977, on an extraordinary dawn following a spectacularly busy and astrally historic night for both Lucifer and Leianna, and for Hell, Earth and Heaven, the High Council of Hell reconvened when Lucifer summoned them again to the palace throne room.

Some had waited out Dagon's challenge in their sumptuous palace apartments; others simply stayed in their balcony seats, expecting Leianna to fail quickly and miserably. Some even voiced an opinion that the challenge was pointedly unfair: true evil, they said, never regrets its behavior. If Lucifer's abdication was a "done deal," why make matters worse by demanding the impossible from Leianna? Many councilors felt this would only tax the patience of Lord Baelzebub, making his new wife and rookie political player in Hell look like a cockeyed, optimistic fool.

Ashtoreth, having heard all this in their brief absence, now related it to Leianna, Bael and Lucifer in the private corridor beyond the dais of the throne room.

Azmodeus stood behind his eldest brothers, arms folded, impatient and disgruntled. "Well, did she lose?"

Lucifer took a deep breath and let it out. "She won. Change is upon you, kid, and you're going to have to accept what Bael said about that."

"I have, Father," said Az, his tone and posture both reproachful and regal. "I know what you did last night, utterly blinded by Heaven's wiles, was irrevocable, unless you have a change of mind with an eye toward breach of contract. But I don't think you have such an inclination. That was why I told the people I would not abandon them. Even if I could."

The hum of voices outside in the throne room swelled. No doubt Dagon had appeared in the balconies of the High Council, reseating himself, and Horace and his news people were once again in the news box. But neither would speak until Lucifer officially reconvened the meeting. And right now, he was glaring at Azmodeus. "You have nerve, boy, judging me. You were part of the reason for my rebellion in Eliom. Your mother and I grieved deeply when the Seraphim snatched you away from us in the Canyon of the Winds and sent you to Earth."

"Oh, come now, Father. There was no great love between us before that, when I taxed your patience with my free-thinking and rule-breaking behavior. In fact, I doubt that you'd have fought as fiercely for our freedom from the Creator's demands, if I had not shown you the way by my own disobedience."

Lucifer had listened patiently, and now he responded, his words measured, his voice low but clear. "Az . . . I stood up for the rights of our people with forethought as to how those rights should be ethically expressed and preserved. You, since your return to Hell, following your only mortal life, forced on you by the Seraphim, have shown me that you equate freedom with ego gratification. Because you are my son, I looked the other way, when your motto seemed, 'I'll do what I will,' instead of 'I'll do what is best and just.' You and those like you promote the constant, mortal misconception of what Hell and the Satan's job is all about. Now, you accuse me of running out on you and our people and doing it by kissing our Creator's ass. No, don't say anything! You know you're thinking that. Well, listen clearly. I am not completely responsible for the choices made by those who supported my rebellion in Eliom. None of us expected to be flung into Hell and forced to survive here. But survive we did, and I led them and governed them fairly for tens of thousands of years. And neither they nor you can upbraid me if I choose to seek a better venue than we've had all these past centuries. Nor can anyone fault me for desiring resolution of a conflict that has festered between Hell and Heaven since the angelic war. A new resolution might benefit my followers as well. And the High Council knows this. We have all discussed this possibility before, although any chance of it occurring seemed so remote then as to be nonexistent."

Az brought his arms to his sides, looking upset and lost, which Lucifer considered an improvement, although he still grieved for his youngest in new and troubling ways.

"I'm still in charge of the military?" Az asked.

Lucifer nodded. "But Bael and Ash can override any decision you make that endangers their own trusts and responsibilities, if the High Council approves their veto. As can you override their decision, if you feel it threatens our military, its strengths and needs, if the High Council supports your challenge. But I expect the three of you to work together fairly with the High Council for the good of our people."

Az clenched his fists. "After my mortal life as Adam's son, when my true self returned to Eliom, I continued your protest there, so fervently that those Seraphim flung me down to you in Hell, as was my plan. And now my loyalty is rewarded with your chiding and disapproval." He turned and headed through the door to the throne room dais, growling, "I *hate* your politics."

Lucifer raised his eyebrows, looked at his elder sons and Leianna, and gestured that they, too, should return to the throne room. Bael nodded back, took Leianna's arm, and escorted her through the door, Ashtoreth following them.

Lucifer offered his own arm to Affaeteres, who had quietly arrived from her quarters as he took Azmodeus to task.

She linked her own arm with his. "I can hardly believe we are returning to Eliom later today. Will anyone know us now? Will we know them? And will our family and friends here be able to follow someday?"

Lucifer patted her hand. "It's been a long haul, Aff. Our friends here will have their opportunity, now that I've been given mine. At least our eldest sons and Leianna have access to Heaven, and we can hope that Az will one day resolve his own inner demon, so to speak. By the way, Leianna told Quatama that your release was part of an unwritten addendum on the contract we signed. She said she was keeping a promise."

Affaeteres nodded, as Lucifer and she returned to the throne room, and reseated themselves on the dais.

"As far as whom we will or won't know," Lucifer added, "we can start with our parents, who have also finally returned to Eliom from their own journeys that took them from *us* 35,000 years ago. We will all adjust and hope it will be for the better."

"Then we will have good advice," she said, "and someone to listen patiently."

He saw that tears trailed down her face, and she lifted her hand to wipe them. He gently grasped her hand. "Your tears are the release of centuries of unfair dishonor. Let the people see them and know that a good woman has been lifted up again to her rightful place." He let go, and she lowered her hand to her lap.

He stood up before his throne, addressing the assembly packing the room, for more of Hell's denizens, as the news spread, had swelled the rank and file. They stood quietly waiting for him to announce the outcome of Dagon's challenge. Horace Pearleigh stood with television news reporters and other media press, but he already had his scoop and would share it with his colleagues.

Lucifer began: "Dagon's challenge has been met! He watched Leianna, through sharing her experience as a Holocaust victim, bring Adolf Hitler to tears concerning his persecution of the Jews. We have also filmed the event for all of you to view it as it happened.

There is no doubt the Alliance and the reformation of Hell will now be a great challenge to all of you, and I trust you will meet it as bravely as you have met the other challenges we have triumphed over in Hell."

Before him, his people cheered in loud waves of approval.

"One other thing, which Bael, who also relived Leianna's past life as a Polish Jew in Lódž and finally in Auschwitz, has told me. A private thing which you will not see, as the techniques of reenacting these lives is a silent one going on in the re-enactor's mind. But you will read of this, in condensed form, which will be provided to *The Heliom Hornblower:* As Leianna, then a young victim of sixteen years, died in the gas chamber in December 1943, she called out the name of Prince Baelzebub, grieving that he had not found her through the centuries since the Fall and could not save her from the Holocaust. In that most horrid moment, her love surfaced, proving to us all that these lovers were destined to reunite. Now they have, and to do so, she agreed to love and nurture you as well.

"Dagon, inasmuch as Leianna has caused Hitler to reconsider his view on the Holocaust, will you give her your vote of confidence?"

Dagon stood again in the balcony. "I will accept Leianna as your designated replacement in Hell under the conditions she stated to Naamah. What is more, I have conveyed Hitler's response, following my challenge, to Moloch and to Behemoth, and they, upon hearing of Leianna's triumph, have agreed to grant her a chance to prove herself in Hell. And so the High Council in its entirety will accept her as symbolic leader of the Heliomese Hierarchy with one small change. Symbolically, there must be a Satan, a judge. And Leianna will be called by a feminized version of that title. She will be known as Satana."

"Leianna? Do you accept that?"

She came forward hesitantly, standing beside him to the right, and spoke softly, but her voice carried in the utter silence about her. "That which we call a rose, if called by any other name, would smell as sweetly, as Shakespeare wrote. I accept your title of Satana. I will still be Leianna."

"Then," Dagon called down, "the High Council will record these events with one final event. Lucifer, you have not formally abdicated the throne of Hell."

Lucifer nodded. "I am about to do so. A copy of my signed statement is being brought to you." He paused as a messenger approached Dagon, handing the official document to him in the balcony. "It says that I, Lucifer Morningstar, relinquish my rule and my holdings in the Netherworld known as Hell, on all seven levels, and bequeath its governance to the High Council of Hell, as previously proscribed, and to my sons, Baelzebub, Ashtoreth and Azmodeus, and to Leianna, who shall act as Satana in my stead over the damned and the fallen, those here by choice and those here by circumstance. As to my personal holdings in Hell, I bequeath them to my sons and Leianna, and although I shall, upon this new day, return to Eliom and the heavens, let it be known that I now support the Alliance between Heaven and Hell. I believe it will bring greater understanding for all involved, and one day may bring to the citizens of Hell and for the souls incarnated upon the Earth a brighter future in the beyond. So saying, I, Lucifer, abdicate, with love for you all still within my heart and the hope that my future endeavors will still benefit you, that your souls may rise as you see fit in the future."

Now, in a hush, those who had been seated stood, and cries of "Fare thee well" were heard, and some wept openly. Lucifer beckoned Bael over and grasped Bael's hand with his left hand and Leianna's hand with his right hand and, facing the people, raised their hands high, then stepped back between them, letting go.

Bael now took Leianna's hand. Both stood quietly as Lucifer beckoned Affaeteres over. They kissed their son and Leianna upon their cheeks, and the former Emperor of Hell and his wife quietly left the throne room through the private door into the corridor beyond. Lucifer paused beside his wife as the guards shut the door behind them. He smiled at them. "Thank you."

The guards wore solemn faces. The older guard asked, "Permission to speak, sire."

"I am no longer your sire, but permission is granted."

"You will be greatly missed, sire."

Lucifer inclined his head gratefully. "Look after Leianna."

The younger guard said, "As you wish."

The elder one said, "As you command, my Lord."

Lucifer took Affaeteres's arm. "Goodbye," he said, moving on, hearing a great cheer ring out in the throne room beyond.

Bael had just announced that he and Leianna would have an official Heliomese wedding in Domain on December 21, 1977, and the coronation of Leianna as Satana and Queen of Hell would follow the wedding.

The crowd in the throne room became jovial and teasing now, as Naamah leaned over her balcony and called, "And will she give birth following the coronation?"

Bael laughed, and Leianna felt herself blush, but he answered:

"We may have that blessed event beforehand or a few days afterward. She starts her ninth month on December 15th and her due date, in astral time, is December 25th." He turned to Leianna. "Beloved, if you manage to deliver our son early, your dressmaker can save on fabric for your wedding gown."

She stared at him as the crowd roared with amusement, his grin wide and infectious. She realized he was playing to the audience. She looked down at her swelling belly, ran her hands over the green velveteen gown, smoothing and covering it, looked back up at him and then at the crowd, saying loudly, "I'll see what I can do!"

The people laughed raucously, nervous laughter, she realized, in the face of immense change. Every nation, every country needed a leader they could believe in and trust. They wanted to believe in Bael, whom they had considered Lucifer's heir, and now one-third of the triumvirate, and they, oddly enough, wanted to believe in her, because Bael did. She and Bael were the fairy tale queen and king who would rule and protect the realm, and she was soon to deliver its prince.

But she wondered if the finale of their performance tonight was to be a stand-up comedy routine, and when they might get the last drum roll — *Ba Da Boom!* — and she could finally get some rest, with time to reflect on all that had occurred.

The laughter had died down now and, in the balcony, Lothan stood, and Sharlan stood beside him, and she called out: "It doesn't matter if you have the baby before or after your Heliomese wedding and the coronation, Leianna, as long as our baby is healthy, and you are well!"

Shouts rang out in earnest agreement with her from the throng, and then Sharlan did a strange and wondrous thing. She bent on one knee, calling out: "I pledge my loyalty to Leianna, whose coronation will bring light to Hell, beforehand as well as afterward, as she is already our Satana and Queen, and I know she will be just and kind."

And then, many of the men and women who stood before Leianna bent on their knee, and even those who remained standing seemed to eye her with respect, some looking both surprised and amused.

Bael, of course, turned it to his own humorous advantage, staring up at his head concubine. "What? You're not going down on your knee for me anymore, Sharlan?"

"My Lord," she laughed, "may I ask if this is the proper place for such levity?"

Exhaustion got the better of Leianna. "Bael! For *God's Sake!*"

The giggles, chortles, guffaws and titters from the audience faded. Silence.

Leianna put her hands on her hips and glared at them all. "Oh, for cryin' out loud, people, it's *just* an expression! *Lighten up!*"

The laughter resumed, and someone shouted: "Is that a command, my Lady?"

"Yes, it is. And if it's all right with you, Bael, I need to close this party down and get some rest."

He wrapped his arms around her, hugging her fiercely, and then loosened his hold, addressing everyone: "I call upon the High Council to note that this meeting is adjourned, by order of Leianna."

Dagon stood. "We note its adjournment. Well wishes to all until next we meet."

Leianna leaned tiredly against Bael. "Does that mean we can go now?"

"Yes." He shouted, still grinning, to the assembly. "Later, people! But be ready to party on December 21st!"

The crowd responded enthusiastically as it broke up, leaving the throne room. Bael kept his arm about her as they waved and headed back to his royal quarters. She said sleepily, "I swear you would have made a great flim-flam man."

He snorted. "Where have you been all these years, girl?!"

"Waiting for you to get real, honey, at least, on the astral planes where I can see you." She looked up to see a tender smile crease his lips.

"I'm here, baby. I'm here for you. And together we're going to make the greatest comedy team since Burns and Allen!"

Leianna rolled her eyes at him. "You know, I *liked* Gracie Allen, Bael!"

"That's fine, Lei. Every woman needs an outstanding role model, babe. And I liked George Burns."

"Let's go say goodbye to your parents, George, okay?"

"Sounds like a plan, Gracie."

She sighed.

Mephistopheles grumbled under his breath as he continued to neatly pack Lucifer's personal belongings into the astral traveling trunk, checking each item off the list Lucifer had given. "Hell is going to Hell!" Mephistopheles had not been a major player at the Fall from Grace, in fact, few barely knew who he was then, but as the centuries passed, he had succeeded at various positions, including becoming a famous procurer of souls for Lucifer's realm.

But the last one he had snared, a young girl named Regan whom he had fooled into believing herself damned — her mother's death had not really been her fault despite that belief — had become his downfall.

The girl resembled Queen Affaeteres in her ancient youth, and Lucifer took the girl into his personal harem, which infuriated his wife. What she had once grudgingly accepted, she suddenly rebelled against, her wrath ominously directed toward anyone associated with the girl.

Regan was quickly transferred to Prince Azmodeus's harem. Mephistopheles hoped that would be the last he'd hear of her, but the young prince had a tendency to taunt and punish the girl loudly, *because* she resembled his mother. These incidents traveled back to the queen, enraging her more, and she sought to punish Mephistopheles for damning the girl, as if he had deliberately done so to harass Affaeteres.

And so he was called before Lucifer, who apologized for having to fire Mephistopheles, no pun intended, from his procurement job, and reemploy him, at the queen's insistence, as a servant in their royal apartments. Lucifer made amends for this drastic ploy to shut his wife up as best he could by installing Mephistopheles in his own quarters as his personal butler.

While Mephistopheles considered this quite a step down from the fame he had previously achieved, he did not argue with Lord Lucifer, knowing the mad queen probably had a much lower position in mind for him. Being head butler to the Emperor was at least a respectable place, and so he strove to serve his master as best he could.

But tonight everything had changed; Lucifer had abdicated the throne, and he and Affaeteres would be leaving. Another woman, that strange girl, Leianna, was replacing the Emperor, unbelievably. She had stopped Prince Azmodeus from torturing Regan, and word spread that Regan had been removed from Hell, presumably taken to Heaven. Rumor was that Heaven intended to save the lost souls through a reformation program. That certainly wasn't the way things worked before!

At one point he had jestingly called himself a case worker for the potentially damnable. Now it appeared there might be case workers in Hell trying to undamn its souls.

"Mephisto, have you finished loading my things onto the travel trunk?" Lucifer had come into his bedroom behind him.

Mephistopheles nodded. "I just added the last items. Your books, my Lord."

"Then please lock it, and I'll send it ahead."

Mephistopheles closed the locks, securing them, and stood back. Lucifer placed his hands on two small silver symbols on the trunk. It faded before Mephistopheles's eyes, being astrally sent to Heaven. "The new technology, my Lord, is quite amazing."

"Yes. It is. Mephistopheles, I am going to release you from service today. I have left you a pension and a small apartment in Domain to live in. Leianna would probably have no need of your services, and I suggest you lay low until one of my sons, probably Bael, appoints you to a new position in the new order of things."

"Do you think they might do that for me, Sire?"

"I've spoken to them about it. They'll be in touch with you. In the meantime, treat this as a leave of absence."

"Yes, Lord Lucifer."

A knocking sounded. Lucifer gestured. "Please go find out who that is. Oh, by the way, Affaeteres is in the drawing room, but I've told her not to bite you."

"Very good, Sire," Mephistopheles said dryly and strode through the drawing room, nodding politely at Affaeteres, who ignored him, past the waiting room to the vestibule.

He opened the door to see Lord Baelzebub and his wife Leianna. "My Lord, my Lady. I will let your father know you are here." He sighed. "Your mother is also here."

Bael held up his hand. "Wait, Mephisto. I want you to announce us as George and Gracie."

"My Lord?"

"You heard me. Tell my parents that George and Gracie are here to see them."

"I understand, my Lord. Humor makes the parting less bitter."

He saw the grin on Baelzebub's face disappear.

"Exactly as you wish, my Lord." He came into the drawing room, paying no mind to the sullen look Affaeteres wore, and saw that Lucifer had joined her. "My Lord, I have been asked to tell you that George and Gracie are here to call upon you."

To his surprise, Affaeteres burst into laughter. Lucifer smiled. "Show the smart alec and his bubble-brained wife in, Mephistopheles."

He bowed and returned to the vestibule. "Your father and mother will see you now."

They moved into the drawing room. Leianna immediately sat beside her mother-in-law, hugging her. "I said I'd get you back into Heaven."

"Yes, dear. But I only wish you'd be there, too."

"But I will be, Mother Aff! I'm not barred from Heaven. This is like a job where I have to commute."

"A very serious job, dear!"

"All jobs are serious if you take life seriously, and I work in all three realms: Heaven, Earth and Hell. But I won't be alone. I'll have lots of help."

"Leianna," Lucifer cut in, "you will bring the child to Heaven for us to see it?"

"Yes, of course. Bael, explain to them."

"Dad, you'll also be permitted to visit us in Hell. Heaven knows you'll honor the contract. In fact, Quatama has suggested that you act as an advisor to the Alliance people."

Lucifer remained silent, seated beside his wife. Leianna leaned over to touch his arm. "I'm sure your insights and knowledge would be invaluable, Father Lucifer, in setting up the reformation."

Lucifer patted her hand. "Perhaps so. But, for now, I think that Aff and I want to reacclimate ourselves to Eliom. We understand it's quite changed."

"For the better! It's very modern now. When I visit, Mother Aff, we'll go shopping. Great department stores downtown. You pay with skane points: the tally of your good works."

Affaeteres studied her wonderingly. "I think you might possibly have some normal traits within you."

"Nah. Those rumors are totally unsubstantiated. But Eliom is now quite expanded, beyond the small geographical areas we knew as our village, the Garden, the prairie and elven woods, and the Shore of the Seraphim, although they're all still there. The original Canyon of the Winds and the Seraphic Hall where the colored winds carry souls to and from their mortal incarnations are still there as well. But the rest of Eliom has grown beyond it, miles upon miles, into a vibrant, active city."

Lucifer asked, "We can still return to our village, Leianna?"

"Yes. According to Quatama, they've restored your old *thachka* . . . the cottage you owned."

"I do remember the language, Leianna."

"Sorry. But the thing is, the village now is larger, and most of its inhabitants are public workers maintaining all of these historic areas we once called home."

"The original Eliom is, what? A public park and museum?"

"It's more than that. It's treated sacredly, the boundary of the eighth physical astral plane before the ninth and tenth planes, where the spirit masters and Seraphim live. And many souls visit Old Eliom, as it's called. Some come to walk in the Garden and to taste its fruits and vegetables. An elven community still maintains the woods, although many of the elves have also traveled to many other realms and places, and they have their own city far across the Seraphic Sea."

"Avalon?" Lucifer asked.

"It has many names. And souls come to breathe in the vapors of the Well of Being. As you saw, its mist, conveying long life, once again rises from its shaft. But the secret was, once you had inhaled its gift, it was yours forever. As you, by now, should know."

"I suspected as much. Well, Affaeteres, are you ready to return to Eliom?"

His wife stood. "I'm almost afraid."

Leianna said: "Don't be. Your parents are waiting for you both. They'll be there when you arrive." She hugged Affaeteres, and said to Lucifer. "Goodbye, Dad. Don't worry about Heliom. We'll take good care of it."

When she extended her hand, he squeezed it, and then turned to Bael, grasping him by the shoulders. "I know I'm leaving Hell in capable hands: yours, Ashtoreth's and the Council's. Possibly Leianna's!" he laughed.

She smirked and then laughed back.

"Watch over Azmodeus. Keep him out of trouble."

"I will, Father. Did you say goodbye to him and Ash?"

"Yes. I'm going to miss you the most, Bael, although in the beginning, I thought you were going to Heaven in a hand basket, son."

Bael grinned, shot a glance at Leianna. "The lady towing the basket knew where she was going."

Lucifer nodded. "Goodbye, then, for now." They hugged in the hearty manner of men, thumping each other's backs, then let go.

"Mother." Bael hugged her tenderly. "Say hello to my grandparents for me."

"You haven't seen them yet?"

"No, Mom, not yet. And not all of the angelfolk who volunteered for that intergalactic journey eons ago have returned yet. Some won't finish their work until 2001. I hope they find this section of the universe has improved when they return. But your parents, Marcellus and Venea, and Dad's, Othorah and Ise, were called back early to greet you upon your return to Eliom." He paused at the surprise registering on his parents' faces. "Yes, the Creator knew you would be returning there. Give them our love. We'll be up to see them with your grandson — their great-grandson — soon."

"Have you decided on a name yet?"

Leianna answered. "Stefan Nicholas. Nicky, for short."

Lucifer laughed. "How traditional."

"Hey," Leianna said, "Santa Claus was a Nick, too!"

Bael put his arm around her again. "We're also honoring Shar-lan. Our child is hers as well, reborn, and Leianna has embraced her as a sister. Besides," he chuckled, "we have to keep some of the old legends going. Otherwise, we'll lose our edge."

Lucifer grinned, "Then, may the Powers That Be watch over us all."

"I hope so. Are you ready?"

"Yes."

Affaeteres nodded, tears again in her eyes.

Bael and Leianna stood back. A beam of light came from above, bright and blinding, enveloping Lucifer and Affaeteres. When it cleared, they were gone. Leianna moved into Bael's tight embrace, both holding each other silently, until Bael gently pulled away. "Now it begins, my love."

He looked at Mephistopheles and pulled a set of keys with an address tag attached to them from his pocket, handing it to him. "Your new digs, Mephisto. You'll like them. I'll be in touch."

"Thank you, sir . . . Sire."

"I am," Bael said, leading Leianna away. "Lock up before you go. Palace Housekeeping will change the locks and wards later."

19

Two Mornings After

The buzzer roused her from sleep at 6:30 A.M. with a vague memory of Bael's hand caressing her face, telling her it was time to wake up. Leigh Ann moved groggily toward the bathroom, knocking on the middle bedroom door as she passed it, calling, "Fred! Time to get up for school." Her brother, now 19, attended Community College part-time and worked part-time, assisting their father. Bill Elfman wanted Fred to study to become a journeyman plumber, but Fred wasn't sure where he was heading careerwise. It was a source of contention between father and son. Fred's only ambition seemed to entail eventually getting a bachelor's degree, majoring in computer science with a minor in philosophy. Bill Elfman didn't think either of these would earn his son a proper living.

Fred was emerging, bleary-eyed, as she headed back to her bedroom to dress. She asked, "How much beer did you down on that fishing trip?"

"More than Dad," he said, and shut the bathroom door behind him.

In the bedroom, Danny had turned over on his side, falling back to sleep in the other bed after Leigh Ann had turned off the alarm. She moved quietly, getting dressed. She wouldn't have to wake him until 7:15 A.M. Then he'd dress himself, eat breakfast with her and Grandmom Miriam, and then Leigh Ann would take him to Paley Day Care, where they would escort him back and forth from the Farrell Elementary School. At 6:00 P.M., Leigh Ann would pick Danny up at the daycare. It was the same routine every weekday.

Danny seemed so mature at times, but right now, she saw him as the child he was, vulnerable, curled up in sleep. She murmured, "I love you, kid," unwilling to believe that an ancient soul lived in her little boy's body.

She trudged down the steps, feeling heavy, through the living room and dining room and into the kitchen. Her father ate his eggs and toast as he looked over his list of plumbing calls to make that day. He picked up his coffee cup, downed the last gulp, and stood up. "Gotta go. Gotta pick up Sammy. Damn fool kid got a busted tire on his car. I told him a week ago that tire was going bald, and he needed a new one." Bill kept a motley assortment of plumbing helpers, who never quite satisfied his need for perfection, except for his apprentice Jerry, who had just passed his journeyman's test, a source of pride for her father. "You know, Fred," he said as Fred came into the kitchen, plopping textbooks and a notebook on the table and going to the cupboard for a coffee mug, "you could make three times more money as a plumber. I don't know why you want to repair those computers."

"Program, Dad. Program computers. And believe me, there will be money to be made." He lifted the coffee pot, filling the mug, drinking it black.

"As long as it's not just a fad and something bigger and newer comes along."

"Believe me, Dad, if it does, it'll be computerized. Can you drop me off at Bridge and Pratt to catch the El train? After you pick up Sammy, I mean. My class isn't until 10:00 A.M."

"Yeah, yeah. Come on, then." Bill was pulling on his green winter jacket.

Leigh Ann noticed his face looked craggier, its lines becoming deeper as he neared his 55th birthday, but his eyes remained alert, forever filled with a questing curiosity. "Hey, Dad. Have a good day."

"I will, kitten. You do the same." He went down the steps and out the side door. Fred put on his navy blue coat and followed him out.

Miriam still stood by the stove, sipping her coffee, watching her. "Do you want something to eat? Besides your coffee."

Leigh Ann sat at the table and poured a cup from the still hot pot on the trivet, spooning sugar in and adding milk. "No, Mom. I want to talk. Where's Ginnie? Still asleep in the basement?"

Ginnie had fixed up the central basement room into a space all her own, with a sofa bed, dresser and mirror, a wardrobe, a bookcase and a desk and chair. Bill had paneled the walls for her and painted the small lavatory that housed a sink and toilet to the right of the laundry room. Ginnie insisted she preferred it to bunking in the front bedroom with Leigh Ann and Daniel. Leigh Ann couldn't deny that they'd all be too cramped in one room.

"No. She worked a double shift until 7:00 A.M. this morning. Mary Ann called in sick last night, so Ginnie filled in for her." Miriam joined her at the table, refilling her cup. "So what did you want to talk about? Your astral pregnancy?" She glanced at the wall clock. "We have about fifteen minutes before you have to get Danny up."

"Yeah. By the way, I've gained about ten pounds."

Miriam sighed. "It's sympathy weight. It'll go away after your astral son is born."

"I hope so." Leigh Ann pushed up the arms of her green sweater.

"Are you warm? You may be overdressed in that grey wool skirt and your sweater. I can turn the heat down."

"A little. Don't bother with that now, Mom. Mom? Umm . . . do you know about the contract I signed last night . . . with Lucifer?"

Miriam slowly put down her cup. "The Alliance? Did he agree to it? Finally?"

"Umm . . . yes. We exchanged places, Mom. I mean, I still have access to Heaven, but I'm Lucifer's replacement. The High Council has declared my title to be *Satana*."

"The High Council of Heaven."

"No, Mom, of Hell. They have a High Council, too."

Miriam nodded, pulling her bathrobe collar closer. "And the Heliomese? Do they accept you? Accept this?"

"Somehow . . . yes. For the most part. Lucifer declared a triumvirate between his sons, and the Council members still maintain their jobs and authority, but somehow I'm in charge of judging the lost souls and setting the reformation of Hell in place, and seeing it, I guess, enforced. Quatama says I won't be alone. The Heliomese seem to regard Bael and me as their king and queen. It was quite a night. I'll tell you more about it when we have more time and privacy. But Bael wants us to marry and have the coronation on December 21st, whether or not I've had the baby by then."

Miriam glanced at the clock again. "When are you astrally due?"

"December 25th."

Miriam raised her eyebrows. "Well, my gut feeling is that you won't be having a Christmas child."

"It would be a bit strange."

"No, just an uncomfortable coincidence. I'm sure the Heliomese would actually love it, because fanatics would say you bore the Antichrist, astral child though he'd be. But I think you'll deliver earlier, and end stupid misconceptions on either side. And when you do start labor, you tell Quatama to come and get me, astrally."

Leigh Ann stood up. "I've got to get Danny up. But I'll tell Quatama. What I want to know is, what if I'm awake when I go into labor? You know, physically awake."

Miriam smiled. "You won't be. They'll probably induce labor when you're close to your due date, to make sure you're physically asleep. Or hold your labor off, if you did start it while awake, until you could sleep and have the child in your astral body."

Leigh Ann offered a dubious nod. "I'm going to get Danny.

We'll talk more later." She headed upstairs, and under her breath, lips pursed, out of her mother's earshot, she murmured, "It's all so weird, I'm not sure *what* to call reality anymore!"

Lucifer gazed about the *thachka* — the two story cottage he had once shared with his wife and their sons. Affaeteres had been greatly surprised at its modernization. Its kitchen now had a stove and oven, a refrigerator and a sink with faucets for hot and cold water. He expected the Eliomese no longer used their radiant energy as a heat source. In the large front room, instead of broad wood stairs leading to the sleeping alcoves, a smaller, banistered staircase rose upward and a new wall blocked any view of the loft. The bedrooms — his and Affaeteres and the one his three sons had shared — now had doors, where once curtains had covered their entrances. At the end of the corridor between them, a small table held a vase of bright flowers below a circular window in the wall. Sunlight streamed through it.

Lucifer pointed to it. "That wasn't there before, either."

Behind him, Affaeteres glanced at Gabriel, standing beside her as quietly as a house agent showing off a property. "It wasn't," she agreed, "but I love it."

Gabriel nodded. "It brightened things for the staff we had living here before . . . your return."

Lucifer turned. "Staff?"

"One of the Garden custodians and his family resided here. They've been given other quarters now."

"So my house was occupied all these centuries?"

"Put to good use, Lucifer. You didn't expect us to treat it as a shrine, did you?"

Lucifer let out a snorting laugh. "No, I suppose not."

"It's good," said Affaeteres. "It's good that somebody took care of it for us."

"It's yours now," Gabriel said, "again. Unless you'd rather live elsewhere."

Affaeteres shook her head. "I want to be here. Perhaps the children can use the other bedroom when they return for a visit."

Lucifer watched her face. A timid joy suffused it. "This is perfectly fine. We'll need time to adjust, and where better than in the home we once knew? But where did they send our traveling trunks? Aff's and mine?"

Gabriel opened the door to the left bedroom. Both trunks sat on the floor. "Just arrived. We wanted to make sure you were satisfied here."

Lucifer nodded, unwilling to show how overwhelmed he felt. His emotions ranged from relief and gratitude to guilt and shame. Some Heliomese could condemn him, unless the events following his leave-taking reaped solid benefits for them. This Alliance! Had he made the right decision, even with the careful preparation he and his Council members had set in motion, devised for that time when this could indeed become a reality? And now it had.

Or had he, as Azmodeus so crudely put it, been utterly blinded by Heaven's wiles, finding himself on the Shore of the Seraphim, finding himself forgiven by the Creator, because a young woman could fulfill the challenge made so long ago, and because Heaven had new plans for Hell, had he been led to believe this was destined? "This plan of our Creator's, the reformation of Hell, do you realize that my people will expect free will in accepting or not accepting any changes Heaven proposes?"

Gabriel seemed surprised by Lucifer's question, pausing before answering it. "All things must change, in Heaven, In Hell, and on Earth. Innovation is preferable to stagnation."

"That doesn't answer my question."

"No. Because I cannot. Time will answer it. Your people, our Creator, and time. Let us hope that they will freely accept those changes. Otherwise, decay and destruction may set in. Change, one way or another, is inevitable." He lifted his gaze to meet Lucifer's, no longer the arrogant angel Lucifer had once known. The simple brown robe he still wore now seemed to match a humility learned over the centuries since the angelic war. "You and Affaeteres will understand better when you speak with your parents. They're waiting for you downstairs now."

"What?!"

"Lucifer!" A rich, baritone voice sounded from below. "The table is set, refreshments are served, and we have much to discuss. Did you think your sudden elevation in stature, employment and location only has to do with you and those that followed you? Can you not conceive of vaster causes and implications beyond your influence and circle of friends?"

"Father." He whispered the word.

He watched Affaeteres sway, as if she might faint, and moved toward her, but Gabriel, as tall as she was, caught her, saying, "It's all right, Aff. The news they bring is hopeful."

Lucifer couldn't conceive of his meaning. He linked his arm around Affaeteres's, steadying her, and they slowly descended the staircase together. Two men and two women sat before the table on the long wooden bench. The bench on the other side awaited

Lucifer, Affaeteres and Gabriel. Teacups were set with spoons in saucers and napkins beside them. Three steaming teapots graced the table, along with bowls of fruits and nuts and two plates of biscuits.

Othorah, like his son, was not tall. His blond hair, unlike Lucifer's full mane, was close-cropped. His wide-set eyes, patrician's nose, full but well-shaped mouth, and strong, cleft chin all resembled Lucifer's. But his face was thinner, his cheeks almost hollow, a gauntness Lucifer did not recall his father having.

Ise was as he remembered her, except that the ends of her black hair curled about her neck and over her ears, no longer long and flowing over her shoulders and back. Her eyes were black, flecked with gold, like Bael's, and she was still tall, her figure firmly slender.

Marcellus appeared the same: a jovial, blond-haired, round-faced man. If anything, he appeared fuller in girth, but it seemed muscle rather than fat. Although in Heaven and in Hell, as on Earth, what one consumed affected what one became, regardless of fey tricks, Marcellus and Venea always seemed well-proportioned, both tall, both fair. In that, they hadn't changed at all. Venea's beauty had been inherited by her daughter, but neither was vain. And Venea now shocked Lucifer: while his parents and Marcellus, like Aff and himself and Gabriel, wore the traditional winter robes of old Eliom, Venea stood up, moving towards Affaeteres, arms flung outward to greet her, wearing tight blue jeans, long black boots and a green, fluffy, scoop-necked sweater. "My sweet child," she said, hugging her.

Affaeteres returned the hug, then let go. "Not a child anymore, Mother."

"Yes, darling. I understand. But you're home now. And we have so much to tell you." She gestured toward the benches. "Sit." She took her own seat again beside Marcellus. "This sector of the universe has changed so drastically in our absence: a war in the heavens, the creation of Hell, the incarnation of the angelfolk, and the chaotic, genetic rebalancing of humans on Earth. If I didn't know better, I'd believe our Creator had failed with the latter, humankind is so violent. And now they hold the very atoms of existence hostage with nuclear weapons!"

"They've already used them, Mother, in Japan." Affaeteres slid onto the bench across from her, Gabriel sat beside her, and Lucifer sat on the end, opposite his parents.

"Yes, I know, in Nagasaki and in Hiroshima. Terrible! And the evil of Hitler's Germany — all horribly tragic."

Lucifer cut in, "If this is rebalancing, I'd like to know what the final genetic mix is supposed to produce? Mankind's self-extinction?"

Othorah picked up a tangerine and slowly began unpeeling it. "In a way."

Ise reached across the table, patting Lucifer's hand. "Don't look so shocked, my son. Your father exaggerates. It is not extinction, but a new phase of evolution that humans will enter into in the next century. And the angelfolk will also share that change."

Lucifer shifted uncomfortably, looking at all four elders across from him. "Will our brains swell up — like space aliens on pulp science fiction magazine covers? And why are you so unemotional at seeing your son and daughter again after a 35,000 year absence? Give or take a decade or two."

Marcellus smiled sadly. "Our emotional natures have changed. We are overjoyed at seeing you both. But we now control our emotions and never display them intensely, improperly or indecorously."

Othorah put in, "In the newly formed world we helped to develop, its natives knew no emotions. They neither felt love nor hate, joy or sorrow, desire or fear. They also had no anger nor conflict that thrived on violence. It was the elders' job to teach them the positive use of emotions, while blocking their experiencing any negative or destructive emotional impulses."

Affaeteres asked, "And did you succeed at such a challenge?"

Venea smiled beneficently. "Yes. Not only with the primary sentients, but with ourselves. We have developed complete emotional stability and rationality, a state of mind where one cannot, literally, act irrationally. And where we cannot, directly or indirectly, choose to act destructively toward another." She lifted up her filled teacup, sipping at it delicately. "When all the elders have returned here, we will help humanity to relearn control of their own emotions."

Lucifer stared at his own empty cup. He slowly picked up the nearest teapot and filled the cup. "Sounds rather benign."

Venea offered a tiny, lilting laugh. "It's not boring, if that's what you mean. There is still music, laughter and dance."

Marcellus leaned toward her, putting his arm around Venea affectionately. "There are still enough intellectual challenges to fill many books and launch intriguing debates. But we have found the way to stop the emotions that hinder, hurt and break down societies, human or alien."

Lucifer warmed his hands around his cup. "And how do you propose to do that with mankind?"

Othorah answered. "We don't propose anything. It will occur naturally, and then we will help shape the result. You see, Lucifer, human violence and other negative reactions are caused by a currently diseased DNA code, normally present in all sentient beings as a protective, but not destructive gene. Call it the war code. And there is another string which controls what I'll call the peace code. They normally balance each other out, cooling our angers, or causing us to react heroically when endangered. When one or the other of these codes is unbalanced, the psyche becomes irrational, reacting with either great timidity or great aggression."

Marcellus interrupted: "Let me explain it. You see, the mingling of angelic and mortal DNA triggered, eventually, a strange immune system deficiency in the resulting hybrid children and their children's children. And a virus mutated to take advantage of that opening in humanity's immune system, to fill that weakness with its own evolutionary needs. Mankind has no conception of this virus because it co-exists with human biology and seems to do it no physical harm. And mankind hasn't yet perceived what it does and has done for thousands of centuries as a problem, because humans think it is a part of their nature. What this virus does is feed on and deplete the peaceable code, regulated by the DNA, by mutating it into the warring code instead. But stage two evolution is about to end this imbalance."

"Yes," Othorah said. "A new strand of DNA is building, shall we say, a fort against the virus, creating an antidote, which will produce new antibodies to attack it and restore the balance again. And although I called the negative impulse the war code, it was never meant to cause violence and aggression on a personal or mass scale, but rather to protect the human by rationally correcting any difficult or dangerous situation, whether individually or as a group. Mankind was never meant to kill or to destroy wantonly as a solution to any problem or challenge. He was supposed to use his brain and find rational methods that would benefit humanity, not destroy it."

"But the virus stopped that," Ise said, "and now most of mankind considers violence and evil as unfortunate but natural human traits, for which nothing can be done."

"That isn't true," Venea added somberly.

"No," Ise continued, "but mortals had no way of knowing that. Eve and Adam and their children caused the imbalance, the immune deficiency and the virus spiraling humanity's impulse for good versus evil out of control. They couldn't know that angels were incarnating into human fetuses to rebalance the DNA and eventually eradicate the virus that brought such misery to Earth. They couldn't know that their very beliefs in the nature of good and evil were spawned by that virus, or that the war in Heaven was not caused by Lucifer's arrogance and fall, but by a challenge to re-balance humanity's DNA. Over those thousands of centuries while that rebalancing was taking place, mankind set up religions and philosophies explaining that dichotomy, the misconception of absolute good and evil, to control it until the virus could be mutated further by the rebalanced DNA, forcing it into something either harmless or possibly beneficial."

Lucifer asked, "And this evolutionary change is going to occur naturally?"

"Of course," Othorah said. "In 2001, the human genetic code, now fully balanced with the angelic code, will begin to evolve fur-ther, just as I have said. And it will eventually wipe out the destruc-tive impulse causing war and violence, which mankind has suffered with for 35,000 years."

Lucifer spread his hands, palms out, in a gesture of inquiry. "So . . . in 2001 . . . all human conflict will cease? No one will act evilly anymore?"

Suddenly their elders were silent.

Affaeteres asked quietly, "What? What will happen?"

Venea reached over and clasped her daughter's hand. "The new century will not be violence-free. The rebalancing will indeed start a new stage of human evolution. But as with all births and new beginnings, there will be a long period of readjustment and a sloughing off of the discarded beliefs and behavior, a panic among some humans experiencing true emotional stability for the first time — and an initial rejection of it with blame cast on everything except the return of sanity." She laughed again, but this time it held an edge of ruefulness. "If there is unfinished business that the virus has not attended to, a last ditch effort to safeguard the human destructive impulse will occur. This may sound contradictory, but it means that mankind will find excuses to cling to its violent nature, for one last, unresolved conflict or one final battle before the genetic evolution wipes out the virus, freeing mankind from it for-ever, ushering in an age of rationality and peace."

Marcellus nodded. "It will take most of the new century to chart the initial changes in human evolution and the subsequent changes in human behavior. But modern medical science will prove all this to be accurate by 2100, when the Golden Age will start."

Ise looked intensely at her son. "Everything will be affected: philosophical and religious teachings, how troubled souls are taught a new path and are led to a new manner of existence, what constitutes this new reality, developing new criteria for judging right and wrong, and finding innovative remedies to resolve conflicts appropriately and positively in a world that no longer experiences rage and human destruction. And because of this, Hell will need to be reformed. The original concepts you built it upon will become obsolete."

Lucifer sat utterly still, staring back at her, trying to condense the immensity of their news. Finally he whispered, "The Creator knew this, when I and my people were flung into Hell?"

"Yes," Ise said. "Our Creator knows All That Was, All That Is, and All That Will Be. And you will eventually forgive and understand better. Humans are not the only ones whose evolution is about to continue. For every angel who did not incarnate on Earth, there are three times as many who did. And when they return home to the heavens after death's release, they will also still carry the new DNA codes within their angelic bodies."

Affaeteres murmured, "Then the Curse of Cain is about to be lifted."

Venea nodded. "And peace and love will finally triumph over war and hatred. As they were originally meant to, before Eve and Adam, philosophically speaking, bit into that apple of curiosity, came to Earth, metamorphasized into mortal flesh and produced an altered genetic code in their offspring."

Gabriel had sat utterly silent, listening to Othorah, Ise, Marcellus and Venea and their interchange with Lucifer and Affaeteres, enlightening them. He had watched their reactions and their final comprehension. Now he rose up from the bench, turning to Lucifer. "We still need your expertise, if you're willing to lend it to us. You've seen the worst of human nature in your long exile, and there's still a good three decades to go. No doubt, we'll see the last great conflicts of mankind before its new evolution begins to heal them. Your observations as these occur, along with your past knowledge, would be invaluable in aiding and smoothing the evolutionary transition. Will you join us on Heaven's team? Will you join the Alliance?"

Lucifer stood up. "Will you give me a minute to myself?" The others nodded, and he stepped outside, closing the cottage door behind him. They had preserved old Eliom well; he had missed it bitterly. And now he knew that his exile had been predestined, unwittingly aiding the repair of the genetic breach. And yet he knew, if he lent his expertise to the Alliance, it would comfort the two women who had always held his heart. Affaeteres would be glad for the sake of their son Bael and his wife Leianna. And Eve, while glad for the same reason, would benefit in another way. It would help to clear the chaos she and Adam had created and ease the burden it had placed on her.

Lucifer re-entered the cottage and gazed at his parents, his in-laws, and at Affaeteres, who smiled gently, waiting for his decision.

"Well," he said. "It will be nice working in the sunlight for a change."

20

And Baby Makes Four

On Friday morning, December 16, 1977, Leigh Ann dragged her-self out of bed and went through her routine, taking Daniel to daycare and then going to work. She was now employed at a Center City CPA firm, again as a secretary. She had switched jobs in 1975. It was just too traumatic working around terminal patients and not being able to try to heal them with her psychic ability — something most medical authorities discredited, even when it worked.

She had managed to help one young patient's recovery, giving a four-year-old girl with Wolmer's Tumor a teddy bear, which Leigh Ann and Terence had filled with healing energy. The child had been given one month more to live. Initially, she ignored Leigh Ann's gift. But the next day, the nurse told Leigh Ann that the child, after her radiation therapy, had clutched the bear to her. She and the bear became inseparable and, three months later, Leigh Ann saw the child return for a follow-up appointment, her disease having gone into remission. The cancer had just disappeared, the nurse told Leigh Ann.

Despite that triumph, so many of the patients were elderly. Sometimes healing energy wouldn't work, if the illness was the soul's way to exit this world, and not always because of age. But their suffering saddened her, and so she chose to move on, leaving Heaven's work at the hospital to its skilled doctors and nurses. They, too, had the healing touch.

The hardest part was leaving Willa and Kate. They all agreed to keep in touch.

Now she sat in the accounting firm's typing pool and tran-scribed letters once again from a dictaphone. Her two friends, the other secretaries, sat near her, their desks all in a row. Suddenly Leigh Ann hunched over, a dull, pulling sensation traveling down her back toward her abdomen. It wasn't painful, but was definitely palpable and uncomfortable. She sat straighter, but the pull re-peated itself, tensing her.

Molly, a sweet-face Irish girl with long blonde hair stopped working. "What's wrong, Leigh Ann?"

"I don't know. It feels like I've strained a muscle in my lower back."

Marge, brown-haired with solid Polish features and build, the head secretary, glanced at the wall clock. "It's nearly 4:00 P.M. Do you think you'll be okay until five?"

"I think so. Molly, do you still have that heat rub?"

Molly rummaged in her desk drawer. "Yeah, sure. Do you need help applying it in the ladies' room?"

Leigh Ann took it. "No, thanks, I think I can manage. I'll be back in a few minutes." She grabbed her pocketbook and headed past the receptionist and into the hall where the rest rooms were. No other employees were in the ladies' room. She immediately sensed Bael and Terence beside her, seeing them through her mind's eye. "About time," she muttered, and then switched to thought-communication. — *I think the baby's coming.* —

She felt Bael's hand on her only slightly swollen mortal stomach. — *Dr. Mateus will be here in a second.* —

The doctor appeared. She saw him telepathically as a dapper, thin man with short black hair and a thin, black mustache and goatee. He opened his medical bag and took out a small hypodermic needle, saying, — *What I'm going to give you will hold off the birth until late tonight, when you're asleep. Then we'll reverse the process when you're out of your physical body, in your eternal one on the upper planes.* — He gave her the needle. — *You'll be fine. Don't worry.* —

She had barely felt the needle and, almost immediately, the discomfort lessened and stopped. — *I'll be all right?* — She was smearing Molly's heat rub on, just in case.

— *Yes. We've temporarily stopped the contractions. I'll see you tonight.* —

— *My mother wants to attend the birth.* —

She mentally saw his smile. — *She won't be the first extra mother in a delivery room,* — he said.

She felt Terence give her a hug. — *You'd better get back to work now,* — he said.

At one A.M. on December 17, 1977, Leianna rested between astral birth contractions in the maternity ward in New Eliom on the eighth plane. She was only vaguely surprised to see three other women waiting for the birth of their own astral children.

On the nearest gurney, an older woman, her long, black hair braided down her back, leaned toward her. "I'm Veta."

"I'm Leigh Ann, on Earth at least. My soul name is Leianna."

"You're still in your mortal life?"

"Yes, but I have an astral marriage." She glanced at her belly, fully swollen in her astral body. It would probably be best not to mention having two husbands.

Veta nodded. "It's not unheard of. Not common, but it happens. Your first child?"

"My first eternal one. I have a seven-year-old on Earth."

"Well, don't worry. You'll get a nanny, I'm sure, to watch over this child, when you can't be here with it."

Leianna felt another contraction, but it still only felt a bit uncomfortable. She smiled at Veta and the two other younger women. "I'll worry a bit anyway. But my astral family will take good care of the baby."

Veta smiled back and patted her own pregnant girth. "It's so much easier in the heavens. Mostly because our bodies are in spirit form, including the baby's. Oh, dear!" Her eyes widened. "My little one wants to come now." She reached over to the nightstand near her and rang a buzzer.

A nurse came swiftly into the room and over to her, checked her briefly and said, "Dr. Ott, I'm bringing Veta to the delivery room. She's ready."

Leianna wondered how she could communicate so accurately and instantly with the obstetrician, but apparently she did, releasing the brake lock on Veta's gurney and wheeling her from the waiting room. Veta waved, and Leianna and the others waved back. No one wished her luck or an easy delivery; this was Heaven.

She wondered if she should continue conversing with the remaining women, but suddenly a great cacophony of chatter arose in the hall outside. One of the mothers-to-be, a short blonde, turned her head to Leianna. "Your entourage is approaching, your majesty." Her tone held humor, but not sarcasm.

"Huh?"

"We know who you are," she said, grinning. "Most people in Heaven do. Probably in Hell as well, but I couldn't vouch for that."

"I could," said Leianna. "But that other woman didn't know who I was."

"Yes, she did." The other woman grinned again. "As soon as you said your name, we all knew. She just wasn't sure about your still being mortal. Anyway, if you don't mind telling us, which of your astral husbands got you in the family way?"

Leianna's mouth hung open, caught off guard and unsure of whether she was famous or notorious. Her entourage came through the doorway in classic Stooge fashion, knocking against each other in their rush to get through. Bael got through first.

"Speak of the devil," Leianna said and suddenly felt herself blush as the small blonde said, "So you're to blame," and the other girl laughed.

"I'm innocent," Bael assured her and leaned over Leianna's gurney, kissing her. "How are you feeling, honey?"

"Weird," she said.

"Well . . ."

Her mother Miriam, Sharlan, Dr. Mateus, and Terence all crowded around her. "What," Miriam asked Bael, "did you expect her to say? It's not every day a mortal woman gives birth to an astral child."

Sharlan took Leianna's hand, squeezing it. "A very special child!"

Terence stared quietly at Leianna. "A child with two mothers, one from his past life, one in the life about to begin."

Leianna met his gaze solemnly. "A child with two fathers as well. Even if you're not officially his father, I want you to love him and I want him to love and respect you." She looked at Bael. "You don't mind that, do you?"

He shook his head. "The more dads, the merrier, babe. He'll know he's my flesh and blood, metaphorically speaking, but that alone doesn't make a good father, and jealousy doesn't belong in our lives." He grinned at Terence. "You agree, of course, when it's your turn to fatten her up?"

"Bael!"

"I do agree, which shows how far we've come, Bael. But fattening her up isn't the way I'd put it."

"Just a joke, Terence. She looks good to me skinny, plump, or in between."

Leianna laughed. "Sharlan, what are we going to do with such an indiscriminate man?"

Sharlan still held her hand, as if by doing so, she would share in the birth. "Love him, I guess."

"Ooph!" Another contraction hit her. "It's strange. It doesn't hurt, but it feels like pressure is pulling everything downward inside of me. But it's nothing like Danny's birth."

Sharlan used her free hand to smooth down Leianna's loose hair. "Did Danny's hurt?"

"Enough that my moaning and cries woke patients on the floors above me and below me. When the day nurse came on duty at 7:00 A.M., she taught me how to breathe through the contractions. Ooph! I think I'd better start breathing now. Dr. Mateus, it feels like the baby's coming!"

They made room for the doctor as she bent her legs, spreading them to let him see the progress. Two extra pairs of eyes peered at her below the sheet with him. Leianna gave an exasperated sigh. "Bael? Sharlan? Do you really need to check that out, too?"

But Sharlan was beaming. "Oh, Leianna! I can see the baby's spirit energy!"

Dr. Mateus offered them a chagrined smile. "It is time." He released the brake on the gurney. "Bael, make yourself useful. Wheel Leianna to the delivery room. Sharlan, I know why you're excited. You can continue to hold Leianna's hand during the birth. Bael, you can hold your wife's other hand until the child emerges. Miriam and Terence, I need you to stand off to the side until the baby is born."

They all scurried behind Dr. Mateus as he talked and led the way down the hall, Bael steering Leianna into the brightly lit delivery room as the pressure between her legs increased, and helping her onto a long table with soft bedding and foot stirrups. Dr. Mateus lifted her feet into them, and said. "Now just push. You know how."

She squeezed Sharlan's hand on her left and Bael's on her right as she bore down. A thick, white mist poured painlessly from between her legs, billowing up and congealing into a vague shape. It *felt* as if she had expelled a baby-sized bulk from within herself. "Where's our son?" she asked, becoming alarmed. "And what is that white glob of goo?"

Dr. Mateus only said, "Bael?" He moved back.

Bael let go of her hand, came around, and stood facing her legs. He reached out with his hands, cupping them palm up under the floating, white mass, its nebulous wisps and tendrils fading the moment his hands formed a cushion beneath it.

Miriam's voice soothed Leianna. "Remember that birth is different here, as it was in Eliom when I was Eve and gave birth to you there, your first lifetime. Our children emerge as pure energy and then coalesce into their individual self. Watch Bael's hands."

She did, also remembering her mother's words, six years ago, describing birth in the heavens, when Leianna had reenacted and experienced Miriam's original life as Eve. What she had called a white glob was quickly developing a human shape: arms, torso, head, legs. Color quickly replaced the white energy as the baby appeared, softly cradled in Bael's hands, the white light now an aura around it. The baby's hair was black as midnight. His eyes, scrunched shut, now opened, also black like his father's. She heard Sharlan let out a deep breath, which she no doubt had been holding, and heard her say, "Is he . . . is he whole?"

Bael said, "He's got all his fingers and toes, Sharlie, and his thick head of hair reminds me of Nikki. Oh, son!" His voice held his own relieved emotion, knowing this child, conceived through his Leianna, was also the son he and Sharlan had lost so long ago.

Sharlan still had not left Leianna's side nor relinquished her hand. Now she asked, her voice cracking, "May I . . . Leianna . . . can I please hold him?"

"Yes, you may hold him, and then please bring him over to me."

As Sharlan moved toward the baby, Dr. Mateus handed her a soft blanket. She took it, holding it out for Bael to wrap the baby in it. She held the swaddled child, murmuring, "Nikki, Nikki, oh, my Nikki, you've returned and you're whole!"

Leianna saw tears unabashedly streaking Sharlan's face, and saw that Bael, too, was crying, his arm around Sharlan as she cooed to the baby. But he smiled poignantly at Leianna, as if she had gifted him with the greatest treasure in the universe.

Sharlan visibly struggled to control her display of emotion. She brought the child over to Leianna, who cradled her newborn son, feeling both happiness and awe, for he seemed perfect. She could feel the child's contentment, that his little soul had traveled countless centuries to regain what he had lost in that terrible previous life.

The baby had kicked the blanket open, exposing his tiny legs and feet. "Of course, you and Bael will name him as you see fit. But he'll always . . . remind me of Nikki."

Terence and Miriam still stood quietly off to one side.

"Mom? Do you want to hold the baby?"

Miriam nodded wordlessly, beaming, and took the tiny boy into her arms. Terence smiled down on him. "So, Leigh Ann, have you and Bael actually chosen a name yet?"

"We have," she said, glancing at her mother. "His name is Stefan Nicholas. S-T-E-F-A-N and Nicholas, as it's normally spelled."

Bael, grinning, added, "We thought we'd call him Stevie, for short."

Leianna smirked at him, and gazed at Sharlan, who was looking overwhelmed and perhaps felt a bit alone, despite her joy. Leianna remembered Sharlan's sorrow, so many centuries ago, and she knew Bael had been joking. She knew what they had really decided for the baby's nickname, the only one that it could be.

"Actually, Sharlan," she said, "Bael is only teasing us. Stefan is far too regal sounding to be shortened. And Stefan Nicholas is such a fine royal name for a prince. But as far as a familiar name, we're going to call the baby Nicky. N-I-C-K-Y. A small change from the Eliomese spelling, but it sounds the same. I think the baby will like it, too."

"Oh, Leianna!" Sharlan's tears started again.

Bael came over, hugging her, reaching out to clasp Leianna's hand. "Of course, we've joked about this name raising a few eyebrows for a totally different reason. I mean, my father had a similar nickname."

Leianna let go of his hand, gestured to Miriam for the baby. Miriam lowered Nicky into her arms. Leianna stroked his soft cheeks. The baby yawned. "He's so quiet. Why isn't he crying?"

Dr. Mateus came over. "He's healthy, if that's what's worrying you."

"Don't they usually cry?" Leianna also saw her concern reflected in Sharlan's face. "Or is he just a very calm baby?"

Dr. Mateus pulled a long feather out of his pocket and began to tickle the baby's throat with it. Nicky's eyes widened and his tiny hands tried to push the feather away, but the doctor kept tickling him. Unable to stop the annoying sensation, Nicky let out a healthy, bawling protest.

Dr. Mateus removed the feather, but Nicky, once started, obviously felt the need to chastise them all with further loud, wailing sobs.

"Oh, dear," said Leianna. "Ssh, Nicky, shush!"

Sharlan knelt immediately beside her, smoothing the baby's hair. "Sha, Nicky, sha. It's okay, my little one, your mamas are here and your daddies both love you."

Nicky stopped crying, hiccupped a few times, and moved his small head to look at both Sharlan and Leianna.

Terence bent down, his face close to the baby. "Hi, there, mate. I'm Daddy Terence. Welcome to Heaven." Nicky let out a small, cooing sound. "Hey, look! He's smiling at me!"

Bael peered at his son. "Nah. I think it's gas."

"Bael," Leianna chided him, then yawned. "So does this new astral mother get to have some sleep?"

Bael picked up his son, rocking him.

"And, Doctor," Leianna asked, "is there afterbirth with an astral birth?"

"It already dissipated when Nicky took form. And I think you and the baby will stay here until you have to wake up physically later this morning. Sharlan and Bael will take care of the baby while you're attending to your mortal days."

"Where?" She yawned again.

"That's up to you, Bael and Sharlan. And Terence might want to have a say in that, or at least have his opinion known.

Leianna said, "I want the baby raised in the heavens."

Bael shook his head. "Our son is a Prince of Hell, and you are Hell's Satana. He should be raised in Domain."

Leianna sat up as they wheeled her down the hospital corridors. "I don't think he'll be safe there. He's a target if someone is against us."

They brought her to a room filled with flowers and into a warm hospital bed.

Bael handed Nicky to her. "He'll be protected."

Terence butted in. "She has a point there, mate. Leigh Ann and I have been living in her house here. If Sharlan is willing, she can stay there and take care of Nicky. You can bring him down to the lower planes for a visit, bit by bit, you know, show him off to the people, but tell them his mother feels the vibes down there are a little strong for such a wee babe."

Leianna nodded to Sharlan. "Sounds okay with me."

"Oh, Bael! Can I stay here to take care of our son while Leianna's away on the mortal plane?!" Sharlan suddenly quieted. "I mean, if they'll let me back in Heaven."

Bael eyed her incredulously. "Sharlan, you *are* in Heaven."

"I mean, beyond tonight."

Miriam waved toward the doorway. "Maybe you should ask this fellow."

Quatama stood there, smiling. "I come to congratulate the parents of Stefan Nicholas, or Nicky as he will be known familiarly. Bael, Sharlan and Leianna, may you and your child be blessed with happiness. And I have brought four others who wish to see their grandson. He stood aside and let Lucifer, Affaeteres, Lothan and Tia into the room.

Sharlan rushed over to her parents. "Mom! Dad! He's fine!"

Leianna unfurled the blanket to show them the baby. Lothan whispered, "Nikki. Restored."

Leianna smiled tiredly. "This is going to be one spoiled baby."

"Deservingly," Tia said.

At that point, the conversations about her, and the oohing and aahing over Nicky swelled into a lulling susurration. Leianna had a strange sensation of being rocked to sleep. Somewhere or sometime during it all, she heard a murmur of approval concerning Sharlan's mothering Nicky on the eighth plane, while Leigh Ann was attending to her mortal life, or even attending her new duties as Satana, when that called her to Hell. She felt Nicky gently lifted from her and heard Sharlan babytalking to him.

Leianna would feel up to handling anything, just so long as her children were safe, loved and watched over, both Nicky and his mortal brother Daniel.

Just before she nodded off entirely, she heard Quatama say, "You needn't worry, Leigh Ann. Every thing will work out, for the Creator will give you strength and wisdom and will protect your loved ones as well as you." She opened her eyes and saw Bael place Nicky back in her arms, as he leaned down and kissed her.

Someone must have snapped their picture, because she saw a flash, although she wasn't sure if they used flash photography in Heaven.

And then she fell fast asleep until she woke up in her mortal body on Saturday morning at 9:00 A.M. She could psychically see Bael sitting on her bed, grinning ecstatically at her.

— *Where's the baby?* — she asked.

— *Sharlie and Terence are with him on the eighth plane, just as you wanted. Nicky's fine.* —

— *So why are you grinning like that? Just happy?* —

— *Of course, I'm happy. But I also just rescheduled our Heliomese wedding ceremony and your coronation as Queen and Satana for January 1, 1978. What do you think, Leianna? New Year's Day . . . a new day in Hell.* —

She sighed. — *I think it's going to be quite a year.* —

He kissed her. She felt the soft, ghostlike brush of his lips. — *I think* you're *going to have quite a life.* —

No one else was in the room. Danny was probably in the living room watching his cartoons on TV, so she mumbled her reply aloud: "But no one in this world will believe it!"

She got up, put on her robe and slippers, and padded downstairs. Danny was indeed watching television, while eating a bowl of Captain Crunchberry cereal with milk. Apparently both Fred and Ginnie were still asleep, but both her parents were in the kitchen. Bill Elfman was reading the newspaper; Miriam was frying eggs for breakfast.

Her father looked up from the business section. "Good morning, princess. Everyone thinks they're royalty in this house, they sleep so late."

"Good morning, Dad. Good morning, Mom."

"Good morning, sweetheart. I hope you had a good night." She winked.

Well, Leigh Ann thought, *maybe one person will believe it.* "Absolutely wonderful," she said. "Now, all I need is some coffee."

21

All Things Change

She would always remember three things happening in the early dawn of January 1, 1978: adoring her Heliomese wedding gown, waking up in the middle of the ceremony, and the sunrise in Hell, signaling the Creator had begun to change the Netherworld.

She and Danny had stayed up past midnight on Saturday night, December 31, 1977, watching the New Year celebrations on TV, the sparkling ball in Times Square, the crowds surrounding it jubilant. Leigh Ann drank Manischewitz cherry wine and allowed Danny a small glass, toasting the arrival of 1978 together with the cat, Lucy Angelina, curled up between them on the sofa.

Her parents and Fred were out to separate parties, and Ginnie was dining and dancing in Center City with a new beau, Larry, a medical intern at the hospital. Leigh Ann and Danny finally went upstairs to bed at 1:00 A.M., the wine making them drowsy. Both fell quickly asleep.

Bael gently called her out-of-body about ninety minutes before the Heliomese ceremonies, set to begin at 3:00 A.M. She glanced at her sleeping mortal self and at her son, dozing in his bed.

She wondered, "Does Danny go out-of-body?"

"Not tonight. He'll sleep through this night. Let's go, Leigh Ann. You have to dress for the wedding and coronation."

She placed her astral arms around Bael, murmuring to Danny: "Sleep well, son. I love you."

Bael lifted her up, like a man carrying his wife across a threshold.

And he was.

The gown's sleek, white satin hugged her recently reclaimed figure curvaceously and yet slenderized it, its strapless bodice, waist and long skirt studded with full-sized cultured pearls. Instead of sleeves, wide, silver-threaded satin armbands extended from the bodice, encircling her upper arms with more pearls, and the edges of each armband were bordered with fire opals. Thin, silver chains descended from each armband at three-inch intervals around the circumference of Leianna's arms, connecting with a thinner wristband of the same pearly and opalescent composition. Set in the silver chains from upper arms to wrists were brilliant diamonds.

They flashed as she turned in the soft light of her royal dressing chamber, viewing herself in the full length mirror.

A diamond and silver tiara circled her head, and her feet were shod in delicate, small-heeled, silver sandals, their straps also covered with tiny gems.

She wore no veil, signifying that this was a ceremonial wedding, the real marriage performed months before in the heavens. Still, it was important, an affirmation before all of Hell of the love and commitment between her and Bacl.

Her auburn hair was pulled back into an elaborate twist, more jewels woven into it, casting golden gleams throughout her coiffure, with curlicue wisps adorning her forehead and sides. Sharlan adjusted the tiara, making sure it sat firmly. Terence stood nearby holding Nicky in his arms. Both he and the baby wore a dark blue tuxedo, Nicky pulling on his miniature cummerbund, fastened loosely around his small frame.

Leianna gave Sharlan, her Maid of Honor, an anxious look. "You're not upset about this, are you, Sharl?"

"About what?" She smoothed down her own gown, appraising it in the mirror, a strapless gown of bright green that also hugged her ample curves and flared out dramatically in a fishtail below the knees. Long white gloves adorned her arms and hands, a diamond necklace and earrings accentuated her throat and earlobes, and her rich black hair was also styled in an alluring upsweep. Leianna knew her shoes were green satin flats. Sharlan was tall enough without heels, and she'd be holding Nicky during the ceremonies.

Leianna sighed, feeling like a fairytale princess about to break her new friend's heart. "About my marrying Bael. About Bael marrying *me*. After all the years *you* spent with him."

"What am I supposed to say? You've always been first in his heart. And your own heart is so large, you can love both him and Terence equally." She smiled at Terence. He would symbolically give Leianna in marriage to Bael, in place of a father, also a show of good will on Terence's part. "And I've told you: I've lived with Bael's memories of you for so long, it's better now, having the real woman to interact with and work things out with."

"That's truly magnanimous of you, all the more so because I know you're sincere."

Sharlan leaned down and hugged her, careful of their hair. "I've always held only the highest opinion of you, of your courage, and as they say in heaven," she glanced again at Terence, "if you truly love someone, you don't deny your loved one the desires of the heart, if those desires are beneficial and aren't harmful. And I also have a large heart and can share Bael's love with you."

Leianna felt her own emotions swell. "I love you, too, Sharlie, like a sister. I'm so glad you're here for me. And for Nicky."

Sharlan turned her gently to face the mirror. "You look beautiful, Leianna. Enjoy your Heliomese wedding day."

Terence added: "Not to mention your coronation as Satana."

Leianna smiled quietly at him. "That's a commitment to the lost souls in Hell and to the future of humanity, strange as that sounds." She had already begun to think of them as her people, much as a mother would say *her children*. Hope must spring eternal; it could not be abandoned anymore.

Terence nodded, looking at Nicky. The firstborn of Hell. Born twice. "Whatever happened to my vision of a family cottage in a sunny glen?"

"Maybe another time."

The door to their dressing room opened. Ashtoreth, the best man, came in, his tux of midnight blue matching Terence's and Nicky's. He looked handsome, his wavy golden hair framing his face, his sea green eyes solemn, almost sad. "It's time. Are you ready?"

Leianna took a deep breath, steadying herself. "As ready as I'll ever be." She lifted the short train of her gown and placed the small loop sewn into it through her left-hand middle finger. Terence's wedding band rested on her right-hand first finger, which in Jewish lore led to her heart. "Do you have the rings?"

Ashtoreth nodded. "I have them."

"And the betrothal bands?"

"Quatama has them."

The golden wristbands, with which she and Bael had pledged to one another 35,000 years ago, had survived Bael's exile and Leianna's countless incarnations following the war in Heaven. Had there been no war, they would have married one year after the betrothal. Bael had asked that the bands be given, at long last, in the Heliomese ceremony. All of Hell's High Council would see the bands placed permanently upon their wrists, signifying full commitment. All of the Council members had been present, millennia ago, at Bael and Leianna's betrothal ceremony in Eliom. All things change, but some things are renewed.

Terence transferred Nicky into Sharlan's hands and crooked his left arm for Leianna. She put her right arm through. He picked up her wedding bouquet, an elaborate latticework of moonflowers circling its leafy vine with sprays encrusted with seed pearls surrounding them, from the dressing table, and placed it in her right hand. They walked down the hall to the throne room; Sharlan, Nicky and Ashtoreth followed behind them. Leianna saw her mother, Miriam now, but also Leianna's mother from 35,000 years before, when Miriam was Eve in Eliom before the Fall from Grace. All things change, but some things are renewed.

"Mother?" Leianna asked. "Are you crying already?"

Miriam slid the back of her hand across her cheek, towards her curly red hair, wiping the tear. "I never thought we'd see this day." She wore a demure, blue, brocaded gown, looking every inch the mother of the bride. "I mean, I missed your upper plane ceremony with Bael, it was so quick, although I enjoyed your and Terence's beautiful wedding ceremony."

"We kept things simple."

"Yes. Well, so long ago, I thought to see you and Bael marry with a great celebration. So I get a little emotional, okay?"

"Okay, Mom. Here comes Lucifer and Affaeteres. Mother Aff, you're crying, too! Wait until Bael and I exchange our vows at least."

She was beginning to feel lightheaded and nervous.

Terence squeezed her hand. "Mothers are allowed to cry at weddings, Leigh Ann. It's a law, with no clause as to timing."

She took another deep breath. "Okay."

Affaeteres leaned down to kiss her cheek. "Creator bless you, Leianna, and my son." She wore a long-sleeved, velvet gown of viridian green, its scooped neckline set off by a velvet choker with an emerald set in gold hanging below her neck.

Lucifer, in a silver tuxedo, also bussed her cheek. "And us all," he added. "Shall we begin?"

She nodded, and signaled the guards to open the huge central doors to the throne room.

The room was packed with guests seated left and right of the aisle, the High Council and their families and friends filling the balconies. The news people crowded the center back balcony, cameras at the ready, with space set aside in other areas for photographers and cameramen to record other angles of the wedding promenade, wedding and coronation. The guests swiveled around in their seats as Lucifer and Affaeteres began their slow march down the aisle, carpeted in gold and red, to the dais, followed by Miriam, who was Eve, a susurration of surprised murmurs following her.

Leianna looked at the beautiful decorations, the banners of gold and red, and the countless vines of moonflowers and other flowers and greenery draping the balconies, circling the pillars supporting them from below, and overflowing huge pots upon the dais.

Bael stood to the left of the three centered steps leading up to it, his right hand extended toward her, waiting.

He was dressed in white like a Renaissance prince: white satin trousers, white boots nearly to his knees, a loose, white, satin, long-sleeved doublet that covered his hips and was cinched with a white belt at the waist. Upon all of these white surfaces were studded jewels of many colors, scintillating in the throne room light.

His thick black hair fell in rich waves over the modernized collar of the doublet, and a silver coronet circled his head and fore-head, set with gems of fire opal and onyx. Leianna had never seen him wear his crown. He could have sprung from a fairytale, he looked so royal.

She and Terence approached Bael. On the dais, Lucifer and Affaeteres stood on the left side, Miriam, on the right. Dagon, the Elder of the Heliomese High Council and Hell's spirit master, stood just beyond a wide bower of moonflower vines, and Quatama stood between him and Miriam.

Dagon asked, "Who gives this woman to be wed to our Prince?"

Terence answered, "I offer this woman's love, given freely from her heart, to be shared with your Prince." He released Leianna's arm and moved to stand beside Eve.

Leianna reached out her hand. Bael clasped it and led her up the dais steps to stand to his right before the bower.

"And who," Dagon asked, "will accept this marriage in the name of Hell and declare it to be for the good of Hell?"

Sharlan rose up the steps and stood to Leianna's right. She made a small bow, holding Nicky firmly as his small hand played with her hair and earring. "I accept this marriage in the name of Hell and declare it to be good for all of the Heliomese people."

"And who," asked Dagon, "brings the symbols of unity to join our Prince and his bride?"

Ashtoreth ascended the steps to the dais and moved to Bael's left side. "I bring the symbols of unity to join them." He pulled a ring box from one pocket and opened it to reveal two thick rings, Bael's ring, silver, Leianna's ring, gold; both had small diamonds circling the band. He gave Leianna Bael's ring, and gave Bael her ring. "I bring rings of silver and gold that they may place upon each other's fingers."

Dagon nodded. "Leianna, place Bael's ring of silver upon his finger."

She did, upon his left-hand, third finger.

"This symbolizes the mystic power of the moon, which only shines on Earth and on Eliom, but never in Hell. Yet we are connected to the moon, powerful in the night, and magical to all things subjected to darkness. Silver is the moon and our symbol of the Netherworld on Earth, and the diamonds are the stars, circling Heaven, Hell and Earth, connecting them. And so you marry the moon and take him as your husband."

Dagon paused and turned to Bael. "Bael, place the ring of gold upon Leianna's finger."

He did, sliding it onto her left-hand, third finger.

"This symbolizes the indestructible power of the sun, which shines on Earth and on Eliom, but never fully in Hell. Yet we are connected to the sun, bringing light and life to the day, magical to all things subject to warmth, growth and renewal. Gold is the sun and our symbol of Heaven's light on Earth, and the diamonds are the stars, circling Heaven, Hell and Earth, connecting them. And so you marry the sun and take her for your wife."

Dagon stepped away from the bower, nodding to Quatama, who took his place.

"We have a second symbol of unity," said Quatama, "the bands of betrothal Bael and Leianna wore 35,000 years ago to declare their love to their families and friends in Eliom. They had hoped to exchange them once again when their betrothal year came to an end and they could marry. But the war in Heaven — the second Fall from Grace — took them from each other . . . until now."

He waved his left hand in the air, and the rounded wrist bands appeared, seemingly out of nowhere. He held them up for all to see. "Magic!"

The ancient spirit master smiled beneficently, as only he could. "For those who never knew Eliom, these bands were fashioned from the sand on the Shore of the Seraphim, where the sea leads to even higher places in our Creator's universe. Betrothal bands are formed while linked to one another and, during the betrothal ceremony, worn by those betrothed, they are separated while on their hands, suddenly linked no longer, and yet retaining the link spiritually between the betrothed couple. Magic! Bael and Leianna have waited 35,000 years to give one another their betrothal bands, exchanging them now as marriage bands."

He held Leianna's smaller band in his left hand and Bael's band, slightly larger, in his right hand. "For those who do not know me, I am Gautama Buddha, although I was not known as Buddha when I became the spirit master to Bael and Leianna 35,000 years ago in Eliom. I am still their spirit master, and I will now lead them from betrothal into marriage, for they have fulfilled their betrothal vows and will now pledge to each other eternally." He held up the betrothal bands again. "Bael and Leianna, take the band you each wore throughout the long separation you endured." They took their own bands, holding them. "Leianna, although in your many incarnations, you had to wed and be wife to many others, you never ceased, within your secret heart, to love Bael. And although you love and have married Terence Dearborn, you still also cherish Bael. Even in those days in Eliom, when we asked you to be faithful to your beloved, we meant that you be sincere in your love and that it be enduring. It is possible to love more than one in that sincere and enduring manner, and so in the name of Eliom and our Creator, I recognize your reunion with and declaration of marriage to Bael. Place your betrothal band upon his wrist."

Bael held out his right hand. She pushed her band onto it. It glowed as she did so, resistance fading as it slid over his larger hand to his wrist, enlarging itself slightly to fit.

Quatama turned to Bael. "What I have told Leianna applies equally to you, Bael. Your reputation as a lover has been well-established in Hell, but you did not love these other women. You buried your loss of Leianna in their arms, but their hearts never merged with yours in true unity, but for one exception. You, too, have loved another woman sincerely and enduringly, and her name is Sharlan. And you have learned upon Leianna's return to you, that your heart can be faithful to both of these loves. But now you must pledge your faithfulness to them, and allow no other to falsely intrude upon that faithfulness. I know you have now regained your heart's desire, and so, in the name of Eliom and our Creator, I recognize your reunion with and declaration of marriage to Leianna. Place your betrothal band upon her wrist."

Bael drew his own larger band over her hand, now sleek like her own, which he now wore, not textured and ridged as these bands had originally been at their betrothal ceremony. Her band had changed into smooth gold when she dared to breach the electrical barrier separating the compliant angels from the rebels during the war in Heaven, desperate to reach Bael and badly burned in the failed attempt. She had often wondered if his betrothal band had changed when he and his family and Lucifer's followers had been exiled to Hell. She recently found the answer to that question. His band had sympathetically altered at the same time as hers, as the rebels were lifted into a blinding light and flung far from Eliom. When he and the other fallen angels regained consciousness, he found his betrothal band had also become smooth gold.

Now his band glowed in the same manner, becoming smaller, fitting Leianna's wrist perfectly.

Quatama asked, "Do you both vow to love, cherish, respect and nurture one another, your marriage a meeting of your minds, your hearts, your souls and your flesh, to share joy, to share knowledge, to share pleasure all your days and to meet all challenges with faith, hope, love and determination?"

Bael and Leianna clasped their hands. She knew his beatific smile matched her own.

He said, "I do!"

She said, "I do," and then the throne room faded before her eyes, and she awoke abruptly in her mortal body in her bedroom in Philadelphia.

The house was dark, everyone asleep. The illuminated bedroom clock read 4:00 A.M.; Danny lay asleep in the other bed. And she psychically heard a soft, sneering, and recognizable laugh. — *Sorry to break up the party, dear sister-in-law. Why should you have all the fun and not let me have any?* —

— *Azmodeus!* —

— *None other.* —

Bael and Terence appeared, nearly colliding astrally.

— *Watch it, mate!* —

She felt Az flee.

— *Leianna, this is a fine time to need a bathroom break.* —

— *I don't, Bael! Azmodeus woke me up. Deliberately.* —

— *Az? I thought I sensed his presence just as we arrived. I'll deal with him later.* —

She asked, — *Wasn't he invited to the wedding and coronation?* —

— *Yes, of course. He was seated in the front row. Just go back to sleep, babe. I'll have someone restrain him the rest of the night.* —

— *I'll try. Do I have to get dressed all over again?* —

— *Of course. Your gown and all fell to the floor the moment you jetted back here.* —

She sighed. — *Well, let me use the bathroom anyway, so maybe we won't be further interrupted. Some Queen of Hell I'll be if I can't control my astral body. Or my bladder.* —

She shambled off to the bathroom, Bael and Terence following, relieved herself, and shambled back to bed. She felt a third presence in the room, a benign one.

Quatama patted her hand as she pulled the covers over herself, and then he touched her forehead. — *Shut your eyes. You will be asleep again in a minute, and stay asleep until morning,* — he said.

She did as he asked.

She was back in the dressing room again, clothed in the astral version of her nightgown, with Sharlan, Affaeteres and Miriam all pulling it over her head, frantically redressing her.

Affaeteres fumed. "That stupid son of mine!"

She hastily pulled on her undergarments, and they lifted the gown carefully back over her head, adjusting it. Her wedding and marriage bands had remained on her fingers and wrist.

She slipped on the jeweled sandals as Sharlan fixed her hair and set the tiara back on her head. "I'm ready."

Miriam held up a small wooden box. "Wait. One more thing." She opened the box, a small gold ring with a brilliant blue stone within it. "Your eternal grandmother Deianna gifted you with this ring on the seventh day of your eternal life, just before your Naming Ceremony. Quatama kept it safe. Deianna said to give it to you on your wedding day, but I missed your earlier ceremony with Bael and forgot the ring when you married Terence, you had the ceremony so quickly. A disadvantage of living my own busy mortal life." She offered Leianna a wry grin. "But perhaps it's for the best, giving it to you now. We were surprised when Deianna gave an adult's ring to an infant and asked that it be held until the baby's eventual marriage, but perhaps this is the right time, as this ring has a special legacy. I remember her exact words. She said it will impart wisdom and direction." She held it out to Leianna.

Leianna took it, trying it on her left hand's middle finger, next to Bael's gold and diamond wedding band. It fit. "Where are your parents, Mother? I've heard nothing of Deianna or of Grandfather Mercurius, not since my memories of old Eliom, of the Fall and its aftermath, were awakened in 1971."

"Deianna is on Earth, honey, also undergoing an incarnation. Mercurius just finished an incarnation; he's getting reacclimated to the heavens. It takes time, switching from mortal to immortal mode, getting over the restrictions of an Earthly lifetime. He remembers you, but it's very confusing for him. He said to send you his love, and he'll see you when he's more his old self."

"A bit of a pun, Mom."

"Actually a fairly accurate statement."

Sharlan opened the dressing room door. "We have to go. They're waiting."

"Okay. Let's go." They moved quickly to the throne room, Leianna admiring Deianna's gift. "What kind of stone is this, Mom? I've never seen a blue this bright. It's nearly a metal."

"On Earth, it's called a Spectralite, and scientifically known as an orthoclastic feldspar. In Eliom, we called it a *chahbel*, meaning stone of wisdom."

"It's beautiful," she said, looking down at it, and nearly ran into Azmodeus, abruptly and angrily exiting from the throne room.

"Watch where you're going, bitch!"

Her temper flared. "Get out of my way, Az."

"Sorry about my being nonplussed, but you took my favorite concubine from me. Against her own will. And now you think you're the Queen of Hell."

The huge doors eased open and Bael came out quickly, closing them behind him. He smacked Az against his chest, knocking him backwards, away from Leianna. "If it's war you want, little brother, I'll declare it. But for now, you either leave and fume in your quarters and all our guests will note your rebellion, or you go sit down, as a member of our agreed-upon triumvirate. You obviously dressed for it." He waved his hand at the elegant suit Az wore. "Either way, if you make one more disruptive move, I'll personally pound your ass into the seventh level of Hell! And Ash will hold you down while I do it. Your choice."

Leianna put in tersely, "It's also your choice to respect or abuse a woman who loves you, but you have to pay the consequences for that choice, too. The society you live in has now changed. It no longer accepts abuse, or the myth of a willing victim. Regan is protected now, even from herself, if need be."

Az did nothing, staring at all four women and Bael.

Bael held the throne room door open. "Ladies? A dignified walk now to your places on the dais. The coronation awaits."

Sharlan and Miriam headed in. Affaeteres glared nastily at her youngest son as she went in. Az cringed, recovered, shot a sullen glance at Bael and Leianna, and went in to his seat without further words.

Leianna gave Bael a disgruntled grimace. "You owe me a kiss on that dais," she whispered.

"Stop scowling, get up there, and I'll oblige you."

She walked briskly back to the dais, smiling to hide her anger, Bael right behind her, absolute quiet in the throne room as they took their places before the bower.

Quatama seemed merely amused as they returned. "An interruption is like an obstruction in a river, which blocks its flow. The water may back up for a period to accommodate the disruption, but eventually it will overflow it and continue in whatever direction it needs to . . . to overcome it.

"I believe that your rings and bands were exchanged and your vows taken. And now, the marriage sanctified here tonight shall be sealed." He nodded at them.

Bael pulled her to him without hesitation, bending down, his lips claiming hers. She kissed him back passionately; when they pulled away for decorum's sake, her mouth still hungered for his.

Quatama now stepped away, and Ashtoreth and Terence, on either side of the bower, wheeled it to the back of the dais, while four, strong guards rolled Lucifer's former, elaborate marble throne of state forward to where the bower had stood and lowered it down. Bael whispered, "Retractable wheels," to Leianna.

The throne's sculptures of the four Seraphim glared down at Leianna: the ox and the lion rose from its back, the eagle and the wolf extended from its arms. Leianna remembered these Seraphim at Eve's trial 35,000 years ago on the Shore of the Seraphim, remembered Lucifer challenging them and their chastisement of him. She remembered their names: Gehtat, who wore the head of an eagle, who had first appeared as a sparrow; Elat, who wore the head of an ox, who had first appeared as a gazelle; Seheer, who wore the head of a human female, but who had first appeared as a grey wolf, and Chahtai, who both wore the head of a lion and had first appeared as one. They had worn these images to represent some of the species on Earth which were endangered by the genetic disruption caused by Eve and Adam, if the other angelfolk did not help its repair.

Lucifer had depicted Seheer as the wolf, not as a woman, perhaps because that looked more menacing, but now this throne was to be Leianna's. She remembered that the Seraphim had given her and Bael and the other angels foresight, to know within their soul why the Fall from Grace had occurred, and how it would one day be healed.

The Seraphim were not her enemies. Their images upon this throne would now represent their strength and *their* foresight.

She also hoped Lucifer realized that there was no need for revenge, that it would serve no purpose, for all had played a necessary part in the genetic journey of humanity's rebalanced DNA.

Guards rolled three, less elaborate marble thrones in, a large one flanking the sculptured high throne, and two smaller ones on either side of them. The wedding party had retreated to the sides of the dais. Now Lucifer came forward, standing beside the high throne, carrying a long, flat, velvet jeweler's box.

Bael held out his hand to Leianna, who took it, and he led her to the sculptured throne. She stood before it, between Bael and Lucifer.

Dagon came forward, dressed in his black, silver and blue robes as the elder of the High Council of Hell. "We are gathered to formally witness the ascension of Leianna as our Satana."

Lucifer opened the jeweler's box, holding up its contents for all in the throne room to see. It held a strange, thick ornament composed of three golden circles, each the size of a silver dollar, set together into a large triple ring. Three golden symbols were set in each of the gold circles.

The top circle held the letter Y right side up. The bottom circle held the letter Y upside down. The stems of each Y, on either side, created the illusion of a three-dimensional, golden line separating the top and bottom circles through the arms of each Y.

The central circle held a symbol resembling a lightening bolt, its zigzag line traveling diagonally down from right to left in perfect symmetry with the opposing Y's.

Between the arms of each Y, and surrounding their stems, were thin triangles of emerald. The recessed spaces unclaimed by the lightning bolt held tiny sheets of diamonds cut to fit. The emerald, diamond and gold ornament was suspended on a short but thick chain of gold. Leianna knew it would fit perfectly just below her neck and above the bodice of her gown, and was the reason she wore no other jewelry there.

"This," Lucifer began, "is the Taleis-Yalin, composed of three pendants, once separate, now joined forever."

"The Taleis, the central pendant with its lightening bolt, was once lost for centuries, after it was crafted in Hell with wards set upon it for its protection and control. Prince Ashtoreth recovered this powerful talisman a hundred years ago and has kept it safely hidden until now. It can bring great destruction if used wrongly. But now it is warded further with two powerful pendants set above it and below it.

"The top pendant with its upright Y and the bottom pendant with its inverted Y were both created in Eliom before the war in Heaven. Michael and his wife Eve, and I and my wife Affaeteres, commissioned it as mirror-talismans of our avowed friendship. They, too, are symbols of power, but only for good. Affaeteres kept the upright Y, and Eve kept the inverted Y, and then handed it to Quatama for safekeeping when she began her incarnations.

"Upon this precipitous occasion, the Taleis, which represents Hell's power, which I wore upon my later coronation as your Emperor, and these conjoined Eliomese friendship symbols, called Yalin, representing Heaven's power, have been made one. The Taleis-Yalin represents the Alliance, the new hope for Hell through the ending of humanity's genetic imbalance. It represents the friendship, now renewed, between us and Heaven through the marriage of Bael and Leianna. It represents Leianna's willing ascension as one of the *lamed vov,* a pure soul, to the throne of Hell as our Satana and eventual Redeemer."

Shouts of "Leianna" and "Blessed be," followed by her new title echoed in the throne room. He held up his hand for silence and removed the Taleis-Yalin from the jeweler's box. "Leianna, come forward." She did. He fastened the ornament around her neck, and turned her to face the assemblage. The necklace's three rings, its golden symbols and shining emeralds and diamonds glowed under the throne room lights. "With the placing of the Taleis-Yalin upon you, I recognize you as my successor in Hell and hope that Heaven's blessings will be visited upon the people of Hell through you, Leianna. I have relinquished my place to you and, with my blessing, I proclaim you to be Satana of Hell."

He stepped back.

Quatama came forward. "With the placing of the Taleis-Yalin upon you, its essence shall meld with your spiritual essence, never to be removed until such time as your duties here are completed. As do your wedding rings and marriage bands, it shall only appear as and when needed. Do not speak of it to any on Earth until Earth's rebalancing is complete. When it is, the Taleis-Yalin shall represent the protection of Earth and everything upon it. The potential for destruction within the Taleis will then be contained between the two sides of the Yalin. The nature of humanity will be balanced, and then, Heaven, the Earth and Hell shall be healed."

She whispered so low, only he could hear it. "A large order, master."

Quatama's eyes merely twinkled with silent mirth, the corners of his mouth barely creasing upwards. He bowed gracefully and moved to the right of the thrones beside Eve, Sharlan and Terence.

Lucifer, nodding to Dagon, moved to the left of the thrones beside Affaeteres and Ashtoreth.

Dagon turned to face the guests, the news media, the elite guards dressed in Romanesque military garb, standing alert, chosen for their devotion to the royal family, including Leianna, should trouble erupt. "Now," his voice broke the silence, "the triumvirate will take their places upon their thrones to witness the ascension of our Satana to her own. Prince Ashtoreth."

Ash moved to the smaller throne to the right of Leianna's and sat down.

"Lord Baelzebub, henceforth King of Hell."

Bael seated himself on the larger marble throne to the left of Leianna's.

"Prince Azmodeus." Dagon nodded to Az, seated in the front left row of the guests.

He rose very slowly, but walked at a normal pace up the steps to the dais. He kept his gaze away from Leianna, but she saw him glance covetously at the sculptured throne Lucifer had commanded Hell from, pausing before it before moving to the far left and seating himself on the smaller marble throne to the left of Bael.

Dagon continued. "The triumvirate is acknowledged by the High Council of Hell as the second successor to our Lord Lucifer. Does the triumvirate acknowledge the High Council and its representation of the people of Hell and their laws?"

"I do," said Bael.

"I do," said Ash.

Az waited three heartbeats and slowly said, "I do."

"Leianna, Satana, and henceforth known as Queen of Hell, do you accept the High Council and its representation of the people of Hell and their laws, with the exception that, if you find fault, you shall work with us fairly and respectfully to repair that fault?"

Leianna quietly said, "I do and I shall."

"Then . . . as elder of the High Council of Hell and in the presence of the triumvirate of Hell, I bid you ascend to your throne as our Queen and Satana." He offered her his hand as she turned and sat upon a green velvet cushion placed there for her comfort.

Dagon walked off to the left, but returned a moment later holding small, black velvet cushion upon which lay a crown of silver adorned with diamonds, opals, pearls and black onyx along its band. He bowed slightly to Bael, cushion and crown held outward.

Bael stood up, taking the crown in his hands. Dagon bowed again and moved on to the left, standing beside Lucifer.

Bael lifted the crown up and placed it on Leianna's head, fitting just beyond and covering the small tiara she already wore. He then took her right hand in his left and drew her gently from the throne. They walked to the edge of the dais, Bael drawing their hands up high in a triumphant regal gesture. The crowd about them roared and shouted their approval as she and Bael slowly descended the dais steps and walked down the aisle, the guards drawing open the throne room doors for their passage.

Ashtoreth, Azmodeus, Terence and Sharlan holding Nicky followed, and behind them came Miriam, Quatama, Affaeteres and Lucifer. They all formed a line to greet their guests as they emerged from the throne room.

The banquet hall awaited them all. The rest of the night would hold further festivities, and Leianna would find herself too tired, as fireworks continued above the sky in Domain, to sleep or even appreciate Bael's attempts to seduce her.

They had finally escaped the exuberant revelers, Bael hinting broadly to them that wedding night pleasures took precedence over partying. He had spirited her away to the completely renovated royal suite once occupied by his parents, which included a lavishly furnished balcony filled with potted plants of night blooms.

Bael had lifted her lavender negligee and was planting small kisses on her stomach. She started to laugh. "You're tickling me."

"That wasn't my intention, babe."

"It never tickled before. I must really be tired." She sighed and hugged him. "Let's go sit out on the balcony and watch the stars. It must be nearly dawn on Earth. Thank God, it's New Year's Day, even if it is a Sunday, so I get two more days off from work to recuperate from all of this fun." She grinned at him.

He grinned back and kissed her mouth lightly. "Fine." He threw on a black silk robe; she pulled on a white satin robe against the night chill.

More moonflowers, their scent performing the air, adorned the balcony as she and Bael cuddled on a chaise lounge, gazing at the black, star-studded sky. She must have dozed off, for she suddenly awoke when Bael shifted abruptly. "Wake up, Leianna! Look at the moonflowers!"

She did. They had closed their large petals up as they would on Earth when night ended. But here in Hell, with the day that never grew brighter than a milky grey, the night blooms had never closed completely.

Bael was scrutinizing the sky. "Yes! Over there!" He pointed to a thin golden line traveling along the horizon.

They stared as the early morning twilight of the sky became a rich blue without a trace of its expected, dull greyness. The blue paled as the golden light suffused the lower half, and suddenly red and purple and orange hues streaked across the sky, painting the dome of Hell vivid with sunrise.

Bael, mouth agape, murmured, "Dear God . . . dear God."

Leianna wrapped her arms around his waist, leaning against his chest, staring wide-eyed at the multicolored, brightening sky. "Yes . . . this is the Creator's doing, Bael. It's a miracle! A new day in the truest sense."

Bael clasped her tightly, continuing to stare, unable to speak further while he gazed up at the wonder.

Leianna sat up, leaning forward, her right arm still hugging him. "Isn't it beautiful?"

A frantic knocking sounded on the doors to the royal suite. Bael and Leianna answered it, having dismissed the servants for the night. Terence, Ash and Sharlan, still carrying Nicky, all still in their wedding attire, rushed in, all talking at once about the sunrise, the miracle of a sun, perhaps Earth's, perhaps a new sun, shining on Hell.

Lucifer and Affaeteres followed them in. "Have you gone outside?" Lucifer asked.

"We know, Father," Bael said. "We were on the balcony when the sun rose. Come look."

They all stood on the balcony, watching the remnants of the sunrise, its colors fading to a brilliant blue, clouds of white, standing out sharply against it, as they had never done before when only set against grey.

Lucifer swallowed hard, Affaeteres clinging to him, tears in her eyes.

Leianna, Terence and Bael all hugged one another, and drew Sharlan and Ashtoreth into their embrace, Nicky vocally protesting being a bit squashed and then giggling as they kissed and cuddled him. But Ashtoreth pulled away to stand by the stone balustrade of the balcony, staring out at the phenomenon, tears running down his cheeks. Leianna approached, putting her arms around him, resting her cheek on his shoulder.

"It's a wonder," she said.

Ash turned to her and gently kissed her forehead. "You're a wonder."

She smiled up at him. "I didn't have anything to do with it." She turned to Sharlan. "I think Nicky has to get changed and go to bed *upside*."

Sharlan glanced at Terence, who nodded, kissed Leianna's cheek, and put his arms around Sharlan and Nicky. All three of them faded out. Leianna yawned. "He's getting very good at that *beam me up* stuff."

Bael smiled, looking dazed, up at the sky, for the sun had actually appeared and lit up Domain.

Miriam and Quatama walked out onto the balcony.

"A new day in Hell," said Miriam. She hugged Affaeteres and then Lucifer, who added, "We've waited a very long time for it."

Quatama merely beamed at them all, something he was very good at. "There have always been candles to light the darkness," he said, "but the gift of bright natural daylight is always valued. It gladdens the heart and helps us to see things as they are in many directions in the distance."

He placed one hand on Leianna and another on Miriam, telling Bael, "Say good night to your wife and mother-in-law, or follow us when they awake on Earth. For now, morning has come and they have mortal lives to lead."

Leianna had just enough time to blow Bael a kiss before she drifted off and drifted home.

Between multidimensional commuting, royal responsibilities in Hell, finding a legacy to leave as the current Keeper of the Earth, meeting Heaven's expectations and criteria, and being a wife and mother in various dimensions, she might not mind life becoming a bit boring once in a while.

22

Leianna's Legacy

The teapot is empty. My tale has been told. M— sat very still as I related it. Now he leans forward. "So Hell has changed."

"Yes."

"And the rebalancing of humanity's DNA is now complete."

"Yes, but the new state of evolution will take about a hundred more years or so to get off the genetic ground, and finish wiping out the virus that caused irrational violence and unethical behavior."

"And when this happens, religion will change?"

"Yes, of course. The concept of sin will become obsolete. The idea of fearing God will become obsolete. Humans will be able to trust each other to do the right thing, and there will be many 'right' things to choose from. No one will dictate to one another or play God with one another. Because we're not God, and we shouldn't go around pretending to be."

M— steeples his hands, considering this. "And the words of His messengers? Are they the words of God?"

"You'd have to ask *Her*," I tell him and grin somewhat impishly. He smirks, and so I answer as seriously as I can. "If a messenger's followers believe his words come from God, that's their right. But it is not their right to force their beliefs on others. And when the evolutionary change is complete, all religions will know this."

M— nods, rubbing his chin thoughtfully. "But until this virus you say exists is completely conquered, the violence you detest shall continue, no? And you shall have to punish the sinners, even as you try to reform them in Hell." He holds up a finger, making a point. "In your own lifetime as a mortal, you will not see the full fruits of your labors of the last thirty years. So what legacy can you possibly leave as the Keeper to help the people before you leave this world? For the Keeper must leave the legacy on Earth, a gift created by his or her mortal labors."

I sigh. "I've been considering this since 1978. And I've started to write down a philosophy based on the principles of universal love."

"A new religion?" he asks me, his tone a tad disapproving.

"We don't need more of those. We have more than enough, and they always gum things up, always arguing and fighting, not just between religions, but among their own followers!"

"Then what do you propose?"

The air around us suddenly shimmers. Quatama and Yeshua appear, and also a blue-skinned Hindu god, who smiles and confirms, "Hello, I am Krishna." Various other deities of differing ethnic groups are also crowding M—'s patio. I see Aishah staring at them, wondering if she should offer them tea. I catch her eye and shake my head.

"What I propose, as I've said, is a philosophy of universal principles that will promote peaceful behavior. Peace on Earth. It has to start with individuals, of course. I'll call it *Universophy*, a philosophy for universalism.'

M— offers me a dubious look. "Do you really think this would change the world?"

"Not right away. But we need to interpret God's nature peacefully in our multireligious world and learn to share God's love and our lives together peacefully despite our differences."

He spreads his hands in frustrated inquiry. "So what could you possibly say to achieve this? And why are all these people here?" He waves his hands at them.

Krishna answers. "We are sorry for the intrusion, but are here to listen to Leianna's principles. Our people also must benefit from her legacy, must make it their own." He adds, "May it please you," and steps back as all the other deities nod their agreement.

M— sighs and nods at me. "Go ahead."

I nod my own head respectfully and begin, hoping my words make sense. "When all of the followers of all of our religions realize that our Creator, God, is greater than all of them put together, then they will see how foolish it is to wage wars over questions of faith. Universophy will allow us to reach out in peace, understanding and tolerance towards other religions, races and countries while strengthening ourselves through others treating us with equal courtesy and respect. And so I've written the ten guiding principles of Universophy."

I look to Quatama, who hands me two typed sheets. "Tell Rosemary I said, 'Thank you,' to her for typing them."

Quatama inclines his head. "She says you are welcome. Please proceed."

I read from the first sheet. "Principle 1: Universophy is not a religion. It is one way, hopefully, among many others, to encourage humanity's peaceful co-existence.

"Principle 2: Universophy affirms life. It recognizes that bodily death comes to all living beings in a mortal lifetime, and so it reveres life, both our own and the lives of others who share life with us.

"Principle 3: Universosophy recognizes the belief in a supreme creative force, but recognizes the sacred right of choice, open to all individuals, in how they choose to commune with, praise, or worship that force, if they choose to do so. All spiritual pathways must be free from coercion, or they will not be effective.

"Principle 4: Universosophy recognizes both the positive and negative aspects of life, but seeks understanding, balance and control of these opposing forces, that harmony might be the keynote of our universe and not dissension.

"Principle 5: Universosophy recognizes hatred as love thwarted and seeks to heal hatred. It recognizes evil as good thwarted and seeks to heal evil. Hatred and evil are recognized, but never condoned.

"Principle 6: Universosophy does not condone unethical fighting, whether by individuals, by groups or by countries. It believes in resolution of conflicts, and in necessary self-defense, should a tyrant disturb the peace, or when attacked by unethical individuals, groups or countries, but not in blatant retaliation, reprisals or wars of conquest. Universosophy does not condone an endless cycle of egotistical, aggressive human behavior.

"Principle 7: Universosophy recognizes that basic evil does exist, until such time as mankind evolves beyond it, but not because of devils or demons set apart from the universal creative force. Evil is an action, not a being, and all beings can learn to control their actions toward spiritual balance. Evil can also be controlled and restrained for the sake of the person inflicting it and for the sake of those affected by the evil act."

I switch to the second sheet.

"Principle 8: Just as we cannot claim to know God completely and therefore cannot force another to accept our belief as all-knowing, we cannot know the universe scientifically or spiritually enough to claim a closed standard for what we call *reality*. Therefore, Universosophy gives a measured but open consideration to all theories, beliefs and experiences concerning our universe, to accept or reject them only after studying them fairly. To ridicule new ideas or concepts without first honestly appraising them is an exercise in egoism and minimizes the universe and its vast potential. You can always change channels if the program sounds stupid, but don't censor the broadcast network of the universe."

I look up to see that grins have popped up on a few of their faces. "I was just checking to see if I put you to sleep."

That gets a few chuckles, but not from M—. "Go on please," he says.

"Sorry. Principle 9: If there are other worlds or other levels or planes of existence," I smile at all of them, conspiratorially, and they smile back, "Universophy hopes that these principles will reach and be welcomed there as well.

"And lastly, Principle 10: Universophy recognizes that we are more than the sum of our individual traits. We are connections, beyond our individual selves, to the rest of our world and to our universe. We will always try to consider our words before we speak them, and consider our behavior before we act, that our words and actions will offer hope, respect, love, and peaceful co-existence in the world we share together."

I put down the pages, look about me and then at M—. "So what do you think?"

He is silent for a minute and then says, "I think you are a dreamer. Even if this new evolution eradicates man's violent tendencies, do you really believe that you can ask humans not to criticize their neighbors and never fight again over who is right and who is wrong on any given subject? That they will do this because you say they must?"

"Excuse me for responding for the lady," says Krishna, "but she did not say that anyone *must* follow these principles, only that they might consider following them. This Universophy is presented with hope and courtesy to its potential followers. It does not demand that they follow."

"Exactly!" I chime in, and turn to M—. "We're like a tapestry with different threads askew. We need to mend our connections to see the big picture, showing each of us as children of God, each traveling the path that is best, no one path exclusively right or wrong, only different. Yet all will lead us to our Creator and to lives freed from intolerance. Because each human being is unique, and the connection between each of us and God is unique. And Universophy will help each of us find our way, whether we run with the crowd or go it alone."

I turn to Quatama and Yeshua. "So what do *you* think?"

Yeshua says, "I think it will take some time before all humanity can understand such tolerance, but it cannot hurt to suggest these things to them ahead of time."

Quatama says, "I find it an excellent legacy, Leianna, and you should put these suggestions before humanity before you leave this Earth. It is not for you to decide who will read it and who will follow it. That decision, according to your Principles of Universophy, is up to the individual who discovers and considers it. And he who is the previous Keeper before you must know that the coming evolution will stop the chaos and suffering of his own people and heal their lives."

M— turns tiredly to me. "If all this is true, then write your philosophy. Perhaps some will put it to good use. My own people have need of a future where they can live in peace and harmony with those of other faiths and nations. Perhaps the future will turn brighter, once this sickness which has blighted humanity's soul for over thirty thousand centuries becomes extinct. For all of our people were infected with it."

I reach out my hand, offering it to him. "And all of our people will be freed from it forever, in the not too far off future."

He very slowly reaches out to me. We clasp hands.

"Salaam."

"Shalom."

EPILOGUE

It's 2008 now.

I am getting older now; I have just turned sixty. Daniel is 37-years-old now, is married, and has five children, three girls and two boys.

I'm married now to a very nice fellow, a history teacher, who puts up with all my crazy notions about astral planes and spirit guides and even astral husbands watching over me. I'm required to tell the truth, and Bael and Terence insist that Tyler, my mortal husband, knows spiritually about them and that he understands. Tyler's a lot like my father was, a realist.

My father passed away two years ago, and my mother — Miriam — will be moving in with me this spring. She's eighty now, but in great shape, and even though the genetic rebalancing is completed, she asked Heaven for the right to stick around on this good green Earth a bit longer. Heaven approved. After all, she completed her last project: me, Ginnie and Fred.

Ginnie's married to a doctor now, but they have no children, so she sponsors children for various charities all around the world. She's also still a nurse. Fred never married. He recently moved to Florida, where he works for a computer firm and hangs out on the beach.

If this all sounds too normal, well, not everything is weird in my life. I'm still overseeing the reformation in Hell as Satana, and I still have loving astral friends and families. There are many other tales I could tell about them and our interdimensional lives over the last thirty years, but as someone once said, *that's another story*. Perhaps these other tales will get told someday. Maybe.

Life keeps us busy. I've got other things to do. *You've* got other things to do. And I've been told that our Earth will keep turning.

As far as the world, well, change is indeed upon us, isn't it? People from all cultures are starting to speak out against violence, against terrorism, against war.

Tyler says war is always about solving a conflict, and sometimes wars provide an ethical solution. The good guy wins.

I, too, want the good guys to win. But I want peace to resolve the conflict and provide the solution.

It'd be nice if that could happen sooner. If not, one hundred years will pass quickly enough.